PRAISE FOR JANE POR

ODD MOM OUT

"Jane Porter knows how to scoop
of her hand. She knows her characters intimately and makes
sure the readers get to know them, too."

—Stella Cameron, *New York Times* bestselling author

"Nobody understands the agony and ecstasy of single parenting better than Jane Porter. Alternately funny and touching,
ODD MOM OUT champions a woman's right to be herself,
even at a PTA meeting."

—Vicki Lewis Thompson,
New York Times bestselling author

"Fresh, fun, and real, Jane Porter's writing is a delight!"

—Carly Phillips, *New York Times* bestselling author

FLIRTING WITH FORTY

"Calorie-free accompaniment for a pool-side daiquiri."

—*Publishers Weekly*

"Strongly recommended. [Jane] Porter's thoughtful prose
and strong characters make for an entertaining and thought-
provoking summer read."

—*Library Journal*

"This is an interesting coming-of-age story...It asks the questions, how much should we risk to find happiness, and is
happiness even achievable in the long run? True-to-life dialogue and, more important, true-to-life feelings."

—*Romantic Times BOOKreviews Magazine*

more . . .

"An interesting May-December...romance between two nice individuals who...must defy societal relationship taboos of the older woman and much younger man. Readers will want the best for Jackie...fans will enjoy this fine look [as] Jackie gets her groove (or does she?)."

—*Midwest Book Review*

"Don't miss the sexy story of Jackie, a forty-year-old divorced mother who finds a romance she wasn't even looking for with a much younger man."

—*Complete Woman*

"A terrific read! A wonderful, life and love affirming story for women of all ages."

—Jayne Ann Krentz,
New York Times bestselling author

THE FROG PRINCE

"Witty, smart, sophisticated...I loved this book!"

—Christine Feehan,
New York Times bestselling author

"Entertaining and witty...tugs the heartstrings in a big way."

—*Booklist*

ALSO BY JANE PORTER

The Frog Prince
Flirting with Forty

ODD MOM OUT

JANE PORTER

WITHDRAWN

5SPOT

NEW YORK   BOSTON

Copyright © 2007 by Jane Porter

5 Spot
Hachette Book Group
237 Park Avenue
New York, NY 10017

Visit our Web site at www.5-spot.com.

5 Spot is an imprint of Grand Central Publishing.
The 5 Spot name and logo are trademarks
of Hachette Book Group, Inc.

Printed in the United States of America

First Edition: September 2007
10 9 8 7 6 5 4

Library of Congress Cataloging-in-Publication Data
Porter, Jane
Odd mom out / Jane Porter.—1st ed.
p. cm.
Summary: "Jane Porter returns with another entertaining tale
of a bohemian, single working mother who finds herself at odds
with the stay-at-home, alpha moms"—Provided by publisher.
ISBN: 978-0-446-69923-5
1. Single mothers—Fiction.   2. Working mothers—Fiction.
3. Stay-at-home mothers—Fiction.   I. Title.
PS3616.O78O34 2007
813'.6—dc22
2007004366

Dedicated to my mother, Mary Elizabeth Lyles Higuera.
Thank you for teaching me all things are possible
(although it will probably take a lot of hard work).

Acknowledgments

Being a single mom requires courage as well as immense support, and I couldn't do what I do, or write what I write, if it weren't for friends and family who (try to) keep me sane: my brilliant sister Kathy Porter for knowing me since birth and still enjoying my company; Jamette Windham, who somehow manages to organize my home and my life; the gifted University of Washington graduate Lindsey Marsh, for taking such good care of my boys—and me— these past few years; the dedicated Leena Hyat of Author Sound Relations for making sure my writer life doesn't take over my home life; and finally, the one and only, and very funny, Lorrie Hambling (who really needs to star in a book of her own), for making sure I always have somewhere to go for Thanksgiving, Christmas, and Easter dinner . . . as well as when the power goes out.

Odd Mom Out was inspired by real women, women like Lucy Mukerjee, who was once my editor in London and now works in the movie biz in Hollywood, and Liza Elliott-Ramirez, founder and president of Expecting Models (Liza inspired me so much that I had to include her in my book). Lucy and Liza, I love seeing women take the world by storm. Brava!

To my true-blue writer friends Susanna Carr, CJ Carmichael, Barbara Dunlop, Elizabeth Boyle, and Lilian Darcy—thank you for trudging through the publishing peaks and valleys with me.

To my wonderful Bellevue friends, who nearly all juggle work and mommy hats—Joan, Lisa, Sinclair, Kristiina, Janie, Cheryl, Julie, Mary, Wendy—keep on keeping on.

To my beautiful young nieces Krysia Sikora, Maddie Porter, Betsy Porter, and Callen Porter—may you grow up to be brave, creative, and tenacious. (And never forget crazy Aunt Jane loves you.)

To young girls, young women, and old girls—don't be afraid to go for it. Expect to get knocked down. Just make sure to get up again.

To my very own maverick, Ty Gurney, thanks for continuing the long-distance romance. It's always interesting and it's certainly an adventure. You're my guy.

To my editor, Karen Kosztolnyik, and my agent, Karen Solem, thank you for helping me write the books I want and need to write. This is what I've always wanted to do.

And last but not least, this book is for you, my readers. Thank you for all your letters and insights and support. I want to be a better writer for you.

ODD MOM OUT

Chapter One

"Mom, can you still wear white if you're not a virgin?"

My nine-year-old daughter, Eva, knows the perfect way to get my full attention.

I push up my sunglasses and look at her hard. This is supposed to be a special mother-daughter day. I took off work to bring her to the country club pool, but lately, being Eva's mother is anything but relaxing. "Do you know what a virgin is?"

"Yes." She sounds so matter-of-fact.

"*How?*" I demand, because I sure as hell didn't tell her. My most gruesome memory is my mother sitting me down on my bed and explaining in horrendous detail "the story of the sperm and the ovum." I've vowed to find a better way to introduce Eva to the story but haven't found it yet. "You've had sex ed already at school?"

Eva sighs heavily. "No, Mom, that's in fifth grade. I've still got a year. But I read a lot. Between Judy Blume and Paul Zindel, I know everything."

That's as scary a statement as I've ever heard. "So you know about sex?"

"Yes." Her lips compress primly beneath the brim of

her straw hat. It's actually my hat, but she claimed it once we sat down.

I push my sunglasses even higher so they rest on top of my head. "You know about getting your period?"

"Yes."

"You know how babies are made?"

"Doesn't that fall under the sex question?"

Wow. She does seem to know quite a bit, and I watch her as she returns to the magazine she's reading.

"This is so ick," she says in disgust, turning a page in the bridal magazine on her lap. She brought three bridal magazines to the pool today and has been riveted for the last few hours by the oversize glossy publications. "There's nothing nice in here at all."

"Which magazine is that?"

"*Seattle Bride.*" She tosses aside the slender magazine with a contemptuous snort and reaches for another. "They don't know how to do weddings in Seattle. The styles are so ugly. The best weddings are always in the South."

I can't stop staring at her. So hard to believe this little girl came from me.

"So, Mom, back to my question," she says, flipping through the next magazine, *Southern Bride*. "Can nonvirgins wear white?"

"Yes," I answer reluctantly, thinking this is a discussion I'd very much like to avoid. "It's done all the time."

"So you don't have to wear ivory or pink?"

"That's an old rule. No one follows that anymore." Or there'd be no white weddings, either.

Eva pauses briefly to study a beaded gown with an equally ornate veil. "Obviously, virgins can't have babies.

Well, except for the Virgin Mary, but that was an exception to the rule, so if you've had a baby . . ." Her voice trails off as she looks up at me. "Probably not a virgin."

"Probably not," I agree.

"So you're definitely not a virgin."

"*Eva.*"

"I'm just asking."

"It's none of your business, but no, I'm not a virgin. Not that I had sex to make you."

"Gross. Don't talk about making me."

"You're the one talking about virgins!"

"That's different."

"*How?*"

"It just is. Ew." She shudders and slams *Southern Bride* closed before turning on the lounge chair to face me, her long dark hair falling over her thin shoulders. She's so skinny that her hipbones jut out and her long legs look vaguely storklike. "Too bad you can't wear white at your wedding, though, because ivory dresses are u-g-l-y. Ugly."

I don't know who this child is or where she came from. I know she's biologically mine—she looks just like me at nine—but what about the rest of her DNA? Whose sperm did I buy, anyway?

"I could wear white, Eva, but I don't have, nor do I want, a boyfriend. And the last thing I'm interested in is ever getting married."

She sighs wearily. "But if you don't even give marriage a try, how can you say you don't like it?"

Advil, Advil, Advil. Need Advil badly. "Marriage isn't like broccoli. You don't nibble on a stem to see if you like it."

"You're comparing men to vegetables?"

I almost liked it better when Eva thought I was a lesbian.

Two of the kids in Eva's New York preschool class were raised in lesbian households, and the kids were fantastic, funny, bright, well adjusted. At three, Eva was crushed when I told her that there would never be two mommies in our family. We were a one-mommy household.

"Just one mommy?" she'd cried. "But what about the Ark? All the animals came in twos."

It seemed like a good teaching opportunity, so I explained that Noah's pairs weren't female and female, but male and female, and I hastened to add that the decision wasn't so the world could live in harmony, but for reproductive reasons. The animals on Noah's Ark had a serious job. They had to repopulate the world that had just been drowned in the forty days of rain.

The drowning part of course caught her attention.

As did other Old Testament favorites like Cain killing Abel, Sodom being set on fire, Lot's wife turning to salt, and Abraham laying Isaac on an altar as a sacrifice. The dramatic illustration in her children's Bible of Abraham holding a knife over his son particularly fascinated her. Gave her some nightmares, too. But she never forgot the story.

She never forgets anything. She has the memory of an elephant.

"I thought we were here so you could swim," I say, trying to change the subject, wanting her to go play, be a normal little girl, although that's probably pushing it. "The pool closes next week once school starts, and it'll be nine months before it opens again."

Eva glances past me to look at the crowded deep end. The pool is packed today, as it's in the mid-nineties and nearing the end of summer.

"I am hot," she admits, fanning herself.

"So go swim."

But she doesn't move. She lies there on her side, studying the girls playing in the deep end. She's scared. Scared of being rejected again.

With me, she's brave and funny. Articulate and confident. But around the little girls here, her confidence vanishes. She just doesn't fit in, and I don't know why. She had no problem making friends in New York City. She was reasonably popular at her school in Manhattan. Why doesn't she have friends here?

"Should I go off the diving board or go down to the shallow end?" Eva asks, leaning against her arm, her dark green eyes tracking every move the girls make.

"Do what you want to do."

She hesitates and then slips off the lounge chair and drops her towel. "Okay. I'll swim in the deep end."

I shouldn't be, but I'm nervous as I sit in my lounge chair at the edge of the Points Country Club pool, watching Eva paddle around the deep end trying to get the other girls to notice her.

Just as she's done all summer. Just as she did last summer after we'd moved here.

I try not to stare at the group of girls playing just out of Eva's reach. Why don't they like her? Why won't they include her?

Eva's staring at them, too. She's clinging to the tiled wall and watching with wistful eyes as they splash and laugh.

Despite my studied nonchalance, I worry. I hate that wishful expression on Eva's face. It's so not who she is, so not who she should be.

Eva's brilliant. In kindergarten, she read at a sixth-grade reading level. This summer, she's managed many of the classics quite nicely. Her favorite cities are Tokyo and London.

So why doesn't Eva fit in?

Eva's decided she wants to be popular, and not just popular, she wants in with the most popular girls, the exclusive clique of the very rich, very pretty girls who aren't at all interested in being friends with her. And instead of accepting their lack of interest, she's determined to change them. Or her. Neither being a winning proposition.

Earlier in the year, I tried to explain to Eva that wanting to be liked, and wanting to be popular, is the kiss of death. I told her that she was just giving away her power, giving it to girls who don't deserve it, but Eva shook her head and answered with that martyred saint expression of hers, "Some people like to be liked."

She's right. I never needed people the way she does. I never cared what people thought. I still don't. My parents say I marched to a different drum from the time I could walk, and I've made my living being different. Apart. Unique. First as a graphic designer, now as the head of my own advertising company. My vision creates my art, and my art isn't just what I do, it's who I am.

I knew the move from New York to the Pacific Northwest would be difficult for me. I never expected it to be so hard on Eva. I grew up here, in Seattle, and left as soon as I turned eighteen. I never planned on returning—this was where my parents lived, not me—but then eighteen months ago, a work opportunity arose and I took it. Despite my misgivings.

I watch Eva, my stomach in knots. We should have stayed in New York.

"Eva!" I lean forward and call to her. She turns to look at me, her long dark hair streaming water. "Want to go?"

She scrubs a hand across her wet cheeks, her gypsy eyes too wise for her years, eyelashes long, dense, and black. In the last year, I've begun to see the hint of the cheekbones that will one day come. She has my face. I wasn't pretty as a child, either; my looks came much later, when I was older, sometime late during college.

"Not yet, Mom." Her attention's caught by the cluster of little girls climbing from the pool and race-walking to the diving board.

The little girls are pretty in that golden shimmer of late summer—tan, long limbed, sun-streaked hair. They have cute little noses that turn up, wide wet-lashed eyes, and gap-toothed smiles where baby teeth come and go. Children of privilege. Children who grow up belonging to country clubs and private tennis clubs and, if you're very lucky and live on the water, one of the exclusive yacht clubs, too.

Hugging the pool wall tighter, Eva watches the giggling girls take turns jumping and diving off the board, trying to outdo one another with big splashes and new cool maneuvers.

And behind the diving board are the little girls' nannies and moms. You can tell which girl belongs to which mom. Children and parents come in matching sets here, neat, tidy, incredibly groomed. Most of the moms wouldn't dream of actually getting in the pool with their children, despite being in outstanding shape (thanks to private fitness trainers and visits to a local, exceptional plastic surgeon who never names names).

I'm not pointing fingers, though. I wouldn't get in the pool here, either (although I have, when Eva's been especially lonely and desperate for companionship), not when every woman on the side will stare, sizing you up and down as you peel off your clothes, drop your towel, and climb in the pool.

They'll give you the same once-over as you climb out, too.

Each time. Every time.

And I guarantee nearly every woman is silently measuring. Comparing. *Do I look that fat? Is her figure better than mine? Does she have flab? Dimples? Do my thighs jiggle like that, too?*

These thoughts remind me of why I loved New York. New York was cool and sharp, beautiful in a hard, glistening way Bellevue isn't.

Bellevue, a suburb of Seattle, is soft, squishy, with exceptional public schools, big shingle houses fronted by emerald green lawns, sprawling upscale malls, and a Starbucks on every other corner. In this place of affluence and comfort, I feel alien.

Like Eva. But not. Because I don't want to fit in. I don't want to be like these women who have too much time on their diamond-ringed hands and who drive immaculate Lexus and Mercedes SUVs.

The girls swim close to Eva, and suddenly Eva is pushing off the wall and swimming toward them. I'm torn between exasperation and admiration. She tries every day. She doesn't give up. How can I not respect her tenacity? I never liked no for an answer. I should be glad she doesn't, either.

"I can dive," Eva says to them, smiling too big, trying too hard, setting my teeth on edge. "Want to see?"

One of the girls, I think it's Jemma Young, makes a face. "*No.*"

But Eva, now that she's finally made the first move, persists. "I'm hoping we're going to be in the same class again this year."

Jemma rolls her eyes at the other girls. "Yippee. That'd be fun."

I press my nails harder into my palms at Jemma's smart answer. Why didn't Jemma's mom teach her any manners?

"*So* fun," another little girl chimes in sarcastically, playing Jemma's game.

The little girls are all giggling and looking back and forth from Jemma to Eva.

I feel wild on the inside, like a mama bear needing to protect her cub. But I don't get up. I don't do anything. This is Eva's battle. She must learn to fend for herself. Even when it breaks my heart.

Jemma and girls flick their wet hair and swim toward the side of the pool. As Jemma hauls herself out of the pool using the ladder, she glances at the others, lined up little duck style right behind her.

"Let's go get ice cream," she announces imperiously.

The little duck friends follow.

Eva tries to follow.

She starts to climb the ladder, and she's smiling, keeping that too wide, too hopeful smile fixed on her face just in case Jemma turns around and asks her to join them.

But of course they don't ask her. They walk away, heading toward the snack bar.

And Eva's smile starts to fall. Her face is so open, so revealing. The anger in me rises again. I want to take Eva by the shoulders. Shake her. *They're not going to ask you to play. They're not going to include you. Stop hoping. Stop making them so powerful. Stop allowing them to hurt you.*

Eva doesn't know yet what I know about the world and being female. She doesn't understand that you have to establish yourself, establish your identity and boundaries, young. Girls can be vicious, far more cruel than boys, because their world is made up of language, stories, and secrets. Too often, little girls and women start a conversation with, "Don't tell anyone . . ." Three words I've learned that too often lead to pain.

In the boy world, any boy can join in provided he can spit farther, ran faster, hit harder. The boy world isn't an inner circle, but a totem pole hierarchy based on strength, guts, courage. Bravado.

It's the world I'd give Eva if I could. Instead, Eva's world makes me sweat. Bleed.

Goddamn town. Goddamn country club. Goddamn girls who won't let Eva in.

I gather Eva's magazines, placing the copy of *Elegant Bride* and *Modern Bride* in my tote bag before rising from my chair and holding up her striped towel. "Eva," I call to her, "want to go to Cold Stone?"

She's still watching the girls drip their way around the pool, past the mothers clustered at tables and lounge chairs, toward the snack bar nestled against the country club's shingled wall.

"I could just get a Popsicle here," she says, her wistful gaze never leaving Jemma and gang.

I spot Jemma's mom, Taylor Young, across the pool. Taylor blows Jemma a kiss as her daughter passes. Taylor Young, the original Bellevue Babe in her fitted light blue Polo shirt and short white tennis skirt.

Taylor, Taylor, Taylor. Wife of VP of Business Development Nathan Young, room mom, school auction chair, president of the PTA. *Why? Because nobody must do it better.*

Blech. I'd rather shoot myself between the eyes than spend every afternoon at Points Elementary.

But that's not nice of me. Taylor can't possibly spend every afternoon at school. She obviously does other things. Like highlight her hair. Visit Mystic Tan. Botox her brow.

Am I bitter? Hell, no. I'd hate Taylor's life. I love working, love my career and my colleagues, the intensity and challenge of it all. My life is one of taking risks. That's what brought me back to the Pacific Northwest, after all.

"Can I ask Jemma for a sleepover?" Eva asks timidly.

I'm jolted by Eva's question. Jemma Young for a sleepover? *Oh, Eva. Jemma Young doesn't even treat you nicely. Why do you want her as your friend?*

But I don't say it. I hold my breath instead, count to three, and then exhale. As I exhale, I draw Eva toward me, wrap her towel around her shoulders. "She might already have other plans."

Eva shrugs. "She might not." Her shoulders are so thin. She's tall, bony, delicate.

"That's true."

"And I haven't had a sleepover all summer."

When I was growing up, playdates and sleepovers weren't the thing they are now. Maybe now and then you had a friend over, but it wasn't this almost daily round robin of going to friends' houses that dominates the Points Elementary School scene. "That's true, too."

Eva smiles at me. "So it's okay?"

"Mm-hmm." I'm biting my tongue, biting it hard, knowing that Jemma's just going to reject her, wanting to protect her from the rejection, but not knowing how to. For the first time in my life, I wish I were someone else, wish I'd been crafted from different material. If I were like other women, if I were more domestic, more maternal, I'd know how to handle this, wouldn't I? I'd know what to say, what to do, to make my daughter more secure, more popular. More like the people she wants to be.

"Will you go with me?" she asks, pressing her towel to her mouth and chewing on the thick yellow terry cloth.

Will I go with her?

I don't even have to look at my Eva to see her. She's imprinted so deeply on my heart that I just know her, feel her, love her with the love of a mother lion or tiger. The love of a protector. I would do anything for her. "Yes. Let's go ask."

We—Eva—asks. Jemma says no. It takes all of five seconds to ask and be refused. As Eva heads into the girls locker room to get her clothes, I see Taylor Young rise from her chair and walk around the pool. She's stopping now to say hello to some women who've just arrived. Her smile is big. She's so shiny and pretty. So perfectly assembled.

My dislike doubles, grows. I want to punch her in the

face. Not nice, but I've never claimed to be nice. I'm honest, and that's something altogether different.

Jamming my hands deeper in my slouchy cargo pants, I'm acutely aware of how different I dress from the other women here. Even though it's a country club pool, I'm wearing an old faded black T-shirt, old cargo pants that ride low on my hips and are frayed at the hem, and gray paint-splattered rubber flip-flops.

My hair, a dark brown that people like to call black, is loose and reaches almost to my waist and doesn't have a style. It's just long, but it's how I've worn my hair since college, and I like it. I don't try to be soft or pretty. I just want to be me.

Eva emerges from the locker room as Taylor Young walks our way. Eva, still in her swimsuit and with her clothes balled in her arms, stands at full attention as Taylor approaches. She's looking anxiously at Taylor, smiling too big, waiting to be noticed.

When Taylor is about to pass without making eye contact or acknowledging her, Eva shouts out, "Hi, Mrs. Young. How are you?"

My hand clenches. I wish Eva hadn't done that, but now Taylor pauses, turns in her short tennis skirt, and looks at Eva, and then me, and back to Eva. Her lips curve smugly. "Hello, Marta. Eva. How are you?"

I nod my head. "Hello, Taylor."

"I'm good, Mrs. Young, thank you," Eva answers breathlessly, smiling hard. "Are you having a nice summer?"

"Very nice. I hope you are, too." And with a smile at Eva and a brief incline of her head in my direction, she moves on toward the locker room.

Eva's wide, tight smile fades as Taylor disappears into the locker room. Her shoulders seem to curve in. "She's the nicest mom. Everybody says so."

I say nothing. What can I say?

We head to my truck, and I toss the wet towels in the back of the pickup. "You okay?" I ask her as we climb in.

She nods once but doesn't say anything.

As I drive, I play my favorite Wyclef Jean CD. Eva just sits next to me, staring silently out the window. Her eyes are watery, but no tears fall. I tell myself it's the chlorine from the pool, but I know the truth.

For a moment, I think I could hate Taylor and Jemma and all of them at the pool, but hate is such a useless emotion, and I don't want to hate anyone.

Besides, Jemma's just a little girl, and Jemma's entitled to like who she wants to, even if Eva's not one of them.

"Want to go see a movie? Go out for dinner?" I ask, glancing Eva's way again, thinking of fun diversions.

She shakes her head, her long black hair hanging in inky tangles down her pale back. "No."

"Is there anything that sounds good? It's only Friday night, we could go home, pack up, head to Grandma and Grandpa's cabin at Lake Chelan—"

"I just really wanted to have someone stay the night at *our house*. Play at our house." She's pressing her towel back to her mouth, chewing relentlessly on the corner. "I just think it'd be fun."

For the first time in a while, I see the world as a nine-year-old, not a thirty-six-year-old, and she's right. A sleepover would be fun.

*   *   *

That night, Eva sleeps with me in my bed. We're calling it a "slumber party," and I'm trying hard to make it different from the other nights Eva's crept into bed with me because she's lonely or had bad dreams.

For the first few years of Eva's life, she slept with me or in a crib next to my bed. From the very beginning, it was just the two of us, and I couldn't bear to put her in a separate room. It was hard enough leaving her every day to go to work. I hated having her so far away at night. But then my insomnia returned, and I couldn't sleep—would lie awake all night, fidgeting in the dark, trying not to wake Eva—and eventually I decided she was better off in her own room.

But she's back tonight, along with a stack of her ever-present bridal magazines, and we're watching a Hilary Duff movie on cable and eating popcorn and hot-fudge sundaes; and even as Eva snuggles close, using my lap as a pillow, I know I'm a poor substitute for a best friend.

Remembering my own best friends, I stroke her long hair; the black tangled strands that hang down her back are still chlorine rough. I should have made her wash her hair and condition it when we returned. But that's so not my style. Instead I ordered out for barbecue chicken pizza. Trying to distract her. Trying to distract myself.

Growing up, I had best friends, great friends, friends my parents hated.

The corner of my mouth curls as I picture Sam and Chloe, friends who wanted to be as different as I did. Sam dressed punk and Chloe Goth, but both rode skateboards as I did before we got our driver's licenses and went for funky muscle cars and barely running sports cars. We weren't soft, pretty girls. We were too angry. Which is probably why I got shipped off to boarding school my senior year.

Sending me to boarding school had been Dad's idea. Dad was old school. A retired major from the Deep South. All his life, he wanted sons. In the end, all he got was me.

Slowly, I untangle the tangles in Eva's hair, hearing the movie dialogue but not listening. I understand what Eva wants, more than she knows.

I never did get my dad's approval, and I adored him for much of my life. But nothing I did was good enough, nothing was right. He wanted sweetness, goodness, charm, docility. And I wanted fire.

Glancing down at Eva, I see the crescent of black lashes, the slight curve of future cheekbones, the full upper lip, and the firm, rounded chin.

This, I think, is the child my father wanted. My fingertips trace Eva's cool brow. This is the daughter he would have cherished, adored. A delicate girl. A brilliant yet eager-to-please child, one who could be molded into a southern belle, his idea of the ultimate beauty queen.

The movie ends, and Eva scoots down beneath the sheet. It's a hot night, and we've no air-conditioning, and even with a fan pointed at the bed, the air is still, hot, thick, heavy.

"Mom?" Eva's cheek nestles in the pillow, her feet reach out and wrap around my legs.

With the window open and moonlight spilling, I can see her face. Her profile is pale, goddesslike in the dark. She was born with an old soul, and even though she's nine, she's mastered the pensive look perfectly, a troubled line etched between her brows. "What, baby?"

"Do you think Jemma's mom is pretty?"

I feel like a cat with a hairball. I want to retch. Instead I touch that furrow between Eva's eyebrows, willing it to go away. "Mmmm."

"I love her clothes, and her hair. I think she's so stylish and pretty."

I can't even come up with an appropriate answer, but fortunately, Eva doesn't seem to need one.

"You'd look beautiful in dresses and outfits like that, Mom. Don't you think? You could be so beautiful if you tried." Eva smiles up at me, and her smile briefly dazzles me with its innocence and hopefulness. Eva can be so serious, and then when she smiles it's like the full moon at midnight. So big and wide, glowing with light.

I lean toward her, kiss her. "I love you."

She's quiet for a long time, and I think maybe she's fallen asleep. But then a moment later she whispers, "So white would be okay? Because I saw the most beautiful dress for you, Mom. It looks like a ball gown—"

"Don't make me send you back to your room, Eva."

"Mom."

"You know weddings aren't my thing. The whole idea of dressing up like a Madame Alexander doll and marching down an aisle while everyone watches curdles my stomach."

"That's rude," she protests, cold feet rubbing against my calves.

"But it's true, and Eva, you don't have to get married to be happy."

"Maybe not, but there's no reason to make fun of people who want to get married."

"I'm not making fun of them. I'm just saying, don't try to be part of the pack. Be the wolf. It's so much more fun."

Eva giggles. "You're weird."

"I know, and I like it. Now go to sleep."

"Good night, Mom."

"Good night, my Eva."

Eva scoots closer and tucks her hand into mine. "You know what I want, Mom?" Her voice is pitched low, and it sounds strangely mature in the dark room.

My fingers curl around hers. Her hand is warm and small in mine. "Please don't mention weddings or marriage."

"No, it's not that."

"Then tell me. What do you want?"

"I want Jemma to like me."

The pressure is back, a weight on my chest. I clear my throat. "I'm sure she does—"

"No, she doesn't." She sighs softly, sounding far too old for her years, but maybe that's what being an only child does to you. "I can tell she doesn't like me. But maybe she'll change her mind. You know. When she gets to know me."

I squeeze Eva's hand tighter. "Let's hope so."

Chapter Two

Eva's shaking my shoulder and talking too fast. "Mom, Mom, Mom. The class lists! They should be up. Wake up."

I squeeze my eyes tighter and try to roll away from her. I roll right onto a crumpled magazine. I reach for her magazine and shove it off the bed. "Eva, why do you do this to me?"

"You have to wake up sooner or later. Might as well wake up now. The class lists are up. We've got to go check it out."

"And this is why you're waking me up?"

She climbs over me, her knobby knee banging my hip, and puts her face in front of mine, her long hair falling on my cheek. "We've got to find out who my teacher is and get my class supplies. It's already Saturday. School starts in three days, and I've got to get organized."

Another curious difference between us, I think, slowly opening one eye to peer at her. I hated school, and Eva loves it. She excels academically, reads and writes as if she's fifteen instead of nine, and aces every test.

"Mom. Get. Up." Eva impatiently rips back the covers.

The early morning air is way too chilly for that, and I yank the covers back. "What time is it?"

"Almost seven."

Glancing past her, I see the clock next to my bed. Six twenty-three. Arrrgh. "You lie. It's not even six-thirty."

"You might as well get up. With school starting soon, we've got to get on a routine again. Get back to normal."

Normal? Routine? Schedule? Whose kid is this?

Growling, I bury my head under my pillow. "Give me another half hour. I need a half hour. Okay?"

And Eva, my delicious little daughter, agrees and returns to wake me up at six forty-five on the dot.

I see the red numbers on the alarm clock, and so does she, but Eva just grins, happy to rob me of fifteen minutes if it means she wins.

As soon as Eva sees me up, she bounds out of the bedroom, long legs flying. I'm moving much more slowly, and I stumble toward the kitchen to start the coffee.

Leaning on the counter, newspaper spread out in front of me, I scan the headlines as the coffee brews.

"Are you going to go for a run?" Eva asks, taking the DVD of *Father of the Bride* off pause.

She's watched that movie a dozen times this summer, along with her other summer faves: *Runaway Bride*, *The Princess Bride*, *My Best Friend's Wedding*, *My Big Fat Greek Wedding*, *The Wedding Planner*, and let's not forget *Four Weddings and a Funeral*.

As Steve Martin's emotion-choked voice fills the room, I close my eyes. "I will run if you insist on watching this again."

Eva temporarily mutes the sound. "But there's nowhere else to watch it, Mom, this is our only TV."

"Maybe you don't need to watch it."

"Maybe you need to run."

Maybe I do.

Grumpily, I head to my room and change into shorts, a T-shirt, and my running shoes before strapping my iPod on one arm and my cell phone on the other.

I reappear to say good-bye to Eva. She beams at me, sinks deeper into the couch cushions. "Have a good run."

"I've got my phone. Call—"

"I know. I know the number. I know the house will be locked. I know what to do." She waves me toward the door. "Now go. The best part of the movie is coming up."

I glance at the screen. Steve's about to cry. This is definitely my exit cue.

Opening the door, I'm confronted by the morning fog. In summer, we often get a marine layer that blankets the city and lake with a soupy gray mist. I know it'll burn off later, but it doesn't make me think *fun run*.

"It's icky," I call to Eva, who knows already because she was the one who brought in the newspaper earlier.

"Then come back and watch the movie with me. It's coming up to the best part."

Eva knows how to get me moving. "I'll be back in twenty-five."

"Bye."

Outside, I start slowly until I wake up properly. I don't run as often as I used to. I used to run a lot in Manhattan, meeting up with Shey in Central Park. Whenever Tiana was in town, we made her run with us, too. And running was good for us, made us feel powerful. Strong. The point of exercise isn't to make you skinny, but to armor your mind. We are fierce, tough, warrior women. We are not fragile or helpless. We do not need to lean on anyone. In fact, the world leans on us.

With my iPod on, I'm able to maintain a quick tempo, and as I run I take deep breaths to try to clear my head, help me relax.

At the corner, I pause, glance in both directions, and start to cross when suddenly a black Hummer appears from nowhere, brakes hard, and lays on the horn.

The horn jolts me, but what pisses me off is that the driver of the Hummer ran the stop sign. It didn't even come to a full stop, just barely slowed before nearly mowing me over.

As the Hummer passes, I see the driver, a skinny blonde, on a cell phone.

I'm tempted to shout at her to be careful, but I know it won't do any good. Skinny blondes in Hummers don't have the best listening skills.

Instead I quicken my speed, pushing myself to go a little faster than usual to burn off my anger.

So many of the women around here seem so oblivious to real life, preoccupied as they are by perfect hair, teeth, and nails.

Must be nice to have a rich husband who takes care of all your needs.

Almost immediately, I picture Taylor in her cute tennis skirt. Taylor didn't take the day off work to be at the pool. Being at the pool—and on the tennis court and in the gym—is Taylor's job.

Disgusted, I turn toward home, running along 84th Street, heading toward Points Drive, when I'm passed by a man who is running, too. He's huge, head and shoulders taller than me, and I'm not short.

As he moves in front of me, his head turns ever so slightly and his gaze briefly meets mine.

Light eyes, an intense expression. Hard jaw. A face that's more chiseled than beautiful.

I shiver a little as he takes the lead. He's wearing long baggy shorts and a navy long-sleeved T-shirt, yet he's so big, so thickly muscled, I imagine he's got to be a professional athlete. Maybe one of the Seattle Seahawks or perhaps a Mariner.

Either way, he's definitely amazing, and as he disappears into the fog in front of me, I slow, suddenly light-headed, almost dizzy.

I slow even more and then stop running altogether. For a moment I just stand there, hands on my hips, trying to catch my breath. And my breathlessness has nothing to do with my physical conditioning.

Eventually, I start jogging again and head for home. Back at the house, everything is just as I left it, and Eva's still on the couch, watching the end of her movie.

Our Yarrow Point house isn't huge, but it's got a modern floor plan with a soaring ceiling—no formal living room, just a great room with kitchen, family room, and dining room all combined—and I love it because I can see Eva no matter where I am or what I'm doing.

I kick off my running shoes, leaving them by the front door, and after stripping off my socks head into the kitchen. Without looking away from the TV, Eva asks, "Good run?"

"Yes."

"See anybody?"

I think of the man who passed me, the man of mythic

proportions. "No." I reach into the glass-fronted cabinet for one of my thick, hand-painted pottery mugs I bought in Mexico aeons ago. "There was a lady who nearly ran me over, though."

"Was she putting on makeup?"

"Talking on her cell."

"Typical," Eva drawls, and then looks at me. "So. Are you almost ready to go?"

"Go where? I just got back," I answer, filling the mug with coffee.

"To the school."

"It's *early*. And I haven't even had my coffee yet."

"You can pour it in one of those travel mugs."

"I can drink it here."

"Mom—"

"*Eva.*"

"I'm just saying—"

"And I'm just saying there's eager and there's absurd. You can be eager, but you can't be absurd, okay?"

She makes a humphy sound and twirls the tips of her long ponytail around her fingers. "So when will we go?"

"Nine."

"*Nine?*" Her voice rises an octave. "And what will I do until then?"

"You haven't watched *Monsoon Wedding* lately." I smile, grab my coffee, and head through the back door into the garden and to the office studio at the back. Once upon a time, I kept a laptop on the kitchen counter, but I ended up checking e-mail way too many times in the evenings and weekends, so now all e-mail happens in the office studio.

The office studio is why I bought this house, although

the studio was in shambles, with a leaking roof and small dark windows that didn't get any light.

I use the hidden key to unlock the studio door, then put the key back and flick on the lights. I'm just booting up my computer when Eva appears in the office doorway. "You said you were taking the weekend off!"

"I am," I say, typing in my password before dropping into my chair. "And working isn't checking e-mail. Checking e-mail is checking e-mail."

"You spend *hours* doing e-mail."

"That's business these days, baby."

"Mooooom."

I glance up, grimace. "I know, sweetheart, but this is what I do. This is part of my job, and I won't be more than fifteen minutes."

"You always say that—"

"*Eva*. This is how I pay the bills, and you said you liked me working from home instead of at an office downtown. You said you'd rather me work from here because then you wouldn't have to go to day care."

"But it's Saturday."

"Lots of people work Saturday."

Eva sighs dramatically and marches back to the house. I watch her go, trying not to feel guilty. I'm not doing anything wrong. I'm a single mom. I have to work. But maybe I feel guilty because most of the time I *like* working.

In New York, I was a vice president at the huge ad agency Keller & Klein, and when they approached me about opening a West Coast branch for them, I jumped at the opportunity. It was a huge honor as well as a risk, and I craved both.

Unfortunately, Keller & Klein got bought by a big German media conglomerate shortly after we moved to Seattle. The German media giant shut down the Seattle office, and that's how I ended up starting my own company, Z Design.

I couldn't yank Eva out of school once again, and not away from her grandparents. She's still just getting to know them, and now she knows Mom is sick.

It's good, owning my own business. The hours are long, but I'm living my dream. I've a great staff, a thriving company, and financial stability. What more could I want?

Outside, the fog is beginning to lift and a brave bee buzzes around the potted roses. I catch a whiff of the herbs—mint and lavender—planted outside the studio door, and after hitting send and receive, I wait for the e-mail to download.

I love summer. I love sleeping in and the slow mornings where Eva can sprawl on the floor and watch her movies or cartoons while I have my coffee and do my thing. So many moms seem relieved when summer ends and their kids go back to school, but I dread the start of the school year. Sure, I accomplish more when Eva's in school, but I resent how the school system superimposes its schedule on ours, limiting our trips, our adventures, Eva's and my time together.

I've thirty, forty e-mails, with nearly half being spam. I delete those and then skim through the rest of the e-mail. Nothing seems to require immediate attention, and I happily forward several to my staff members for them to handle. Eva thinks I love e-mail. She doesn't realize it's a necessary evil.

But she is right about me not working today. I've promised to take the weekend off. It's our last weekend before
school starts on Tuesday, and Eva and I didn't have enough
time together this summer. I ended up working far more
hours than I'd anticipated.

Sipping my coffee, I breeze through the various e-zines
and business bulletins that I skipped yesterday because of
lack of time. I'm still reading one of the bulletins when
the studio phone rings.

"Marta, Frank here. How are you?"

Frank is Frank Deavers, one of the former executive vice
presidents of Harley-Davidson who'd left Harley a few years
ago to do his own thing. I'd worked with Frank on some
small jobs for Harley, but Keller & Klein wasn't the right
agency for Harley and they took their account elsewhere.

In the meantime, Frank and I remained friends, catching up by phone or e-mail every couple of months. Frank
knew I owned a Harley but dreamed of owning a restored
Indian or Freedom bike one day.

"Found that Freedom bike yet?" he asks.

"Have you found your Indian?"

"They are opening an Indian factory in North Carolina."

"Heard that." I draw the blinds in the studio, brighten-
ing the office. Until the rest of the fog burns off, it'll be
rather gloomy outside.

"Did you hear Freedom's building a factory in your neck
of the woods?"

I sit at the edge of my desk. "Here in Seattle?"

"Apparently they've found some land outside of Renton,
and with the various Boeing layoffs they believe they've
got the skilled workforce needed."

"You're serious."

"Completely."

Wow. I love, love, love the old bikes and have dreamed of putting together a vintage Freedom chopper, but that will be a labor of love, as well as some significant money.

"I've signed on with Freedom to handle franchising and merchandising."

If you don't love bikes, you won't know what this means, but it's huge. It's wonderful. Bike lovers have dreamed about the day the legendary bikes like Indian, Victory, Triumph, and Freedom will be manufactured again. There's nothing wrong with Harley or any of the Japanese motorcycles, but it's like having only two car companies to choose from—Honda and Chevy.

Car aficionados want choices. Consumers want choices. Bike lovers want choices.

"But we're talking years, right?" I ask, trying not to get ahead of myself too much with bike fantasies.

"We're unveiling our first bike in January, in a thirty-second TV spot during the Super Bowl."

I'm shocked, and thrilled, and impressed. This is great news, and I'm already thinking how I can get a piece of the action for us at Z Design. "That's expensive."

"We're going to do this right."

There are so many questions I want to ask, so many things I want to know. "You'll have bikes in production by then?"

"We'll be taking orders. The first bikes will roll out late April, early May."

"Just in time for summer." Damn. I really want to be involved. Working with Freedom Bikes wouldn't be merely revenue, it would be a chance to work with a product I enjoy, an opportunity to support something I believe in.

"So, Frank, did you call just to torment me, or are you going to tell me there's a way I can be part of this? Because you've got to know I want to be part of this. How many years have I known you? Six? Seven? And we've shared how many bike stories?"

"I know." He pauses, hesitates. "So how's business going?"

I notice he didn't answer my question, but that's okay. Advertising's always a cat-and-mouse game. Fortunately, I'm a very patient kitty. "Good. We're handling some significant regional and national accounts."

"How significant?"

"What's that?"

"How big are the big accounts? What are you dealing with nationally?"

"You want my client list, Frank?"

"I want to know if you've got the balls to handle the launch of Freedom Bikes."

My heart races. I'm practically salivating. If Frank weren't twenty years older than me with a wonderful wife and three kids, I think I'd fall for him. "What's the bottom line? What do I need to do? Who do I need to win over?"

He chuckles, his deep, rough voice growing rougher. "All of them."

"Who is my competition?"

"Everyone."

Sounds like my idea of fun. "Frank, count me in."

"We're in Seattle in a week or so to tour the job site and sign leases on our downtown office space. I want to

introduce you to the executive committee then. It's not
the time to present anything conceptually, but I'd like you
to come to dinner, meet folks, put faces with names."

"In a heartbeat."

"I'll have my secretary e-mail you Tuesday with the
details. Make sure you save the date."

"I wouldn't miss it for anything."

"Marta, I'd love it if it worked out, but this is a long
shot. I don't want you disappointed if it doesn't happen."

I would be disappointed. Beyond disappointed. "Why
is it such a long shot, Frank?"

"Don't make me state the obvious."

"Because I own a Harley?"

He laughs, deep guffaws that make me smile. "Yeah,
and it has nothing to do with you being a woman."

"Being a woman just makes me better."

"I know that. But we're talking about the bike industry."

I know. Macho, male dominated, no room for women
at the top. Just at the bottom. Underneath 'em. Right where
men like to keep 'em. "Frank, you can't scare me."

"So let's just take it a step at a time and see what
happens."

"You've got yourself a deal."

I hang up the phone and smile at nothing in particular.
Frank just made my day.

Two hours later, Eva finally gets us to Points Elementary
to check out the class list. She bounds out of the car, and I
trail behind more slowly, still thinking about Frank's call.

I want to be part of the Freedom Bikes ad campaign. I
want to be involved.

Despite it being a Saturday morning, there's an impressive crowd grouped in front of the school office window where the class lists have been posted. Eva's pushed toward the front to get a look at the fourth-grade class sheet.

I'm learning here in Bellevue that class assignments determine the kind of year it's going to be, and it's not only the teacher who influences the class but the kids in the class as well.

Parents want their children to have a good class, too, but I'm beginning to sense that to some here, good doesn't mean behaved. Good means connected. Good means rich.

I've heard the names bandied about, too, and the most desirable kids to have in your class are those sired by Microsoft millionaires and billionaires, the founders of Amazon, or one of the McCaw brothers, those fathers of wireless technology.

If you don't get a technology heir, you could always hope for a Nordstrom or an offspring of the professional athletes filling the Seahawk, Sonic, or Mariner roster.

Good kids from good money.

Long live the Eastside communities of Medina, Hunts Point, Yarrow Point, and Clyde Hill.

"Mom!" Eva's reaching through the crowd and grabbing my elbow. "Did you see who I've got? Mrs. Shipley, the one I was telling you about last year, the one who does the school's literary magazine."

"Oh, not Mrs. Shipley," groans a mother in the group. "She's impossible, the hardest teacher by far at Points. It's common knowledge that she gives twice the homework any other fourth-grade teacher does. *Twice.* And her expectations for writing! Absurd. These kids are still just learning to write. How can you expect them to be doing essays every week?"

Apparently, Mrs. Shipley was moved over from Bellevue High School, where she taught honors students, and she approaches her fourth-grade classes as though she were still teaching ambitious Ivy League–dreaming teenagers.

Eva lets out yet another squeal. "Mom! You won't believe it. Guess who's in my class?"

I don't have a clue, and Eva, bless her, doesn't make me wait.

"Jemma," she breathes, her grip tightening on my wrist. "Jemma's in my class! We're going to be together in the same class this year. Finally!"

We're heading to the car now, but Eva continues to jump and twirl. "This is so great. It's so wonderful." She turns to beam up at me. "This is going to be the best year ever."

Chapter Three

Eva's dancing through the aisles of downtown Bellevue's Office Depot, her mood so ebullient that you'd think we were in a bridal salon instead of an office supply store.

Although to be completely fair, Eva truly does love office and school supplies. When she was a young child, her favorite purchase at the grocery store or drugstore was a spiral-ring notebook. *Seriously.*

While Eva searches for the correct supplies, I'm left to push the oversize shopping cart and check off items as they're found. I'm also thinking about Eva and Jemma being in the same class and what an ungodly long year it will be if Eva insists on trying to make Jemma her friend.

This summer, Eva and I went to the Yukon for our summer vacation. We flew on Air Canada from Vancouver to Whitehorse, where we rented a car and spent a week exploring the Yukon Territory.

Growing up, I'd read everything I could by Jack London (my two favorite authors being Jack London and Mark Twain), and one of the places I'd always wanted to visit was the Klondike, so this summer Eva and I went.

We traveled the Top of the World Highway, panned

for gold, had a drink at Diamond Tooth Gerties, and we laughed so much. We hiked and batted at mosquitoes the size of my fist. (Only a slight exaggeration.) We had such a good time, and I thought—somehow—that when we returned, Eva's confidence would be back, too.

And it was, for all of one day, until Eva tried to tell the girls at the pool about her trip and the girls laughed. *Laughed.*

"Why did you go there?" Jemma asked in disgust. "Why didn't you go to Hawaii like everybody else?"

Okay. That's why I don't like Jemma Young, and this is why I never wanted to be part of the popular-girl clique. Being popular seemed like such a drag. All those girls trying to say the same thing, do the same thing, pretend to be just like one another.

How horrible.

Eva peers around the school supplies display. "Mom, is it twenty-four or forty-eight crayons? I forget."

I smooth the supply list that I've inadvertently crumpled and look for Eva's class. Fourth grade. Crayons. "Twenty-four."

Her hand hovers over the Crayola boxes. "I like the forty-eight better. More colors. More choices."

"Then get the forty-eight."

"But we're supposed to get what's on the list."

"The list is merely a suggestion—"

"It's not, Mom. It's required." Eva dumps the crayons and colored pencils in the cart. "Everything on there is required."

How did I get Little Miss Schoolgirl for a daughter?

I specialized in cutting class and forging my parents' signatures. Eva won't miss school even after a dentist appointment. She insists on going back after getting a filling, showing up for class drooling with a thick wad of cotton clamped between her teeth.

Now she continues to select the just-right binder, the exact plastic-coated colored dividers, the specific number of number two pencils, the set of highlighters, the precise style of notebook.

Eva's still crouching in front of the plastic space makers, trying to find one that's twelve inches long—not nine—when I spot my favorite kind of Bellevue mom, one of those women who are perfectly done even for a Saturday morning trip to Office Depot, with two kids.

I don't recognize her, but the kids look familiar, particularly the little girl, and I hear their conversation even before they reach us.

"I have to have a new backpack, I hate my old one."

"This year I want everything purple. A purple binder, purple folders, purple pens."

"Why can't I have an iPod? Or an iPod shuffle? Everyone has an iPod shuffle."

Eva hears them, too, and her face lights up. She shoots me a significant look, as though to say, *See?* as she scrambles to her feet. "Hi, Paige," she says breathlessly, the turquoise-lidded space maker clutched to her chest.

"Hi, Eva."

Eva and Paige size each other up from across a safe distance of mothers and shopping carts. Awkward silence unfurls even as I place Paige. Yesterday, at the pool. She's one of Jemma's friends.

"Buying your school supplies?" Eva asks, and her voice quavers nervously.

"Yeah." Paige is chewing gum, and she pops a little purple bubble. "Who's your teacher?"

"Mrs. Shipley."

"Jemma has her," Paige says, cocking her head and rubbing her foot against the back of her calf. "I've got Mrs. Lewis. She's supposed to be easy."

"You're so lucky," Eva breathes, making me think she's got the IQ of a tree monkey.

Why is she playing dumb? Where the hell did her feisty personality go? And what is so special about these little girls that she feels the need to earn their approval?

Paige's mom in the meantime has been studying me, and when I look at her, she forces a quick smile. "I don't think we've ever met. I'm Lana Parker, Paige's mom."

I hold out my hand. "Marta Zinsser, Eva's mom." We shake hands, and she winces at my firm grip. I didn't expect her hand to feel like pudding.

Lana Parker removes her hand as fast as she can from mine. "Are you new to the area?"

"We've been in the Pacific Northwest over a year now."

"Where did you move from? California?"

"New York."

Lana's eyebrows try to lift but can't go far, as her forehead is very taut and smooth. A little too taut and smooth. "That's a big change."

"Yes, it is."

"How do you like it here?"

"It's good," I answer vaguely, not bothering to mention I'm relatively local, raised in tiny Laurelhurst just across the 520 bridge. I never was comfortable with my father's wealth or social status, a status my mother enjoyed tremendously. Instead of hanging on Dad's coattails, I've tried to make my own way in the world, wanting to succeed on the basis of my talent and reputation versus his.

"Was your husband relocated?"

My husband. Great. I love these kinds of questions. "No. I was transferred."

"And he followed you out? There's a good husband for you."

I just smile, the small, close-lipped smile that I use for moments like these. I had plenty of them in New York when I'd take Eva for walks in her stroller and then again when I enrolled her in school. *Does she look like her daddy or you? Her father isn't listed on the emergency contact forms. Will her father be coming to the parent orientation?* I used to try to answer all the questions, but it just got old and repetitive, and now I do my best to ignore them. "I'm lucky I have an interesting career."

"What do you do?"

"I have my own advertising agency, Z Design."

"That must keep you busy."

"There are some long hours," I admit, feeling vaguely uncomfortable and unsure why. There's nothing alarming about Lana Parker. A dark blonde with hair swept off her face, Lana reminds me a bit of Faith Hill in *The Stepford Wives.* She's pretty, quite pretty, but not quite real, either.

"I couldn't work," Lana says, lips pursing. "Not when the kids are little. They're only children once, and I don't want to miss a thing."

This is why I was feeling uncomfortable.

I have to work—it's not a choice—yet my work isn't just a paycheck, it's who I am, what I love to do. "I agree. That's why I've made a point of working from home."

"So smart. Because those full-time jobs are so hard on families and children."

I don't have a part-time job. I definitely have a full-time job, and I think Lana knows it. I think Lana's being clever and slightly unkind.

"You're very lucky you have such a supportive husband," Lana adds sweetly. "He must really help pick up the slack."

"Is that what men do?" I ask just as sweetly. "Pick up the slack?" Either Lana is living in la-la land or she's just trying to push my buttons. Virtually all of my friends are married, and while most are still happily married and most would marry their husbands all over again, most also wouldn't say their husbands make their lives, or their work, easier.

Lana blinks, taken aback. "Uh . . . well . . . I don't know."

Her expression looks about to crumple, and I feel a ping of remorse. "So how many children do you have?" I ask, trying to change the subject and move us into safer territory.

Lana grabs gratefully on to the new topic. "Just these two, Paige and Peter. They're twins." She pauses. "Fraternal."

Yeah, I guessed that.

Lana leans toward me to whisper conspiratorially, "I just wish we'd thought a little more about the names. My son gets teased at school all the time."

"For Peter, Peter, pumpkin eater?"

She stiffens uncomfortably. "*No.* For Peter Parker." She pauses, waits for me to get it. I don't get it.

"Peter Parker," she repeats a trifle impatiently. "As in Spider-Man."

"Ah. Sorry. I haven't read the comics in years."

"But the movies . . . ?" she persists. After a moment she shakes her head, her cheeks flushed nearly as pink as her fruity Juicy Couture tracksuit. "So are you going to the emergency parent meeting this afternoon?" But she doesn't wait for me to ask, launching immediately into an explanation. "It's about the kindergarten nightmare."

"What nightmare?"

"You haven't heard?"

"I'm afraid we've been . . . traveling."

Lana shudders. "It's a disaster. A complete fiasco, that's what it is. Those poor kids. And their parents!"

I just shake my head.

Lana leans even closer, her hand pressed to her throat, and whispers, "They're sending all the Points kindergart-ners to the Lakes."

She delivers the information with a note of triumph, and I stare at her blankly. Obviously I'm missing the point. "Forever?"

"No, for the *year,* until the school board can figure out what to do with all the kids. Despite the remodel a cou-ple years ago, Points Elementary has already outgrown its space, and so all the incoming kindergartners are going to be bused to Lakes Elementary." She pauses, stares at me. "Can you believe it?"

"Bused," I repeat, wondering why children are being bused to a school that is less than half a mile away from their own.

"Exactly! Those little children bused and then mixed with kindergartners from the other school. They're not even being kept separate. No, Lakes teachers will be teaching

Points kids, and Points teachers will be teaching Lakes kids—awful, that's all I can say."

"But it's just for one year, isn't it? And don't most of the kids play on the same sports programs anyway? I know Eva's soccer team last year had children from Enatai, Points, and the Lakes—"

"But families, siblings, *separated*. And now the Lakes wants one-sixth of our auction money, too. As if we wanted our children to attend their school!"

Now is one of those times I think I should read the Points school bulletins more closely or maybe attend a PTA meeting or tiptoe into the back-to-school brunch so I can put faces to names and learn the school news firsthand.

"There's going to be a parent meeting today, before tonight's beach picnic," Lana continues. "It's at Taylor's house. You do know Taylor Young?"

"Oh yes." I nod and smile. "I do."

Eva is hanging on every word as well, and she nods furiously. "I do, too."

Lana shoots Eva a condescending smile. "You know where Jemma lives, sweetie, don't you?"

Eva and Jemma ride the school bus together every day. They even share the same bus stop. Not that Jemma ever talks to Eva, but, hey, just standing on the same corner as Jemma rocks Eva's boat.

"Join us at the meeting," Lana urges. "You'll hear from the committee about what's been done and what we still need to do. There's no time to waste."

With a glance at her watch, Lana shakes her head. "Oh dear, look at the time. Tennis in less than an hour. Have to hustle." She points at me, jabs her finger. "Four o'clock at

Taylor's. If your husband can't watch your daughter, she's of course welcome to come. There will be other kids there."

Now Lana wiggles her fingers in a wave and moves on.

Eva is staring after Lana Parker, her forehead furrowed. "Why did she keep saying 'your husband'? Doesn't she know that you're not married and I don't have a dad?"

"I guess not, and I didn't feel like correcting her."

"Why not?" she asks, turning to look at me. "Does it bother you?"

"No." At least it didn't bother me in New York.

"So tell her. It's weird listening to her say 'your husband, your husband.'"

"I will. Next time."

Eva's still looking at me. "We are going to Mrs. Young's today, aren't we?"

Going to Taylor Young's? Going to a ridiculous committee meeting to protest kindergartners spending a year at another local elementary school, a school that leads the state in WASL scores? Do those women have no life? And is my daughter completely out of her mind?

"Go?" I ask her, my voice calm, clear, although on the inside I'm fairly frothing at the mouth. "I don't think so."

Eva deposits the space maker in the cart and faces me. "Why not?"

I hear that cool, steely tone, and it amazes me how Eva can sound so much like my mother. It's one thing to hear your mother's disapproval come from her lips. It's quite another to hear it from your nine-year-old daughter.

I take a deep breath. "Because for one, I don't agree with them. These moms are making a mountain out of a molehill—"

"They just want what's best for their children."

I stare at Eva and try to see who AS1V677 really was, AS1V677 being her sperm donor father.

I ordered AS1V677 off the Internet, choosing AS1V677 over the other sperm donors because (a) AS1V677 had a great résumé. He was thirty-two, raised in a big Jewish-Irish-Catholic family, had gone to William & Mary, played sports throughout high school and college, and was now a practicing pediatrician in upstate New York. And (b) AS1V677 was taller than me.

At nearly five ten, I've felt huge next to most women and have tended to tower over many male colleagues, so I thought it only fair that I give my offspring height, too.

Height and résumé aside, it didn't hurt that AS1V677 was also described as very attractive, with blue eyes and thick, wavy brown hair.

But facing Eva, I'm not seeing that attractive element, I'm seeing stubbornness as well as a frightening need to play follow the leader.

"Eva, I hate committee meetings."

"But you're a mom. You're supposed to do mom things."

"Committees are mom things?"

"*Yes.*"

"Says who?"

She throws her hands into the air. "Everybody knows. Ask anybody here. They'll tell you. Moms meet and . . . do things."

Anybody here being the choice words.

"What about working moms?" I ask her, leaning on the cart, fascinated by her view of mothers' responsibilities.

"When are they supposed to have time to attend all these meetings?"

"I don't know. They just . . . work them in. And you could. If you got up a little earlier or stayed up later. You could, I know you could. If you tried."

If I tried. Wow.

"Well, thank you for that, Eva. I'm clearly missing pages in *The Perfect Parent Handbook*."

She rolls her eyes. "Meetings can be fun, Mom. Just give them a try."

"Like men and marriage?"

Eva grabs the shopping cart and begins pulling it to the front of the store, her green eyes snapping with temper. "Mom, I love you," she says, pausing by the electronics, "I really do. But one day I hope you'll realize there's nothing wrong with being normal."

I watch her huffily haul the cart all the way to the checkout line, and I know I've had this conversation before, but that time it was with my mom, not Eva.

Eva barely speaks to me on the way home, so I call my dad to remind him that he and Mom were invited for a Labor Day barbecue on Monday.

He says he hasn't forgotten and that Mom is looking forward to seeing us in a few days.

Mom. My mom, who used to play bridge, and once belonged to a million women's civic clubs, and successfully used the school's bake sale as a chance to prove her worth. Her cakes were always the fanciest, her cookies the best.

When I think of my mom, I still have this one picture

from when I was a child. Mom and Dad were going out to a party, and she's wearing this gorgeous white silk hand-painted kimono-style gown. It was the late 1970s, and it suited her. Full hair, long sleek gown with hand-brushed strokes, flames of yellow and orange, like a starburst or a jeweled candy. I remember shouting her name from the top of the stairs, and she turned in the doorway down-stairs and looked up at me, and she was like a movie star. Beautiful dark hair piled high on her head, with dangly jeweled earrings and a gold clutch in her hand. Her eyes shimmered and her lips curved, and she was the most regal queen of all.

My mother.

My mother, who is losing her mind because of Alzheimer's. And how is that fair? She was the main reason I took the job in Seattle and moved us across the country.

I remember all the things I used to throw in her face as a teenager. I remember how and why I left home, angry, bitter, too damn cool for wealthy suburbia with its Junior League meetings.

It wasn't until I became a mother myself that I realized I wanted my mom, but I wanted her the way I wanted her, not the way she was. I wanted my mother to care about the things I cared about, to validate my view of the world. Not hers.

And the crazy thing is that now that she can't talk to me about anything, I realize she wasn't just a dumb beauty. She wasn't a shallow mom. She simply didn't talk about the things she felt very strongly about. It wasn't that she didn't feel. She just didn't believe it was polite to show it. Tell it. Reveal it.

I get it now, but that doesn't take away all my anger, because the problem is—and, yes, it's my problem—she's slowly dying, and we never really talked, never really shared, never really came to an understanding about anything. She was the impeccable wife of the CEO, and I was the hothead rebel daughter who lived in New York and smoked pot and enjoyed sexual intercourse.

"We're looking forward to seeing you guys, too, Dad." My voice suddenly has a lump in it, and I swallow hard. "It'll be a fun barbecue. Nothing fancy, so we can all relax."

"Sounds good, Marta. See you Monday. Have a good weekend."

"You too. Bye, Dad."

Hanging up, I glance at Eva. She still has her nose jutted in the air. My righteous little Mensa child. So brilliant at home. So socially pathetic at school.

"Grandma and Grandpa are coming over Monday for a Labor Day barbecue."

"How's Grandma feeling?" Eva asks, her tone softening. She's amazing with my mom. Far more patient than I am or ever was.

"Okay, I guess. Grandpa didn't really say."

She nods and looks out the window, her brow creased again. Something's on her mind, but she doesn't talk about it and I don't push her. She's a bright girl, sensitive, and let's face it, she's got me for a mother and no father. Considering the odds stacked against her, I think she's doing pretty well.

At home, I make lunch while Eva begins to sharpen the first of thirty-six number two pencils.

She's sharpened only six in the electric sharpener, but my nose already itches and burns while thoughts of lead poisoning dance through my head.

"Why don't you sharpen just one twelve-pack?" I suggest, making Eva her favorite sandwich, two slices of bland turkey with a smear of mayo on extremely white bread.

She doesn't even look up as she jabs in the next pencil.

"We have to have all pencils sharpened."

"But you can't use all of them on the first day."

"The school supply sheet said they had to be sharpened."

I rest the mayo knife on the cutting board. "And it would just kill you to break a rule, wouldn't it?"

She glares at me and pushes another pencil into the sharpener, measures the progress with what's quickly becoming a practiced eye. After drawing out the pencil, Eva studies the tip, then puts it back in for another whirr, whirr, whirr.

Now sharpened, the pencil is returned to the box and she reaches for another.

I go back to finishing her sandwich.

I didn't want to return to the Pacific Northwest, and I definitely didn't want to live in suburbia. I love big cities, and none suited me better than Manhattan with its river of taxicabs and racing engines. I like the sirens at night and the bright lights and how just two blocks off one noisy street can be another all narrow and quiet, lined with the leafiest green trees.

The heavy humidity in summer suited me, and I never felt alone or lonely, not with the thousands of impatient pedestrians, not with the battles for cabs or the ridiculous cost of housing. All the things that made it hard were positives for me. All the difficulties were challenges I enjoyed meeting.

"Your lunch is ready," I say, cutting her sandwich and putting it on the plate.

"Can I have an apple?"

"Yes." I reach into the fruit basket beneath the counter.

Eva watches me slice the apple. "Are you going to the meeting today or not?"

"You really want me to go."

"Yes."

"Why?"

"For the same reason you ask me to brush my teeth."

I put down the knife. *What?*

"Some things we do because we have to do them. That's what you're always telling me. Brushing your teeth, seeing the dentist, getting shots." Eva presses the next pencil into the sharpener for what seems like an endless moment. But when she removes it, the point is perfect. She blows the dust off the tip and places it in the box. "Going to meetings is the same thing. You don't like it, but they make things better."

"For whom?"

"Everybody." Her shoulders lift, fall. "You. Me. The school."

I can see even more clearly the reason why Eva's struggling socially. She doesn't talk or think like a typical nine-year-old. She talks and thinks like a little adult. Because we're alone together so much, Eva talks to me about everything, feels comfortable challenging me about anything, but then she gets to school and can't find the right nine-year-old tone and banter. Girls her age gossip and whisper. Eva discusses culture, education, and politics.

My fault, I'm afraid.

She was born in New York, and we had a great apartment in TriBeCa. From the time she was a toddler, Eva went to preschool and then elementary school with children whose parents were as diverse as the names in the phone book, parents whose work ranged from jobs with nonprofits, to the struggling musician and artist, to coveted positions with the United Nations.

Now my East Coast Eva tries to fit in with children who view adventure as a four-star resort with twenty-four-hour room service and an eighteen-hole golf course.

"I'll go," I say, still leaning against the counter. "We'll go. Happy?"

She beams at me and immediately starts cleaning up her pencil mess. "So what are you going to wear?"

"No."

"No what?" she asks innocently, stacking the remaining boxes of unsharpened pencils on the counter by the phone.

"I'll go to the meeting, Eva. But I'm going as I am."

"Don't you think you want to dress up a little?"

I know in her eyes I'm the mom who doesn't volunteer very much in the classroom. I'm the mom who doesn't know all the kids' names. I'm the mom who sits alone at the country club pool. "I'm not going to dress to impress."

"Other moms do." She's gotten the Formula 409 and a paper towel from under the sink and is spraying and wiping away all pencil residue.

"And if that works for them, great. It doesn't work for me."

She almost slams the 409 on the table. "Why not?"

My hands go up. "I think it's fake."

"Why? Because you want to make a good impression?"

"It's more than that, Eva. It's changing who you are just to satisfy others. It's worrying about what people think—"

"Which is important—"

"*No!* No, it's not."

She stares at me long and hard.

She's such a pack animal, and I appreciate her need to be part of a group, but there are dangers in a group. If you're part of a pack, you must think like the pack and follow the pack leader, and I won't do it. I'm not a follower. I'm a lone wolf. Leader of my own pack.

"I will go to the meeting," I say more quietly as I carry our sandwiches to the table. "But I won't change who I am."

Chapter Four

The Young home is something straight out of *Traditional Home* or *Renovation Home* or perhaps that iconoclast *Architectural Digest*.

Like other houses circling low on the lake, it's a big shingled house that rambles on a full acre with a huge green swath of grass that seems to unroll right into the lake itself.

"Mom," Eva breathes, lifting a hand to shield her eyes from the bright midafternoon sun. It's clear and hot today and almost too dazzling with the sun shimmering off the lake.

This, I know, is Eva's idea of paradise. In her mind, the only thing that could make the setting more perfect would be the addition of an outdoor wedding reception. She's shown me her idea for my wedding. A big party tent. Strings of pink Japanese lanterns. Tuxedoed waiters.

"It is pretty here," I say. Movies are filmed in locations like this, movies and the illustrations for books and magazines. I grew up across the lake in a big, proper house surrounded by other big, elegant houses, but these new shingled confections on the Eastside of Lake Washington are almost otherworldly with their fairy-tale touches of arbors and trellises, towers and cupolas. For a split second I have total house envy, thinking that anyone in a house like this must have such a beautiful life, a life blessed.

It is Taylor who opens the door, and her smile is wide, welcoming. She recognizes Eva and greets her by name.

Taylor's wearing a white sleeveless sheath with aqua stitching around the square neckline and strappy sandals that show off sleek legs and pedicured toes. "The girls are upstairs, Eva," she says, "in the media room, and they'll be so happy to see you. If they're not there, check the game room. They might be playing on the computer."

Eva smiles and dashes up the stairs, and I wish I had an ounce of her enthusiasm as I trail after Taylor into the living room, where everyone has gathered with notebooks and pens.

Taylor introduces me around the room. There must be about twelve women there, but their names and faces are just a blur during the introductions, and they all seem to be the same—perfect tawny-haired bronzed mommies.

The kind who wear Prada loafers and 7 for All Mankind jeans.

The kind who have three-plus-carat rocks on their fingers.

The kind who wear size two clothes and call themselves fat.

The kind who dress their children in miniature designer duds.

I find the only empty seat, the piano bench pulled away from the baby grand in the corner, and sit down, still smiling and nodding, first to the woman on my right, a woman whose long hair hangs well past her shoulders, falling in soft Grace Kelly waves, a tiny bobby pin holding back the first sleek wave in a new-old school preppy sort of way. She's wearing a snug tangerine knit tank cropped at a flat waist, belted dark narrow-legged jeans, and dark stylish expensive loafers. The bling-bling on her wedding finger sparkles so brightly, I turn to my left.

The woman to my left wears her dark blond hair just above her shoulders, and she's got one side tucked behind her ear, revealing a diamond stud the size of my left nostril. She's dressed in a sleeveless silk turtleneck, pencil slacks, and leather loafers.

Glancing down at my nineteen-dollar flip-flops, I realize I'm way underdressed for this meeting.

"Would you like something to drink?" Taylor offers.

Actually, I could use something to drink. Like a shot of chilled vodka or a good dirty martini. "Just show me where to go. I can help myself."

"Absolutely not!" Taylor cries in mock horror. "Sit. I'll bring it to you. What would you like?"

What would I like? I'd like to go, that's what I'd like, I think, glancing around the enormous living room with the antique beams and the huge arched window with the multitude of true-light divided panes. I feel like a total fraud. This whole place is too pretty for me. This whole world is everything I never wanted.

I am not like these women. I don't belong here. I don't fit. And it's not my flip-flops or the camo pants. It's not that I rode a skateboard in high school or used to work on my own muscle car.

It's me. *Me.*

I feel too rough, too raw, too strong, too emotional, too

intense, too passionate. I feel real, wild, bordering on out of control.

And these other women, these neat, fashionable, slim, tanned, toned women, aren't out of control. They're together. They're organized. They're orderly.

"What do you have?" I ask, feeling increasingly awkward.

"We've everything," Taylor answers as one of her friends appears at her elbow and hands her a cocktail. "Nathan's made sure we have lots of girls drinks—pitchers of watermelon cosmos, chilled white wine, iced tea—it's green sun tea—and sodas. Regular and diet."

"Iced tea," I say, going for the safe over sorry choice. Even though part of me would kill for a drink, I'm not comfortable enough here to have one, not at four in the afternoon and not when I still have work to do later.

Taylor's friend disappears to fetch the drink, and I try to sit on my piano bench and look confident and comfortable.

When Taylor's friend returns with my iced tea, the tall glass ornamented with a thin lemon slice, I thank her, smiling as widely as I can, trying to be charming. I keep thinking charming thoughts, pretend I'm Maria from *West Side Story* rather than one of those tragic circus sideshow freaks in the novel *Geek Love*. That's a sad book, very twisted, and not the thing to be thinking about as I sit here trying to look as if I belong.

Finally Taylor calls the meeting to order, and everyone applauds her. I'm not sure why they're applauding, but I clap once or twice, too. Then Paige's mom—Lani? Dana?—reads the letter sent to the school superintendent along with all the families who signed the bottom. There must be at least twenty signatures, and some of the names are familiar from the school bulletins and the notes from Eva's room mother, but with the exception of Paige's and Jemma's moms, I don't know who is who.

Must get better at this.

Must make a bigger effort.

It was fine to be a stranger when we first moved here. It was fine to be an outsider when Eva started third grade last year. But it's been months. This is supposed to be home. This is where we live.

I want to be a good mom, I really do. I want Eva to make friends and be happy—popular—and I'm here resolved to get more involved. The discussion moves from the unfairness of the decision to bus little five-year-olds to another school, to the concern over mixing children from two different schools in one classroom, to the auction money raised last year, which is now under attack. Apparently, the parents representing the Lakes school feel entitled to a portion (one-sixth is the number mentioned) of the funds raised last spring since they are going to have to spend some of their money on "our" kids. My smile becomes increasingly stiff.

It's not that I don't want to care about their concerns, but there are so many real worries in the world, and I can't help thinking this isn't one.

I'll walk/run to aid cancer research. ALS. Diabetes. And my new favorite, thanks to my mom, Alzheimer's.

Better yet, I'll donate for the poor in my own community, those who live on the other side of Bellevue, families confronted by crisis, poverty, and change. Women, children, and families in need of shelter, transitional housing, protection from domestic violence, literacy education, and health care.

In short, I think we in our cushy community have enough. Our own children have enough. When will we fight as hard for other women's children?

When will we see we're all in this together? What about everyone else?

Suddenly, I can't stay another minute. I can't watch ladies talk about fighting with their school district over a temporary situation when there are huge, urgent needs right at our door.

My mother and her friends were the same way. While I was in school, she organized endless bake sales, car washes, raffles, dinner dances . . . for what end? So she could make sure her child had more? A bigger piece of the pie?

My mom said I was ungrateful, but I don't see how she could think I'd enjoy more pie when others were starving.

Taylor sees me shifting in my chair. "Marta? Were you wanting to say something?"

No.

Yes.

I uncross my legs, sit tall, try to manage my expression so I'm warm, supportive, nonthreatening. But the moment I open my mouth, the words come out too clear, too strong, too blunt. "What about all the other children? What about the kids in Crossroads? The kids without two parents or where both parents work? Why don't we donate some of our money there? Why don't we help them?"

My words are greeted by strained silence, and then Taylor smiles pleasantly and smoothes her short skirt over her long, tan legs. "We hold the school auctions to help pay for classroom aides. It's one of the ways we keep our teacher-to-student ratio low and ensure that all children get more teacher attention."

"All children in our school."

Taylor's brown eyes hold my own. She's still smiling, but underneath I feel a tough, "don't mess with me" tension. "It's not as if they can't do what we're doing. They could have their own school auctions. They could do the wrapping paper sales and walk-a-thon, too. It's not that hard."

"No, it's just time, money, and energy."

"Exactly," Paige's mom chimes in, and she's nodding earnestly. "It's something they could do with a little effort, too."

But these other families don't have the time, money, or energy. They're strapped, stressed, barely getting by.

And I say as much, knowing I shouldn't, knowing this isn't the place. "Is there a way, though, to include these other schools? Maybe include them in our efforts, ease some of the burden on them?"

There's only silence when I stop talking, and twelve-plus women stare at me, their expressions ranging from unease to outrage.

"Maybe we can adopt a school," I conclude quietly.

Taylor's staring at me, her expression chilly. "Well, thank you for the input, Marta. I'll make a note of your suggestion, and maybe if there's enough interest from other parents, we can discuss it at a future meeting." She draws a breath. "Now, back to the issue of auction funds."

One of the women clutching a watermelon cosmo raises her hand. "I can understand giving the Lakes PTA a tiny portion of last year's auction income, but won't that set a precedent for this year?"

There's a loud murmur of agreement, and the discussion moves on.

The meeting drags on for another hour but is eventually brought to a close when one of the women—a mother to an apparently athletic, popular son—glances at her watch and sees the time.

"The picnic!" she exclaims, gathering her purse and notebook. "I promised Eric I'd have him there early. The guys are going to be swimming."

Another mother rises, and so do I. I've been waiting for this moment since I arrived, and I can't collect Eva fast enough. The girls upstairs barely look at her when she says good-bye.

We're outside, heading to the truck, when Eva suddenly lets out a shout. "My watch!"

I stop and drag a hand through my long hair, combing it off my neck. I left it loose today, and it's too hot and heavy for such a warm day. "You took it off?"

"I was just showing them."

I stifle an irritated sigh. "Go get it. I'll wait here."

"You won't come up with me?"

"No. But I'll wait here. Just go in, grab it, and come back."

Eva knocks timidly on the door before going in, shutting the door carefully behind her.

I stand on the porch, inspecting the glossy white veranda running the length of the house. There are a cluster of big wicker chairs and hanging baskets of ferns and colorful impatiens. One would almost think we were in the Deep South instead of Greater Seattle.

The living room windows are open, and as I wait for Eva to return, I hear voices spill out from the living room.

The moms aren't in any hurry to leave. Most are enjoying a second cocktail or a refill on their wine.

"Who is that?" I hear one of the women ask just after the front door closes behind Eva. "The little girl with the long dark hair? I see her at the pool sometimes with her mother."

"The girl who just came through?" Taylor's laughter tinkles. "That's Eva Zinsser, Jemma's little shadow. Her mother was the one who just left. Marta's her name. Different, aren't they?"

There's a giggle from the living room. "Did you see what Marta was wearing? Those pants? That ratty-looking T-shirt? Certainly didn't seem like she took any pride in her appearance."

"A bit too bohemian for my taste," another replied.

"I don't think they have a lot of money." It's Taylor again. I recognize her voice. "Apparently they've moved from the East Coast, and I can imagine their sticker shock at the price of homes. Nathan says you can get a lot more for your money there."

"So is she married? Divorced? Haven't seen a Mr. Zinsser," someone said.

"I don't know if there is one," Taylor added, her voice dropping slightly. "And that could explain why the little girl's a bit clingy. Eva seems very sweet, but she really needs to make some friends of her own. Poor Jemma's beginning to find Eva's hero worship claustrophobic."

The women all laugh, but I don't. I stand there in the overhang of the doorstep, shielded by the soft leafy shade of an enormous Japanese maple, with a furious lump filling up my throat.

I don't care if they talk about me, but how dare they talk about Eva like that? How dare they discuss my child? Who the hell do they think they are?

My legs shake, and I'm trembling with rage. I will show them. I will teach them. I will—

The front door opens suddenly and Eva tumbles out, her cheeks a mottled rose against white. Her expression is stricken, and her wide eyes hold mine. It's obvious she's overheard the same thing I did.

"Eva," I say.

She's shaking her head. "My watch," she whispers. "I couldn't find it."

So she didn't hear them, then. Thank God. My relief is huge, staggering, and I almost sag against the oversize Craftsman-style column supporting the front porch.

"Will you go in and look for it with me?" she asks, her voice shaking.

I'd shave my head before I'd go back in that house. "Let's not worry about it now. Let's go to the beach for the picnic, and I'll give Mrs. Young a call later."

"But the watch," she protests.

"We'll find it." I steer her toward the Ford truck, a meticulously restored 1957 classic with a glossy paint job somewhere between vanilla and buttercream. It's my prized possession, and another f___ you to those (like my father) who would have us believe a woman isn't complete without a man.

But Eva's still fighting tears as she opens the passenger door and climbs inside. "Grandma and Grandpa gave me the watch for Christmas last year."

The watch does have sentimental value—especially

since my parents had it engraved for her—but I just want to get the hell out of here.

Our house is only a few blocks away. We could have walked to the Youngs', but since we're heading straight to the beach, I've already packed the back of the truck with our folding chairs and cooler.

But as I back out of the Youngs' circular drive, Eva announces she doesn't want to go to the beach after all.

I brake at the stop sign and turn to look at her. "But the picnic is a big deal. You've been looking forward to this all summer."

She just shakes her head.

"Eva."

Eva takes a deep breath. "We're just going to end up sitting alone again. Aren't we?"

I grimace inwardly. Ouch. "I don't know—"

"We are. We always do."

The steering wheel feels clammy against my hands. "I'm trying very hard, Eva."

"Why did we even move here?" she cries, her voice breaking.

I pull over to the shoulder and park in front of yet another huge shingled house. The beach park is just at the end of 92nd Avenue, and we're going to have to park along the side of the street anyway.

"We came for Grandma," I say slowly, wondering what it is she wants to hear from me, what it is that would reassure her, make her feel better. "Because she's sick, and she's not going to get better."

"But it's not as if we see her very often."

"We go to her house once a week."

"More like every two weeks."

Holding my breath, I look at Eva. Right now, nothing I say or do is correct. Right now, I feel as though I'm just failing as a mom, yet I'm trying my best. "You've been upset with me all day," I say carefully, trying to keep my tone neutral. "What's wrong?"

Eva does that preadolescent shrug she's getting so very good at. "Nothing."

"Nothing?" I echo, trying to be brave because it's hard to open yourself for criticism, especially from the one person you love most in the world. "Are you sure there isn't something that's eating at you, something you're mad at me about?"

"Well, maybe. A little."

A little. Okay. I take a quick breath, tell myself not to be hurt. "What am I doing that's bothering you?"

Another shrug. "I don't know."

"Do I embarrass you?"

And a third shrug. "Not exactly."

I feel as if I'm wading into very deep waters here, and I take a big breath for an added shot of courage and calm. "But you're not proud of me?"

"No, it's not that. Oh, Mom. It's just that . . ." Eva's shoulders slump, and she squeezes her eyes shut. "The kids that are popular, they're popular because . . ." She sinks even lower on the seat. "Because they have nice clothes and nice things, and everybody wants stuff like that."

I don't say anything. I just look at her and wait. Because there's more. There's always more.

"Jemma, Paige, Devanne, and Lacey do really cool things, too. They go on all these neat trips with their families—"

"We went to the Yukon this summer."

"The Yukon! The *Klondike*." She makes a big whoopee motion with her hands. "And guess what? Everybody thought I was a big fat geek."

"You're not fat."

She ignores my feeble joke. "I want to be like the others, I want to go to neat places—"

"Maui is not that neat."

"Maybe not to you, but it is to me. And it is to the people that go every Christmas with their families."

"And what does one do in Maui, Eva, that's so cool? Sit on a beach? Go swimming? Get a tan?"

"Yes. Sit on a beach, swim, play in the pool, get a tan, wear cute clothes. That sounds really fun to me."

"I think it sounds dumb," I mutter.

"Well, I think you're dumb," Eva flashes furiously.

"That's enough."

"It is enough. I've had enough." Eva grabs the handle and flings open the car door. "You don't look like a mom. Not like a real mom. Not like the moms here. And you don't even try to act like a real mom—"

"Eva, you're my daughter. That makes me a real mom."

She jumps out of the truck and slams the door shut, but with the windows open I can hear her quite clearly when she yells at me. "Real moms don't have motorcycles!"

"Real moms do," I retort, leaning out the window, "and I don't ride it around town anymore. I stopped riding it because you asked me to."

Her cheeks burn red. "I asked you to sell it, not stop riding it."

"Eva—"

"You just love to be different. You wear your hair too long, and you don't even wear normal clothes, just jeans and boots and guys' army jackets." Her voice cracks. Tears fill her eyes. "I know you're an artist, but this is Bellevue, Mom, not New York."

I know. Oh, do I know. I barely survived growing up here, took off first chance I got, and if my mom hadn't gotten sick, I wouldn't have come back.

"That was unkind and unnecessary," I say huskily, more deeply hurt than she knows. "You owe me an apology."

She just shakes her head and knocks away tears with the back of her hand. "Do you know what I ask God every night? I ask about my father, and then I pray that God will make you more like everybody else." And then without another word she stomps back to our house, which is less than a block away.

I would cry if I knew how to.

I haven't cried in so many years that I think my tear ducts have forgotten how.

But Eva has hurt me in a way I didn't know I could be hurt. I love her and fear for her. I lie awake at night worrying about her. My nearly every thought revolves around Eva and helping Eva, yet apparently it's not enough.

I'm not enough. Not good enough. Not right.

I press two fingers against my eyes, try to block the picture of her storming out of my truck, turning on her heel, and marching away.

I try to stop her angry, hurtful words that are echoing in my head.

The problem when you're a small family, when you're a family of two, is that there is no one else to give space, distance, perspective. There is no one else to go to, to lean on, to reach for.

As a single mom, one becomes strangely adept at the concept of self-comforting.

I'm still sitting in my truck on the side of the road attempting to self-comfort when my cell phone rings.

I reach for the phone on my dash, and it's Shey.

I haven't talked to Shey in weeks, and her call couldn't have come at a better time.

"Hey," I greet her, my voice pitched low. "So you finally return my call."

"What's wrong?" she asks immediately, knowing me so well.

Shey's one of my two best friends, and she's still in New York. I've missed her more than I imagined. Even though we didn't see each other in New York more than every week or two, I always knew she was nearby and knew I could grab her for lunch if I really needed her. Now I wait for a phone call, but even a really good long chatty call isn't the same thing as a good long chat in person.

"Kind of having a bad day," I say.

"Work?"

"Eva."

"So what are you doing right now? Feel like taking a trip?" she asks.

Suddenly I have a ridiculous lump in my throat. It's so good to hear Shey's voice and hear her throaty laugh. I felt like such a freak in Taylor Young's living room and then so hurt when Eva attacked me here. "I wish we could come to New York, but Eva starts school Tuesday."

"I'm not in New York, baby. I'm on Orcas Island, just across the Puget Sound."

"You're *where*?"

She's amused, and I can picture her smiling like the fat Cheshire cat. "Orcas Island. Hop on the six-forty seaplane and come see me."

"Get out."

Shey laughs, and she sounds exactly the way I remember her—beautiful, laid-back, very much in control. "I'm here for a shoot, and the shoot wrapped up early. I was supposed to fly home tomorrow, but John called and he's decided to take the boys fly-fishing, and I thought maybe, just maybe, you might want to come and hang out with me."

"Yes," I breathe. "Yes, yes, yes."

"Do you need to ask Eva?" Shey says. "She might not be so eager."

"Eva might not adore me," I said, the husky note back in my voice, "but she loves her Aunt Shey."

"I'll see you soon, then."

Chapter Five

I drive up to the house and park without pulling into the garage. As I head in, Eva comes tumbling out.

"Sorry," she chokes, tears on her cheeks. "That was so mean, and I'm really sorry."

I hug her. I don't know what else to do but hug her. She's just a person, and so am I. "I love you, Eva."

"I know, Mom. And you can't help being different. You were just born that way."

I'd laugh, but I'm afraid this time I *would* cry. "Your Aunt Shey called," I say, dropping a kiss on her forehead before letting her go. "She's on Orcas Island for the weekend and wants us to join her. Feel like going?"

"*Yes.*"

"We'll miss the beach picnic and bonfire."

"I don't care. I didn't really feel like going to the picnic after all."

"I could change, Eva, put on a cute dress and curl my hair—"

"No." Eva giggles. "Going to see Aunt Shey on Orcas Island sounds much better."

"All right. Then let's get packing."

I've two best friends, Shey Darcy, a New York model who started an agency, ExpectingModels, with another top model when both of them became pregnant, and Tiana Tomlinson ("Tits" for short), a popular face and name in the entertainment industry, buried deep in the Hollywood Hills with a Mensa mind, dazzling teeth, and . . . well, a great pair of tits.

Shey, Tiana, and I met during our senior year of high school when we'd all been packed up and sent off to the St. Pius Academy by the Sea in Monterey, California, where we were to finish our education in a more rigorous academic and moral environment. It was definitely more rigorous than my high school in Seattle and thankfully only slightly more moral.

From the time I met her, Tiana wanted to be an actress or entertainment reporter, a career entailing cameras, lighting, and makeup artists, and it did take her a while to get from behind the cameras to in front of them, but she's succeeded beyond her wildest dreams. Now her social life is news of the day. Want to know what she's wearing, where she's shopping, or whom she's hooking up with? Open *Us Weekly* or *Star* and it's all there.

I tell Tiana the mags are better for our friendship than the BlackBerry, and she just laughs. I think she likes it that I tell her to f___ off and respect her bizarre rocket ship to fame about as much as I respect the mommies at Points Country Club comparing manicures and waxed brows.

Shey, on the other hand, didn't know what she wanted and bummed around Europe after college before running out of money outside Budapest. Her parents wouldn't wire her any cash (they were furious she'd spent a year screwing around Europe instead of going to law school after graduating from Stanford), so she took a job for minimum wage making beds at a Budapest luxury hotel and ended up being spotted by a European modeling agent, who convinced her she could find work on the catwalks in Milan. It wasn't long before she appeared in Italian *Vogue*, and then she was back in the United States commanding an impressive fee.

These are my friends, these are the people I admire—courageous, creative, risk-taking women. Shey's married with kids, Tits was married briefly and there weren't kids, which is a good thing since her journalist husband died covering the war in the Middle East just months after their honeymoon. Both my friends adore Eva and supported me in my decision to become a single mom. Shey even drove me to the fertility clinic for the artificial insemination. As thanks for her help and support, I made Shey, a mother of three, Eva's godmother.

I'm hoping Shey will know what I should do about Eva now.

It doesn't take Eva and me more than five minutes to throw our swimsuits, tennis shoes, and change of clothes into an overnight bag. Orcas Island, like the rest of the San Juan Islands, is casual, sporty, and not very developed, meaning there's not much to do on the islands but play on the beach or go for a bike ride, but people don't go to the islands for the activity. They go for the lack of it.

Happily, there's no traffic on the 520 bridge, and we arrive at the seaplane terminal at Lake Union with time to spare.

One of the best parts of living in Seattle is Puget Sound, with its endless islands, islets, and waterways. Usually we take one of the ferries to the islands, so flying on the seaplane is extra exciting.

There's nothing quite like taking off from the water and then flying low enough so you can see virtually everything. The world from the seaplane isn't like the world from a Boeing jet. Life below still seems so close, yet the colors just pop—stunning sapphire blue, rich emerald green, scattered fields of brown, tan, and gold.

Eva's glued to her window, and I'm sinking into my seat, taking some deep, calming breaths, thinking that Shey's call was divine intervention.

God knew I needed some help.

"I heard what they said," Eva suddenly says in a soft voice.

My body tenses immediately. I long to reach out and touch Eva, but at the moment I don't think she'd welcome it. She's in such a strange place now. Maybe all fourth graders go through this—angry, wistful, confused.

Finally she turns to look at me, and her expression is shuttered. "I heard what Jemma's mom said. About me annoying Jemma by being her shadow. Following her everywhere."

That explains Eva's strange color when she left the Young house. I thought she looked shocked. Bruised. "Mrs. Young didn't mean anything by it. She was just talking, just being silly."

"But I heard what they said about you, too. I heard how they thought we didn't have any money and that maybe it's too expensive for us here."

I start to protest, thinking she's misunderstood them, but stop myself. Maybe she hasn't misunderstood. Maybe she's understood them better than me.

She looks at me with wide, pain-darkened eyes. "But we're not poor, are we?"

"No."

"And we have an old truck instead of a nice new car because . . . ?"

"It's a classic. It's a beautiful truck and a piece of history." I reach out and lightly smooth back the hair from her brow. "And driving it is fun. I have fun in it. I feel . . . pretty. Sexy."

"*Sexy?*"

I shrug and make a face. "Pretty is different for every woman. Mrs. Young likes designer clothes, Gucci, Prada, Ralph Lauren. I like vintage stuff. I like things that don't match, that have a masculine edge, things that contradict standardized ideas of beauty."

"But you're so pretty, Mom, and you could be so beautiful."

"And I feel beautiful when I'm me."

"In guys' jackets and army boots?"

"Especially then."

Eva's quiet a moment, then looks up at me. "I don't like it when the other moms talk about you. It made me really upset. I was so mad."

"I don't mean to embarrass you, Eva. And I'm sorry that I didn't change before the meeting. I was underdressed, and you're right—this isn't New York. I can't do the things here I could do there."

"People like things nice here, don't they?"

I nod. Thank God we're going to see Shey. Thank God we're getting out of Bellevue, even if it's just for the night. "Eva, I promise I'll try harder to be more like the other moms, if you try not to listen to everything people say. And that includes Jemma Young."

"But what did I ever do to Jemma?"

"Nothing."

"So what am I doing wrong?"

Just being yourself, I think.

Outside, the sun gleams like liquid gold on the water of the sound. Tall pine trees jostle between rocky island coves.

"I've always been nice to her," Eva adds softly. "I've always tried hard."

"Maybe that's the problem. Trying too hard is sometimes worse than not trying at all."

"Why?" she demands even as the plane's hum changes. We've begun our descent.

Do I tell her people can be animals? Do I tell her this is why I don't trust women more? That I keep most women, except for my closest friends, at arm's reach?

I glance out the window and watch us sail low, lower, down toward the sapphire water. Ten to twelve thousand years ago, Orcas Island and the surrounding Puget Trough lay beneath a glacier said to be a mile thick. The glacier eventually receded and new life formed, with humans appearing six thousand years ago. Six thousand years later, the affluent humans in the Pacific Northwest liked these islands very much.

"Why, Mom?" Eva repeats.

I look back at my daughter, who is still waiting for a response, who still thinks I have all the answers. Bless her. How wrong she is.

"I think trying too hard makes people uncomfortable, it changes the dynamics," I say as we touch down, the seaplane's rails bumping and then sliding across the water's surface, "giving others too much power."

Eva just looks at me. She doesn't understand. I don't blame her. I didn't get it until I was an adult.

Shey's at the small terminal to pick us up. She has a rental car, a small Toyota four-by-four, and I spot her as soon as we emerge into the light.

But it'd be hard not to see Shey. She's a Texas girl and gorgeous, the kind Rod Stewart would have wanted for himself had he met her. Nearly six feet, very slim, and strawberry blond, Shey stands out in a crowd, but when she smiles, she stops traffic dead. Her smile is huge, wide, as generous as her Texas drawl and big old Texas heart.

Shey is the sister I've always needed.

Grinning, I hug her and pull back, check to see if she's aged—she hasn't—and then hug her again. How she juggles motherhood, work, and being a wife to a sexy photographer is beyond me, but she does it, and she never complains. She's just freaking positive. And maybe that is how she does it.

With faith, good humor, and a dose of Norman Vincent Peale.

Shey's now scooped Eva into a bear hug, and she's showering my daughter with ridiculous kisses. Eva's squealing and giggling, and her skinny arms are clinging as tightly to Shey as they do to me.

If I had a sister, it'd be Shey.

If Eva had another mother, it'd be Shey.

People look at Shey and see the external beauty and assume the worst, that she's vain or narrow or shallow.

But Shey's secret weapon is that she's far more lovely on the inside than she is on the outside, and I think that's why God made her so beautiful. Because He knew she'd never take advantage of her gifts. He knew she'd use her beauty and love for others.

We toss our bags into the backseat, climb into the car, and buckle up. Shey's rented a cabin for the weekend, and we head there now, a slow ten-minute drive to the other side of the island.

Eva immediately wants to go down to the beach, and Shey tells me to go with her while she carries our bag into the cabin.

Wandering toward the lake edge, I hear the screen door bang shut behind Shey, and I tip my head back to see the towering evergreens sheltering the half dozen scattered cabins.

It was beautiful in Bellevue, but it's even more lovely here with the rustic charm of fifty-year-old cabins and ancient islands and lakes carved out of the Puget Sound.

Because in summer, the sun doesn't set until sometime between nine and ten; at eight p.m., the lake's beach is still warm and drenched in sun.

Eva's standing at the edge of the water, wearing her favorite sundress—it's simple and cream colored, with just a scattering of green ferns and leaves.

There's nothing fancy about the dress, but as she stands at the water's edge, the wind blows the hem, and her dark hair trails down her back, and she's laughing at the breaking surf, which is particularly big at the moment thanks to the wave riders and water-skiers out on the bay.

Eva's been watching some kids jump waves, and she's

caught off guard when the water suddenly rises and crashes on her legs, drenching the hem of her dress. Laughing, she turns to look at me, and I just smile, shake my head.

She laughs again.

It's been a long time since I've heard her laugh like this. A long time since she seemed like a little girl. And for the first time in weeks, I feel some of the tension inside me ease. Eva's going to be okay. Eva will find her way through the intricacies of girl friendships and girl power struggles.

She will. I did. Shey and Tiana did. It's part of life, one of those rituals called growing up.

"I'm so glad you called," I say to Shey as she heads down to the water's edge with a couple of bottles of chilled water. "How did you know I needed you now?"

Shey tosses a bottle my way. "Because I knew I needed you. I miss you. The city's not the same."

We sit on the patch of grass before it gives way to pebbles and stone. I unscrew the cap of my water. "How's work?"

"Amazing. Incredible. We're so busy. The agency just keeps growing. We can't keep up sometimes with the demand."

"For pregnant models."

"For models that are moms."

I look at her, unable to hide my admiration. "I'm so proud of you, so glad you're doing what you do." With her agency she's changing the way the world looks at women and helping celebrate the beauty of the pregnant woman. "To think it all started when you were pregnant with Harry."

"I didn't want to stop working," Shey answers with a slight shrug.

And she shouldn't have had to, but the agency she worked for sent her home, told her not to come back until she'd had the baby and dropped the baby weight, and oh yeah, don't get stretch marks or ruin your looks or you'll not have work when you return.

Fortunately, her friend Liza had a better thought, and Shey went to work with her.

It's been ten years and some serious blood, sweat, and tears, but Shey's now a mom of three and vice president of ExpectingModels, one of New York's premier model and talent agencies.

"How are you?" Shey asks. "How's Eva? You sounded pretty upset earlier."

I sigh as I watch Eva dance along the water's edge. "She wants to be popular. She wants to be part of the in crowd, and it's not a very nice little clique."

"It never is."

"And right now, nothing I know, nothing I suggest, seems to help. Right now, being me seems to make everything worse."

Shey grimaces. "The life of a mother."

"But we've never had these problems before. My daughter once liked me."

"She loves you, Marta."

"She was screaming at me today, screaming at the top of her lungs."

"She's growing up."

"She's nine."

"That's what I mean. We're entering the preteen years, and you have a girl. It's only going to get harder."

"You're not making me feel any better."

"I don't think you will. Not until she turns twenty-five."

"You're just feeling smug because you have three boys."

"I'm feeling smug because they're with their dad." Shey stretches her arms above her head and sighs deeply, appreciatively. "God, it's a beautiful night. You're here and I don't have to work. This is my idea of heaven."

"You're not missing your guys?"

Shey shoots me a look as if to say I'm crazy. "I love it when they all go. Get those stinky boy germs out of the house and indulge in all the girlie things I want to do. Bubble baths. Pedicures. Chick flicks on DirecTV."

I lean back on the grass, consider Eva, who has sunk to her knees to begin scooping sand and pebbles into a little mound.

With her long black hair swirling with the wind and her long smooth child arms trailing along the sand, my own heart catches, overcome by love, love, love.

Stop the clock, I think, freeze everything right now. I want to remember this—this second, this moment— forever. I want to remember how lucky I was, how lucky I am.

And I want Eva safe, I don't want her to struggle, and I don't want to worry about her so much.

Shey shoots me a speculative side glance. "That's a pretty heavy sigh."

Had I even sighed? I didn't realize. "Was it this hard when we were in school?" I ask, making a little face.

"Probably. You just didn't happen to notice because you were the one making all the girls' lives miserable."

"I wasn't."

Shey rolls her eyes. "Did you or did you not live with your middle finger raised, your own little American flag flipping everyone off?"

I laugh softly. She's right. I did. I couldn't help it. I could skate, ski, and snowboard better than most guys, and no girl could come close to doing what I could do. I took ridiculous chances, lived dangerously, pushing the ex in extreme. And if any girl dared to make a snide remark, I was pretty damn comfortable giving her a smack-down.

Shey drains her water and puts the plastic cap back on the empty bottle. "I don't know about you two, but I'm starving. How about we go find some dinner?"

Eva falls asleep in the car on the way home from the restaurant. We ended up having nearly an hour wait for our table, and service was slow, which meant we didn't even eat until close to ten-thirty.

Back at the lake cabin, Shey parks the car and I try to wake my zonked-out girl. She doesn't even stir. I end up scooping her up and carry her into the bedroom she's sharing with me.

Shey pulls back the cover while I lay Eva on the exposed bottom sheet. After covering her, I lightly kiss the top of her head and smooth the cover once more over her shoulder.

"You better keep her grounded," Shey whispers as we tiptoe out. "Because she's going to be a knockout later."

"You say that because you're her godmother."

"I say that because I own a modeling agency and have

worked with Tyra Banks for four seasons on *America's Next Top Model*."

We wander into the cabin's kitchen, where Shey uncorks a wine bottle and fills our glasses. "And she's got you for a mom," she adds. "You're not exactly hard on the eyes, if you know what I mean."

"Looks might get you a good table at a Manhattan hot spot, but they don't guarantee happiness."

"Touché." Wine in hand, Shey goes into the small rustic living room, drops onto the couch, and stretches out her long legs, then runs a hand through her thick, shoulder-length, strawberry blond hair. "I could get work for you two, you know. I get lots of calls for mother-daughter teams on the West Coast—"

"No."

"You used to model."

"For one blink of an eye, and I hated it."

"You were amazing."

"I still hated it."

"Let Eva model and she'll be very popular."

"Now I hate you." I make a hideous face at her. "That's such a sellout, and I will not sell out."

"That's right. Take the hard, high road. That's so much more satisfying," Shey mocks me, her eyebrows arched, eyes lit with mischief.

I lift my wineglass, salute her. "Life's about the journey, not the destination."

"That's because you haven't picked a very fun destination."

"Feck off."

She just laughs her throaty laugh.

I love Shey. I love her humor, her spirit, her feistiness. And I love most of all that she refuses to let me take myself too seriously. Every time I get up on my soapbox, she just cheerfully knocks me off.

Damn Gaelic fairy.

Drinks like a fish, eats like a linebacker, and is as tall and delicate as a prima ballerina.

I'd have to hate her if she weren't so wonderful.

Wineglass in hand, I join her in the living room. "You took the only good place to sit, you know."

She pats the saggy cushion next to her. "Come sit next to me, baby."

"Don't try anything."

"You wish."

I laugh and sink into the saggy cushions. It feels good to just sit and relax.

I sip my wine and tilt my head back, and the wine's warm and feels so good in my mouth, throat, going down. It's a big robust red and perfect for a night like this. "You've always had excellent taste in wine."

"John educated me," she says, referring to her husband of thirteen years. Shey and John met on a shoot and they've been together ever since. "He said I can't skate through life on my good looks alone."

"Thank God for that. Otherwise you'd be useless. Over five feet eleven and bonier than hell."

Shey's laugh is low and husky. It's one of my favorite sounds in the world, and I open my mouth to tell her how damn glad I am to see her, how much I needed this time together, but that lump is back, the one that makes me doubt myself.

It's been tough moving back to Seattle.

Leaving New York, leaving her, leaving everything that was good and comfortable, has really thrown a curveball into my confidence.

I've begun to feel more like Loser Mom instead of Super Mom.

I'd planned on being a single parent, but there are times—days—when I'm just so bewildered by all that isn't what I thought, knew, dreamed, expected.

I knew I'd love Eva, and I'd hoped Eva would love me, but I didn't realize that Eva would have problems I wouldn't be able to help her with.

"I saw him," Shey says quietly, laughter gone. "For a minute I wasn't sure it was him, but it was." She turns to look at me. "He's still with her. They were together. The kids were there, too."

I would like to pretend that I don't know who or what she's talking about, but Shey and I don't have that kind of friendship. Our relationship is quick, sharp, honest, real. "How does he look?" I ask, my insides tangling, emotions suddenly chaotic.

"Good." Shey presses her lips, tries to smile, but her expression is tender, protective. "You did the right thing, Ta. You did."

I nod once, bite the inside of my lip, and will the stinging sensation out of my eyes. This is so many years ago, so long ago, it's not even news of this century.

Shey reaches out, touches one long, dark strand of my hair, and then tugs it gently. "You'd be over him if you had someone else in your life."

"I am over him."

"You need someone else—"

"No. I'm not—" I stop myself, shake my head, my jaw beginning to ache. "No. Not like that. Never again."

"Marta, it's been ten years."

"I'm happier now than I've ever been."

"Ten years and no sex, no men?"

"I have great toys, sweetheart, and they give tremendous satisfaction for a very small investment."

"They're plastic dildos."

"Yeah, and the only tenderness they need is a battery change now and then."

"You're saying a battery-operated toy is better than a man?"

"Yeah." I ignore Shey's guffaw of laughter. "Vibrators don't have wives."

For a moment Shey says nothing, and she sits, long legs out, ankles crossed, her green eyes narrowed, expression catlike. "You told him to go back to her."

I shake my head slowly. It feels as if she's yanking out my fingernails one by one. "Let's not talk about it."

But Shey isn't ready to drop it. "He asked about you."

I swing around toward her, my hand shaking so much that I wildly slosh wine onto the ugly college plaid couch. "You *talked* to him?"

Her gaze is calm. "If it's any comfort, I'm pretty sure Scott still has feelings for you."

Just hearing his name jolts me all over again, and unsteadily I put the wineglass on the coffee table. I get to my feet under the pretense of getting a damp towel to mop the sofa, but in reality I've got to move, got to put distance between Shey and me.

She's killing me.

And no, it's not a comfort knowing he might have feelings for me. It's no comfort at all.

I didn't just love Scott, I craved him, the way you'd crave a drug like cocaine.

I knew from the beginning, too, that wanting anyone that much couldn't be good, feelings that intense had to be bad.

I was twenty-five when I first met him, and we were together a year, and I fell hard right away. When I wasn't with him, I missed him. When I'd be on long business trips, I'd begin to miss him so much that I felt ill, as though I were lacking warmth, light, oxygen.

But when we were together, it was heaven. When we were together, it was perfect. He seemed close to perfect, and that was good enough for me despite my crazy, passion-infused addiction for him, his smile, his voice, his skin.

But then I discovered he had a wife, who he was merely separated from, not yet divorced, when we first met, and two young kids, the youngest only eighteen months. Scott had told me he'd been married, and we'd discussed his divorce, but I'd never really gotten the whole picture until his wife showed up at my office and spread pictures of their babies on my desk.

I didn't even look at the pictures of the kids. I just stared at her. Karen was small, slim, with a blond pageboy bob and the saddest blue eyes that watered constantly. As she talked, tears kept falling and she kept wiping them away as she told me anecdotes about baby Jordan and big boy Jason, who was all of three and a half.

Three and a half. Is that when little boys become men?

I ended it with Scott less than a week later. I actually asked him to leave after we'd had the best sex ever, and maybe the sex was so good because I knew it was the last time we'd be together.

But just because I ended it didn't make it easy. Like an addict, I had to get him out of my system. I went through complete withdrawal. It was hell.

Those first few weeks were so bad, so unbelievably difficult, that I didn't think I'd survive to get to the other side. The loss was so real, so intense, it felt as though I'd amputated part of myself.

I never called Scott, although I wanted to. I couldn't let him know I missed him or wanted him, couldn't give him an opportunity to run from Karen, the kids, and his responsibilities.

About two months after our relationship ended, I was finally able to eat and keep food from sticking in my throat. Finally able to sleep without waking up in tears. Finally able to work without feeling as though my legs were about to give way.

And when I recovered sufficiently to function, and even halfway smile again, I vowed to never, ever love anyone like that again.

And I haven't. I won't.

Just because I wear combat boots and black eyeliner and have a small, well-inked tattoo high on my right shoulder doesn't mean I know how to cope with my feelings.

In the minuscule kitchen, I grab some paper towels and dampen them at the sink before attempting to clean the red wine, but the plaid is so dark, and the couch is so old,

I can find only a couple of burgundy dots. But I scrub the hell out of them anyway, creating grayish brownish fuzz on the paper towel.

Shey just watches me go at the couch, and eventually I give up on scrubbing. Squeezing the damp towel into a ball in my fist, I exhale. "I'm glad they're still together. It would have sucked to send him back to her to discover that they parted ways a few years later."

"You never hoped he'd come back to you?"

"*No.*"

Shey's voice softens. "You'd only be human if you did."

My heart hardens. Everything is so tight in my chest, I can barely breathe.

I knew what it was like as a child to long for your father's time, your father's attention. I couldn't come between Scott and his kids. I've got enough guilt as it is.

"I had Eva," I say, going to the kitchen to throw away the paper towel. But it takes me a moment to locate the garbage can, which has been hidden in a skinny pantry between the oven and the wall. "I made Eva. And he had children who needed him."

"You did the right thing. You created good karma."

I stand up, cross my arms over my chest. "I didn't do it for the karma. I did it for myself." My voice is too high, too sharp. And for a moment, the old pain returns and it feels almost alive.

Shey shrugs. "The fact is, he would have stayed with you forever if you'd let him. You were the grown-up. You did the mature thing."

Did I?

I broke up with the man I loved most. I told my soul

mate to take a hike and never come back. Then I went out and got pregnant on my own.

Back in the small living room, I pick up my wine-glass and, ignoring how my hand still shakes, take an unsteady sip.

I swallow and then laugh. A small, rough laugh. "Damn, girl," I say, my voice as unsteady as my hand, "but you sure know how to throw a punch."

Chapter Six

Shey and Eva sleep, but I can't and I'm miserable lying in bed wide awake. Eventually, I get up and make a cup of tea and go outside to curl up in one of the Adirondack chairs on the cabin's front porch.

The big trees cast shadows around the cabin and on the beach, but the water itself is dappled with moonlight. Leaning back in the chair, I stare up at the glittering, star-lit sky and listen to the breeze rustle and whisper through the pine boughs.

I feel as though I'm losing control. And it's not just Shey's mention of Scott, but the morning run where I saw that guy and I felt absolutely rocked, as though everything in me suddenly wanted something different from the life I've planned. And then there was the afternoon meeting at Taylor's as well as the fight with Eva in the truck. Eva seems to be changing right before my very eyes, and I want to be such a good mom and yet sometimes I don't know how.

But even as panic bubbles, I squash it back down. I don't want or need a man. I don't have to be like Taylor to be a good mom. Eva's a child, and she's fine.

The point is, there's no quitting, and being negative solves nothing. I'll just keep moving forward, sticking with the game plan, and everything will be fine. I can do this. I've faced tougher challenges.

Like when I nearly miscarried Eva and had to go on bed rest. And then going into labor early, in the middle of a meeting, so I had to rush in a cab through traffic-snarled Manhattan, trying desperately not to give birth there on the backseat while the foreign-born driver screamed at me, "No, lady, no baby here! No baby here!"

My lips twist. Did the driver really think I *wanted* to have my baby on his backseat?

But thank God, Eva hung in there, held off until I could be plopped on a gurney and wheeled into a delivery room.

Eva might be a handful, but she also has impeccable timing. If she hadn't come early, she probably wouldn't have made it, as she arrived with the umbilical cord wrapped dangerously tight around her neck. My obstetrician said if Eva had stayed in the womb much longer, it would have been too late.

I go back inside and lock the front door, and before I climb into bed, I lean over and lightly kiss my daughter.

This is how it's always been with Eva. Great drama and excitement, lots of emotion and passion, and honestly, I wouldn't have her any other way. I love my girl. I do.

We sleep in late the next morning, and when we finally wake, we go in search of breakfast, stumbling on a local coffee shop that serves enormous slices of warm home-made blueberry coffee cake with good strong coffee and hot chocolate for Eva.

After breakfast, we hike along an island trail, Eva's long, thin legs taking long, efficient strides. When she walks she looks as if she's attacking the trail, black ponytail swinging, brow creased, expression focused, determined.

The hike is followed by a swim, and then we all work together on a jigsaw puzzle we find tucked on a shelf inside the cabin before Eva reminds us we haven't had lunch yet and it's already three o'clock. Heading to town, Shey discovers a place where we order sandwiches piled high with tomatoes, avocado, sprouts, and more. Shey loves sprouts so much, Eva and I give her ours.

Wandering through the shops in Eastsound, we get ice cream and buy two freshly caught and cooked crab, a huge loaf of still warm cracked-wheat sourdough bread, grape soda for Eva, and a bottle of chilled white wine for us. It's while I'm waiting for the crab to be wrapped up that I see a very tall man with an enormous pair of shoulders, and my heart does a crazy leap, and I think it's that man, the one from my morning run.

Breathlessly I watch him, waiting for him to turn, waiting to see if he'll recognize me, but when he finally does turn around, my heart falls. The man's old, with a thin, weathered face and no chin to speak of.

I'm surprised by the depth of my disappointment, and as I take the paper-wrapped crab and tuck it into my basket, I give myself a hard talking-to. The guy I saw during my run probably doesn't even exist, or if he does, he's probably not half as gorgeous or interesting as I'm imagining. He's probably dull and vapid. Slow, thick, and not at all charming.

Besides, I don't want a man. I don't need a man. I'm a single mom. End of story.

At the cabin, we work on the puzzle again before we can't resist the crab. We all eat until we're stuffed—Eva eating nearly as much as Shey, as she's a crab and shrimp girl, has been since she was born—and then we collapse on chairs on the porch and talk until we can't talk anymore.

It's Eva who convinces us that since it's our last night we have to sleep outside, beneath the stars. We carry out all our bedding, set it up on the porch, and try. Shey—the girl who grew up on a Texas cattle ranch—gives up after an hour, complaining she heard a mosquito.

Eva and I make fun of her as she leaves, and we vow to tough it out. We even come up with a pledge:

I, _____ Zinsser, am not a wuss and refuse to be afraid of the dark. I will not let other people's fears and cowardly actions chase me back into the cabin.

We take turns reciting our pledge before we shake on it.

Eva falls asleep immediately. I lie awake and look at the sky, reminded of a book I loved when I was Eva's age. The book was about a white pioneer girl kidnapped by Indians and taken captive. The girl grew up and married the son of the chief.

I used to want to be adopted by a Native American family, too, and I pretended I had animal spirits to protect me. My spirits were the eagle, the wolf, and the sacred buffalo.

Looking up at the immense sky with its sheath of stars,

I like to think the eagle, wolf, and buffalo still protect me today.

The next morning while I start breakfast, Shey's in her room doing yoga and then emerges in her swimsuit to go to the lake for a swim.

Eva quickly changes into her suit and tags along after Shey. Fifteen minutes later, Eva and Shey return to the cabin, shower, and change. Now they take their places at the small dining table, their wet hair still drippy but their faces glowing pink.

"That was great," Shey says cheerfully, chomping on a strip of bacon. "What do you think, Eva? Did you have a good swim?"

"Great," Eva echoes, matching Shey bacon for bacon.

"Get going on the pancakes," I say, still standing at the stove and flipping the final batch. "Don't let them get cold."

Neither needs any encouragement, and by the time I pull the last pancakes off the griddle, Shey looks as if she's ready for more.

"It's not fair that you can eat so much," I complain, passing her the platter after I've taken my three.

Shey smiles her dazzlingly white smile. "It's payback for everyone making fun of me in sixth grade."

Eva looks up, intrigued. "People made fun of you, Aunt Shey?"

"Heck, yeah. Stilts. Grasshopper. Giraffe legs." Shey leans forward, elbows on the table, and whispers conspiratorially, "And Eva, it wasn't just the girls making fun of me, it was the boys, too. You see, by fifth grade, I was the tallest kid in my class. By sixth, I was taller than nearly all the teachers. I hated how tall I was. I hated being so skinny and ugly."

"You're not ugly. You're beautiful," Eva protests indignantly.

"But I didn't look the way I do now, back then. I was just plain skinny then, and awkward, and uncomfortable."

I watch Eva's face. She's staring at Shey hard, as though she hoped to see something else, see something new. "Didn't everyone know you were going to be a famous model?"

Shey chuckles, and it's southern and comforting. "No, darling. I didn't even know I was going to be a famous model. It just kind of happened."

"How?"

Shey's brows furrow, and she looks at Eva and then at me and then back to Eva. "I got confident," she says. "And I learned to trust myself."

Eva's puzzled again. "But what does that mean?"

Shey's lips curve. "It means I stopped listening to what other people said about me and started listening to myself."

We take the ferry back to Seattle early afternoon. By walking on, we avoid the lines that have been queued up for hours.

One of my happiest memories of being a kid living in Seattle was taking the ferry. It didn't even matter where we went or if we even got off at Bremerton or one of the islands. I just liked cruising around the sound in the big white-and-green boat.

Eva wants to stand outside at the rail and watch the cars board, so Shey and I take a bench against the side and let Eva watch the loading of the cars while we finish catching up. And now that I know Shey will be leaving soon—she'll be catching a flight back to New York tonight—there's suddenly so much to say.

Shey looks at me. "She's going to be fine, Ta. She's smart and kind. Sweet and sensitive—"

"And that's what's getting her hurt," I grouse, leaning against the bench. "She's too sensitive."

"She's stronger than you think. Stronger than you were."

"No."

"Yes. That's why she wants to be in the in crowd, she thinks she can handle the in crowd. And you know, I think she can, too."

"But why this desire to be popular? What's that about?"

Shey shrugs. "It's about power. Dominance. Eva is confident enough, she wants to compete—"

"But on whose terms?"

"*Her* terms."

"No."

"*Yes.*" Her shoulders lift, fall, and in the sunlight I see a smattering of freckles on the bridge of her nose. "Eva can handle this. She's not going to crash and burn. The person I'm worried about is you."

"Me?"

"Running my own business has taught me that we don't exist in a vacuum. We're part of a community, something larger than ourselves, and we need to be involved in the community. Not just Eva, but you, too."

"It's not easy to make friends here. They're not like you, Shey—"

"You don't know that, though. You don't really know who they are or what they think because you're not giving them a chance."

It dawns on me that my daughter has been talking to my best friend. "What did Eva say?" I ask grimly.

Shey just grins. "You can't dislike women on the basis on their having nice things."

"I'm not."

"Just like they can't dislike you for owning a motorcycle and an old truck."

I adore Shey, but right now she seems more like a turncoat than a best friend. "Your point being?"

"You need to reach out more, find the people you have things in common with. They do exist, Ta. They're out there."

But I don't know about that, and I fear I'll have to slice off the best parts of me to fit in.

When I was growing up, Mom was always correcting me, criticizing me. *Marta, not so loud. Marta, cover your mouth when you laugh. Marta, that's not proper. Marta, behave. Marta, think of what others would say.*

I hated it then, and I hate it still. I won't be stuffed in someone else's mold of good and proper woman. I'm good because I am. And that's what I want Eva to learn. That she's good and beautiful because she exists, not because she's succeeded in earning someone else's approval.

I blink, turn to look at Shey, who is still smiling, but the curve of her lips is faintly ironic. We both know it's not easy. Never has been, never will be.

For a moment, neither of us says anything, and the only sound is that of metal clanging and the shouts of the ferry workers down below.

"I am going to get more involved," I say, breaking the silence. "I'm going to volunteer to help out at Eva's school—"

"But it's not just for Eva, it's for you, too. It's so you can have friends here and be included—"

"With the Bellevue Babes? The Eastside Barbies?"

Shey laughs, and it's low and throaty and very Texan. "Now I remember why we became friends." She looks at me sideways. "You needed me. No one else could handle being your friend."

"We're off!" Eva cries from the railing, and I can feel the deep vibration from within the ferry. We are indeed moving.

Shey and I rise from our bench and join Eva at the railing. The water churns blue green with foamy white, and as we move we gradually begin to pick up speed.

The wind blows our hair, and the sun shines down, hot, bold, reckless. The sun doesn't have anything to worry about. It's old, it's strong, and it's seen everything.

Eva, I think, circling her shoulders with my arm, is still just learning everything for the first time.

And as I stand behind Eva, my arms around her shoulders, her heart beating beneath my hands, I think I am, too.

After we disembark from the ferry, Shey catches a cab to the airport, and we grab one to take us in the opposite direction, north to Lake Union, where we left our car at the terminal for the seaplane.

Once I'm at the wheel again, I drive to Bellevue and stop at the grocery store to pick up what we'll need tonight for the barbecue.

Eva wants to stay in the truck and read one of her magazines she found stashed behind the bench seat. It's a tattered issue of *Town & Country Weddings*, but she's delighted to reread an old friend.

I park near the front, tell Eva to lock the doors and if she gets nervous at all to come inside and find me.

Eva just buries her head in a Mexico beach wedding layout, and I finish talking to the top of her head.

I shop quickly, knowing exactly what I need: chicken, barbecue sauce, corn on the cob, some cans of baked beans I'll doctor to make taste even better, and some garlic bread. Eva wants to make a cake, she'd mentioned it earlier, so I'm hustling to get all the shopping done so we can go home to get the cake made on time.

I've just grabbed four white husked corn when I step back and ram right into someone. I was moving quickly, so I hit hard, a slam of bodies and red baskets that sends me reeling backward.

"I'm sorry," I exclaim, certain I've just run over a little old lady. But it's not a little old lady.

It's him.

The real him, the guy who passed me in the fog on Saturday, the man who literally took my breath away.

I stare at him, and he's even bigger now, up close. "Are you okay?" he asks, putting out a hand to steady me.

I feel the warmth of his hand on my arm even as his deep voice registers somewhere inside me. He's big, thickly muscled, with a wide chest and long legs and an intense gaze. I can't tell if his eyes are blue, green, or both.

"Yes," I answer, dazed, far too fascinated by everything about him. I'm tall, but he's huge. He's a mountain. His shoulders would fill my truck.

"That was a pretty good hit." His gaze meets mine and I can't read his expression, but there's such an intensity in his eyes that I don't look away.

I exhale hard even as I grow warm. He intrigues me on so many different levels. He's big. He's powerfully built. And he's flat-out gorgeous.

Just as I process that he's not like anybody I've ever met before, and certainly not like the men around here, I also realize I'm staring openly.

I'm blushing now, all the way from my chin to my forehead, my skin so hot that I'm grateful when the water in the produce section kicks on, misting the vegetables. "You're really okay?"

"I'm *fine*. I'm more worried about you."

"I'm fine, too."

I see a flash of white, straight teeth as he smiles. "That's good."

He's teasing me, and flushing, I shove the ears of corn into a plastic bag. "Well, have a good day."

"You too."

I rush off then, my legs not entirely steady, but knowing that Eva's in the car keeps me hurrying. I grab a pint of strawberries and then look for the right selection of chicken breasts, legs, and thighs. Scooping up the chicken,

I see him from the corner of my eye. He's picked up a case of beer—Alaskan Amber—and now he's selecting steaks, a pack of big, thick New Yorks.

I'm so afraid of being caught staring that I head for the checkout line. Honestly, I haven't felt this gauche in years. You'd think I'd never been with a man before.

I'm standing in line when I realize I forgot garlic bread, but as I still have time before it's my turn, I leave my basket on the ground to hold my spot before dashing to the bakery for a loaf of French bread.

He's behind my little red basket when I return.

I peek into his basket as I slide back into my spot in line. Steaks, beer, potatoes, and lettuce. My kind of meal.

My kind of guy.

I can feel him behind me in line, too. I can tell he's looking at me, watching me, and I want to say something to him, want to turn and speak to him, but nothing comes to mind. What would I say, anyway? *Nice day. Great weather for a barbecue. Looks like you're eating steak tonight.*

Ridiculous. I'm feeling very ridiculous, yet when the young female cashier takes my basket to start ringing up my items, I glance over my shoulder and end up looking him right in the eye.

Crazy, I think, this is crazy, but I totally dig this guy. I've been thinking about him ever since my run on Saturday morning, and here I am, feeling practically dizzy with desire.

I've always thought how clichéd romance novels are. Around the hero, the heroine's pulse races so fast that she can hardly think, much less breathe, but that's exactly how I am right now.

It's exactly what I feel.

Dizzy, breathless, dazed.

"Are you a QFC Advantage member?" the clerk asks, and I jerk myself back around, force myself to finish the transaction, my hand trembling as I input my home number, which is also my Advantage number, and then swipe my debit card.

The cashier's phone rings, and as I wait for her to finish the call, to push whatever buttons she must push to let me escape, I just grow warmer.

I'm so aware of the man behind me that my nape, back, and hips burn, my skin hot and sensitive everywhere. I'm also now aware that my jeans are frayed and my red tank T-shirt is faded and has some bleach marks near the hem. In short, I'm a mess, and my hair needs washing, and I wish I looked better, wish he weren't so close.

Then like that, the cashier's call is ended, she pushes the approval button, rips off my receipt, and hands it to me. "Have a good day," she chirps.

"Thanks." I smile self-consciously. "You too."

I'm leaving now, exiting through the sliding glass doors, and as I go, I feel a whoosh of disappointment, the same disappointment I felt in Friday Harbor when I spotted the man who wasn't the right man.

But this one—the one I bumped into in the store, the one who stood behind me in line—this one has done something to me, and my body's acting as though he is the right man.

My body's acting as though he is my man.

I leave the store, searching for my sunglasses in my bag, as I walk out into the late afternoon sunshine, and then my keys. I'm still digging around in my bag when Eva leans out the truck window.

"Mom," she calls to me, holding out the cell phone. "Grandma's on the phone."

As I near the truck, she covers the phone and adds, "And I think she's mad at you."

I drop the bags in the back of the truck and take the phone from Eva. "Hi, Mom, it's Marta."

"Where are you? What happened? I've been trying to reach you for days."

"We've been gone just two days, Mom."

"It's not been two days."

"It has," I say, leaning against the truck, the door smooth and warm against my back. It's as I'm leaning there that I see him again, and this time he's climbing into his own truck, a battered Land Rover.

His Land Rover isn't the typical Range Rover driven in Bellevue. No, this is a proper Land Rover, an old beat-up beige four-wheel-drive vehicle that looks as if it's really seen service in Africa, bouncing up and over rain-gutted roads, tracking big game, logging serious miles beneath a blazing sun.

He drives past me, his window down, his tan left arm resting on the sill, and as he drives past, his gaze meets mine once again. Our eyes lock, and for a moment I forget my mom, I forget Eva, I forget everything but those intensely focused eyes of his and that firm, not quite smiling curve of his lips.

"Marta? . . . *Marta*," my mom repeats, trying hard to get my attention.

"I'm listening, Mom," I say quickly, pushing dark, heavy

hair back from my hot face and watching the Land Rover disappear from the parking lot.

He's hunky, too hunky, with a body to die for and an ass and legs that look perfect in faded Levi's.

"So where were you?" Mom demands.

"With Shey, on Orcas Island," I answer, gathering my wits and climbing into my truck.

"Shey?"

"My friend from St. Pius." I start the truck and back out slowly, the phone wedged between my neck and collarbone. "The one who's the model."

"Her husband died in Afghanistan."

"No, her husband is still alive. Shey's husband's a photographer."

"So who died in Afghanistan?" Mom's voice quavers.

"Tiana's husband."

"They're both photographers?"

I merge with traffic and head down Bellevue Way. "No. Tiana's husband was a journalist. He worked for CNN. He died just a few months after their wedding. You went to their wedding. It was in Carmel, at the mission. Remember?"

Mom sighs, her tone increasingly cross. "I can never keep them straight."

"The point is we're home now, Mom, and you're coming for dinner tonight. We're having you over for a barbecue."

"You're not coming here?"

"No, Mom, you and Dad are coming here."

As I jump onto the 520 to take a shortcut home, I think there are days when Mom sounds like herself and we talk about normal things and then there are days like today, when we talk and I feel like a parent with a very young child. God knows how Dad deals with it. He was never very patient, not while I was growing up, but somehow he has found an extraordinary gentleness, as though Mom's illness has made him not just an officer but a gentleman. I picture Richard Gere lifting Debra Winger and swinging her in his arms, carrying her away from her factory job.

"I get tired," Mom says. "I'm tired right now."

"I know, Mom, which is why we're going to eat early."

"I don't like being out late. I don't like your father driving late."

"Mom, it won't be late, and Dad can drive just fine."

"Maybe we shouldn't have dinner. Maybe it's not a good night."

I wish for more of my father's patience. I've never been strong on patience. "Eva's looking forward to seeing you, Mom. She's even making a cake for you."

My mother, who once had impeccable manners, the sort of manners that ensnared a southern boy, snaps irritably, "All right. But I want to be home early."

Five-thirty on the dot and the doorbell rings. Dad and Mom are here, and Eva rushes to the door to let them in.

Dad, who never, ever used to enter a room before Mother, steps forward first, and Mom trails after him obediently. This is how they go places now. Dad leads. Mom follows. And if Dad doesn't walk, Mom doesn't move.

I watch Eva hug her grandparents, noting that she's up to my mother's shoulders now. Eva's going to be tall, probably as tall as me.

Mom actually looks good today, more like the mom I

grew up with. Despite her disease, she's still slim, and she's wearing her favorite pink dress with the starched polo collar and the fabric belt tied at the waist. In her pink poplin dress, she looks like my mother with the trim ankle, the high-arched, narrow instep, the mother who loved shoes even more than she loved clothes. But as Eva moves away from my mom, Mom just stands there. No motion, no movement, just still. Lost.

I have a thousand stories I could share about my mom, and in not one is she lost.

To cover my unease, I go forward quickly, hug my father, kiss his cheek, and then go to my mother. She stands semialoof in my arms, as though enduring my hug and kiss. Then, just as I'm about to pull away, she pats my back, once, twice, so absently that I wonder if she even knows who I am.

Despite my wild, rebel ways, I've always loved my mom—well, maybe not so much when she tried to turn me into a debutante, but that was years ago, and I eventually escaped to New York, the half dozen cotillion classes ostensibly forgotten. And now I'm back, and I've brought Eva with me. I thought it only fair that Eva should have a chance to know her only grandmother before her only grandmother won't know her.

As we separate, my mom takes my hand, her fingers thin around mine. She smiles distractedly. "Marta."

"Hi, Mom." I dread the day she will not know me. Mother is young for Alzheimer's. Since she was diagnosed, even before we moved back to Washington, I read everything I could on the disease, ordering every book I could from Amazon, researching endless nights on the Internet, even going to a clinic on Long Island that treated Alzheimer's patients.

The cause of Alzheimer's might not be known, but the outcome is always the same.

"Come sit down," I encourage, taking my mother's arm and walking her slowly toward the patio, which blooms red and purple and orange with late summer roses, zinnias, and dahlias.

I point out the State Fair zinnias and roses to my mother, who smiles kindly, blankly, as though she were asked the time by a stranger.

"Those were your favorite combination," I remind her as Eva emerges from the house with my father. "The dahlias and roses are constants, but every year you had to plant your zinnias as seedlings. One year you were furious when Molbaks didn't order State Fair but another zinnia. You said you'd never go back to them again."

Mom, Dad, and Eva all look at me, listening to the story, but Eva can't believe that's all there is to it. "Did Grandma ever go back?"

Mom blinks, and her lips lift. "Yes," she says triumphantly, "I did. But I made them wait a week."

We all laugh, and no one looks happier or more relieved than Mom, whose blue eyes crinkle mischievously, her elegant gray hair with the thick white strip at the brow—all natural—dancing.

Dad has made sure she still gets her hair done once a week, and she's just been, on Saturday.

I never understood my father growing up, didn't like him very much when I was a kid, and his relationship with my mom was equally perplexing. Yet I have nothing but respect for both of them now. Life isn't for the faint of heart, and Dad embraces the aging future the same way he approached Korea and, later, Vietnam.

Cool, calm, courage, conviction.

I disappear into the kitchen to retrieve the pitcher of strawberry lemonade that Eva and I made earlier while the cake was cooling. We used fresh lemons and nearly the entire basket of organic strawberries I picked up at the store earlier.

Dinner goes well, and the night's a success, at least until dessert time, when Eva proudly carries in the cake she baked by herself.

This afternoon, I stepped in to help her only when one of the round layers broke coming out of the still warm pan and I showed her how to press the pieces together and then glue it all with frosting. No one will know, I told Eva as she heaped more frosting over the broken layer. Once a cake is frosted, it's impossible to see the cracks and flaws.

Kind of like us women and our makeup.

Now Eva slides the glass cake stand onto the table, placing the cake in front of Mom.

"Eva, where's your watch?" Dad asks, leaning over to tap her bare left arm.

Eva casts a reproachful glance my way. "I lost it."

"Lost it?" he booms, suddenly the military man.

I can't help sighing. "It's not lost, Dad. It's at a friend's."

My dad crosses his arms, puffs out his cheeks. "It's an expensive watch."

"We know where it is, Dad. It's at the Youngs' house, and we'll get it back tomorrow."

But Dad ignores me. "Why did you take it off in the first place, Eva? If you don't take it off, you can't lose it."

Eva hangs her head. "I was just showing my friends."

"Showing off, were you?"

"*Dad.*"

"That was your grandma's and my present to you."

"Dad . . ." I rise, put out a hand to Eva. "She understands."

But he can't seem to shift gears. "Kids nowadays don't respect anybody or anything—"

"Go inside, Eva." I give her a push toward the house, wait for her to close the door before I turn on my father. "What are you doing? Why are you talking to her like that?"

"It was a two-hundred-dollar watch, Marta."

"I don't care if it was a two-thousand-dollar watch, Dad. You don't talk to my daughter like that." Even as my temper flares, I realize that for my dad, this isn't about Eva or the watch. It's about me.

He still doesn't approve of me. He doesn't approve of how I dress, what I drive, what I do. He doesn't approve of how I parent Eva, either. "If you have a problem with me, Dad, then talk to me. But don't humiliate Eva—"

"This isn't about you—"

"Yes, it is. You don't think I'm raising her properly. You even said so last year. You said, quote, Eva would have been better off in a normal family. But Eva and I are a normal family. We're *our* family—"

"I'm tired," Mom suddenly says, her voice quivery. "I want to go home. I want to go to bed."

"So do I," Dad agrees grimly, getting to his feet and helping Mom up.

I don't try to stop them as they head for the door. I don't get Eva, either. But Eva rushes out as she hears Dad start the car. "Where's Grandma and Grandpa?"

I feel as if I swallowed a piece of glass. My throat and stomach hurt. "They went on home. Grandma was tired."

She turns toward the kitchen. "They didn't even try my cake."

I can't tell her how upset I am. I can't let her know that her grandparents, my parents, have disappointed me badly, too. "Well, let's have some now."

"But I made it for Grandma."

I give her a quick hug, then turn her around and march her into the kitchen. "We can take her a piece tomorrow, after school. But I can't wait till then. I've got to have some of that yummy cake now."

Chapter Seven

Eva and I sit in the kitchen facing each other on stools at the counter, each of us with our slice of gooey chocolate cake.

One woman, one child, I think. It's a very tidy, compact life, this life of ours. Unlike the families surrounding us, cocooned in large elegant shingle houses, we have just us. And that's good. It's all we want. All we need.

"Have everything you need for school tomorrow?" I ask, licking frosting from the prongs of my fork.

Eva nods, a mouthful of chocolate cake preventing her from speaking. When she swallows she drinks some milk and wipes the back of her mouth on her hand. I push a napkin toward her, but the damage is already done. The back of her hand is smeared with frosting now.

"If I'm going to volunteer, what do I do?" I ask Eva casually.

Eva jerks up her head, her mouth stained with chocolate. "What?"

"I'm thinking that maybe I'll volunteer more this year."

Eva just stares at me agog. "Is this a joke?"

I nearly choke on my last bite of cake. Am I that bad

of a mom? Do I lack that much legitimacy? "No, it's not a joke, but if you don't think I should, then—"

"No, no," she interrupts, taking the napkin to scrub her mouth clean. "You should. So what are you going to volunteer to do?"

"I don't know. Help out in the class, probably."

"Last year each teacher had their own sign-up sheet. All the moms that helped in the classroom signed up on that. They came in the first week of school to sign up," Eva answers. She's always been better at reading the packet sent home from the school office than I have. She likes knowing all this stuff, whereas the details just give me a headache. "If you want to help out in my class, that's what you'll have to do."

"Okay."

She's staring at me again. "You're going to do that?"

"Yes."

"Really?"

"Yes."

"Why?"

I can't help laughing at her stunned expression. "Why not? I've decided I'm going to try to be different from now on. I'm going to be like the other moms. Sign up for things. Do committees. Have meetings."

And do you know how my darling Eva thanks me? She laughs so hard that she falls off her chair.

The weatherman might say summer doesn't officially end until September 21, but ask any kid and you'll be told summer ends the first day of school. And today is that day.

Eva sleeps in her new clothes to make sure she'll be ready for school on time, and now she's up, pacing the house at six in the morning, no longer smirking, no longer finding humor in anything.

She's scared. Worried sick.

I don't know how to calm her, so I make her breakfast, a Belgian waffle topped with strawberries and a big whiz of canned whipping cream. But she eats only a third of her waffle before she puts down her fork, saying she's going to throw up.

While I finish making her lunch, I listen to her making retching sounds in the powder bath near the kitchen. She's gagging, but no throw-up, at least not yet. Eventually she emerges, pale, ghost eyed. "I didn't throw up."

"Do you feel better?"

"No."

"Would you like some SevenUp?"

"I just want to go back to bed."

"But you've been so excited about school starting."

"But I'm not anymore. What if the teacher hates me? What if Jemma doesn't talk to me? What if I never make friends?"

"Your teacher won't hate you."

Eva nearly cries. "But what if no one else ever likes me?"

She and I both know that being teacher's pet doesn't exactly help popularity contests. "There are four classes of fourth grade at Points Elementary. Half of those kids are girls. You'll make friends. You've just got to give some of the other girls a chance."

I'd meant to be reassuring, but from Eva's alarmed expression I think I've done just the opposite. She rushes from the kitchen and flings herself in the bathroom, and I hear her retch again.

And this time she does throw up.

Twenty minutes later, I tell Eva, who is now lying on the couch staring woefully at the ceiling, that it's time to go.

"I don't want to do this," she says mournfully, rolling off the sofa and onto her feet.

"I know. But it's the law. It's what kids have to do."

She makes a face at me. "Is that the best you can do?"

"Well, it is the law. And be glad, otherwise you could be a child laborer, slaving away in a factory—"

"Mom. Let's just go."

I hide my smile. I might not be the most "normal" mom, but my methods work. After grabbing my keys and wallet, I head to the garage door, but Eva stops me with one hand.

"Are you going to school like that?" she demands, indicating my tattered jeans with the holes at the knees and one high on the right thigh.

Suddenly, Eva sounds eerily reminiscent of my mother, who is giving me yet another lecture during my "coming out" year, the year she insisted I enter society as a privileged Seattle debutante. Each of those achingly boring lectures would begin with, *There comes a time in a young woman's life when appearances matter.*

I hated my mother's lectures, but I learned she was right.

There was a time right out of college when appearances did matter and you did whatever you had to to get the job.

If you were applying for a financial position, you

dressed like a banker in a navy suit with a white shirt and serious sensible dark pumps.

If you wanted a job in education, you chose something brown—tweedy skirts or slacks with another crisp white blouse and maybe a single strand of pearls or a gold chain with a pretty locket.

A job in advertising? Lose the pearls and gold chain with locket. You wore bold, clean designs in unfussy neutrals—black, white, gray—and then just for pop, a jolt of lime, orange, or cherry red.

I glance down at my supersoft faded Levi's and then lower, at my favorite combat boots, the laces loose, the toes scuffed. I've worn these boots for years, and no one had a problem with them until now.

"Mom, can you just put on nice slacks or something?" Eva asks delicately, as though aware that she's broaching a sensitive subject.

"Sure. But my boots are okay?" I ask in mock seriousness.

She frowns. "You want to create a good impression."

Do I?

Do I really?

Um, no. Because I don't really care about pleasing everyone else or wanting everyone's good opinion. I don't even know why I should want everyone's good opinion.

And my boots are just boots. They're not hurting anyone, are they?

But that's not really the point, and I know it.

In my jeans and boots, with my hair in a long ponytail, I feel tough. I feel cocky, confident, brash. And feeling this way, I walk with a little more swagger in my step. To quote Nancy Sinatra, these boots are gonna walk all over you.

And this is what keeps me from blending in at school. It's not the boots. It's the attitude.

I try to stick out. I like being the sore thumb.

But I change. And I swear, I wouldn't do it for anyone else but her.

Although Eva usually takes the bus, today I drive her as promised. As we cross from the parking lot to her new classroom, she carries her book bag gingerly, holding the supplies as if they're the most precious thing on earth instead of a school bag stuffed with plastic binders, boxes of tissues, and a dozen yellow number two pencils already sharpened.

"Are you sure about this?" Eva asks as we near her classroom door. "You don't have to volunteer—"

"You're making me nervous, Eva."

"I just don't want you to do something you'll regret."

"I'm not going to regret pitching in and helping out in your class. That's what *real* moms do," I say, stressing her choice of words. *Real moms.* I haven't forgotten her little dig last Saturday as we sat in the truck after leaving the Youngs' house.

I've always prided myself on being a good mother—a mother unlike my own mother, who was too busy, too involved, too interfering—yet now I discover that just might be the kind of mother Eva secretly wants.

"Real moms," I say with a tight white smile, "*love* spending time with their kids."

She gives me a strange side glance. "Are you watching Dr. Phil again?"

"I've never watched Dr. Phil."

She makes another of her funny little hmph sounds and mutters, "Maybe you should."

We've reached her classroom door, and with a huge gulp Eva smoothes her short brown skirt over her long legs and opens the door. We go in.

Feeling oddly out of place (what kind of mom goes to school on the very first day?), I walk with Eva to the back of the room, where Mrs. Shipley is receiving boxes of tissues and zipper plastic gallon-size bags.

I introduce myself briefly to Mrs. Shipley, tell her I've never been a room parent before but I'd love to help out, do whatever I could do, and Mrs. Shipley thanks me, asks me to leave my name and contact info, and then that's that. I give Eva a quick kiss and go.

As I step outside, I walk straight into Jemma and Taylor Young.

"Well, hello," Taylor says brightly, her straight golden hair brushing her shoulders. "You're just the person I was looking for!"

"I am?" I'm not sure why I'm so uneasy around women like Taylor Young, women who always look immaculate, women with hair the color of honey who wear pearls at their throats and loafers on their feet.

Maybe it's because they're so put together.

Or maybe it's because I'm afraid they'll judge me.

"An invite to our annual back-to-school brunch," Taylor explains, extracting a sheet of paper from her purse. "It's thirty-five dollars and a must-do. All the moms attend— as well as a couple of the more modern stay-at-home dads.

Jill makes fabulous mimosas, and we just have a ball. It's Thursday at nine-thirty. Hope to see you there."

It's not until after she rushes off—she's just spotted a mom she has to talk to—that I remember Eva's watch.

In the studio at my desk, I study the invitation.

Brunch at the Belosis!
Champagne, great food, and great conversation.
Catch up with all your friends and hear the exciting news
about what's happening at Points Elementary this year!

I don't know the Belosi family. But then I don't know most of the families here, unlike our neighborhood pre-school in TriBeCa. There, I knew almost everyone at least by sight, if not by name. Clearly, I've played the lone wolf card in Bellevue a little too long.

What the hell, I'll go to the brunch. What's the worst thing that could happen? I get food poisoning and die?

I reach for the phone, call the number at the bottom of the invitation—get voice mail, thank God—and RSVP that I will be coming and that I'll pop a check in today's mail.

Hanging up, I feel good about myself. I feel fantastic. In fact, I think I'm on my way to Mother of the Year.

Five hours later, I'm still at my desk and so immersed in my work that I've lost complete track of time.

At Z Design, we're in the final stages of putting together the newest proposal for Jet City Coffee, a regional coffee company in the Pacific Northwest. Keller & Klein handled their account two years ago (which means I handled the account), but when Keller & Klein was bought out and the Seattle office closed, Jet City Coffee took their business to another Seattle ad group with disappointing results, so they're back with me now and I want them happy.

We're known at Z Design for our quirky designs as well as what we like to call "retro reborn," where we take a style popular in one time period and reintroduce it with a twist, like the new series for Jet City.

The cheeky 1940s- and 1950s-inspired ads (think Ward and June Cleaver, smiling housewives with aprons, retro Maytag washers, fin-tail Cadillacs) will appear in the big Pacific Northwest newspapers—Portland, Seattle, Olympia, Boise—as well as the regional lifestyle magazines with the biggest circulations. The graphics in these ads are strong, and the colors are bold reds, blues, golds, and bronzes.

I'm still playing with one of the final mock-ups when Eva trudges into the studio, her book bag slung carelessly over her shoulder.

"Hi, Mom. Hi, Chris, Allie, Robert," she says, greeting my team with a heavy sigh before sinking in a heap at my feet.

This isn't the nervous but buoyant Eva I dropped off at school this morning. "What's wrong?" I ask, pushing back from my desk and leaning over to tug on her shoe.

Eva lies back on the ground, closes her eyes. "Nothing."

"First day didn't go well?"

She stretches her arms over her head. "No. It's fine. If you like—" She breaks off, shoulders rising and falling in an evocative shrug. "Being laughed at."

"You were not," I say.

She opens her eyes and looks at me. "I had no one to eat lunch with, so the duty made me eat with the boys, and then the girls all laughed and started saying I'm in love with one of them."

"Are any of the boys cute?"

"No. They're the grossest guys in fourth grade. They were doing weird things with their food and then talked with their mouths open just to make everyone sick."

"It sounds like it worked."

"Yeah, too well." She slides her arms slowly across the floor, reminding me of a snow angel on a Pergo floor.

I reach for the invitation now buried on my desk. "Well, I have something to tell you."

"What?" She rolls up, sits cross-legged.

I wave the invitation in front of her before letting it fall into her hands. "I'm going to the back-to-school brunch at the Belosis' on Thursday."

"You're not!" she exclaims, doing an amazing Lindsay Lohan imitation.

"I am."

"Do you know who the Belosis are? Only the richest family in the whole school."

I actually think there are other families that are probably richer, but I don't correct her.

"Devanne's dad has his own jet," she continues excitedly, "and when they go on vacation they use his jet, and Jemma's gone with Devanne in the jet and says it's so cool. There are no airport security lines and no waiting to board. You just go to this terminal near Boeing Field and get on. How cool is that?"

"That's pretty cool."

"I want to go on the jet. I want to go to Aspen or Vail or wherever it is they go for Christmas."

"I thought everybody went to Hawaii for Christmas," I tease her.

She sticks out her tongue at me, knowing exactly what I'm referring to. "Well, lots of people do, but the rest go skiing. You know, Whistler or Sun Valley. Aspen. Jackson Hole."

In New York, Eva had no idea this world of wealth even existed, and now she sounds like a writer for *Vanity Fair* or *Travel & Leisure*.

"Can we do that sometime? Go with everybody to a ski resort?"

That doesn't sound fun at all to me, but I smile, try to appear enthused. "Maybe."

Behind Eva, Robert and Chris are trying to keep a straight face. The team has heard everything by now, and it's one of the negatives of working from a home office. We sometimes have too little separation between the personal and professional lives.

Our office, "the studio," is really a guesthouse I converted into a work space. It was a savage remodel to make it work where I gutted the guesthouse's kitchen, knocked holes in all the walls, and added skylights to the ceiling, but I now have what I need: a bright, white, light-filled professional space with large windows that overlook the garden.

Eva grabs her backpack. "Well, I'm going to get started on my homework. I've got a lot to do. Mrs. Shipley has already assigned an essay we're supposed to turn in tomorrow."

She blows kisses to everyone and breezes out.

"Isn't she the little drama queen," Chris says, bursting into laughter as soon as Eva's gone.

"She's not a drama queen," Allie defends. "She's just a girl. If you think she's intense now, wait until her teens."

Like that's not scary at all.

I take a break an hour later and find Eva working diligently at the kitchen table. She's not writing her essay, though, she's doing math problems.

"How's it going?" I ask, coming behind her to drop a kiss on the top of her head.

"Okay. But I hate math. I really do."

"You're great at math."

"I don't know. Not anymore." She hesitates. "I think this year I might need help. You know, get some tutoring."

Tutoring? *Eva*?

I pull out a chair at the table and sit down. "What's going on?"

"School can be hard, Mom. I don't get everything, and it's not a big deal to get tutored. Lots of people I know do."

"Like . . . Jemma?"

She nods, unaware that she's just revealed her hand. "Jemma and Paige and maybe even Devanne, although Devanne's pretty smart. She does really well in most subjects."

"Eva, there's no shame in being bright."

"I know." But from her swift shrug, I don't think she knows, and I don't think she believes it. "Oh." Eva reaches into her backpack, pulls out a big brown envelope stuffed with papers, and pushes it across the table. "You've got to read these and send some back signed tomorrow."

More paperwork to fill out. Tons of paperwork. Yuck. Sometimes I feel as though school is more work for the parents than it is for the kids. "So what's your essay about?"

"It's the usual back-to-school getting-to-know-you stuff." She flips her carefully organized binder open to the first page, where she has a bright orange, pink, purple, and lime green assignment calendar, and reads aloud her notes. "Five-paragraph minimum. Introductory paragraph. Paragraph about each member of the family—" She breaks off, looks at me. "Guess I'll have to write about my sperm donor father."

Ah. I know where she's going with this, but I don't rise to the bait. "Tell her we have a small family, or write about why we moved to Washington so we could be closer to Grandma and Grandpa."

"So I *shouldn't* tell her that I don't have a father?"

"You could tell her whatever you want to tell her. It's your essay."

"It's okay then to tell her my mom ordered sperm off the Internet and had it sent to a clinic in New York where they used a cat catheter to transfer the sperm into your—"

"*Eva.*"

She looks at me innocently. "What?"

When Eva was a baby, I dreamed of all the warm, wonderful mother-daughter things we'd do together. Shopping, reading books together, going to the movies, having lunch, trips to the theater to see good plays and the annual holiday ballet, *The Nutcracker.*

I never thought about these sparky little mother-daughter talks where daughter makes snide comments to mom. I should have. I specialized in snarky with my mom.

And it hits me all over again that it's true what they always said, about payback being a bitch.

Which means I'm going to be suffering for a long, long time.

"What, Mom?" she repeats, a little less cocky than before.

"Do you want to write about sperm donors and sperm banks for your fourth-grade essay? Is that what you want to read out loud to the class?"

I don't even wait for her to answer. "If so, then go right ahead. Educate your classmates. Mention that most women who do this are like me, professional women with the resources to support a family. Mention that the adoption rules are more restrictive for single women than for gay couples. Mention that using a sperm donor is faster, and cheaper, than adoption as well. And while you're at it, mention that, yes, I short-circuited the traditional method of procreation, but I wasn't going to wait for Mr. Right. I don't believe in Mr. Right. I believe in you.

"And that," I conclude, standing, "should give you at least five paragraphs."

Eva stares up at me, eyes wide and, I hope, suitably impressed. "Okay," she says with a little cough. "I will."

"Good. And then we'll go to Grandma's when your essay's done."

I head back to the studio via the garage, and as I pass my truck, I spot my bike parked in the far corner, covered with an old paint-splattered dropcloth.

My bike.

It's been so long since I rode it. So long since I've even looked at it.

I open the second garage door bay and let the light stream in. There aren't any cobwebs in the garage, I keep it too clean for that, but there is a neglected feel in that half of the garage. Nothing's there but the bike, and that's hidden.

On an impulse, I strip away the dropcloth and let it fall to the ground. Dust puffs, and the sun catches the particles.

I stand back and admire my bike. It's a big black muscle bike, far from ladylike, and when I sit on it I feel strong, female, powerful.

In the sunlight, I can see fingerprints on the chrome and more smudges on the black-painted gas tank. Using the hem of my cotton T-shirt, I buff the fingerprints out of the chrome and paint.

Still wiping off smudges, I swing my leg over the seat and sit down. I put my hands on the handlebars. It feels good just to be sitting on the bike again.

Eva appears around the garage door. "Allie's looking for you."

"Tell her I'll be there in a minute."

"What are you doing?"

"Just checking out my bike."

"You're not going to go for a ride, are you?"

"No." But with my feet on the ground, I stand straight, balance the bike, feeling the weight of it, the heaviness and size. It's like a very old friend.

Eva frowns. "Why are you on it?"

I pretend to shift gears, remember how when first learning to ride the Honda YZ80, I shifted gears too fast and ended up doing a ridiculous wheelie. Got thrown, and while I didn't break any bones, my pride took a beating.

The guys I was with at the time laughed their asses off.

It made me even more determined to learn to ride, and ride well.

The first bike I bought was an outlaw. It'd been stripped and pieced together. It was ugly. I loved it.

Eva clasps her hands behind her back. "I'm not going to write about the whole sperm bank thing. Okay?"

I carefully buff the cap on my gas tank. "I know you miss not having a dad. I'm sorry. It's hard on you."

She shrugs. "It's not that hard."

I climb off the bike. "You've always wanted one."

"And I used to want a Barbie Dream Castle, but I survived without one."

Just when I want to throw in the towel, Eva surprises me, making me remember why I love our family.

Smiling, I reach for the paint-splattered cloth to cover the bike. Eva bends over, takes a corner of the dropcloth, and helps me settle it over the bike, hiding it once again.

"It's a nice bike, Mom," she says awkwardly as the fabric flutters from her fingers.

"Thanks."

"Maybe you should ride it again. You know, since you like that sort of thing."

Chapter Eight

Every member of the Z Design team looks at me agog when I appear Thursday morning in the studio in a pretty summer dress and heels.

"Going to church?" Chris asks, grinning.

"Or a funeral?" Robert quips.

Allie makes a face at all of them. "I think she looks very nice." But even she is curious. "But where are you going? It can't be business if you're wearing . . . peach."

"It's not *peach*," I say disdainfully as they all fight fits of giggles. "It's *apricot*, and Eva picked it out for me to wear to this morning's brunch."

"Brunch . . . now?" Allie repeats.

Chris flexes his muscles beneath a too snug knit shirt. "I thought brunch was a weekend thing."

"For country club folk," Robert adds.

I roll my eyes. They're worse than little kids. "It's a school fund-raiser."

"Because Points Elementary doesn't have enough of those," Susan, our office manager, sings as she peels off her thin sweater and settles her purse in a desk drawer. She's only just arrived, she never comes until she's dropped off her kids at their various schools and preschool, and her middle son attends Points, too.

"I'm glad you all approve." I lean over my computer, check e-mail, make sure nothing's come up in the last half hour, then straighten up. "Okay, I'm off. I'll see you in a couple hours."

"Toodles," Robert calls as I head to the door, and again they're all in gales of laughter. Their support is tremendous.

The Belosi home isn't on the lake, but on a huge chunk of land smack in the middle of Clyde Hill with an unbelievable view of the lake and the Seattle skyline. It's one of my favorite views, as high on the hill you can see the entire length of the Olympic mountain range. I've always found it breathtaking, the city with its skyscrapers and famous Space Needle centered in front of the Olympics' snow-capped peaks and ragged edges.

As I pull through the impressive wrought-iron gates, a valet attendant takes my car and I'm ushered up the stone front steps and into the "villa," as the Belosi family and friends refer to their home.

It does have the makings of a villa, but—and this may be my own snobbery—villas belong in Italy, overlooking Portofino, or nestled along the banks of Lake Como, not in the rugged Pacific Northwest.

However, the Belosi villa entry is probably grander than the classic Italian villa, with marble covering every exposed surface—pillars and columns, stairs and floor—with enormous tiered chandeliers everywhere, never mind the gilt-framed mirrors at the top of the stairs and another on the front wall behind the round table with its opulent arrangement of flowers.

Music tinkles from one of the great rooms to the right of the entry, and I see a uniformed waiter passing flutes of champagne and goblets of mimosas.

I take a mimosa, try not to think about all the work piled on my desk, and try to remember my goal—to meet more moms and to find women I have things in common with.

Glancing around, I see everyone is already in groups, and the loud voices and laughter boom from every direction.

I need to find someone who is standing on her own. Someone approachable. Someone hopefully friendly.

And there she is. A medium-height, medium-build woman in a sober navy dress with sensible navy pumps. She has brown hair with just a few strands of gray and, unlike most of the women here, looks quite normal.

I approach her and introduce myself. "Hello, I'm Marta Zinsser," I say, smiling warmly. "I have a daughter in fourth grade."

"Oh." Her lips barely curve; she looks at me and then past me. "I've a son in third. My son's Hunter."

It's so loud that I lean toward her. "I'm sorry. I didn't catch your name."

"I didn't say it."

"Is it a secret?" I joke, feeling increasingly awkward.

She looks at me, doesn't smile. "No. It's not a secret. My name is Mary-Ann Lavick."

"It's nice to meet you, Mary-Ann."

She just looks past me again. I force myself to keep smiling, although I'm smiling at nothing.

Uncomfortable heat rushes up from my collarbones past my neck to my face.

We stand there for another moment, not quite shoulder to shoulder, in painful silence while I try to figure out what I should say or do next.

Mary-Ann saves me the trouble. "There's my friend," she says bluntly. "I'm going to join her. Good-bye."

She goes.

"Good-bye," I say as she weaves—rather solidly—through the crowd of happy, beautiful ladies.

I'm back on my own again, so very glad I spent thirty-five dollars to come to this fabulous brunch party. This is exactly what I like to do with myself. Dress up, squeeze my feet into painfully high heels, and stand around with a fixed smile as though I'm a department store mannequin.

My hair's the problem, I tell myself. I'm the only one wearing it up. Everyone else's hair is down, all swingy and shiny. I shouldn't have pinned up my hair. I was just trying to be a grown-up, and now I feel as if I'm one hundred years old. Old and weird.

Why am I wearing peach—because it is peach, not apricot!

Why am I here?

I'm not a country club mom. I don't play golf. I don't play bridge. And I don't belong to the Junior League.

Why aren't I wearing black, as I would have in New York?

Better yet, why aren't I wearing my camo pants and flip-flops and a comfy T-shirt, because then I'd at least be myself?

All these women look so comfortable, and it's not just

hair and flawlessly applied makeup, it's something else. They're . . . fresh and scrubbed. Their skin glows.

Lana Parker spots me, nods, and almost smiles. I nod back, almost smiling, too. This is an interesting event. I feel vaguely like a diplomat at an embassy party. This house—villa—could be an embassy. It'd be perfect in Buenos Aires. Now we're just waiting for the ambassador from Chile to arrive so we can sit down and eat.

"Marta . . ." A nearly familiar voice says my name.

I turn around to see Taylor Young. She's got Eva's watch in her hand. "I believe this belongs to you."

"Yes, it's Eva's. Thank you so very much. My parents gave it to her for Christmas last year, and my father was very upset when he thought she'd lost it."

"Nathan thought it looked like an expensive watch."

I slide the watch into my purse. "Too expensive for a little girl," I answer, "but you know how grandparents can be."

"Mmmm, yes," she says, her attention caught by Lana and another woman. She waves, smiles, and nods. "One second," she mouths to them before turning back to me.

"Isn't this just a marvelous thing the Belosis do for Points Elementary?" she adds, her hand sweeping around to include the house, the flowers, the waiters with champagne. "They open their house for us every year. Don't know what the school will do when their youngest moves on to Chinook."

I just shake my head. I can't even begin to imagine.

"So have you been meeting people? Lana said you don't know everyone yet."

I think about my nice conversation with my new friend Mary-Ann Lavick and mention her name.

Taylor nods knowledgeably. "Oh, Mary-Ann is a jewel. She does so much for the school. Her husband's a physicist, I believe, and very highly thought of by the Gates Foundation."

"Really? And what does Dr. Lavick do?"

"Oh, I don't think he's a doctor. He's just a physicist. Or something like that. But apparently it's quite impressive work."

"I see." And I do. Apparently it's important to be connected around here. If one's not comfortable name-dropping, then one should at least be properly subservient to those in high places.

Lana is waving madly at Taylor. "Come here!" she shouts. "Hurry. You've got to hear this story."

"You better go," I urge. "Sounds like a great story."

"You're all right on your own?"

"I'm great. I'm having a ball."

Taylor hurries away, rushing toward her friends, who throw their arms around her and hug and kiss, cheek to cheek, as though they hadn't just spent last Saturday afternoon together in Taylor's living room discussing the kindergarten disaster.

Suddenly, I miss Shey and Tiana all over again. I feel like such a dork here. So raw and rough around the edges.

But I remember my promise to Eva and my conversation with Shey. There are women here with whom I have things in common. I just need to find them.

I join a group not far from me, women who are animatedly discussing what appears to be a controversial topic. I casually join them, curious about their passionate discussion. Turns out they're discussing the pros versus the cons of laser hair removal.

"I used to swear by it, too," says one attractive brunette. "I thought it was the best thing since sliced bread. But then the hair grew back less than two years later."

"They do say follow-up treatments will be necessary—"

"And it's not as thick as it was before—"

"But you can't laser with a tan, and the whole laser process takes months."

Someone advocates a return to shaving, and there is a roar of disapproval. Not shaving. Maybe waxing—but oh no, not waxing, either, because one, you've got to wait for the hair to grow out, and two, there's the problem of ingrown hairs. Everyone is in agreement now. Nothing worse than nasty ingrown hairs in the pubic area. Talk about a turnoff.

I'm really enjoying this conversation. It's fascinating. And I do feel much closer with everyone, but there's so much work at my office, and I feel guilty leaving Allie, Chris, and Robert to take care of advertising headaches while I learn about my neighbors' preferences for personal grooming.

I find a waiter, hand off the barely touched mimosa, and am scooting to the front door when I bump back into Taylor and her crowd.

"Remember," I hear Taylor telling the others, "first field trip it's all us girls."

"The A team," one cheers.

"Only the A team," another cheers, and they all giggle and raise their flutes and make a toast.

The A team, I repeat silently as I slip out the front door. Didn't know they played that way here, but I shouldn't be surprised. This is a stunning area of haves and have-nots. Someone's bound to be part of the have-nots. Just didn't know they had a team name.

Outside, the late morning sun shines on the broad, sweeping front steps and the line of luxury cars parked on the side of the half-circle driveway—Lexus, Lexus, Mercedes, BMW, Volvo, Saab, Porsche, Hummer, Mercedes, Infiniti, Range Rover.

And then there's my car. My restored 1957 Ford truck.

Okay. So it's a little like *Sesame Street*'s "one of these things doesn't go with the others," but I'm trying. I really am. I wouldn't go to brunch as a peach for just anyone.

"You're back early," Allie says as I walk in through the studio's open door.

At my desk, I kick off my heels and sit down. "It wasn't the most comfortable place to be."

"A little too rich for you?" Robert laughs.

"A lot," I answer, rubbing my face and feeling exhausted. What a horrible way to spend your morning. I suppose if everyone there is your friend, and if you've nothing else to do, it'd be fun, but for the moms who work, long, leisurely brunches just don't fit into the day. "I was a total fish out of water."

"Did you give it enough time?" Allie persists.

Allie's our traditionalist. A graduate of Seattle U, she's twenty-seven, strong, smart, spiritual, and anxious to be married. She's dating someone at the moment and praying it'll end in a trip to the altar followed by a glorious wedding reception for four hundred and then maybe a baby in the next year. I love Allie's graphic designs but can't relate to her driving ambition of marriage and motherhood. Motherhood's all very well, but how is marriage the answer to women's problems?

"It wasn't a waste of time. In fact, it was highly educational," I say, leaning over my drafting table with the poster-size ad of a pert, pretty 1950s housewife in a fitted blue-and-yellow polka-dot dress pouring her smiling husband a delicious cup of Jet City coffee.

The woman's wearing pearls and fashionable blue pumps. The husband's sitting at the kitchen table. It's a scene of perfect domestic tranquillity.

Of course, this ad was Allie's concept and design.

"There's an A team at work here," I conclude, reaching for my drafting stool, "and now I'm thinking that the whole A team concept applies to the children, too."

"Of course it does," Chris answers, taking a break from typing. He's spent much of the week drafting a proposal for a chain of health clubs. "Children learn from their parents. Parents are the ultimate role model."

"It's more than that, though," Allie argues. "All girls want to be popular. All girls want approval and acceptance."

"But what is popular?" Robert interjects, hands folded behind his head. "And does popular mean good or right?"

I grab a pencil and jab it in Robert's direction. "Exactly my point. Why are these little fourth-grade girls the popular ones? Is it because their parents have the most money? Is it their clothes? Or is it because there was once a power struggle and these 'popular' girls won?"

"Everything's a power struggle," Chris says bluntly,

downing his favorite protein-mix drink. Chris is buff, built, spends a lot of time in the gym, and owns expensive clothes and an expensive car. "Life is about competition. It's one of the things kids have to learn."

"But not all girls are competitive," Allie protests, tucking a blond spiral curl behind her ear. Her hair is naturally curly, and the first time I met her, I thought she reminded me of a young Sarah Jessica Parker. "And I don't think competitive or 'bitchy' girls"—and here she does the word-in-quote thing—"are necessarily popular. I think confident girls are popular, and Eva can be one of those girls. All she needs is more confidence."

I don't like the headache I'm developing. I don't know if it's from the brunch, the sips of mimosa, or the very personal turn this conversation has taken. "So we're in agreement that Eva isn't on the A team?"

"Yet," Allie emphasizes, "but she will be." She hesitates. "As soon we get you on the A team."

"I'm not on the A team?"

My question is met by a deafening silence. I guess I've had my answer. I'm one of the B team.

Maybe even the C team.

"Interesting," I say, clearing my throat. "Good. This has been a most enlightening morning. And now could I suggest we return to our slogans, graphics, and ad campaigns?"

I don't even wait for an answer. I grab my pencil, duck my head, and start making notes for Allie about changes I want made in the mock-up before we present the final design.

A team. B team. *Blech.*

* * *

By the time Eva gets home from school and she's tackled her homework and I've wrapped up business for the day, the last thing I want to do is make dinner. We're still in the first week of school and I'm already wiped out. How the hell are we going to get through nine more months of this?

Eva suggests we go to P. F. Chang's at Bellevue Square for dinner, and I second the suggestion. Chinese food and an icy cold beer sound like heaven.

It's still dazzlingly bright outside as we drive to the mall, trees profusely green and heavy with leaves. Traffic in downtown Bellevue is always congested, especially this time of night as commuters clog the streets en route to the freeway. I take all the back streets, enter the parking garage closest to 100th Street, and park on the third level before cutting through Nordstrom to reach the restaurant.

We arrive early enough to be seated within fifteen minutes, and we order immediately, choosing our favorites off the menu.

Over the lettuce-wrap appetizers, we talk about our day. "You haven't told me about brunch," Eva says, scooping the seasoned diced chicken mixture into the crisp, cold lettuce cups. "Is the Belosis' house as nice as everyone says? What did you eat? Did you have fun?"

Calling the brunch fun would be an exaggeration by any stretch of the imagination, but it was rather exciting to go someplace new and get a glimpse into how the other half lives. "It was really interesting. It's good I went."

"Yeah?" Eva looks at me over her bite. "So who did you talk to?"

"Um . . ." I picture not-so-smiling Mary-Ann and then the radiant Taylor. "Mrs. Lavick, Hunter's mom."

"Hunter's got serious food allergies," she replies matter-of-factly. "And he goes to these special chess camps in summer. Plays Russians and Albanians. Pretty intense."

"I'd say so. They're an interesting family, aren't they?"

"You think?"

"Hunter plays chess with Russians, and the dad's apparently quite connected. He's a physicist—"

"Dr. Lavick's not a physicist. He's a pharmacist." Eva looks at me disapprovingly. "Who told you he was a physicist?"

"Someone," I answer vaguely, not revealing Taylor as the source to Eva, as I don't want to damage Eva's hero worship. Besides, it's an easy thing to mix up. Pharmacist and physicist.

"Was she nice to you?" Eva asks, preparing another wrap, sprinkling it carefully with her favorite soy chili sauce blend.

"Uh . . . you know."

Eva nods. "She's kind of serious. You can see why Hunter's so . . . intense."

"Yeah."

And then I get that crazy feeling again, the one that's hot and sharp, and I look up, glance around, and he's there, being seated at a table next to us.

He's not alone, either.

He's got a tall, statuesque brunette with him, and she's beautiful, beautiful the way my friend Tiana is. Perfect features, thick glossy hair that reaches just past her shoulders, and a stunning smile.

Before I can look away, he sees me staring, and our eyes meet, and the sharp sensation inside my chest heightens.

It hurts. Looking at him hurts. Looking at him with another woman is even worse.

It's so crazy. I feel crazy. I don't understand it. Don't understand why he impacts me, or why I care, or any of it.

Men don't do this to me.

Men don't interest me.

Men don't.

But this one does.

For several minutes, I struggle with my lettuce wrap, suddenly conscious of everything I do wrong—the messy soy sauce spilling, the way food dribbles on my chin, the clumsy way I reach for my beer.

I can't eat dinner like this, feeling so awkward, and so under the pretext of helping Eva dish rice, I reposition my chair slightly so that he's no longer in my line of vision.

Moving my chair helps, and gradually I relax and Eva and I enjoy the rest of our dinner—a mu shu duck with tangy plum sauce and P. F. Chang's version of cashew-nut chicken. And even though we finish our dinner at a leisurely pace, I haven't really tasted anything since he sat at the table across from ours. It's been impossible to taste anything, or feel much of anything, with that rock in my gut.

Someone stops by his table to speak to him, and he rises, unfolding from his chair like a gladiator or mythic warrior. He's so big that he immediately commands attention, and it's not just his height but the way he fills the space.

Eva glances at him, stares, and then turns back to me. "He's so tall," she whispers.

I nod. But it's not his height that fills my insides with wild, uncomfortable butterflies. It's something else. His energy. His focus. His eyes.

I loved it when he looked at me in the store. Shivered when he looked at me here. There is something in his eyes, something in that long, piercing gaze, that makes me feel overwhelmed, dazzled, confused.

He, whoever he is, makes me feel anything but controlled. He makes me crave all the things I've denied myself these past ten years. He makes me want the things I'd nearly forgotten . . . heat, touch, hunger, skin.

Our waiter arrives with the bill and I pay immediately, thinking we're better off going now before my insides start knotting with nerves and adrenaline again.

Eva and I are out the door and heading for Nordstrom's and then the parking garage when Eva remembers her sweater.

"My sweater," she says, stopping in her tracks. "I left it on my chair."

We quickly walk back to the restaurant, and while I wait by the hostess stand, Eva runs to our table to look for her sweater, but she's met partway by my mystery man.

"Thank you," I hear Eva tell him as he hands her the lilac-colored sweater, her voice rising at least an octave.

"My pleasure," he answers, his voice so deep that it sounds like a growl in comparison.

Eva dashes back to me, smiling. "Did you see? That man, the very tall one, he brought me my sweater."

"I saw."

Eva takes my hand as we leave the restaurant again. "He's handsome, Mom."

I feel butterflies in my middle, and my pulse races. "You think so?" I ask, striving to sound normal.

"Mm-hmm." Eva looks up at me. "And his girlfriend, she's pretty, too, isn't she?"

Now my stomach falls. "Yes."

"I think she looks like Aunt Tiana."

I squeeze Eva's hand. "I thought the same thing."

We walk to the parking garage, and I have to be honest. I'm not surprised that my Man as Big as a Mountain has a girlfriend, but I am disappointed.

I like him.

More than I should.

Chapter Nine

The next morning, I wake up before six and my first thought is, It's Friday, thank God. And then my next thought is, It's Friday, and oh God, I hardly got anything done this week and the dinner with the Freedom Bike group is on Tuesday.

I'm still lying in bed, haven't even been awake three minutes, and I already feel stressed.

Have to run.

I change into shorts and running shoes and leave the house before Eva's even awake.

I'm just going down the street, a fast mile or two around the neighborhood just to clear my head.

I slept like crap last night. Couldn't sleep properly, not with all the crazy dreams. The dreams were so real and vivid, too. Bellevue villas, beautiful moms laughing about the poor slobs on the B team, interspersed with my gorgeous mystery man, who is apparently either married to, or dating, Miss America.

I don't understand any of the dreams, much less what my subconscious is trying to tell me.

Do I want a villa in Bellevue?

Am I longing to be on the A team?

Am I really that hung up on this mystery man who was dining with a beautiful brunette and drives a Land Rover?

No, no, and maybe, I think as I head back home, where I discover Eva's awake and eating breakfast at the counter. She has the note I left her in front of her and the cereal box.

"You didn't call me," I say, wiping my damp brow on a hand towel from the powder bath.

"I didn't need to," Eva answers, reading the cereal box. "You said you'd be back by seven, and you were."

"I just don't want you scared—"

"I'm not a baby, Mom. We talked about this."

"Right." I start the coffee and turn to the refrigerator. "Am I making you lunch, or do you want hot lunch?"

"Hate hot lunch," she sings, scooping more Special K with Berries into her mouth. Special K isn't supposed to be her cereal, it's mine, but she likes it better than any of the cereals I buy her.

"Right again."

With the morning paper on the counter, I scan the headlines while making Eva's lunch.

"Can we go to Barnes and Noble this weekend?" Eva asks while I bag the sandwich, which comes closer to jamming two sandwich halves into one snug plastic bag.

"Sure." There are some CDs I've been wanting to pick up. It'd be a good chance to get them. "Is there something special you want to buy?"

"They have a book on hold for me. I wanted to pick it up and then look around for a while."

"What book did you order?"

She shrugs. "Just a kid thing."

My eyes narrow. Eva never reads kid things. "Is it something for school?"

"Kind of." She smiles vaguely and shrugs. "But don't worry. I've got my own money. I'm using my allowance."

I wasn't worried, and she doesn't ask for that much, so I wouldn't have minded buying the book for her.

What exactly is she buying, and what is she not telling me?

Lunch that day is spent at my desk. I eat my salad while trying to do three things at once to make up for the fact that I haven't gotten nearly enough done this week.

A year after starting my own company, I can almost laugh at some of my mistaken assumptions, which included the thought that I'd have more control over my schedule by being my own boss, along with the assumption that by forming my own company and having my staff come here to work from my studio office, I'd be able to devote more time to Eva. The truth is, I'm even busier now than when I was a vice president for Keller & Klein.

Our Friday half days start at one, but today it's already quiet, as Chris has gone to the gym—he's religious about it. Allie's meeting a friend for lunch, and Robert's doing something, I just don't know what.

The phone rings, but I ignore it. We have two phone lines in the studio, an office line and a personal line that also rings in the house. Susan answers the studio line, as I hate being distracted when I'm in the middle of drawing, brainstorming, or problem solving, but I'm the only one who answers the personal line.

"Marta, it's your line," Susan says from the photocopier behind me.

"I know."

"You're not going to answer?"

I stare harder at the computer screen, trying to finish proofing the copy so we can get the brochure order in with the printer today. "Nope."

Susan, whose arms are now full of copies to collate, comes up behind me and glances at the number. "That's the Points Elementary School office."

I look at her. "Are you sure?"

"I know that number well."

Drat. If it's Eva's school, I've got to pick up. "Marta speaking," I say, trying to find the spot where I was just proofing.

"Marta Zinsser?"

"Yes," I answer, scrolling down and beginning the next paragraph. Each of our print materials gets proofed by three sets of eyes to try to avoid mistakes, yet the last print job we did for the Château St. Michelle winery brochure had a glaring error that everybody missed, so now we're doing the expensive job again, gratis.

"It's Mrs. Dunlop from Points Elementary. I'm just calling to verify the contact info for all our new room mothers—"

"Room mothers?" I interrupt even as I place the cursor in the spot I was reading. I'm not a room mother. I just volunteered to pitch in now and then.

"The room parents are encouraged to have a meeting the second or third week of school, and your head room mom, Taylor Young, will be contacting you sometime today or tomorrow about scheduling that meeting." She takes a breath. "So this is the correct number to reach you by phone?"

"It's my home and work number."

"Do you have a cell number?"

I give it to Mrs. Dunlop even as I try not to panic. I'm not a real room mom. Taylor's the room mom. I'm just helping serve punch at a class party.

Aren't I?

"Any questions?" she asks brightly.

"Um, yes. Just one. If Taylor Young is the head room mom, what am I?"

"You're the first assistant head room mom—"

"*First assistant?*"

"The next in command, after Taylor. But it's unlikely that anything will happen to Taylor. Knock on wood." She pauses, and I hear the distinct sound of knuckles rapping a desk.

"Knock on wood," I echo fervently.

"Fantastic. Now don't forget that I'm here, a resource if you ever need me, and look for that e-mail from Taylor. I imagine it'll be arriving before the end of the day. Have a good afternoon, Mrs. Zinsser—"

"Ms.," I correct automatically, thinking that this is a disaster in the making.

I do want to help in Eva's class, and I anticipated contributing. Cupcakes, yes. Rice Krispies Treats, yes again. Holiday art project for sure.

But first assistant head room mom?

First assistant to *Taylor Young*?

Oh, this makes me nervous. This makes me think of bad things, hurt feelings, and lots of Advil.

On the bright side, Eva's going to be thrilled.

I don't get Taylor's e-mail until late that night, as Eva and I head to Seattle to take my parents to pizza and a movie. Unfortunately, we're not even halfway through the movie before we have to go, since Mom wouldn't be quiet. She kept talking to the screen, having her own dialogue with Harrison Ford as though she and Harrison were starring in the film together.

With people practically screaming at Mom to shut up, we hauled her out of the theater and out into the lobby.

Dad's grim as we exit through the front doors. I'm shaken. Eva's undisturbed.

She takes my mom's arm. "Poor Grandma," she says, patting her back. "Those people were so mean, weren't they?"

Dad and I walk behind Eva and Mom. Dad's pale, almost ash toned. "I didn't think this would work," he says tightly. "I told you she wouldn't do well in a theater."

I shrug helplessly. "I thought she was doing better."

Dad looks at me sideways. "It doesn't get better, Marta. It only gets worse."

We walk in silence the rest of the way to the car.

I find Taylor's e-mail waiting when Eva and I get home. I'm sitting on the couch with Eva, using my laptop to check my in-box even though I'd vowed not to do e-mail on my laptop anymore.

But the always rushing out to my studio is proving to be a big pain, and I'd rather sit with Eva on the sofa anyway.

Taylor has sent a mass e-mail to her committee, advising us that there will be a room parent meeting at the school one day next week, once she confirms the time and place with the school. In the meantime, she's working on preparing "informational packets" for all the parents working with her, packets she'll distribute at the first meeting next week that will explain our goals and job descriptions.

I scan the job descriptions just to see how bad it's going to be.

Class Auction Chair
Room Party Coordinator
Field Trip Coordinator
Yearbook Liaison

And the list goes on.

Is this for real? Whatever happened to just a normal fourth-grade experience?

I'm still reading Taylor's e-mail when Eva leans across me to see what's on my computer screen.

"Why did Jemma's mom e-mail you?" Eva demands, catching a glimpse of Taylor Young's name.

She scans the e-mail before I answer and then straightens to look at me with a mixture of awe and concern. "You're really the first assistant head room mom?"

The way she makes it sound, I could either be her savior or a catalyst for catastrophe.

I'm silently thinking catastrophe, and I'd wager so is she. "Yeah. What do you think?"

"I don't know. That's a pretty big step."

Her confidence underwhelms me. "It can't be that hard, can it?"

"Noooo." But she doesn't sound convinced. "But on the positive side, you'll get to spend lots of time with Mrs. Young. You'll probably be seeing her a couple times a week."

That's so not cool.

"And maybe she'll be able to help you," Eva adds more brightly, moving back to her spot on the couch to resume watching her show. She gives me a big cheery smile. "Maybe she'll be able to teach you all the mom stuff you need to know."

Sunday afternoon, Eva and I hit the bookstore as promised, and while Eva shops, I select a handful of CDs. She already has her purchases paid for and bagged when I emerge from the music section. "Ready to go?" she asks.

I pick up an iced coffee from the adjacent Starbucks, Eva gets a Raspberry Tango, and we head home, where we're doing something boring for dinner like meat loaf. It's easy and fast, and I can work in the studio while the meat loaf's in the oven.

As I work I hear the house line ring, but I ignore it, just as I always do. The ringing ends abruptly, and I fear Eva's answered it. I'm right. She appears in the studio a minute later, holding the phone against her chest.

"It's Mrs. Young," she whispers excitedly. "Jemma's mom."

I save up my work on the computer and take the phone. "Hello."

"Hi, Marta. This is Taylor Young, and I'm calling to schedule our first room parent meeting for sometime this week. Thursday's Back-to-School Night so we need to find another evening that works."

"That sounds great," I answer. "Let me just get my calendar."

Eva's two steps ahead of me. She's already grabbing my BlackBerry from where it's charging on my desk and hands it to me.

I tap on my calendar icon for the coming week, and it's more booked than I expected with the Freedom Bike Group dinner on Tuesday night and Back-to-School Night on Thursday.

"I'm free Monday, Wednesday, and Friday evening," I tell Taylor. "I'm wide open on those days."

"Oh dear," Taylor says with a sigh. "That's not good at all. You're sure Tuesday's bad?"

"Very sure. You can't do Monday or Wednesday?"

"No. And, it's not just me," she answers. "It's everybody. After polling the other moms, Tuesday night seemed to be the best night, so it's what we decided on."

I find myself mentally counting the number of times Taylor uses everybody, others, we.

Who is this "we," and when did they decide? "I don't understand. I thought I was the first assistant head room mom—"

"Oh, well, yes, but I didn't want to bother you until we had some sort of consensus, and since Tuesday night was the best night, we're going to go with that."

"Am I the last one you called?"

"Yes, but it's just because I've worked with the others

before, and since they're married I thought it only fair to check with them first."

"That's fair how?" I ask quietly, thinly.

"Well, uh, they have husbands."

"Right."

"And nearly everyone has got to check in with their husband."

"Is that a big deal?"

"Well, um, yes, it can be." She's beginning to backpedal.

"And why is that?"

"It's just more work. They've got to make sure some-one can cover kids, coordinate schedules, things of that nature."

I can tell Taylor's scrambling, but I feel no mercy. In the meantime, Eva is giving me incredulous looks, as though I'm an NFL player and have just thrown the Super Bowl.

Taylor clears her throat. "I'm sorry you won't be able to make it—"

"Where is it?"

"The school library."

"What time?"

"Uh, seven."

"Thank you." And looking down into Eva's pleading face, I add as sweetly as I can, "Have a nice night, Taylor."

I hang up.

Now I know where I stand. I'm evidently the C team.

I don't think there's a chance in hell I'll be able to make the room parent meeting, but at the last minute Frank calls and says a group of the executive team can't fly out because of a problem on the East Coast and the meetings in Seattle have been rescheduled for the following week.

I'm disappointed not to meet the Freedom Bike Group for another week but very glad I'll be able to make the room parent meeting.

Dad and Mom come for dinner Tuesday night and have agreed to stay with Eva while I slip out to the meeting.

I shouldn't be late to the meeting, but a phone call from Tiana has me laughing hysterically instead of getting out the door.

After ten minutes, though, I beg off, promise Tiana I'll call her in the morning, and race toward my truck.

By the time I drive to school, find parking, and make my way into the library, Taylor's leaning against the librarian's desk, talking. The parent meeting has already begun.

Quietly, I shut the door behind me so as not to disturb the others. Taylor's looking quite sharp tonight, very much the professional mother in her brown trousers with a subtle gold-and-green plaid, a white blouse, three strings of fat cream pearls, and brown crocodile pumps.

I slip into the nearest empty orange chair as Taylor's narrowed gaze sweeps over the parents approvingly. "I'm really excited about this new school year. We've got the best group of parents, absolutely the best, and we're going to be the best class, too."

Taylor reaches for a leather binder. She's made each of us, her room parents, a binder, too, and filled it with everything we could need to know. It has four plastic dividers with the tabs already marked and placed inside. Calendar. Contacts. Parties & Field Trips. And last, Class Project.

And in each of the four sections are handouts, schedules, forms, information sheets, and helpful how-to-do directions and then how-to lists.

The information is so detailed, and the to-do lists so cute with cartoon graphics and liberal use of fun color fonts, that I feel as if I'm in high school on the student council or maybe it's the first day of cheerleading camp. Either way, it's so BUBBLY and UP that I feel even more uncomfortable.

High school was anything but the best time of my life. I did well in school, although my grades suffered because of my numerous unexcused absences and tardies.

My high school years are mostly a blur, but two things stand out: (a) I didn't fit in; and (b) I lost my virginity at the junior-senior prom.

I was only a sophomore the year I attended the junior-senior prom. My date was a senior, and I'd just turned sixteen. He wanted to get laid. It was his senior prom, after all, and I was too stupid to tell him no. The sex was forgettable (it hurt more than I expected), and worst of all was the indignity of spending the rest of the evening in a stiff formal gown feeling wet.

I didn't expect to feel so wet the rest of the night. No one ever talked about that. And I never went to another prom. Proms were stupid fake parties full of drunk, overdressed kids wearing the oddest flowers a florist could sell a seventeen-year-old.

Or put it another way—it wasn't me.

As most of adolescent life wasn't me.

Taylor continues to move the meeting along at a nice, crisp pace. She's obviously done this before. Her points are precise. Her tone is friendly and yet firm. I'm in Taylor Young's favorite domain.

"It's our job to make the school more efficient. It's our job to free up Mrs. Shipley's time so she can concentrate on teaching and not all the extras." Taylor's impassioned words generate a nod of agreement among the gathered women.

"We have to do everything we can to support Mrs. Shipley, and the best way we can do that is by taking a one- or two-hour block each week to assist in the classroom," she continues. "If you can come in twice a week, or even every day for a couple hours, fantastic. The more help Mrs. Shipley gets, the better job she'll do with our kids."

I'm trying not to let my jaw drop. Every parent here volunteer in the classroom two hours every week? With seven parents here, that's a minimum of fourteen hours a week. That's nearly three hours of volunteer help a day. And what would we be doing during those hours? This is fourth grade, not kindergarten.

Taylor presses on. "I've put together the schedule and will send it around with the volunteer sheet on a clipboard. Pick your preferred slot before we open it to the rest of the moms. Or if you have an area of expertise, let us know now so we can get you assigned to the right activity. We need moms to make copies, moms to grade, moms to sort papers, moms to record the grades, moms to work on bulletin boards, moms to read with kids who need a little extra help . . ." And at this last part, Taylor's voice drops. "Again, if you can do more, I strongly encourage you to volunteer for a couple time slots. There can never be too much help."

I wait for someone, anyone, to raise her hand and protest.

Someone here, someone besides me, has to wonder if a teacher—a highly trained teacher who once taught at the high school level—really needs this much parental assistance (read "interference"). But no one does. Instead, every maternal head is nodding, intent on her mission of making sure her child has the very best school experience possible.

Even if it means Mom's back in school full-time.

Knowing I'm about to be the lone voice of dissension, I slowly raise my hand. Taylor sees me and calls on me: "Yes, Marta."

I smile at her to show her I know she's the quarterback on the A team and I'm a third stringer on the bench, but theoretically we're on the same big team. "From what I've heard, Mrs. Shipley is an extraordinary teacher, and I'm wondering if this might be too much help."

Taylor's dazzling white smile freezes. She cocks her head ever so slightly, eyebrows lifting as if she doesn't understand the question. But she does. I can tell from the creasing at the edges of her brown eyes and the very unsmiling expression in those eyes that she knows exactly what I'm saying. And from Taylor's taut, terse smile, she's letting me know that we're most definitely not on the same team. "Marta, you're new here—"

"I've been here a year and a half."

"And you're still learning how things work here, and maybe in New Jersey—"

"New York."

"Maybe there moms didn't help out very much, but we

do here. We're committed to making sure our children have the best education possible."

"I agree, completely. I just thought our efforts were supposed to be more . . . behind the scenes."

"There are twenty-three students in the class. And only one teacher and one part-time aide. How can a teacher realistically teach all twenty-three kids without more help? There's only one of her. And nearly two dozen students."

Thank God she did the math for me. I wouldn't have been able to figure out that challenging teacher-to-student ratio on my own.

"Right," I continue. "But what about those of us who work? How can we be in the classroom two hours a week, every week?"

My question's greeted by absolute silence. Am I the only one here who works? Do none of them have jobs outside the house? Does no one else need to contribute to the paycheck?

Taylor's face rearranges itself, her power smile returning. "Most of us have made the decision to stay home and be full-time mothers. We find that it's so much better for the kids having Mom there every day."

My mom didn't work while I was growing up, and I've got to tell you that it didn't make me a smarter or a better person. Did having Mom there every afternoon make me more secure? Possibly. But not having Mom there wouldn't have made me more insecure.

And thinking back, way back, when I was growing up, my mom did volunteer, and she did pitch in with parties and chaperone field trips, but she didn't spend two-plus hours at school every week. In fact, no mom did. They'd come in periodically for a project like a bake sale or the greeting card and candy bar fund-raiser, but they didn't live in the back (or front) of the classroom.

I'm not sure why it bugs me so much to think that moms are there all the time, but it does. We're supposed to help our kids learn to let go, but if we don't let go, how will they?

Isn't school a time for children to learn responsibility and self-reliance?

Taylor hands the clipboard to the woman to her right. "When the sign-up sheet comes to you, just put down whatever you think you can do. And don't worry, Marta," she says, shooting me a smile that whispers of condescension, "I'm sure between all the moms here, we can cover for you."

Chapter Ten

After that wonderful parent kickoff meeting, I'm not particularly anxious for Back-to-School Night. Taylor will be there again, and I don't like having to be away from Eva for a second night in one week.

Happily, Allie agrees to stay with Eva for tonight's Back-to-School Night so I can go and learn about the wonderful year Eva's going to have and how we're helping the Bellevue School Foundation help us. Which is a nice way of saying that they're going to be asking for more money from us very soon.

I've never felt comfortable at Points Elementary parent events, and that surprised me when we moved here, because I always enjoyed the parent nights at Eva's school in New York. Maybe it's because here in Bellevue I feel like the odd mom out—not just a single parent, but a woman who hasn't yet made any friends.

I definitely need some friends.

Speaking of friends, I never called Tiana back. I completely spaced. *Dammit.*

Eva helped me get ready for Back-to-School Night, making a few too many suggestions re wardrobe and hair.

Not that shirt, Mom.

No, not that one, either. It's ugly.

You can't wear those pants, they make you look fat.

Wear something nice, Mom, the other moms always do.

In the end, I leave the house wearing what Eva thinks is appropriate for a parent education night: black shirt and black slacks with a beige-khaki car coat. I'm wearing heeled black boots, and my long hair is combed straight but otherwise loose. In my opinion, I look as if I'm going on a dinner date, but Eva's happy. She seems to feel I finally represent her properly.

I give my little social climber daughter a hug good-bye and head out the door.

Tonight I'm not late, but by the time I reach the school, the parking lot is overflowing and I'm forced to park on one of the residential side streets flanking Points Elementary.

The gym is brightly lit and buzzing with conversation and laughter. The rows of folding chairs are nearly all full, with lots of Asian and Indian families in the middle and back rows, families lured by Microsoft to add to their technical workforce, while the front rows have been taken by the eager-beaver parents who got here early.

I find one of the last open seats on the side near the wall toward the back of the gym. As I sit down, I adjust my coat, put my purse at my feet, and cross my legs to appear properly busy.

It's a rowdy crowd, conversation punctured by raucous laughter, and as I sit in my chair, my hands folded neatly in my lap, I feel something I'm starting to feel more often.

I'm lonely. Not wildly, miserably lonely, but the whisper of lonely, the lonely that makes me think I need to get out more, I need to network and socialize, I need to maybe have people in for dinner or a movie or something.

Maybe this is what Eva's been feeling. Maybe this is the emptiness that's been bothering her. Our lives are a little too quiet here in Seattle. Our world is a little too routine, and this wasn't how we lived in New York. Our lives in TriBeCa were colorful and unpredictable. Friends dropped by all the time. Shey would call and invite us over. We ate out frequently, Greek food one night, Cuban another, the Jewish deli at least once during the week.

Now I'm meat loaf and potatoes.

How sad is that?

Again I think of Tiana and Shey, and I don't want to replace them. But maybe I can't continue being such a lone wolf. Maybe I do need to make friends here, friends who are adults and have perspective, friends who can listen and give suggestions, friends who'll laugh and celebrate the successes and, on the bad days, offer a hug and a glass of wine.

The principal, Dr. Fielding, is at the microphone, and the meeting begins. Every school meeting seems to be filled with the same good-intentioned people making the same good-intentioned speeches that all somehow manage to be achingly boring.

The Korean family next to me with three kids attempts to shush their youngest, a toddler, as she fusses. I look at the child with sympathy. I want to fuss, too.

People continue to arrive even though it's now fifteen minutes past the hour. One man arrives and takes a position against the wall not far from me, and immediately heads turn and people murmur. The man looks quite nice, broad-shouldered, sturdy, a balding head, but otherwise ordinary, and I'm not sure who he is or why he's suddenly attracting so much attention.

"Steve," someone a row down from me whispers, "here, take my seat."

"Steve, do you want to sit here?"

"Hey, Steve, I don't mind standing if you want to sit."

But Steve declines each offer, shaking his head and smiling. "No, no, I'm fine," he answers.

I'm curious about this very popular Steve. He does look familiar, but I'm not sure if it's because I've seen his picture somewhere or if it's because he looks like the wholesome, hardworking midwestern farmer I used in an ad campaign last month.

Tuning out the third speaker, I glance around and spot faces from the Points Country Club pool. Lana. Taylor with her husband, Nathan—he is good-looking in a very scrubbed Ralph Lauren polo ad sort of way. Mary-Ann Lavick, who definitely didn't enjoy my company at last week's brunch.

I continue scanning the crowd, impressed by the number of dads who have shown up. It's good to see so many men taking an interest in their kids' education. I know my dad never attended any school meetings, not even the parent-teacher conferences. That was always my mom's job. But then, anything to do with me seemed to be Mom's job.

Maybe that's why I had a baby on my own. If my mom could do it, why couldn't I?

Then, as I finish scanning the gym, looking for anything remotely interesting, my heart falls and I go all hot and fizzy.

He's here.

He's here right now, standing at the back of the gym with dozens of others, yet he stands out. Head and shoulders far above everyone else.

I take a quick breath, jolted.

I thought he was huge when he passed me in the fog on 84th Street, thought he was imposing at the grocery store, but here, next to the other men, the other dads, he looks like a mountain.

As I sit there gawking, he turns his head and looks at me.

It's the same cool, piercing gaze from before. It's intense. Discomfiting.

Flustered, I look away, shift uncomfortably in my seat.

My eyes burn, and my pulse races. I feel breathless again, which is ridiculous because I'm not running, not even moving. I'm just sitting in a putty-colored metal chair listening to people talk about buying new math technology and fund-raising to afford more teacher aides. Yet I can't breathe. I can't get enough air.

Suddenly too warm, I take the program given to us and fan myself. Hot, I'm so hot, and I wish I hadn't worn all black with this car coat on top.

But it's not me making myself hot. It's him. And I can't let him do this to me, can't respond like this. So ridiculous, so silly. I'm being silly.

Yet I turn my head and look again. I'm like a schoolgirl, completely infatuated and unable to stop myself.

He's so . . . so . . . everything.

He has the coloring of great Scottish warlords, his short, thick hair shades of red and gold, and his features

are strong, male, as though whittled by wind and weather
and war. He reminds me of a time long ago, of battles and
warriors, peasants and kings.

Makes me almost wish I believed in love.

Makes me wish—even if it's just for a split second—that
I had someone like him at my side. With me, to love me,
maybe even protect me.

I never wish for things like that. I'm an independent woman, a fiercely self-sufficient woman, but
lately . . . lately . . .

I blink, give my head an all but imperceptible shake.
The romantic stuff has got to stop. I'm a mom at Back-to-
School Night, and he's not part of an ad campaign, he's
not part of some great sales scheme.

If he's here tonight, he's a dad. He's someone's father.
And most likely someone's husband.

But he hadn't been wearing a ring last Thursday night
at P. F. Chang's, and neither was his date.

Which means he could be divorced or widowed.

He looks my way again, and our eyes lock, hold.

I'm glad I'm sitting. I don't think I could stand right now.

I don't believe in love at first sight. Haven't wanted to
feel anything for anyone in so long, but he, this complete
stranger, does something to me. He makes me feel so
much, it hurts.

I'm not prone to infatuation, but I'm overwhelmed at
the moment. I need to get out of here, need to get home
and out of these clothes and into my tattered jeans and
my paint-splattered clogs and my big oversize men's shirts
I wear on fall weekends.

The principal wraps up his talk, and the moment he's

excused everyone, I'm on my feet, purse under my arm, racing for the door.

I'm literally fleeing the building, practically running for my truck, when I turn smack into a rather unmovable chest.

I know who it is. I can tell. I can feel the size and width and warmth, and every nerve ending in my body screams. I'm wound so tight, I stumble back a step and then another.

"You all right?" asks a deep voice, a voice that rumbles its vowels and consonants.

My chest constricts, growing tighter and tighter, and I still haven't made eye contact. I'm afraid to, yet normally I'm fearless. "Yes."

"We've never met," he says, and thankfully he doesn't extend a hand. I don't think I could touch him. I don't want to touch him.

"Luke Flynn," he adds.

"Marta Zinsser," I answer, finally lifting my gaze and looking up, all the way up. He towers over me. He's taller than six feet six—I'd swear he's at least six seven. I've never met anyone this big who was also so unbelievably gorgeous.

His gaze narrows as it rests on my face. "You have a daughter."

I nod. "Eva. She's in fourth grade." My heart's thumping so hard, I struggle to say the next words. "And you? How old are your kids?"

"Not married. No kids." The edge of his mouth lifts ever so faintly, almost slyly.

He knows I'm interested in him. The heat in his eyes isn't my imagination. He's interested in me, too.

"You just miss your elementary school days?" My voice sounds breathy, unsteady.

"I'm a Big Brother to a little guy here. I come to his school events whenever his parents can't."

I'm speechless. It's the last scenario I imagined.

Luke glances at the throngs of parents heading to classrooms now. "Better go. Don't want to be late."

I nod, and as I look at him, I feel the strangest thing, as though something in me, something fragile, is about to fall. "I need to go, too." I force a smile. "Good-bye, Luke."

"Good night, Marta."

I join the parents moving like great herds of cattle to yet another holding pen and enter Mrs. Shipley's classroom with the others. Lots of parents sit at the student desks, while a few moms and dads line the wall.

I'm about to take a place on the wall, but one of the moms from the room parent meeting gestures to me. "You're supposed to sit at Eva's desk."

"Thanks." I squeeze through the clusters of small chairs to reach Eva's desk and sit in the small chair.

The classroom door opens and a man sticks his head inside, takes a look around, and then just as swiftly leaves. I recognize him from the gym. It's the balding man, the one named Steve.

I turn to one of the dads at the small desk next to me. "Do you know who that man was?" I ask, nodding at the door. "I think I overheard someone call him Steve."

"Yeah, that's Ballmer," the dad answers. "Steve Ballmer. CEO of Microsoft. Gates's right-hand man."

Ah, right. No wonder he's familiar. His face is only plastered over the Seattle papers' business sections every other week. "He seems like a nice guy."

The wife of the man I've been talking to leans forward

and whispers, "His wife's lovely, too. I like her a lot. And you wouldn't know they're . . . *you know.* They're not flashy, not material. Not like a lot of people around here."

Wow. Someone with an honest opinion. I like this lady, whoever she is. Smiling, I extend my hand. "Marta Zinsser, Eva's mom."

"Lori and Jake Hunter, Jill's parents."

"Nice to meet you," I say. And it is.

The next week I'm busier than ever between sales calls, business lunches, and then the rescheduled dinner on Tuesday with Frank and the Freedom Bike Group.

The dinner at Cutter's, a seafood restaurant on Seattle's waterfront, goes better than my wildest dreams. I like the men, all of them, even the guy with the long handlebar mustache who spoke only twice.

I remember what Frank said about this being just a relaxed, get-acquainted dinner, so I go as myself, dressing in wide-legged charcoal black slacks and a white blouse tucked and belted at the waist. I've pulled my hair in a loose knot at the back of my head and am wearing hoop earrings and a silver chain with a red polished stone.

I'm relaxed as Frank introduces me to the various partners and executives in the bar. We talk over drinks for an hour before we're taken to a private dining room for dinner.

Seeing as it's a bike group, I'm surprised at how many order fish entrées instead of beef. There are more drinks during dinner, but I stop at two, knowing I've got to drive, and no one presses any more on me.

Later, Frank walks me out as the valet attendant gets my

truck. "What do you think?" he asks me bluntly. "People you can work with?"

"Yes. I like everyone. A lot."

"They liked you, too."

"So you haven't told them about my Harley?"

Frank cocks his head, and his teeth flash despite the beard. "No. I think I'll wait until you get the job."

I can see my Ford truck approach. The valet driver is almost to us, and Frank checks out the truck, whistles. "Is that yours?"

"Yeah," I answer, pride in my voice.

"You're not like most women, are you?"

I laugh and tip the driver and prepare to climb behind the wheel. "You know what's funny, Frank? My daughter tells me that all the time."

"Does it bother you?"

I start the engine. "Only sometimes."

Eva comes home from school Wednesday afternoon with something entirely new on her mind.

She announces that she's putting my wedding plans on hold to focus on this year's school walk-a-thon, which is just days away now, and it's an idea I want to support, but it still involves my spending lots of money.

"Of course you'll sponsor me," she says, her sharpened pencil poised over the yellow pledge form. "Should I put you down for five dollars a lap?"

I've just made her a quick cheese quesadilla as a snack before I dash back to the studio to continue working. "How many laps are you planning on walking?"

"Fifty."

"*Fifty?*" Like I'm going to cut a check to the school for two hundred and fifty dollars for a walking event when the damn phone-a-thon is less than a month away. And don't think you can escape the phone calls, either. *It's for our kids. It's for the future.*

Well, the future's stressing me out.

"Mom, they're not quarter-mile laps. They're smaller, around the baseball field."

"You're out of your mind."

"Then how much? Two fifty a lap?"

"Two dollars and fifty cents?"

"Mom, it's a fund-raiser."

"Eva, I already pay the school."

"You do?"

"Yeah, it's called taxes."

She makes a shrrmphing sound, blowing air out between her front teeth. "Everyone does that. You're supposed to give more."

"Says who?" She's been going to way too many school fund-raiser assemblies.

"The school. The PTA. The Bellevue Unified School Foundation."

She's got her pencil poised again, hovering over the little pledge box. "So how much, Mom?"

"I don't know." I can't commit just yet, can't promise anything, not when I'm feeling railroaded into something I don't want to do and am not entirely sure I can afford. One fund-raiser, yes. Two, maybe. Three, four, five? Come on. I'm a single mom, and I don't work for Microsoft.

Eva's reaching for the phone. "Fine. I'll just call Grandma and Grandpa. And then Aunt Shey and Aunt Tiana. Oh, and Chris and Robert and Allie, too. Are they still here or have they gone already?"

Lucky bastards. They've gone. "They've headed home."

"I'll just call Grandma, then."

My mom answers the phone at their house, and from what I can hear she's in a chatty mood today. Mom and Eva discuss the weather and then Eva's ideas for Halloween costumes and schoolwork, which provides Eva with the opening she needs to bring up the walk-a-thon.

My mom isn't a hard sell, but then I didn't expect her to be. When I was in grade school, my mom was president of the PTA.

Eva looks smugly at me as she asks my mom, "So will you want to make a flat donation, Grandma? Or would you like to pledge a certain amount for each lap?"

Eva suddenly gasps, her voice strangled. "A nickel a lap, Grandma? A nickel isn't very much, Grandma. A nickel's . . . well, like a penny."

I'm not entirely sure what my mom says, but Eva's now backpedaling as fast as she can.

"Not a penny, Grandma. *No.* You're right, Grandma, a nickel *is* better than a penny."

So my mom hasn't completely lost her mind. She knows how to deal with a money-grubber.

Eva meanwhile turns to me. "Mom, will you please talk to her?"

"It's your walk-a-thon."

"It's your mom."

Touché. I take the phone. "Mom. Hi. It's Marta, and it's great that you're helping Eva. Thank you so much."

"I'm glad, dear," she says. "I always used to help you, but you didn't do walk-a-thons, though. You used to do swim-a-thons, for your swim team. Remember?"

"I do. That's why I knew you'd want to sponsor Eva. And if you pledged fifty cents a lap, or a quarter a lap, you'd really help her."

"A quarter? That's a lot of money."

"It sounds like it, Mom, but if Eva walks twenty laps, that's only five dollars."

"That's not too much. All right, then, I'll pledge a quarter, but tell her not to walk too many because I don't want to spend too much money. Oh, I have to go now. My favorite show is on. Good-bye." Before I can say anything, my mom has hung up.

Eva's standing at the counter, watching me. "Mom, is she crazy?"

I think about my mom, who she was and the horrible disease taking her away from us, and sigh heavily. "Just a little bit."

The much anticipated walk-a-thon arrives just days later, on the third Friday of September.

Eva has hit up my friends Shey and Tiana just as she promised, as well as cornering each of my office staff. Robert and Allie are always great about sponsoring her or donating to the latest school fund-raiser, but Chris hates these things.

As the walk-a-thon is held after school, I wait in the crush of moms as Eva registers and picks up her official lap card. It's a beautiful day, not too warm and not too cold, and the blue sky overhead is a perfect foil for massive maple trees surrounding the school track. The leaves are just starting to turn red, and the nearby poplars are turning yellow.

Tucking my fingers into my jeans pockets, I listen to Dr. Fielding announce that the walk-a-thon will kick off in five minutes.

Eva has her white walk-a-thon T-shirt pulled over her tank T-shirt and shorts, and her long dark ponytail hangs to the middle of her back. Like the other kids, she wears a lap card around her neck. Apparently, every fifth or tenth lap the kids earn a reward called a "yum," which allows them to get something tasty from the snack stand.

The noise grows louder as kids crowd the start point, a mass of eager bodies in T-shirts, shorts, and jeans. Suddenly the music blares and the kids are off, bursting into a mad run that will soon slow to a more sedate walk as they continue to go round and round and round.

It's hard to keep an eye on Eva with the hundred kids all racing the track in matching white T-shirts. It's while I'm searching the crowd for Eva that I see him. *Luke.*

Luke's here today, and he's always taller than everybody, and he stands in such a way that his shoulders aren't just broad, they look as if he's got football gear on.

He's noticed me, too, and he smiles faintly, the same half smile from Back-to-School Night, when everything seemed so hot and electric.

I feel hot and electric again, and it was one thing in my twenties to feel wildly passionate about someone, but I hadn't expected this in my mid-thirties, much less after having a child.

Jamming my hands into my jeans jacket pockets, I try to ignore that adrenaline rush I get every time I see him.

Why does he do this to me?

Why do I do this to myself?

I gave up on love and romance a decade ago, and it's not on my task list of things to do. I have important things on my task list. Things like career and kids and accomplishing my goals.

Suddenly it's bedlam as the children swarm the moms, each one panting and holding up his or her lap card to be marked.

As the kids take off again, I find myself glancing once more in Luke's direction, and he's looking straight at me. He stares long and hard, as if I intrigue him or amuse him somehow.

I look away first. I always do. I'm so attracted to him that it scares me a little.

Eva breaks free from the crowd of running kids to get her last lap counted.

"Five laps, Mom," she pants, showing me her marked card.

"That's great."

"Only forty-five more to go."

My God. That's going to be hours from now. "Then, baby, get going."

Just go talk to him, I tell myself as Eva rushes off.

Go say hello.

But I don't know what I'd say. I know what I'd like to ask: Where were you raised, what do you do, how did you get to be so tall?

Maybe it's not what other women would want to know, but I'm fascinated by his size and shape. I'd love to know if he played sports in college and, for that matter, where he studied and why he decided to become a Big Brother.

In short, I want to know everything. I want to ask everything. I'm curious as hell and turned on, too.

But I don't go to him because curiosity kills cats, and I don't have nine lives. I'm all Eva has, and I can't afford to take risks.

Then there's the whole insecurity thing. While there isn't just one kind of mom here at Points Elementary, the competition is still pretty fierce.

For example, to my left is the classic *Playboy* Bunny mom with the cropped top, snug pants barely covering her hipbones, and rabbit-fur leggings (maybe she's from Russia with love?).

To my right is the dazzling young trophy wife mom with the huge breasts squeezed beneath a very tight knit top, an überflat tummy, flawless complexion completed by a four- or five-carat diamond ring, which is blinding everyone the moment it catches the sun.

Talking to the trophy wife mom is the "I've a better body than anyone" mom with her little top that looks like a lace sport bra and her white pants that belt three inches below the belly button. She's got Marilyn Monroe breasts and the tanned, hard abs of a Dallas cheerleader, and she's got to know every man is staring and every woman hates her.

In a cluster stand three more moms representative of very different women: the grown-up Surf Barbie mom with the long blond hair that reaches her waist; the richer-than-shit mom who drives car pool in the Rolls (or is it a Bentley?); and the sophisticated yet subtly sexy mom, a slim, youthful brunette in designer wear without any garish bling.

I could go on, but I won't. The point is, this isn't what mothers looked like when I was growing up, and while I'm comfortable with myself and like myself, I'm not your Barbie mommy. And for some reason unknown to me, many, many men in Bellevue crave Barbie & friends.

Chapter Eleven

I'm still standing on the school field watching the kids' walk-a-thon when Eva comes racing toward me.

"Mom, I just got a yum," she says, "and I heard they're short volunteer moms, so go over there and volunteer at cotton candy."

"I don't know how to make cotton candy."

"You don't have to *make* cotton candy. It's already made and in mini plastic bags. You just stand there and pass the bags out." She points to the cluster of tables and chairs. "See? It's easy. Even you can do it."

I appreciate her vote of confidence, and yes, she's right. Even I can successfully pass out plastic bags. "I'll go."

"Great!" Eva shouts good-bye, jabs her pointer finger in the direction of the food booths, and takes off, disappearing into the crowd of children circling the makeshift track.

The mother at cotton candy smiles warily as I approach. "I'm Marta Zinsser," I introduce myself. "My daughter Eva's in fourth grade, and she said you needed some help."

"Sure," the mom answers, tearing open a big cardboard box with practiced ease. The box is packed with individual bags of pink and blue cotton candy. "One of us can check off the yum space on the lap card, and the other one can pass out the candy. Which would you prefer?"

"I don't care."

"Fine. I'll mark cards. You do treats."

Moments later, flushed, panting kids flock around us, all holding out their lap cards to show they've earned their yum.

The mom starts marking the yum space, and I pass out candy as fast as I can. Just as fast as the crowd formed, it thins out, and I open yet another cardboard box.

"I'm Kathleen Jones," the mom says as we finish our second frantic round of cotton candy distribution. "My son Michael's in second grade."

Another volunteer mom stops at the booth and gives us bottles of chilled water.

"Have you done this before?" I ask Kathleen.

"I was a lap counter last year."

"You've moved up in the world."

Kathleen makes a face. "Or down, depending on your idea of success."

A little girl suddenly runs back to the table and asks if she can please exchange the bag of blue cotton candy for pink since blue is for boys.

"It's just candy," I tell her.

"I know, but I don't like blue."

I lean over the table and whisper, "It doesn't taste blue. It tastes pink."

The little girl with the dark brown bob stares at me for a long time before slowly extending her arm to hand me the candy. "Pink. Please."

I give her the pink and watch her run off. The next little girl who approaches smiles at me. "I want a pink one, too, please."

"Why pink?"

"I like pink."

"But pink and blue cotton candy tastes the same."

"But I don't like blue."

"Why?"

Her shoulders lift, fall. She's missing teeth as she makes a face. "It's not pink?"

I give her the pink cotton candy and reach into the box for another handful of plastic bags when I see taut denim-clad thighs step into the line in front of me.

Slowly I look up, button-fly jeans, empty belt loops, a lean waist, and one hell of an impressive chest.

Luke stares down at me, light blue eyes narrowed quizzically. "Fighting for blue rights?"

I feel my face burn hot and my eyes meet his, and there's something so intent there, so fierce and curious, that I step back and drag the cardboard box closer. "Did you earn a yum?"

"I hope so."

"Let me see your lap card, then," I say, trying to sound serious.

There's the faintest hint of a smile in his eyes, as though to challenge me. "I don't have one."

Fortunately, I'm not a sucker. "Then you don't get a yum."

"You're pretty tough on the little guys."

"I hope you're not classifying yourself as one of the little guys."

His smile deepens, and I get a glimpse of a rather astonishing dimple.

I don't know if it's his smile or the dimple, but my insides do a funny flip. This man is dangerous. And he's got to know it.

Amused, he asks, "What can I have if I don't have a lap card?"

Half a dozen thoughts flash through my mind, and none of them are appropriate for a public school function, and the fact that none of them are appropriate throws me. I can't want his mouth, body, warmth, skin. I can't be thinking sex. I can't even be thinking kissing.

And I can't indulge in a purely physical attraction.

Beyond the I'm-a-mom factor is the this-is-my-home factor and this-is-a-small-town factor, along with the everyone-here-gossips factor.

My libido has to settle down.

"Where's your girlfriend?" I ask, looking away and pretending to scan the crowd circling the field.

"I don't have a girlfriend," he answers, reaching across the table and into the open box to distribute cotton candy to the kids lining up behind him.

He's so tall, the children look like Lilliputians next to him. "What about the woman at P. F. Chang's?"

He looks at me from beneath dark lashes tipped with gold. "An ex-girlfriend."

"She didn't look like an ex."

"We're still friendly."

"Do you have lots of those?"

His jaw shifts, and his smile is slow and sexy. "Are you always this cagey?"

Heat surges through me, a heat that starts in my belly and makes me think very lusty thoughts. "Cagey?" I mock, grabbing handfuls of the cotton candy bags, which I pass out rapid-fire. "This is me being friendly."

His deep laugh rings out, and I look up at him, see again that hard contour of cheekbone and jaw, the slash of eyebrow about light blue eyes. I like his look. I really like his look, and I know we women aren't supposed to be visual creatures like men, but I feel like all eyes and desire right now.

"Do you give all men this much trouble?" he asks, arms folding across his immense chest.

Kathleen pushes another cardboard box toward me. "You mean, is that why I'm single?" I ask as I rip open the box.

"That's not what I'm asking at all."

"No?"

Kathleen's briskly stamping the lap cards while Luke and I pass out bags of cotton candy to the next rush of kids.

As the last little boy tears off, I step around the table to face Luke squarely. "What can I do for you?"

He stares down at me, his expression so intense that it's almost intimidating. "I'm asking you out."

"Out?"

"Dinner."

"Dinner?"

"I feel like I'm doing the Texas two-step right now," he answers.

I laugh. I can't help it. "I can't do dinner."

"Why not?"

"It's . . ." I look at him, make a face. "Too much like a date."

"It *is* a date."

"Exactly." I tuck long hair behind my ear, slide my hands into the back pockets of my jeans. "I can do coffee, though. Starbucks. Tully's. Jet City."

"You've only mentioned the chains."

"That's because they're the ones that come to me for business."

"So you are a hard woman."

"Fair but tough," I reply, suppressing a shiver as my gaze locks with his. There's something in his eyes, something strong—male and unnervingly primal—that makes my pulse race. "What's wrong with coffee? There are coffeehouses on every corner, and it's cheap. You could treat, and I wouldn't feel guilty."

A corner of his mouth curls. "And you'd feel guilty if I paid for your dinner?"

"Yes."

His gaze holds mine. "Chicken," he says softly, so softly that tiny shivers race up and down my back.

In a dim part of my brain, I think I've met my match. Someone who might just possibly know my game, and it's thrilling and yet also terrifying. I've gotten to where I am today—a single, successful thirty-six-year-old mother—by insisting I don't need anyone or anything when actually the opposite just might be true.

"Why are you so stubborn?" I ask uncomfortably.

"Because you're intriguing." He pauses. "And cagey as an alley cat."

"And that's flattering how? . . ."

His smile heats his eyes, all blue fire. "I think, Ms. Zinsser, you enjoy being challenged."

"You get all that from what?"

He just laughs quietly and shakes his head. "Dinner. Tomorrow. I'll pick you up at six-thirty."

My head's spinning. The guy is way too confident. "You're way too aggressive."

"Assertive, not aggressive, and I wouldn't have to be so assertive if you wouldn't be such a chicken."

My mouth nearly falls open. He's so not what I thought he was, so not what I imagined. "I don't think I like you."

Luke's expression says otherwise. "So six-thirty. And dress casual. Just in case we have to eat at Starbucks."

Now he is walking away, walking from the building's shadow and into the late autumn sunshine.

"Don't you need my address?" I call after him.

He stops, faces me. "No. I already know it."

"How?"

He's walking again, and looking back at me over his shoulder, he mouths, "The parent directory."

The parent directory?

I'd always wondered what that was for.

I make arrangements for Eva to stay at my parents' tomorrow night, as I'm not comfortable with her knowing I'm going out. She'd be fine with me having a date, though. In fact, she'd be thrilled.

I'm the one with the problem. I'm the one who swore off men. Not that that was the most rational decision.

The plan was for me to drop Eva at my parents' late in the afternoon, but I'd totally forgotten that the Huskies were playing at home, so traffic was nightmarish.

After taking an hour to travel five miles, I spend another half hour making small talk before Dad walks me to the door.

"Could you take your mom to the doctor for me on October sixteenth?" he asks as we stand on the front steps of the house. "I've got something I can't get out of and don't want to reschedule Mom's appointment."

I've never taken her to her doctor and am happy to help but also a bit wary. "Is there anything special I need to do?"

"I keep a notebook so I can keep track of symptoms, and I'll send that with you."

"Okay." I look at him a long moment. He seems unusually tense. But then he's been quite tense for the past month or so. "Dad, is everything all right?"

"Everything's fine," he answers briskly. "The appointment's at three. Don't be late."

He kisses me good-bye, and I'm back in my car. By the time I reach my house on Yarrow Point, I have only thirty minutes before Luke arrives, and I'm suddenly so nervous that I sit at the foot of my bed and take deep, calming breaths.

After a minute, I stand. I don't feel much calmer. If anything, I'm in even more of a panic.

I'd like to cancel the date. And I'd do it if I had his number, but I don't. He's just beautiful Luke with the big biceps, thick chest, tight butt, and long, muscular legs.

Since I can't cancel the date, I've got to at least get dressed.

The thing to do, I tell myself, is to just be myself, and that includes wearing what I like to wear. Wearing what makes me comfortable.

Jeans, combat boots, and a big billowy white shirt.

I look in the mirror and sigh. Eva would kill me if she thought I was going out with a man dressed like this. Eva would just about die.

She'd tell me I'm not Lara Croft from *Tomb Raider* and that only lesbians wear combat boots for evening wear. I look down at my boots. From this angle, they do look rather . . . butch. . . .

Oh, shit.

Impatiently, I plop back on the foot of my bed, unlace the boots, and trade them for my painterly clogs. Eva hates these, too, but I like them, and they don't scream different sexual orientation. They just scream . . . different.

For all of two seconds, I consider changing the entire outfit. But then what do I wear? Something clingy? Something silky? Something that shouts, *Hey, I have breasts and a vagina?*

No. That's just too pathetic.

But some jewelry would help, something funky like my carved pendant from New Zealand and the delicate bangles from India. I top my white shirt with a car-length red suede coat I picked up on a business trip to Milan a few years ago and comb my long hair smooth.

A little mascara and a cinnabar-hued lipstick topped with a golden lip gloss and I'm done. This is as girlie as I'm going to get. And you know, Lara Croft from *Tomb Raider* is kind of my style.

The doorbell rings.

I gulp air. Tough girl disappears with the realization that Luke's here.

"You look beautiful," he says as I open the door.

Luke must have called my stylist. He's dressed like me. Jeans, white shirt, no red suede coat, thank God, but he's got on heavy leather shoes, the kind that look as though they'd work beautifully on a hiking trail.

His hair is still damp and he's freshly shaven, and he smells unreal.

"Thanks," I answer, breathing in his scent, very shower clean with a hint of a subtle spicy cologne I don't know but like very much. "You look nice, too."

"*Nice?*"

"Beautiful?" I say, throwing his compliment back at him.

He has a quiet laugh, and the sound is a sexy deep rumble from inside his chest. He holds the door for me. "Do you have everything?"

"Yes."

His Land Rover is nearly as worn on the inside as it is on the outside, but otherwise it's spotless. The brown leather seats have a wonderful aged patina, the dash has been polished, and the floorboard's vacuumed clean.

"It's a great truck," I compliment as he holds the door open for me.

"I've had it forever."

"And before that it did safaris in Kenya?"

Sliding behind the wheel, he flashes me a curious look. "You have a problem with old?"

"Hardly. My car's a '57 Ford truck."

He looks at me even longer. "A gift?"

"A gift to myself. I bought it years ago, love it, couldn't imagine driving anything else."

His blue gaze drifts slowly across my face, studying, analyzing. "So you're not just easy on the eyes," he eventually drawls, starting the Land Rover. He backs out of the driveway and then turns onto the road.

Easy on the eyes. An interesting expression, I think, watching his broad, tanned hands as he expertly shifts gears that I know have to be a bit creaky; yet he knows his truck, loves his truck, and with each shift of his wrist I feel that hot, fizzy sensation in me grow.

I like him, and I don't even know how or why, but once he looked at me, I saw something in his eyes and I wanted that, too.

I saw a mind working. I saw a flicker of heat in a cool blue gaze. I saw curiosity and a desire to be intrigued, entertained. I liked that he made me feel like a sexy outlaw or chopper, something that one doesn't see all the time on the street.

Watching his hands, I think, I want those hands on me.

I want his mouth on mine.

I want his skin against my skin.

I want.

And like that, I'm dizzy and breathless, and the desire I feel is a very grown-up desire, one that doesn't need small talk or a timid, tentative touch. No, this desire says, *I'm all woman and I need a grown-up man.*

We head to Kirkland for dinner, but our reservation at 21 Central isn't until seven-thirty, which gives us time to wander through the downtown art galleries.

It's a perfect night for wandering around downtown Kirkland, a city that always reminds me of Laguna Beach dropped at Lake Tahoe. We stop in at all of the galleries but save my favorite, the Patricia Rovzar, for last because it's just across from the restaurant.

Nothing grabs my eye tonight, but the gallery owner greets me warmly and offers us a glass of wine. "It's a Willamette Valley red," she says, referring to the Oregon wine region south.

Luke and I pass on the wine. I haven't eaten anything since morning and don't want to drink on an empty stomach, and Luke says he prefers a good amber beer over wine.

We stand in front of a huge murky canvas that neither of us pays attention to.

"I know nothing about you, other than the obvious," I tell him, sliding one hand into my pocket.

His eyes have that flicker of heat again. "What's the obvious?"

"You're tall."

"Mmm-hmm," he answers, and when I say nothing more he adds, "That's *it*?"

I smile crookedly, face flushing. "You want more?"

His upper lip barely lifts. "Sure."

I stare at that upper lip that snakes ever so slightly. What a talented mouth to do things to me without even touching mine. I push my hand deeper into my pocket. "You're . . . attractive."

"Ah."

Heat surges through me. "You're confident."

"Think so?"

"Yeah." I grow hotter. "You said at Back-to-School Night

that you're not married, you have no kids, and you sponsor a Little Brother."

"You remembered."

"That wasn't very much to remember." I look at him sideways. "How old are you, if you don't mind my asking?"

"I don't mind, and I'm thirty-eight. I came close to marriage once, about four years ago, but in the end, it didn't work."

"Why?"

"She lived in Charleston, and I live here."

"You wouldn't move."

"My work wouldn't let me move."

"What do you do?" I ask.

"Management," he answers, "sales."

"And she wouldn't move here?" I ask, thinking of the huge move I made to Seattle to further my career.

He shrugs. "She grew up close to her family and didn't want to raise children so far from them."

I nod. It makes sense in a terribly realistic sort of way.

"And your husband?" Luke asks, neatly turning the focus on me, and his blue eyes hold mine. "Where is he?"

I steel myself inwardly. "There never was one."

"You two—"

"There was no two," I interrupt. "Eva's never known a father. I had her, made her, on my own. I used an anonymous sperm donor."

Luke's surprised. I can see it in his expression. But even I'm surprised that I was so blunt with him. Usually I dance around the subject, but for some reason I don't want to dance around it with him. I am who I am. I like who I am. I'm not going to apologize.

"That took guts," he says after a moment.

My shoulders lift and fall. "I wanted to be a mom. I knew I'd be a good mother."

"But you weren't interested in being a wife?"

"I'm not planning on getting married, no."

"Why not?"

"I just don't see it in the cards."

He looks increasingly perplexed. "You don't like men?"

I smile as heat surges to my cheeks, making my face too warm. He's so rugged and so beautiful. Even women who like women would like this man. "I'm straight, if that's what you're asking. It's more the whole marriage thing that I have a problem with."

"Why?" he demands bluntly.

Again I shrug. "I just don't think marriage works. Love doesn't last—"

"Yet you love your daughter."

"With all my heart."

"But you don't think you can love a man that way?"

My breath catches and my eyes sting, and I turn to face the huge dark murky canvas behind me. His question felt like a sucker punch. It caught me by surprise, and it hurt.

I don't quite know how to answer him, as it's not that I don't think I can love a man that way.

It's that I don't think a man can love a woman that way.

And I don't think a man can love me that way.

I believe women fall in love and begin relationships with great hope and expectations, but then we somehow go wrong. Women end up giving too much, yielding and bending and compromising until we're worn out, worn down. My mother spent much of her life trying to please my father. As a child and teenager, I did everything I could to get my father's approval. A decade ago, I wanted nothing more than to make Scott happy.

But for what purpose? And to what end?

Why did my father get to dictate the mood and tone of our home? Why was he the king? The ruler? The head of state?

Why was it so important to me to make sure Scott was always happy, and happy with me?

Truthfully, it was a relief when Scott went back to his wife and children. It freed me. It allowed me to bury my last lingering illusions of romantic love and move on to mature love. Maternal love.

"I think lots of people get married for the wrong reasons," I say at last. "They get married because they hear a biological clock ticking or they want someone's financial support or they need love, crave acceptance."

Luke gazes down at me, his lips curving faintly, mockingly. "And you don't?"

I think for a moment, then shake my head. "No."

He studies me now. I can feel his gaze search my face, lingering on my eyes and lips. "So you believe in living with a man, just not marrying him?"

"I'm not against marriage, and I'm not about to tell someone to live, or not live, with their partner. I'm just not planning on having a . . . partner." I stumble over the last few words even as an uncomfortable heat rushes through me. I can't believe we're even discussing this topic. I don't talk about this with anyone, much less sexy single men.

A small muscle pulls between Luke's brows. "And how do men you date handle this? They're okay with it?"

My mouth opens, shuts. I struggle to think of an appropriate answer, one that won't scare either of us. "I don't date."

"Don't as in . . .?"

"Ever." I shove my hands deeper into my jeans pockets, shoulders rising higher. "You're the first date in . . . um . . ." I swallow. "Since Eva was born."

He stares down at me, his expression part perplexed, part sardonic. "So why are you here with me tonight?"

I meet his gaze levelly, smile bravely back. "I honestly don't know." And dang it, it's the blasted truth.

Leaving the art gallery, we cross Central and get seated in the dim restaurant with the dark wood-paneled walls with the faux leopard fabric on the booths. We both order beers, appetizers, and entrées.

When the appetizers arrive, I eagerly sample one of the crab-and-lobster wontons. "I love food," I say half-apologetically when I realize Luke's watching me, suddenly feeling defensive.

"So do I," he counters.

"But you're a man, and big. You're expected to eat."

"That sounds rather sexist."

"I think men like women slim."

"Men do, or women say men do?"

The corners of my mouth twitch. He's smart, very smart, and he's not who I thought he was. He's more. "Where did you go to school?" I ask.

"Harvard."

Harvard. Right. "And what did you study?"

"My area was primarily business, government, and international economy."

I want to believe him, but it's almost too good to be true. He's built like a Turbo Power Ranger and has a Harvard brain?

He must be able to read my mind, because he lifts his beer in a mock salute. "Would you feel better if I told you that I earned a football and basketball scholarship and that's how I got in?" The soft light from our little shaded wall sconce reflects off Luke's beer and the hard glint in his eye.

"No. The first time I saw you, you were running and you looked like an athlete, and I liked that about you."

He doesn't say anything, he just sips his beer and looks at me.

I just look right back, too.

He's so different from what I expected, so much more interesting, so much more complex.

There's nothing wrong with the men in Bellevue, but after eighteen months here, so many seem the same. They drive pretty prestige cars and work out at fancy gyms and clubs and seem to like to let their possessions do the talking: *Look at my house. Check out my wheels. And oh yeah, what do you think of my wife?*

These guys ski, water-ski, drive boats, pilot their own planes. They're accomplished in every sense of the word, yet for some reason they've left me cold.

If I don't feel comfortable in the 7 for All Mankind jeans and can't shop during Nordstrom's semiannual sale because the crowds nauseate me, how the hell would I fit into one of these men's pampered and well-orchestrated lives?

"Football's a great sport," I say. I don't know if it's because my dad watched it while I was growing up or so many of my guy friends in high school played, but football's one of my favorite sports to watch, whether in person or on TV.

"Who's your favorite team?"

"The Bears, and they're having a great year. They did last year, too."

"Who's the coach?" he quizzes me.

"You don't think I know my Bears?"

"Da Bears," he corrects.

I roll my eyes. "The Bears, 2006's NFC division champion, is led by head coach Lovie Smith, who is now in his fourth season with them and is the Bears' thirteenth coach. An aggressive defense is Lovie's trademark. He came to the Bears in January 2004 from the Rams, where he was the defensive coach, and before that he was the linebacker coach in Tampa Bay." I stop, smile prettily. "Anything else you want to know?"

"Where'd Lovie go to school?"

"Tulsa."

"Is he married?"

"To MaryAnne, and they have three sons."

"Favorite charities?"

"The American Diabetes Association." I reach for my beer. "Anything else you're interested in, son?"

Luke just laughs, that deep rumble of sound that booms from his chest. "You're for real."

I nod and find myself hoping, wishing, that Luke is for real, too.

My first date in ten years is over, and I don't know if he'll ever call again.

And I want him to call, almost as much as I pray that he doesn't call.

I'm honestly that conflicted.

I'm not one of those people who know how to play the field, just dabble with dates and men. I have this horrifying habit of no, thank you; no, thank you; no, thank you—and then *wham!* I fall. Hard. Impossibly hard.

I haven't dated after Scott because I was too ashamed of what I felt, what I went through. I'm brave—nearly reckless—in every other area, but when it comes to my heart . . .

I shift restlessly on the couch and kick off one clog and then the other.

Luke was right at the walk-a-thon when he called me chicken. I am chicken, and what frightens me is me.

Chicken? Hell, yeah. You might as well call me a poultry farm.

But when I stop panicking and think of dinner, all I can see—think of—is Luke. His huge frame, his grace, his intelligence, his intensity.

And then there's that face.

Forgive me for being shallow, but he is really nice to look at, particularly across a dinner table.

Even better was when, during the meal, I stopped worrying so much, dropped my guard a little, and started having fun.

Luke knew how to have fun, and he made dinner fun by bantering with me, coming up with word games, brain games, things that seduced the mind and then the senses.

When he started talking about his family, his childhood on his farm in Iowa, it was all over for me. Despite the bike and tattoo, I have a huge soft spot for country music and life before everything became so harried.

As he talked about the fields of corn, I could hear the young stalks whistle in the wind. I could feel the heat of the sun and smell the rich, pungent soil.

I loved that he was raised on a farm, had learned to drive by driving tractors and then the farm trucks. I didn't want him to stop talking. I wanted to hear the stories, all of them, but he shared only a few.

His parents are still married after forty-seven years. He's never heard his dad say a harsh word to his mother. He believes marriage is forever, which is why this Mountain of a Man has decided he'd rather never marry than marry the wrong woman.

"You don't want kids?" I asked during coffee.

"Not if there's a risk their mom and dad will split and not raise them together."

"You don't think children can survive in single-parent families?"

"I want my kids with two parents. In the same house. With everyone treated equally—with respect. And love."

As I shift on the couch, it crosses my mind that I'd never make his short list. Woman lives with a man. Loses man. Gets inseminated with some stranger's swimmers.

Not that I want to be on his short list. Not that we'll ever go out again.

But as Luke talked, I found myself watching his eyes, his mouth, his hands, thinking, Yes, yes, yes.

I sat there amazed. Awed. Here was the whole package, the package I'd somehow begun to doubt really existed. Smart, strong, successful, sexy, and yet relaxed. Comfortable. *Normal.* If six feet seven and gladiatorlike strength is normal.

The date ended without a kiss. I didn't expect him to kiss me, not after everything I'd said, and he'd said, but that didn't diminish my attraction, any of that raw physical awareness that rippled through me in waves.

Seeing him again would be dangerous. But not seeing him again seems even worse.

Chapter Twelve

I don't sleep well that night, not with dreams of Luke, lust, and sex turning my internal thermostat up, up, up. The dreams felt way too real, too, as though Luke were actually in bed with me, heating me up.

Even after my dad and mom drop Eva off the next morning, I stumble through the day, grateful it's Sunday and not Monday, particularly when I snap at Eva over something that wouldn't normally get a rise out of me.

All day I feel out of step, though. Even when I'm at my desk for part of the afternoon to catch up on work, I can't focus. My thoughts are chaotic, disorganized, drifting again and again back to last night, and Luke. I feel slightly obsessive at the moment, and it annoys me.

Impulsively I pick up the phone, dial Tiana's number. I need to hear her voice, even if it's just her voice mail.

But I don't get Tiana's voice mail, she answers. "Marta," she says happily. "How are you, girl?"

"Crazy," I answer bluntly. "I think I'm losing my mind."

"Shey said you've been worried about Eva."

"But this isn't about Eva, it's about me. I'm . . . I've . . ." I search for the right words, seeing Luke and yet not knowing how to describe him. "I'm confused."

She laughs. "You, confused? Since when?"

"Ha, ha," I fake laugh back before getting serious. "Tiana, I think I'm going crazy. I'm thinking crazy thoughts, and they're not going away, they're just getting worse."

She stops laughing abruptly. "You're not thinking about suicide, are you?"

Her voice has dropped so low and sounds so concerned that I groan. "No. I'm not depressed. It's a man. I'm thinking about a man."

For a moment Tiana says nothing, and then she giggles. "Ta, that's normal. You're a woman."

"But I don't want to think about a man, and I don't want to be attracted to anyone, and I don't understand why I'm so damn attracted to this one." I take a small breath. "But I am. Distractingly so. And I want to stop it. *Now*."

"He's really got you hot and bothered, hasn't he?"

"Yes," I answer grumpily. "But why? Why him? And why now?"

"I think your mating impulse has taken over."

"*What?*"

Tiana laughs. "I just did a segment on a fascinating book called *The Female Brain*, and the author, Dr. Louann Brizendine, would say that your brain biology has been hardwired to recognize this guy as a suitable partner."

"A partner for what? The waltz? Bowling? Wine tasting?"

"How about reproduction?"

"I'm going to hang up on you."

"I'm not making this up, Marta. There is extensive

scientific evidence behind Dr. Brizendine's book, and she says that the intense attraction you're feeling—that sizzling chemistry—is literally chemicals flooding the brain. The euphoria and excitement can be traced to a rush of dopamine, and the dopamine is bolstered by a shot of testosterone, which heightens sexual desire."

I've heard enough about the chemistry of our brains to recognize some of what she's saying as true, but I'm not ready to give myself over to a dopamine, testosterone rush. "I don't want to be attracted to Luke, at least not this attracted. It was never my intention to fall for him, or anyone, not while Eva is still living at home."

"You might have consciously chosen to live the single life, but your unconscious mind recognizes a potential reproductive partner in this Luke and is doing everything it can to get you in bed with him."

"To reproduce."

"To reproduce," she echoes. "Dr. Brizendine would say it's because your brain sized up Luke as a potential partner, a healthy mate who could give you children—"

"I don't want more children."

"—and is now flooding you with cocktails of neurochemicals because he fits your ancestral wish list."

"Bullshit."

"It's in her book."

"I don't care."

"You're biology driven, Ta, whether or not you want to admit it."

"Good, because I won't admit it, and even if it were true, why now? In ten years I must have met someone that my brain would have recognized as a good reproductive partner. Why didn't I notice until now?"

"Because you've had a mommy brain."

"You're supposed to be helping, Tiana, not making things worse."

"You wanted answers. I'm giving you answers, and you'll get even more in chapter five of Dr. Brizendine's book. Motherhood changes a woman's brain. It's nature's way of ensuring the survival of young. First you're flooded with chemicals during pregnancy, and then after birth you're flooded with more dopamine and oxytocin to help bond with the baby. For years you were hopelessly in love with Eva—"

"I still am."

"Yes, but she's older now, nearly ten, and she's more independent"—she talks louder, overriding me when I try to interrupt—"and yes, you're still very attached to her, but you probably aren't producing quite as much oxytocin as you once were, leaving you more open for sexual attraction and reproduction."

I'm just about to protest that I'm not interested in having another baby, that the last thing I want or need is to add to my family, when another little voice inside me whispers, *Oh yeah?*

The *Oh yeah?* stops me. Cold.

"What was the name of that book again?" I ask her after a slight pause.

"*The Female Brain.*"

"So I'm not crazy."

Tiana starts laughing. "I never said that. But research is

showing that hormones shape us and influence us whether we like it or not, and it's been happening inside our brains from before we were born."

After hanging up, I click on to the Internet and look up the book. The cover photo is white and depicts a bundled ball of phone cord with a little phone jack plug at the end.

Hardwired to fall in love?

Hardwired to procreate?

Hardwired to need a man?

No freaking way.

Monday afternoon, Eva comes home with a packet of papers that includes a notice about the first field trip of the year, the fourth-grade class's November trip to the Pacific Science Center to see the new, highly touted anatomy exhibit and an invitation to a mothers-only event, a Creative Memories Night. I've heard of Creative Memories, because in New York I handled a very small ad design for a rival, Memory Delights, and I did tremendous market research before tackling the ad.

I hand the invitation back to Eva. "It's just a scrapbooking party," I say.

"Who is giving it?" she asks, peering at the invite and then exclaiming, "Oh! Diane Hale. Ben's mom."

"Do I know the Hales?"

"You should. Ben's only like the second most popular kid in fourth grade. Behind Jemma, of course. Which makes him the most popular boy, which means this is a really really cool thing."

"Eva, you fill my heart with absolute terror."

"Mom, this is *big*."

"It's a *scrapbooking* party." I make a cutting motion with my hand. "I've got to make things with construction paper."

"And you're so artistic."

"If you weren't my daughter, I wouldn't like you."

Eva just laughs and plops down on the couch with her binder and homework. "But you need me, Mom. You need someone to keep you grounded in reality."

I shoot her a look of disbelief. "You're representing reality?"

"Mom, I'm just trying to help you." She gives me a long-suffering look. "You do need help, you know."

Not this again. No more "make Mom over" plans. "Why? What's wrong with me?"

"Just forget it. You're getting upset," she answers, picking up her pencil.

"I'm not upset."

"Well, you will be. You always get upset when I tell you these things."

"What things?"

Eva sighs and touches the sharp pencil tip to the pad of her finger. "That it's not normal to be alone. That you need to get married, and I need a dad." Her shoulders lift and fall as she catches my expression. "See? Now you're mad."

Whose child is this? How can she be so blasted conservative? What 1950s happy homemaker drug was plopped into her baby food? "I'm not mad."

She rolls her eyes. "Yeah. Whatever."

"I'm not, and I'm trying very hard to be the mom you want me to be, but sometimes your expectations are a little unrealistic. Not every mom—not even the moms that stay home—makes Toll House cookies every afternoon. And not every mom—not even moms like Taylor Young—devote every moment to domestic activity."

Eva just hunches over her open notebook, working away. She doesn't even bother to look at me.

"Eva, I'm more normal than you think."

"Mmm-hmm."

"Cutting my hair and marrying me off wouldn't change who I am, nor will it turn me into a committee-loving parent-meeting-attending mom. It's just not my thing."

She finally looks up. "So you're not going to go?"

"To the scrapbooking party?" My brow creases. "No."

"And the field trip?"

I look at her pinched expression for a long moment. She's the most exhausting child I've ever met. "Yes," I say, sighing. "Yes, I'll sign up to go. I'd love to go."

Her gaze meets mine and holds.

"I can't wait to go," I add. "It's going to be fun."

"Okay, Mom. That's enough."

Checking my smile, I head to the studio to get back to work.

The next day, I send in the parent sign-up form for the field trip and forget about it, which isn't difficult with my long, demanding workdays and Eva's unusual behavior.

Eva's always been a big reader, and I'm used to seeing her curled up with a book, used to her taking notes. But this week, she's practically locked herself in her room, and whenever I catch her unawares, she's reading and note taking and using a highlighter.

At first I thought it was a paper she was writing for class, but when I ask her Friday morning about what she was reading, she answers with a vague, "It's just something I'm interested in."

I finish her lunch, close the paper lunch bag by folding the top over. "It's not a book report?"

She looks up at me and smiles. "No."

I put her sack lunch by her backpack. "So what is it for?"

"To help me learn."

"Learn what?"

Eva shrugs, closes the book, and slides the notebook on top, concealing the cover. "How to do things better," she answers even as the phone rings.

I want to continue the conversation, but Eva's heading to her room as I pick up the phone. It's Taylor Young. She's calling to see if I could cover for another mom who was to work in the class today but now has a conflict.

"I'm sorry, Taylor, but I can't," I answer, glancing at my watch, thinking I've got to get Eva out the door before she misses her bus. "Fridays are really difficult, and today I've got client meetings—"

"It'd only be for an hour and a half."

"I'm sorry, I just can't."

There's a moment of silence, and then Taylor says very flatly, "I've already called everyone else. You were my last resort. But fine. I'll do it. I always end up doing it anyway."

She hangs up, a loud, decisive click in my ear, and although I feel bad, I don't feel bad enough to change my plans. I've a job. It's not a choice. This is how I pay my bills and keep a roof over our heads.

*   *   *

My first client meeting that morning runs late and threatens to slide into the lunch hour that I've reserved for my second client meeting, which can't happen, as this lunch is a "kiss the customer's butt" meeting, one of those I've got to do every now and then when we've either screwed up or the client just feels sensitive and needy.

In this case, the client's very sensitive and needy, and it doesn't help that she—the director of sales for a local four-star boutique hotel—is six and a half months pregnant.

But I get through both meetings, survive the emotionally charged lunch, promise my hotel client the sun and the stars and the moon, and rush back to the studio to update my team—who are putting in a full day of work today despite it being Friday—so they know what we've got to do and when.

We're still in a meeting in the studio when Eva returns home from school. She sticks her head around the door, waves hello to everyone, and tells me she's got to talk to me ASAP.

"Go ahead," Robert says, gesturing me away. "It could be an emergency, one of those 'I'm becoming a woman' things."

Chris makes a disgusted sound. "*Please*. She's a child."

"A nine-year-old going on nineteen," Robert flashes.

He's got a point, I think, heading for the house.

I find Eva sitting cross-legged in one of the chairs at the dining room table. "I don't have any homework," she says, munching on string cheese and a fistful of Goldfish crackers. "It's Friday."

"So what are you doing?"

"Planning my sleepover party." She looks at me hope-fully and smiles very big. "I really want to have a party."

With her long dark hair and big smiley eyes, I think, I'd like her to have a sleepover, too, but a sleepover *party*?

"And I want everyone to come," she adds. "Jemma, Paige, Devanne, Lacey, Brooke, everyone." She's peeling the string cheese, tearing off long, skinny strands so that the cheese hangs pale and forlorn. "Maybe if people came here, saw our house, saw how fun we are—" She looks up at me, her nose scrunching. "We are fun, aren't we?"

I nod my head. "The coolest."

She gives me a reproving look. "I'm serious."

"So am I." I reach for the box of Goldfish crackers and shake some into my hand. But a party, here, to prove it? Sounds dubious at best.

First of all, coolness—like beauty—is in the eye of the beholder, and second, I don't particularly want Jemma and gang running around the house turning up their noses at everything.

"You can help me do this," Eva adds earnestly. "We could send out invitations—you could design some-thing—and it'd be really fun. We'd do things no one else does—"

"Like what?" I interrupt mildly, intrigued by this pas-sionate daughter of mine who doesn't know the word *quit*.

"I don't know. Maybe make it like a spa party. We could do manicures and pedicures. And rent a bunch of good movies and decorate. Like Hollywood. Or Arabian Nights. Something no one else does."

She makes it sound so easy. I know parties aren't so

easy. And it's not even all the work. It's the fact that you need people to come.

I try to imagine the parents looking at the invitation and getting one another on the phone.

Who is Marta Zinsser? What is this slumber party for, and who else is going?

Is your daughter going?

No. Is yours?

No.

"Come on, Mom," Eva pleads. "You're good at stuff like this. You can make it happen."

I've got stacks and stacks of work on my desk and more headaches, but Eva's excited and I love it when she's excited. Her enthusiasm always touches me. "Okay. I'll help you plan it, but limit the list, Eva. No more than ten girls."

"Okay."

"And when are you thinking? It's almost October, Halloween will be here before you know it."

"What about the weekend after Halloween? That gives us lots of time to plan. What do you say?"

"I'll look at the calendar, but I don't see why not."

"Really?"

"Really."

Eva jumps from her chair, throws her arms around me, and hugs me tight. "It's going to be a great party. It's going to be the best."

During the weekend while Eva plans her slumber party, I put in some late nights in the studio to make up for my shorter workdays. Almost every night after Eva goes to bed, I head to my desk in the studio and get to work.

Saturday night I get a lot done; however tonight, Sunday night, I'm so tired that I can hardly focus.

Luke never called again. I told myself I didn't expect him to, but the fact that he didn't call stings. I liked him. A lot. Too much.

It's ridiculous to get so interested in a man, especially as I keep telling myself I don't believe in love and romance. If Tiana is right, that the brain is wired to lust to enable us to reproduce, then it's great that I haven't heard from Luke. It's better not to have contact. It's better to go through my withdrawals and just get this whole fascination/infatuation over with.

Now.

And speaking of now, I've been staring at my blank computer screen for nearly an hour, and I'm not getting anything done. I want to chuck the towel in and go to bed, but I can't do that. Frank said we'd have a chance to present our proposal to the Freedom Bike Group sometime in the next couple of weeks, and so far, I don't have a clear vision for an ad campaign.

Why? Because I'm thinking about Eva and Mom and Dad and Luke and Taylor and everyone and everything but work.

This bike thing's a big deal, too. I can make it work. I know I can. I've just got to start somewhere, take some of my vague, disjointed ideas and find a theme to pull off.

Yawning, I rub my eyes and then the top of my head.

Can't go to bed, can't go to bed, must get work done.

Standing, I open the windows and door to bring in the cooler night air. The cool air helps.

Caffeine would help, too, so I search out the coffeepot in the studio's miniature kitchen, pour the dregs from this afternoon's pot into my mug, and zap the stale coffee in the microwave.

When the microwave dings, I take the hot mug back to my desk and turn on brighter lights before taking my first swig.

God. The coffee is nasty, so damn bitter that at first I don't think I can possibly drink it. But I gag it down.

I take another sip and gag again, but as I swallow, I kind of smile. The coffee's terrible. It's the worst coffee I've had in years.

In the morning I like my coffee smooth, laced with milk and sugar. But there's something evocative about this cup of really awful coffee. The dark, burnt bitterness reminds me of a badness I used to have, the badness I aspired to, denim and old leather and hard-core boots. Tough as in tattoos and long hair and a swagger.

I think of my old bike in the garage, a bike I haven't ridden in months since there isn't time and this doesn't seem to be the place.

But thinking of my bike in the garage reminds me why I bought it, why I needed it.

The motorcycle was an escape. The motorcycle helped me relax, forget, dream, breathe.

My motorcycle wasn't ever for trips around town. It wasn't a form of transportation for two. It was just my way to get out, to find some quiet, to get some peace of mind.

The pleasure of the open road. The freedom of riding my own chopper. The freedom of telling people and society to f___ off, to do what you want. With my feet up on the desk, the nasty coffee curling my tongue, I get an idea.

Leaning forward, I search the music folder on my computer and find what I'm looking for, the 1971 album released by Starbucks last year and on it the song by the Kinks, "20th Century Man."

I click on the song, crank the volume. The guitar strums. Foot-tapping twang. I crank it loud. Louder.

I stop the song, play it again, smiling faintly even as the idea grows, a minimovie playing in my head, a funky film short.

Dennis Hopper. *Easy Rider.* Big sideburns, real choppers, an upper lip in a curl. Shaggy hair. A handlebar mustache. Sunlight. Laid-back. And the open road.

Freedom Bikes. Taking the road back.

Making life yours.

I grab a charcoal pencil and begin to sketch on a huge notepad. I see it. I can do this.

And *Easy Rider* is just the first inspiration.

I'm picturing a whole series of ads based on the 1970s classics, classics popular when Freedom Bikes ruled the road.

But not just white guys like Dennis Hopper. Think the color spectrum from *Hair.* Blacks, whites, Latinos, Asians, men, women. Everyone groovy. Feeling good. None of the Harley-Davidson biker gang associations. No gangs or groups at all. Freedom Bikes isn't about fitting in or belonging.

Freedom Bikes are about being yourself. Doing your own thing. Making your own way. And loving it.

Loving rebelling.

Loving flaunting societal mores.

Loving being outside the pack. Alone. Unfettered.

Aretha Franklin, "Rock Steady." African American woman, big Afro, tan leather knee-high boots, and leather vest over an orange-and-brown-and-white-striped turtleneck.

T. Rex, "Planet Queen." Biker at dawn, riding Highway 66, desert landscape and the sun rising, appearing over the rugged rocks of Arizona.

Nick Drake, "One of These Things First." Rider on Golden Gate Bridge, heading up the coast. Vineyards. Napa. More sun. Sun everywhere, glazing, glossy, blinding. Sun being warm, sun being easy, sun being freedom. Life.

The 1970s color, the 1970s mood, the desire for self-determination, the rebellion against the big corporate giants.

And isn't that what people still need? Isn't that what they crave? Time for themselves? Time to relax, breathe, think?

Living in Microsoft land, I've seen firsthand the price one pays for giving so much of yourself to the company. The burnout's huge, the stress on families immeasurable.

What America needs is Freedom.

A return to Freedom.

And I've forgotten just what started all this until I reach for my coffee and take another sip of really bad java.

I splutter down the bitterness before pushing away

the cup and drawing the halogen lamp lower, bringing it down toward my work desk.

I'm excited. But it's going to be a long night. Especially as I keep thinking about Luke and wishing he had at least called. Just once. Just so I could have told him no, I'm sorry, I'm afraid this can't work. We can't go out again.

Chapter Thirteen

The staff and I meet early Monday morning, and I share my ideas with the rest of the team.

While I can draw, Allie and Robert are the real graphic artists, able to create a visual for virtually anything imaginable.

Chris is the word guy. He's the one who can do anything with copy. Witty as hell, he can take any concept and vision and make it punchy, poignant, clever.

All of us worked together at the Keller & Klein Seattle office, while two of us—Chris and I—moved from the New York office to open the Seattle branch.

We were all shell-shocked when the corporate office decided to close the Seattle office less than a year after opening it. Chris was angry. He'd sold his apartment, ended a relationship, purchased a car. He'd made huge life changes to head to Seattle, and he wasn't ready to chuck it all after nine months. I knew I couldn't go back to New York, either, not after moving Eva here, not after realizing just how quickly my mother was deteriorating.

Robert, another Seattleite, was the one who came to me

with the suggestion that I start my own advertising agency. "You've got the experience," he said, "and the reputation. The rest of us have talent, but you have the ability to woo and sign huge accounts."

In hindsight, I was probably a little too flattered by his praise. As a single mom, I probably should have been more logical and taken a job working for another Seattle firm. Instead I rolled up my proverbial shirtsleeves and got to work.

"Robert," I say, turning to him now, "can you put together a small-budget commercial we can show Freedom Bikes by October ninth?"

"You really want to do that?" Chris interjects. "Even a small budget's going to be serious money. We've got to hire talent, find a film crew, secure wardrobe, makeup, never mind the production services—"

"Yes, I do want to do it," I interrupt. "Because even with facts and figures, storyboards aren't going to be enough to win the Freedom Bike Group. Freedom's been gone for thirty-plus years. No one remembers Freedom. I don't think Freedom even remembers Freedom. So what we need to do is show customers what they're missing, show them what they crave, need, long for. Freedom. Space. Peace. Good times."

"Groovy," Robert mutters.

I ignore him. "The seventies are enjoying a renaissance. We've been dealing with it for the past couple of years in fashion, interiors, cars, entertainment. The seventies represent a larger-than-life attitude, an openness and expansiveness we didn't have in the eighties or nineties. The sixties were exploring change and protest and innocence. The seventies were riding it."

"On Freedom bikes," Chris intones.

But Allie's listening intently. "You mentioned the Kinks' '20th Century Man.'" She turns to look at the others. "Think about the song. The Kinks hated the modern world. They were so antitechnology."

"But not just technology. Bureaucracy, too," I add. "The feeling was that society was strangling the individual, stripping man of his freedom."

"Freedom Bikes," Chris repeats.

I know Chris is hammering me here, but I'm okay with it. This is how we create. It's how we've always worked together. We lock ourselves in a room and brainstorm, bounce ideas off one another, analyze, criticize, and somehow through our differences we find common ground and end up producing amazing things together.

My favorite part of advertising is this collaborative spirit, of working with talented people who are as passionate about being creative as I am.

"We're shooting a commercial, then," Robert sums up, tapping his pen on the table. "And we need it when?"

They're going to love this. "Seven days."

I ignore the collective gasp and smile my "don't f____ with me" smile. "Or would you prefer three?"

Robert sighs. "Seven's great. Thank you."

The next morning, Eva's just left for school and I'm doing a quick dash about the house to tidy things up before I head into the studio.

The Freedom Bikes proposal is heavy on my mind, but it's almost too heavy. It's got my insides tied up in knots. I can't put this much pressure on us about a deal, either. It's not fair to the team, and it's not fair to me.

In just seven days we do our thing. The meeting's been scheduled, and Robert's under the gun to get film made. Allie and Chris worked late last night putting together gorgeous mock-ups that look more like posters for an art gallery than just sample ideas.

Bending down, I grab one of Eva's stray gray socks from under the coffee table, push the magazine basket back under a side table, and adjust the couch cushions, shoving the big ones against the frame and plumping the top ones. It's while adjusting and plumping that I find a book squished between the couch cushions.

I study the paperback with the glossy cover: *How to Be the Most Popular Girl in Your School,* screams the title.

I read the title again, needing time to absorb the full implications. This book has got to be a joke.

I flip the book to the back, read the back cover blurb.

Ever wonder what it would be like to be your school's It Girl? The girl everyone wants to know? The girl who gets invited to all the parties? *How to Be the Most Popular Girl in Your School* will tell you the secrets known by only a select few . . . teenage models, actresses, pop stars . . . and now you! Follow the simple steps in this book, and before you know it, you'll be the Popular Girl everyone wants to know!

I nearly throw up. This is so bad, it's funny. It can't be serious. It's got to be a spoof. No one would really write something like this.

No one would buy something like this.

Yet there's enough doubt that I stop reading the back cover to flip through the chapter titles.

Be Cute If You Want to Be Popular
Keep Up with the Latest Trends
Make the Internet Yours
Don't Stay Home on Weekends!
Become Super Cool

Wow. I've no other words but . . . Wow.

On the back cover, I look for info on the authors, but all it says is, "Written by two Hotties who know what they're talking about."

Oh God. What if this isn't a joke?

What if people are really writing and publishing this crap, targeting insecure girls? I know I've struggled with Eva finding herself, but this . . . this . . . this is a whole new level of scariness.

This must be the book she bought at Barnes & Noble last month. No wonder she didn't want me to see it. She knew I wouldn't approve.

Horrified, I take the book with me to the studio and slide it across the conference table. "Look what Eva's reading now."

Everyone stands to get a look at it. Chris smiles, Robert howls, and Allie says absolutely nothing.

I shake my head, dumbfounded. "Can you believe Eva's reading garbage like this now?"

"That girl needs help," Robert says, tapping the desk with the tip of his pen.

"Not this kind of help."

Allie clears her throat. "You should be pleased she's taking positive steps in the right direction."

"Positive?" I throw myself in my chair, lean back, and shake my head. I can't get the offensive words out of my head. Be the most fashionable, glamorous girl in your school. Wear mostly brand names. Get a boyfriend, pronto. Have rules that make everyone want to be in your group. "A book that tells girls to spend money on clothes, accessories, and to host the party of the year? *That* is positive?"

"The book also encourages girls to be themselves, teaches hygiene, and gives pointers on how to start a conversation."

I get a little twitchy feeling above my left eyebrow. "Eva showed you the book."

The studio is suddenly deadly quiet, and it might have been my tone of voice or the fact that Allie has been privy to something I haven't.

Allie crosses one leg over the other. "I bought her the book."

"*What?*" My voice must have just gone up three octaves. Chris immediately gets busy with paperwork on his desk, and Robert picks up his iMac sketchpad.

"You bought that for Eva?" I repeat, dropping my voice, but not much. I was upset by the book, but that was nothing compared with what I feel now. I'm offended, deeply offended, that someone who works for me would buy crap like this for my daughter.

"This book," I say, jumping up to grab the book in

question, "is about selling out. It's about buying into all the bullshit society shoves down our throats."

"What bullshit?" Allie asks quietly.

"How about the chapter on how owning the right handbag will make a difference."

"It doesn't say that."

"No? Then let me find it for you," I say, flipping open the book to search through the table of contents. "Here it is: 'Get a nice bag to carry all your essentials, your cell phone, physics book, and makeup.'"

Allie gives me a long-suffering look. "It also tells girls to be friendly and nice to everyone."

"Oh, does it? How about this, then? 'Try making conversation with a few girls in your class, the popular ones, but never those who are not as popular. It is nice to meet a lot of people without compromising your image.'" I hold up the book. "Did it not just tell girls not to talk to girls who aren't as popular because it will compromise their image?"

Allie shakes her head. "I was just trying to encourage her, let her know that lots of girls want to be more popular and that there are things she can do to help feel better about herself."

I close the book, look at the cover of two blondes, their heads nearly touching, laughing at some private, secret joke, and I just have to leave.

Outside the studio, I walk around my garden and then through the side gate into the front yard with the lacy Japanese maples and copper-leafed dogwoods. I wander around the lawn, looking at the fall-blooming azaleas and evergreen rhodies that riot in yellow and orange color through the fall.

I know Allie didn't do this to hurt me, but it does hurt; it hurts because this isn't what I want Eva to believe. Yet people believe the media. They buy into anything they see in print.

The printed word has so much power.

One image in a magazine is incredibly influential. Imagine the impact of thousands of words and thousands of images? Photo after photo of half-starved girls and women, words repeating thin, slender, fit, sexy. Words about sex, boyfriend, pleasure, pleasing him, happy. Words about cars, freedom, opportunity, satisfaction.

I know how we link one idea to another. I know how we deal with one insecurity by creating a dozen new insecurities.

We're a consumer society, and we're taught to consume.

We're perfectionists, and we're taught to strive for perfection.

We're relentless in our pursuit of happiness, yet no one's happy.

We have children but work so many hours that we never see them.

Shit. I know how it goes. I know because I work in an industry that sells, sells, sells. It's my job to find the hook, too—locate the consumer's tender spot (the jugular, anyone?) and dig in. Hold on.

I can do what I do because I know the rules and ignore the rules, but children don't understand the big game and what it means and what it does.

But I do.

And Allie should.

"Marta." Allie's followed me to the front yard, where I

stand facing a small tree of no visible importance. "Marta, I'm sorry. I really am—"

"It's okay," I interrupt, unable to bear much more of her apology. Allie is a throwback to Doris Day. She's looking for her Rock Hudson (the nongay Rock), and she, like my mom, is a great believer in social standing.

"I wasn't trying to show you disrespect," Allie fumbles on. "I was trying to do something good, something that would make Eva feel better about herself."

I hear Allie, but I can also hear the "party tip" in the book: Host the party of the year, it's all or nothing, and absolutely don't invite the freaks of your school.

My jaw tightens.

"I love her," Allie says simply. "I just want her to fit in, feel like she matters. You know?"

I do know. And I want the same thing, but I want it on her terms, not on someone else's.

"I understand." I look at Allie and see she's been crying. I take a deep breath, exhale. "But you do realize the book wasn't really intended for kids Eva's age, don't you? It's a book with the teen market in mind."

She nods. "I know, but I wish I'd known some of this stuff before I went to high school, wish I'd had a chance to be popular, too."

Monday, a week later, I come in from the studio, where I've just gone to fax a statement to a client who claimed they never received the September bill, and discover Eva scribbling furiously in a pretty, jewel-toned notebook with a matching jeweled pen.

I've got my laptop, as I'm planning on sitting on the

couch with Eva and doing some work while she reads, but the moment she sees me, she snaps her book shut and shoves the notebook, book, and pen beneath a cushion.

I pretend I don't notice that she's shoved the book and notebook under the pillow and sit next to her. Although I want to talk to her about the book, want very much to discuss the concept of popularity, I don't want to create tension right now. There's so much for me to do, so many accounts and proposals and big meetings in the next month, that I don't need friction, not tonight, and frankly, neither does Eva.

But after she goes to bed, I pull out the book and notebook from their hiding spot. Cautiously I open the notebook, feeling vaguely disloyal, like a Peeping Tom, but I'm curious about what she's been writing, curious what she's been recording so diligently.

She's created a title page, and the heading says, "Project Me."

I half smile and turn the page and read the notes she's making.

1. Always Be Neat and Clean
   - Practice proper hygiene.
   - Feel good about your body.
   - Get in shape.
2. Dress Well
   - Wear cute clothes that fit your body.
   - Keep up with the latest trends.
   - If you can afford it, buy designer clothes, with names that people will recognize (i.e., Juicy, Prada, Gucci, etc.).

- Wear black clothing. It makes you feel slimmer.
- No dress-down days allowed. No sweats or hoodies.
- Accessories are a must.
- Makeup is a must. But go light, be natural.

3. Get a Nice Big Bag to Carry Your Essentials
   - Be prepared to spend some money.
   - A nice bag makes a statement.
   - Always carry your MP3 player or iPod. Have great music available. Be knowledgeable about music and trends.

4. Make Conversation with the Popular Girls
   - Get involved. Popular girls are well-rounded.
   - Give everyone a chance to talk. Don't just talk about yourself.
   - Ask about other people's day.

5. Host Big Parties or Sleepovers
   - Host the party of the year. It's got to be a blowout. All or nothing. Obviously, don't invite the unpopular kids at your school.

I stop reading. I have to stop reading.

So that's where she got the idea for big parties. And that's why she's wearing more and more black. And this is the reason she wanted one of my Coach purses.

I feel my heart sink. It's all part of her popularity plan, along with getting a nice purse, a cell phone, an iPod, and cool clothes.

Shaken, I flip the notebook closed. I have to talk to Eva, and soon, but tomorrow's the big day, the day we make our presentation to the Freedom Bike Group, and until that's over, I can't take on one more thing.

*   *   *

The next day, Chris and I are in downtown Seattle, meeting the Freedom Bike Group in a hotel conference room. We're halfway through our presentation, having spent the last hour going over the proposal, including the budget and numbers. Now we're getting to the fun stuff, the part where we show that we're not only affordable, but brilliant.

Chris has just finished setting up the screen and DVD player and I'm just about to introduce Robert's commercial when my phone vibrates inside my briefcase. It's soft enough that I can hear it, but hopefully no one else has.

As the lights darken, my phone begins vibrating again. I reach into my briefcase and attempt to shut it off but can't quite find the right button. Then I glance at the screen. It's the school calling. It's their third call. I must have missed the earlier ones.

I slide the phone into my pocket and stand against the wall to allow the Freedom executives better viewing. I love this short. It's not as polished as a real commercial would be, but the rawness adds to the 1970s retro feel.

The spot comes to an end. Chris raises the lights. I go to my computer screen, touch a button, and start the PowerPoint presentation of the concept. There will be a total of five or six television ads, advertisements we could also get uploaded onto various Internet sites. And while each ad will feature different genders and ethnicities, it's actually about being inclusive. Much like the Gap ads that featured diversity, our ads recognize the commonalities. We're all people, we're part of this thing called life. And we all have certain needs—truth, opportunity, hope, freedom.

Clicking on some recent marketing graphs, I demon-strate the changing market. "We in manufacturing and retailing know that in category after category, premium entries are growing, low-priced goods are stealing shares, and the middle is shrinking. Today's consumers want pre-mium products that offer tangible and emotional value, which is why each of our ads focuses on the tangible—owning a classic, luxury motorcycle—and the intangible emotional rewards from riding—peace, pleasure, comfort, satisfaction."

As I talk, I glance around the conference table, assess-ing the response to the presentation. There's definitely interest, and more than one man is nodding or leaning forward—in terms of body language, a very good sign.

Frank's expression is probably the most open. He's got a half smile, and his eyes crinkle at the corners. He's impressed and proud.

My confidence soars, and I continue to describe how the TV spots will translate into print ads as well as the vir-tual realm.

Chris explains that more companies are using the vir-tual realm to reach out to potential customers, including appealing to a younger generation, a generation we at Z Design feel is a perfect consumer fit for Freedom Bikes.

As Chris describes in greater detail some of the approaches we'd use—video game advertising, a develop-ment of a virtual world, a free Internet-based game that would allow users to design and build a bike—I slip out the conference room door and check my voice mail.

It's the school nurse. Eva has the stomach flu, has a fever of 103, and is throwing up.

With a glance at my watch—it's one-fifteen, the school day won't end for another hour and a half—I call the school and speak to the nurse. The nurse has Eva lying on the cot, but I hear Eva crying in the background.

"I feel so sorry for her," the nurse tells me. "She's thrown up three times in the last hour, and I wish I could give her something for her fever and pain, but we're not allowed to."

"I'm in downtown Seattle," I tell the nurse, "in the middle of a meeting, but I've got another half hour here, at least, and that's not including the drive. I've no idea if there will be bridge traffic, either."

"Oh dear. Who else can we call? Who is on your emergency contact list?"

My emergency contact list has my dad on it, but I can't have him get Eva and risk exposing my mom to something so virulent.

"Is there no way you can come now?" the nurse presses. "She's just miserable."

Glancing at the boardroom, I can see the flickering colors of the PowerPoint presentation through the frosted glass of the conference room window. Chris's presentation should be nearly over. And then it'll be back to me again.

I'm to bring the meeting to a close with my concluding speech, which again touches on the necessity for brands to engage their audiences emotionally and how we must introduce and rebuild the Freedom brand with edge and relevancy.

I haven't written down the whole spiel since I know it so well, but Chris has seen my notes and is familiar with how I wrap my conclusion into an open Q&A period with the executive members.

My talk will last only fifteen minutes or so, but the Q&A could go an hour or more. It just depends on management interest.

I hear the toilet flushing in the nurse's office, and the nurse is running water, giving Eva a wet towel to wash off her face.

"I'm coming now," I say to the nurse, steeling myself not to think about the presentation. It's nearly over. Chris can handle this. He's smart, talented, together. He can easily wrap up and handle the questions. "Tell Eva to hang tight, someone will be there very soon."

Hanging up I try the office but my call goes straight to voice mail. Next I try Allie—same thing. Robert is my next call, and he picks up but he's in the middle of a meeting.

Back in the conference room, I listen as Chris wraps up his talk. I wait until he's done, and then I thank Chris and ask everyone if we can take a brief recess.

The Freedom management seems happy to have a few minutes to stand and stretch their legs. I use the break to corral Chris and let him know Eva's sick, everyone at the office is busy, and I must go.

Chris just shakes his head. "Don't go now."

"She's really ill."

"She can make it another half hour, can't she?"

She could. She's got the flu, not consumption. But I know she's miserable, and I know she could use a bath and some Children's Tylenol and comfort from me. "Chris, you've got my notes. You can do the wrap-up and handle the Q and A."

"Marta, this is your dream. This is the account of your career."

He's right again. It is. But he doesn't know what it's like, needing to be in two places at once, torn between responsibilities, needing and wanting to let neither side down. "If we weren't at the end of the presentation, I wouldn't do it—"

"Then don't do it now." He drops his voice, looks over his shoulder. "Marta, they like us. They like what we're doing here today. They love Robert's film. But it's not a done deal. You're our closer. You're the one that gets the ink on the deals. You're our big gun."

And I'm also Eva's mother, the only family Eva has. She doesn't have a dad. She doesn't have brothers or sisters. It's just me. And if I don't come for her, no one will. "Chris, I don't have a choice."

He glares down at me. He doesn't approve, not at all, but he's not married, he doesn't have a kid, and he doesn't understand how I can be more afraid of failing Eva than of failing professionally.

"Come on, let's just get this moving," I say, making eye contact with one of the executives and then nodding at Frank, who has taken a seat again at the table. "I'll start us again, let them know I've got to leave due to a family emergency and that you'll be wrapping up."

Chris is stony-faced, but he can't make me stay. Yes, he's smart, successful, and the second in command at Z Design, but boss trumps, and I'm the boss.

Fifteen minutes later, as I take the elevator down to the parking garage, I'm hit by the strongest wave of regret. What I've done by walking out on the meeting isn't acceptable, not in the business world. Successful executives have families, but of course those families don't intrude, and in the workplace, family issues are carefully concealed.

But leaving isn't easy for me. It tears me up. I've worked hard preparing for today, looked forward to it. After starting my truck, I back up and then brake, tempted to park again and run back up. I can nail this account. I can get this.

But what about Eva? What do I do with her? Leave her in the school office until I've answered a dozen questions that Chris is just as capable of answering?

If I were the one who was sick, and if I had been throwing up and running a fever, what would I want?

I'd want my mom to come and get me.

I'd want my mom to take me home and hold me and let me know that I'm not alone.

Fortunately, traffic on 5 North is light, and the 520 bridge heading east isn't too slow. I'm able to reach the 84th Street exit in less than fifteen minutes and have Eva home in another ten after that.

Eva's sick the moment we walk through the door, and after she rinses her mouth and washes her face, she collapses on the carpet in the hall, just so she "can be near the toilet." I get her pillow and a blanket and cover her and then track down Tylenol for her fever.

She throws the sticky pink syrup right back up and then lies down again, wan and exhausted, on the floor.

Once she dozes off, I head to my room, strip off my clothes, and shower, then change into a T-shirt and sweats. Being a single mom is never easy, but when kids are sick, it sometimes feels impossible. Nights like these, I think I'd do just anything, give anything, to have another adult here, helping out, running errands, giving me a smile.

In short, reminding me that this, whatever the difficulty is, won't last forever.

Chapter Fourteen

Nine o'clock comes, and I finally, thankfully, have Eva in her own bed sleeping soundly. I'm just about to call it a night, too, when the phone rings.

The house phone never rings this late, and instinctively I wonder if there's been an accident or if Mom has taken a turn for the worse. But it's not an emergency or Dad calling, it's Taylor Young phoning to discuss the field trip I've signed up for. I think she's double-checking the number of kids I can accommodate in my car, but it's not that at all.

She's calling to lobby on behalf of a friend. Her friend really wants to go on this field trip, especially since all her friends are chaperones, and Taylor is asking me to skip this field trip and wait for another one so Andrea Carter can participate.

For a moment I'm speechless, amazed—even impressed—by Taylor's audacity, but as soon as my shock wears off, resentment sets in. It's been a long day, and I'm not in the mood for this. I'm exhausted, Eva's ill, and it's Taylor's daughter making Eva's life at school a living hell.

It's Taylor's control freak nature that's making this school year more miserable than usual.

Taylor doesn't own the school.

Taylor doesn't get to decide who's in, who's out.

Taylor's not in charge.

"I'm looking forward to chaperoning the field trip on November third," I say in my nicest voice possible, considering I'm so tired that I could fall asleep standing up. "Eva's so excited, too. It's the first time I've chaperoned a field trip since we moved here."

"Would you be willing to chaperone a field trip later in the year instead?"

Maybe Taylor didn't hear me. Eva's excited about my chaperoning the field trip to the Pacific Science Center. She wants me to chaperone the field trip. I'm not going to cancel out on her. "Eva's looking forward to my going."

"Yes, I understand, but we're in a bit of a bind, and I was hoping you could help us out. Andrea really wanted to chaperone this trip, and she'd thought she'd sent her form in early enough to be one of the moms picked."

I'm not sure I see the bind. Andrea didn't get her form in in time. "Hopefully Andrea will be able to chaperone one of those other field trips you mentioned."

"But Andrea is *so* disappointed. She was planning on going on this one, and she's made arrangements for her youngest. She hired a baby-sitter—"

"I'm sure she could cancel the sitter. The field trip isn't for three weeks."

"I just thought perhaps you could switch. It's not as though it's a big deal to you—"

"Why isn't it a big deal?" I interrupt Taylor, the softness in my voice hiding my anger. Taylor should not push me this hard. She doesn't realize I'm not like all the other mommies around her. I don't need her, like her, or want her. She's nothing to me, and I have no problem squashing her, if that's what I've got to do.

"It's not as though all your close friends were going, and if Andrea doesn't go, she's going to feel left out."

"Which confuses me," I say quietly, "as this is an educational field trip for *nine*-year-olds."

Sensing she's stepped into something foul, Taylor backpedals with a faint laugh. "You know what I mean."

I say nothing.

"It's just that we've all been doing this together for years," Taylor adds. "And it's become something of a tradition, as well as a chance to help the school."

"So that's why everyone chaperones field trips? To be with their close friends?" I now laugh a little. "Funny, I thought everyone rushed to chaperone field trips to become the teacher's best friend."

Taylor's not laughing anymore. There's definitely tension here, and I'm glad. I'm so ready to take off the gloves and get down to business. Taylor and her daughter are selfish, shallow, and insensitive, and they represent everything I detest about my gender.

Social climbers, opportunists, and power hungry, they have a double agenda: They intimidate and manipulate others to further their own cause as well as maintain control.

You see, they're not just bitchy, they're bullies. They use language and social intelligence as a form of indirect aggression. Instead of weapons, they use words. Barbed remarks. A sharp tongue.

And until this very moment, I don't think I fully understood what I was dealing with. Taylor isn't merely a pretty petty annoyance, she's a danger, because she's teaching her daughters to perpetuate unkindness toward others. She's teaching her daughters to become hurtful women.

But Taylor doesn't know what I'm thinking, and she presses on in the same sickly-sweet tone of voice. "Seeing as you have only one child, you can't know how difficult it is for those of us with three kids, but we don't have your flexibility. We'd love your flexibility—"

"Then maybe you shouldn't have had more kids."

Taylor laughs, but it's not a light tinkle. She's beginning to sound brittle. "That's funny!"

I will smack her. I will knock her down. I will ride my motorcycle all over her and leave skid marks from here to kingdom come . . . Okay, I won't, but the thought is so highly satisfying that I calm down.

"Taylor, I have to go, and I'm sorry for Andrea, but I promised Eva I'd chaperone this trip and I'm going." As gently as I can, I hang up the phone.

It takes me another hour to realize why I'm so angry.

I'm not on the A team. I'm not even on the B team. I'm on the Team That Doesn't Matter.

I wake up with a raging headache the next morning, pound a huge glass of water and two Advil before going to check on Eva.

Eva's up, curled on the couch with a blanket over her lap. She's holding her book *How to Be the Most Popular Girl in Your School,* but not reading or writing. Instead, she's just lying there with the book clutched against her chest.

It still blows me away that she actually takes notes from that book.

"How are you feeling?" I ask, approaching her to put my hand on her forehead.

"So-so," she answers wanly.

So-so is right. She doesn't look good at all. "Have you had anything to eat or drink?"

She pales, shakes her head.

"Still queasy?" I ask.

She nods.

"But you do need to get some liquids into you." I head for the kitchen, where I make some very watery grape Kool-Aid. "Drink this in tiny sips, see if you can keep it down."

Eva clings to the plastic cup along with the book but doesn't try to drink. I head back to the kitchen, where I make coffee, hoping it'll help my headache.

As I grind the coffee, I glance at her on the couch, see the book under her arm, and wonder how to broach the subject of what she's been reading. I've never had a hard time discussing anything with her before, but suddenly we're on such opposite sides of the fence. I never wanted to be popular. She wants to be the queen bee. How can I help her on this one?

As I empty the ground beans into the coffee filter, I think about the different ways I could bring up the subject. Maybe I should tell her that I know Allie gave the book to her and ask her if she likes it.

Maybe I'll just ask her which chapter she's reading and if the notes help her remember the main points.

Coffee brewing, I wander back into the living room and curl up in a chair facing the couch. "Is that a good book?" I ask casually.

Eva nods, deep purple crescents beneath her eyes. "Yeah."

"Is that the same book you've been reading for a while?"

She nods again.

"It's the one teaching you things?"

She closes her eyes. "I don't feel good, Mom."

"Maybe you should just sleep more," I say, feeling guilty for even trying to have this discussion when she feels so bad.

"Okay," she whispers, eyes still closed, thick black lashes fanning her cheeks.

After her breathing slows and grows deeper, I return to the kitchen for my coffee. Filling my mug, I flash back to a time before I was officially a teenager, a time when anything remotely grown-up sounded wonderful and desirable and the discovery of *Seventeen* magazine's *Guide for Young Ladies* at a neighborhood garage sale seemed to be the most exciting find ever.

I bought the book for twenty-five cents when I was just a little older than Eva is now. The book was at least twenty years old, and for months I pored over it in secret, committing to memory necessary facts and tidbits like how to sleep in rollers to give your hair the proper bounce, why proper hygiene is important, how to sit properly, hold a teacup, file your nails.

I can still see the tips written in big swirly cursive script and illustrated with sketches of a delicate red-haired beauty putting on her gloves or checking to make sure her purse matched her shoes.

I would never have admitted it at twelve, but a big part of me wanted to be like that illustration—lithe, pretty, elegant, so very proper. I wanted to astonish people with my perfect rightness, my delicious sense of etiquette. I wanted to be Audrey Hepburn in *My Fair Lady* after the whole Pygmalion project.

But every time I looked in the mirror, I saw a skinny, big-eyed, big-lipped, fourteen-year-old misfit. A misfit who was teased by the popular girls at school.

We get through the day without Eva getting sick again, and later when she goes to bed for the night, she's managed to get a little soup down. I tumble into bed soon after, as everything hurts.

Even though the night's cool I'm hot, too hot, and with the window open wide I lie on top of my covers, watching shadows creep across my ceiling as the moon shifts in the sky. The moon outside is big, bold, one of those huge harvest moons that cast long fingers of light and illuminate the night.

I don't feel well. I'm hot and ache in funny places, with pain in my shoulders, elbows, and other joints.

I'm not coming down sick, I tell myself. I'm not getting Eva's flu. I'm still just upset about last night's call from Taylor.

Maybe it's because I put my all into the presentation yesterday yet felt criticized when I had to rescue my daughter.

Maybe it's because sometimes your best just doesn't seem good enough.

Something wakes me up, some pain in my stomach, and I sit up in bed.

I lunge to my bathroom and take a crouching position before the toilet. Beads of perspiration form on my upper lip. My head is hot and then cool. I've got a fever and—oh no, I'm going to be sick soon. The gross feeling is getting worse.

I see Eva's shadow just as I start to retch. My eyes burn and tear with the acid bitterness. My nose burns, and my throat's raw and on fire.

And just when I think it's all over, it starts again.

I'm nearly crying when Eva pushes a cool, damp wash-cloth into my hand. "Here, Mom, wipe your face. It helps."

I look up at her, grimace at the acid burning in my nose and mouth. Yet with her standing there, smiling bravely at me, I think she's right. A cool washcloth always helps.

"Thanks, baby," I croak even as my stomach starts churning again.

"Can I do anything?" she asks.

I don't want her here to watch me barf. It's bad enough going through it myself. "No, baby, just go back to bed. I'll see you in the morning, okay?"

"Okay."

She kisses the top of my head and leaves, and not a moment too soon. As she closes my door, I clutch the toilet, gag, and am sick all over again.

Tiana wakes me up the next morning with a phone call. I drag myself out of bed to grab the phone from the bedside table. "Hey," I croak into the receiver. "How are you?"

"Better than you. You sound like hell, Marta. You okay?"

"I've got the flu. Was up most of the night." I shudder just remembering.

"Yuck, poor thing. A bug's been going around the studio here, but I've missed it, thank God." She pauses. "I won't keep you long, then, but thought I'd check. I have a chance to interview Laura Bush. She's stumping with the president, and they're going to be making a last minute campaign sweep through the West Coast, ending in Seattle. Hoped I'd have a chance to see you if I came up."

"When is it?"

"End of next week. Will you be around?"

"Definitely. I'm not going anywhere, at least not anytime soon."

"Okay. I'll call back and set something up with you once the trip details are finalized."

"Promise?"

"Promise. Now take care of yourself and get rid of that bug. Hear me?"

"Hear you loud and clear, Tits." She laughs, and I even manage a shaky grin as we say good-bye and hang up.

But once I hang up, my eyes feel scratchy and I feel horribly emotional. I feel like crap. I can't drag myself from bed. But I can't stay here feeling bad, either. I've got Eva, and even if I feel like death warmed over, I still have to take care of her.

Monday morning, Eva's planning on going to school, and I've snuck out for a very slow run. I still don't feel a hundred percent, and it could be the stress I'm feeling regarding work and cutting short the Freedom Bike Group meeting.

I know it's impossible to have everything. I know

professional moms have to juggle their responsibilities at home and work. But even after nine years, it doesn't get easier.

When Eva's sick, I miss work. When Eva has a school holiday, I miss work. When Eva needs extra homework help, I miss work.

But what else can I do? Hire a nanny again? Someone to step in and be a surrogate me?

Today I run, albeit slowly, to quiet the tumultuous voices inside me, the ones that make me frightened instead of fearless. I'm running to remind myself that I won't be afraid. I won't be timid. I won't be intimidated by life.

As I run, I repeat a silly mantra, but it helps. It works. The mantra goes like this: *I like challenges. I welcome the unknown. I welcome change. I can handle anything. I can do anything. I'm wonderful at what I do.*

It sounds funny when you say it aloud, but as I run, with the music playing in my earphones and my feet hitting the pavement, one step after another, it makes a difference. It reminds me to take the risks I need to take to do what I want to do.

I've traveled down Points Drive to 84th, 84th to 8th Street, and then 8th to 92nd, and I'm on my way home, approaching the stop sign at 24th Street, when I see a beaten-up stone-colored Land Rover coming toward me.

My heart does a funny free fall, and I go cold all over. I know that Land Rover, and I recognize the massive arm resting on the door.

I try to speed up, to pass the Land Rover more quickly, but a squirrel dashes across the road and then stops abruptly in the middle, forgetting why it's running in the first place.

Luke brakes before he reaches the squirrel, braking nearly next to me.

I try not to look at the Land Rover, and I definitely don't want to make eye contact with Luke, but it's way too awkward not to.

In the early morning light, the interior of his vehicle is dark, but as I pass him, Luke turns his head and I see him.

His gaze fixes on me, and it's the same direct gaze it's always been. He's wearing a gray T-shirt, and there's dark color high in his cheekbones and his hair is damp, as though he's just been working out.

He looks at me with that steady, long, unsmiling gaze of his, yet his pale blue eyes always make me think of heat. Fire.

"Hey," I say, nodding and trying to smile even as I push a long dark strand of hair back from my face. My hand is suddenly shaking, and I realize the lower half of me is, too. I'm nervous, and I don't even know why.

"How are you?" he asks, leaning slightly out the window.

"Good," I answer briskly. I will myself to start running again, but my legs don't move.

"How's work?"

"Great," I say even more brightly, yet I don't feel good right now, I feel bad. I feel . . . hurt. He never called. He never e-mailed. He just pursued me and then, after taking me out for dinner, kind of dropped me. "And you? How are things in your world?"

"Uh, good. Busy. I just got back from three weeks in China."

Three weeks in China? Has he been there ever since our dinner? "When did you get back?"

"Last night." A car appears behind Luke's Land Rover, and with a glance into his rearview mirror, he pulls over onto the side of the road.

I slowly approach his driver's-side door. "I didn't know you were heading to China."

He grimaces, runs a hand through his short, reddish gold hair, spiking it on end. "I didn't either. A problem popped up the night we were out to dinner. I was on the first plane out in the morning."

I nod, but I'm still upset, which is silly. My ego can't be this fragile. "So that's why you didn't call?"

I don't know if it's the flinty note in my voice or my question, but Luke arches one eyebrow. "Was I supposed to?"

I've given myself away, revealed that I do care and that my feelings were hurt. How mortifying. I usually play my cards closer to my chest.

"You could have called me," he adds. "Or e-mailed."

"I don't have your e-mail address," I say flatly. "And I don't call men."

"That's old-fashioned."

I glance at my watch, checking the time I've been gone. It's nearly half an hour since I left for my run. "Eva's home alone. I better get back."

But Luke doesn't let me off the hook so easily. "You wanted to go out again?"

I turn and look at him. His expression is hard, almost fierce, and my heart gallops off like a high-strung horse.

"I enjoyed your company," I say simply. "But at the same time, I don't want to lead you on."

The edge of his mouth quirks, and his blue gaze hardens. "Do you always put the cart before the horse, Marta?"

My face flames. I deserved that. I struggle to find the right note. "I just don't like wasting time—yours or anybody else's."

"Spending time with friends is never a waste."

A lump fills my throat. "I'm a friend?"

He gives me a penetrating look. "What do you think?"

I have to go now. I'm feeling disgustingly emotional. "Maybe coffee this week?"

Luke releases the clutch. "You call me."

"But—"

He shakes his head, cutting me short. "You want to see me, you call me." He takes off.

I watch his Land Rover disappear and then force myself to move again. My legs feel impossibly heavy, though, and the run home is hard.

I tell myself it's the morning mist that makes the run feel extra long. I mentally add that I'm still recovering from the flu. But the truth is, it's Luke and the conversation we've just had.

I do want to see him. I'd love nothing more than to meet him for a cup of coffee. But call him? I haven't called a man, pursued a man, in so many years that I don't think I can anymore.

Outside my house, I lean against the wall and stretch my hamstrings. My muscles feel tight, and my mind keeps replaying the conversation with Luke.

Should I be offended or encouraged that he wants me to call him?

Does it make sense to call him?

God, I don't know, and frankly, I hate the way I obsess about him. I dwell on him way too much. And it's not my cavewoman wiring telling me to mate. It's not. It can't be.

I'm not a cavewoman, and he's not a caveman. We're both modern people, and I happen to be one very independent, self-sufficient person.

If I call him, it's because I want to call him, not because my brain is flooded with testosterone, dopamine, and oxytocin.

As I enter the house, I kick off my running shoes and then leave them inside the door before padding in socks to the kitchen, where I spot Eva curled up on the couch, dressed for school and watching TV. "I've already had breakfast, Mom."

"Good girl." I reach up for a coffee mug. "I'll make your lunch now. Just give me a sec."

"I already made that, too," she answers primly, yet I detect a smile at her mouth and eyes. She's pleased with herself. She should be. She's a remarkable girl.

And just like that, it hits me: She should have more.

She deserves a dad, someone else to love her, dote on her. She'd be an amazing big sister, too.

I fight guilt as well as some serious confusion as I doctor my coffee. After nine years of supposed contentment, I'm not so sure our two-person family is the way it's supposed to be.

I'm not so sure—big breath here—that I'm as happy being a single mom as I let on.

Lately I feel almost empty, physically empty, my arms and legs heavy, my body weighted.

Lately I miss, deeply miss, being held.

Lately I want someone for me—an adult, an equal, a *partner*.

I don't know if it's the affluent suburb I live in or if it's meeting Luke, but I'm questioning everything these days, including all those decisions I made years ago.

But what about Eva?

I watch her watching TV, and I feel a wave of total love followed by total fear.

I'm scared because if this relationship with Luke continues . . . and should it work out—a long shot, I know, but that's how I look at life—it won't be just Eva and me any longer, it won't be "the two of us," but the three of us, and just possibly one day the four and five of us.

If I keep seeing Luke, if things get more serious, it will change everything, including Eva. Including me.

Right now, Eva says she wants our lives changed, she says she wants a "real family," meaning a mom and a dad, brothers and sisters, but what if she gets the traditional family and discovers she hates it?

What if she hates me for falling in love with someone else?

Last week Chris gave me a very brief update about how the rest of the presentation to the Freedom Group went, but today, with my head clear, I want a more in-depth report. Chris and I spend an hour talking and I can tell he's still angry with me, but I refuse to buy into his guilt trip. Instead I focus on the positives and turn my attention to the rest of day.

I end up getting through the day on adrenaline and caffeine, trying hard to get three tasks done at once, if only to keep myself from thinking about Luke.

I am not going to call him. I am not going to reach out to him.

But it's just coffee, the sadistic devil on my shoulder tempts me.

You know you want more than coffee, the devil on my other shoulder reminds me.

I do want more than coffee. I want sex.

I finish the workday, make dinner, and then later, while Eva draws, I paint.

Painting often calms me, but tonight it does nothing for my equilibrium. I feel as though I'm wound so tight that I could snap any minute.

My dreams that night are just as perverse.

That evening as I sleep, I dream darkly colored dreams of Luke. In the dream I see him clearly, elbow, shoulder, jaw, face.

In the dream I feel the intensity of his gaze, that way he looks at me, as though he can see something I can't see.

It's long ago, what must be the Middle Ages, and I'm locked in a high tower, awaiting execution. I don't know why I'm to be executed. I don't know what I did, and no one tells me anything.

In my dream they come for me, the executioner in his big black robe. I grab at the bars of my tower cell, but the executioner is stronger and he drags me away.

I wake just as the blade comes down toward my neck. I wake and discover I'm damp with sweat and nearly frozen from fear and panic.

It's just a dream, I tell myself, just a dream.

But it takes me a long time to fall back asleep, nearly an hour of staring numbly at my clock.

Was my dream telling me I couldn't do it alone, or was my dream telling me I could but I didn't want to?

Chapter Fifteen

Luke calls the next morning. "Am I interrupting?" he asks, his voice even deeper and sexier than I remembered.

"No." I sit down quickly at my desk. Robert and Chris left the studio a half hour ago for a meeting with a client, and Allie's at Kinko's getting artwork enlarged, so I'm actually alone for once. "How are you?"

"Jet-lagged, but I'll survive. And while it's fresh on my mind, I thought I'd call and give you my cell number. I realized I'd never given it to you, and perhaps that's why you find it difficult to call me."

I smile as he talks. He's so stunningly alpha and so sure of himself. With such smooth moves, he must have been amazing on the basketball court. "You've got to be in sales," I say.

"Aren't we all?" he retorts.

"Okay, I've got a pen. Why don't you give me your number."

He relays the number to me, nice and slow. Still smiling at his skillful handling of all things related to me, I ask as casually as possible if he's got time for coffee this week.

"You really love coffee," he answers deadpan.

I smile wider. My cheeks actually hurt. "I've got to be careful and take things slow."

"You're a tease."

"I'm not. I'm serious. You strike me as quite dangerous."

"And coffee's slow?"

"It's safe."

"Lots of people consider coffee an aphrodisiac."

"Medieval Turks," I say.

"I should have known. You're an expert at trivia."

I roll my eyes. "I have a coffee client. I make it my business to know everything I can about my client's products."

"That'd be a lot of research."

"One of my favorite things about my job."

"So let's get a coffee today. Noon—"

"That's lunch."

"You don't have to eat. You can just sip your caffeine."

"Thanks."

"Or we could go to one of my favorite Indian restaurants and you can eat a proper lunch."

"I do like Indian food."

"Great. Moghul Palace. Noon. See you there." And he rings off.

I sit and stare at the phone in my hand, a bit dazed but also impressed. Nice work, Luke Flynn. We're having our second date.

I'm at Moghul Palace five minutes before noon, and there's a line all the way out the door. The restaurant is very popular, and the downtown business crowd loves this place for lunch.

Luke, however, is already inside and has secured us a table on the upper level among the booths lining the wall.

We sit facing each other, and I slide the menu closer to me even as his long legs bump against mine beneath the table.

"Sorry," he apologizes, yet his smile is faintly wicked and I know he's not sorry at all. He picks up his menu, opens it, and then shuts it almost as fast. "What do you like? Samosas, paneer masala, tandoori shrimp, naan?"

I don't even bother to open my menu. "All of the above."

"That makes it easy."

Luke knows the owner well and orders vegetable samosas, tikka kebabs, tandoori shrimp, masala, and the restaurant's nutty naan. It's more food than the two of us could possibly eat, but Luke doesn't seem to mind. I don't, either. I'm starving, and as on our first date, I have no problem eating with him sitting across from me.

"So good," I say, munching on one of the juicy shrimp. "I don't know why I don't come here more. It's great food."

"Does your daughter like Indian food?"

I think for a minute. "Yes, she does. And Thai food. Greek. Korean. Vietnamese. She grew up on takeout. We don't eat out here as much. I hate having to drive every time we want to go out. In New York we just walked."

"How long did you live in New York?"

"Fourteen years."

"That's a long time."

"It was home."

"So what brought you to this area?"

"Work. And family." I catch his expression. He's curious, and taking a breath, I attempt to explain. "I was raised in Seattle but hated it. Laurelhurst was a bit posh for me, so after high school I headed to the Big Apple and stayed there until Keller and Klein, the ad agency I worked for, asked me to open a West Coast branch for them. I said yes, thinking the move would be good for my mother—and my daughter—so here I am."

"I'm surprised you didn't settle on the other side of the lake. You don't strike me as an Eastsider."

"A Bellevueite?" I mock, shaking my head. "No, I don't fit in here, but I did some research before we moved, and the schools in Clyde Hill and Medina were outstanding. Mercer Island, too. But it was the house itself that sold me. My house on Ninety-second Avenue has a separate studio office at the back. It's perfect for my company—not that I knew I'd have my own company when I moved, but having space for an art studio seemed like a great idea at the time."

"Why an art studio?"

"I paint."

He looks intrigued. "Are you good?"

Shrugging, I tear off a chunk of the naan flatbread and pop a smaller piece in my mouth. "I'm not bad," I answer after I've swallowed. "I've sold pieces before, but right now it's my outlet more than anything. I love to do it. I'm kind of passionate about art, but at the moment I channel most of my energy into my business. I have to. I need to pay bills, make sure Eva's okay."

He smiles at me, fine creases fanning from his eyes, and something in my middle turns over as he continues to smile.

"I like you, Marta Zinsser," he says after a moment. "And maybe it's because I haven't met a lot of women like you. You're honest. Very smart. And you shoot straight from the hip." He pauses. "Or maybe it's because you're sexier than hell and you're making me work very hard—"

"I'm not!" I protest.

His eyebrows lift. "Either way, it's good. This is fun. I'm having fun, and I hope we can have dinner again when I get back from San Francisco."

His eyes meet mine and hold. I blush even as I smile. How can anyone be so intense and so outwardly relaxed? He's a study in contradictions.

"Dinner would be fun," I finally agree.

Luke Flynn, I silently chant his name as I swing by the Bellevue Post Office on my way home to drop off Eva's party invitations.

Did Luke really go to Harvard? And did he really just get back from China? Or is he a gorgeous con artist trying to blow smoke up my a____?

Pulling into my driveway, I vow to check out his credentials as soon as I have time. I probably should have Googled him earlier, but it didn't seem like such a big deal. Now, with me falling hard for this guy, I think I better do some sleuthing to see just who, and what, I'm dealing with.

Chris is waiting for me as I walk into the office. "We've got a problem," he says before I even step through the doorway. "We need to talk now."

Chris, Robert, and I pull chairs to the conference table, and Chris wastes no time dropping the bad news: Our Walla

Walla winery client hates the new advertising campaign and wants something different, something brilliant, yet something cheap. "And they want it turned around fast."

I just stare at Chris. "But they signed off on the new ad campaign. They approved all the artwork—"

"They changed their mind."

I shake my head. "They can't change their mind at this stage of the game. The ad space is purchased, the artwork has been delivered, everything's done."

"That's what I told them." Chris exchanges glances with Robert. "They're going to walk, though, if we don't accommodate them."

"Then let them walk. They've already been billed. They've paid up. I saw the check come in last week."

"They canceled the check. They've paid nothing for the work done other than the initial retainer fee." Chris rubs his head. "And that was just two thousand."

I'm barely hanging on to my temper. "But the ad space alone is ten thousand."

Robert looks miserable. "I'm sorry. It was my idea, my design—"

"Rubbish," I interrupt. "You've nothing to be sorry for. You gave them exactly what they asked for." I clamp my jaw tight to keep from saying more. I'm livid, really livid. "Get Pauline—no, make that Ray—on the phone," I say, referring to the husband-and-wife team that owns the Walla Walla winery. "We're going to talk. Now."

Susan has just managed to get Ray on his cell when Eva crashes through the studio doors in tears.

"What did you say to Mrs. Young?" she cries, throwing

her backpack at my feet. "What did you say to make Jemma hate me so much?"

I cover the phone's mouthpiece. *"What?"*

She storms over to me at my desk. "You said something to her on the phone last week, and Jemma said her mom was so upset she couldn't eat or sleep all weekend."

I'm even more confused than before, and still covering the phone, I demand, *"When?"*

Eva balls her hands into fists. "Last week. Tuesday or Wednesday. I don't know. Whenever you talked to her."

"But I haven't—"

Yet as soon as I open my mouth, I realize I did talk to her. Last week. She called me Tuesday night about the field trip. The same night Eva was sick. The same day I'd cut short my meeting with Freedom Bikes. "Just a minute." I uncover the phone, say hello to Ray, and ask him if I can call him back in five minutes.

Ray's curt but agrees.

I hang up and turn my full attention on Eva. "Now start over. From the top. What happened? What's going on?"

"You tell me," Eva flashes hotly. "Because Jemma's told everyone at school that you're so mean and you made her mom cry."

"But I didn't."

"So why did Jemma tell everyone that?"

I'm on an episode of *The Twilight Zone*, and pretty soon I'll know the plot and figure out what the hell is happening in this story. "I don't know. But yes, Mrs. Young and I talked. I didn't say anything to hurt her. She called to talk to me about the field trip."

"Then why did she cry? And why did Jemma tell me you ruined everything?"

God, little girls gossip, and they never get the story straight, and I honestly don't want to be doing this right now. I'm furious with Ray and Pauline. They approved artwork months ago, and the fact that they canceled a check they'd cut us infuriates me—and panics me a bit, as I've cut a number of checks against that deposit.

"Eva, you've got the story wrong. Mrs. Young wanted me to not chaperone the field trip to the Science Center so another mother could go, Andrea someone."

"Brooke's mom."

"Right. Great. The point is, I told her no, that I'd already made plans to go, and I was going to go."

My words aren't soothing Eva, though. She's just getting more upset, and I'm getting more impatient. The staff is listening, too, and I know from Chris's expression that he's getting tired of my family life intruding into the professional life.

"Eva, let's take this to the house," I say, standing.

But she refuses. "No." She takes a step back and folds her arms across her thin chest. "I don't want to take this to the house. I don't want to talk to you. Why couldn't you do what Mrs. Young asked? Why are you so selfish?"

I flinch at Eva's accusation. Selfish. Is that what I am? Is that how she really perceives me? As *selfish*?

I'm hurt, angry, and stunned, so stunned that I can't speak and don't even try to defend myself.

When did everything change? When did I become the bad guy? And why am I the bad guy all the time?

"They say you're weird," Eva continues hotly. "They say you're a freak. Jemma's been telling everyone that you have a tattoo and you got kicked out of regular school and went to a special school for delinquent kids."

"*What?*"

"She said her mom knows someone who knew you from high school and you had problems and that's why I have problems." Eva's cheeks burn dusky red. "But I don't have problems. My only problem is you. You turned me into a freak—"

"You're not a freak."

"You did this to me, and I hate it, and I hate you." With that she runs to the house, slamming the studio door shut behind her.

The entire door frame shakes with the violence of Eva's slam, and the office is dead silent for a moment after she's gone. The silence is heavy, too, one of those stifling things that feels oppressive, as though it's New York City in the middle of July.

"Um, Marta," Susan says, clearing her throat uncomfortably. "Sorry to bother you, but your dad is on the line. Something about you taking your mom to the doctor today?"

Oh, Jesus.

I forgot. I completely forgot. It's Tuesday. Mom was supposed to see her specialist today, and I'm late, very late, and this isn't an appointment that's easily rescheduled. We're going to be late, but better late than a no-show.

I swivel around in my desk chair, stare sickly at the others. "I'm supposed to go—I've *got* to go."

"Then go. I'll call Ray back and tell him you'll call him later," Robert says, shooing me with his hand. "And don't worry about Eva. We're good with Eva."

"Yes," Allie agrees, standing and smiling cheerfully. "We love Eva. You go take care of your mom. We'll keep an eye on your daughter."

I nod, grab my purse, root around for my keys. "I'll let Eva know I'm leaving. Maybe she'll want to come. But if she doesn't, I appreciate your keeping an eye on her."

"Don't think twice about it," Robert reassures me. I smile at him gratefully. Maybe I'm not married, maybe I don't have a lot of girlfriends in Bellevue, but these people have become my extended family.

In the house, I find that Eva has locked herself in her room. "Eva, open the door."

"No."

"Don't do this. Open your door. I'm late to take Grandma to the doctor."

Her door opens, and she stands in the doorway staring at me with so much anger and loathing that my breath catches. "Eva," I say softly, reproachfully.

Her upper lip curls, and she shakes her head, tears glittering in her eyes. "Go take Grandma. I don't care. I don't care what you do."

"You don't want to come?" I ask as calmly as I can, refusing to dwell on her rejection or contempt.

"No." And with a wretched sob, she flings the door shut and locks it again.

I stand in the hall listening to her footsteps cross her bedroom and then the thud as she throws herself onto her bed.

Swallowing haid, I push hair away from my face. "Okay," I say, my stomach cramping as though filled with bits of broken glass. "I'll be back by five. If you need anything, everybody's in the studio, and they've promised to keep you company."

"Just go."

I do. With a last glance at her locked door, I head for the garage, back my truck out, and head across the bridge to Laurelhurst, where I grew up.

Laurelhurst is an affluent lakefront community in Seattle with winding, tree-lined boulevards, large homes, and eye-popping views of Mount Rainier and Lake Washington.

Our home isn't the largest in our neighborhood, but it's beautiful, a sprawling white two-story house built in the late 1930s by a renowned Seattle architect, and the garden is just as mature, with towering trees, a sweeping lawn, and lush perennial flower beds. It's the kind of house that June and Ward Cleaver would have lived in, with a garden perfect for entertaining in the summer.

Dad's already gone when I get to the house, and Mom is waiting at the door with the housekeeper, who is doing her best to keep Mom calm.

"She's a little agitated today," Elda whispers to me, handing me the notebook Dad has left for me before walking Mom to the truck.

Driving, I wind my way through the neighborhoods closest to University of Washington's east campus, heading for the university hospital's medical center. At traffic lights, I thumb through the notebook that Dad has kept on the progression of Mom's disease.

I've never seen it before, and it's unnerving.

I read about outings they've taken, her prescriptions and reactions, as well as day-to-day problems, including Mom's increasingly erratic behavior. There are issues of incontinence. Wandering. Rage. Tears. Hiding things. Sadness. Confusion.

There are such good days that Mom seems to be almost her old self again, and then there are days where she's unable to perform even the most basic, everyday task, a condition called apraxia.

Suddenly, Eva's tears and tantrums and theatrics seem less urgent compared with what Mom's going through and the stress Dad's been under.

No wonder Dad wanted me to bring Mom today. He must be overwhelmed. He must have needed a break.

Now and then, I glance at my mom as I drive. She's quiet while I'm at the wheel, content to gaze out the window in silence, but her quiet turns to agitation as soon as we park and head for the doctor's waiting room.

"I don't like this place," she says, grabbing at my arm as I reach for the doctor's office door. "I don't want to be here."

"It's okay, Mom. We're together, everything's okay," I say, taking her hand, sliding my fingers around hers. I'm holding her hand the way I hold Eva's, and I walk her inside the office and toward one of the groupings of chairs. "Why don't you sit here while I check us in."

"No." Her hand grips mine tightly. "No. I want to go. I want to go now."

"Soon, Mom, I promise."

Thankfully, the doctor sees us almost right away and I sit in a chair not far from Mom while he checks her vitals and asks her basic questions.

Mom doesn't answer him. Instead she stares at me, expression fiercely unhappy. She thinks I've brought her here against her will. She thinks I've forced her.

"It's okay," I whisper.

"Don't talk to me," she snaps.

The doctor looks at me over my mother's head, the dark eyes behind the glasses professional but kind. "Any questions? Anything new you or your father has noticed?"

I flip through the notebook, go to today's page, where Dad has written in his small, careful script:

"My wife keeps leaving the house, 'wandering' through the neighborhood. I've put locks on the doors, but that doesn't stop her from trying to get out anyway. Where is she going? Why does she want to leave?"

My stomach knots as I read the entry to the doctor. But the doctor doesn't seem at all disturbed by Dad's observation or questions.

"Wandering is obviously a serious problem," he answers, "not only because it puts the patient in danger, but because it also creates worry and guilt for the caregiver. The secret," he adds, "is to understand why the patient is wandering."

"So there are specific reasons?" I ask.

He nods. "Most often the patient that wanders is trying to go home, and in this case home isn't a house, but a place free of problems and worries. Wandering can also be due to pain or fear, it may be boredom or the desire to accomplish a task. It might even be because your mother is looking for something."

"Can we leave now?" Mom asks, standing.

She's still in her paper dressing gown, and it threatens

to unfold, exposing her thin, bruised body completely. I take her hand, gently seat her again.

"How do we know what the reason is?" I ask, stroking the back of her hand, trying to help her relax.

"That's where you have to play detective," the doctor answers. "Go on walks with her. Take notes. Pay attention to what she's doing. Once you think you've discovered the cause of the wandering, then you can try different things to end the behavior. But always be gentle. Nonconfrontational. Your mother doesn't mean to upset you. She's genuinely confused."

On the way home, I stop at University Place and treat Mom to an ice cream. As the disease progresses, she becomes increasingly childlike, and like the girl she once was, she loves her ice-cream cone again. Today we sit inside Ben & Jerry's, each of us enjoying our treat.

Mom looks at me over her cone and takes a lick. "I miss Eva," she says, looking at me intently.

"You'll see her soon," I answer, reminding me all over again of the situation waiting for me at home.

Mom just smiles faintly, as though she doesn't believe it, and finishes the rest of her ice-cream cone in almost beatific silence.

I drop Mom at home. Dad's there, and I tell him what the doctor has told me. Dad nods. He's read the same thing in one of his Alzheimer's books, but he'd hoped the doctor would have more insight into Mom's particular case.

"I didn't know she was wandering off," I say, watching Mom disappear into the house while Dad and I talk in the driveway.

"Pretty much daily."

"Is that why there are all the childproof locks on the doors?"

He nods, his face heavily lined. "I don't know what she's looking for, but she keeps going for the door, over and over. And when I stop her, she gets angry. Swings at me." His face tightens. "It's getting harder. She's getting more unpredictable."

"You can call me more, use me more. Eva and I can come watch her for an evening or a weekend and you can get away. I know you need to get away."

He nods vaguely, stares off into the distance. He's silent so long, I think he's forgotten me, and then he turns back and smiles wryly. "I thought once we got you off to college we'd be free to travel, do things. I never imagined this. Never once in a million years."

There's nothing I can say. I just give him a quick hug and kiss and head on home, back to the problems that await me there.

The farther I travel on the 520 bridge and the closer I get to Bellevue, the more my stomach knots and the tighter I feel the tension in my shoulder blades.

Ever since I was a teenager I've been aggressively creative, wildly individualistic, and I've tried to raise Eva the same way, but it doesn't take a genius to see that I'm the one out of step here. Not them. It's me.

Every day, I'm surrounded by mothers who defy the description of motherhood. Here it's the norm to get rid of your postbaby tummy as fast as you can, whether through dieting and exercise or a quiet visit to the plastic surgeon. Here it's admired, even respected, to augment one's breasts if one, or one's husband, perceives they're lacking.

Here being fit, being sleek, being groomed, is vital to the mommy job. It's as though mothers have all swallowed the marine mantra "Be all that you can be," which here seems to mean "Be as good as, if not better than, everyone else."

The 84th Street exit approaches. Almost home. Usually I'm excited about going home, but not today. Today I just feel tired and very overwhelmed.

Back at the house, I discover everyone's gone but Allie, and she comes sprinting out of the house the moment I park.

"I'm sorry," she says, panting. "I'm sorry. She did it when we were in the studio working. I'm so sorry, Marta."

Allie's talking so fast that I can't follow what she's saying. "What has Eva done?"

"She was in her room, and the door was locked—"

I don't wait to hear anything more. I push Allie aside and dash into the house.

I see what she's done the moment I enter the living room. Eva's standing in the middle of the floor, arms hanging loosely at her side.

She's cut off her hair.

All of it.

Chapter Sixteen

This can't be happening, I think, staring at Eva. This can't be my child.

I stand there looking at her, jaw dropped, absolutely floored, so shocked that no words come.

Allie's backing out the door. "I'm leaving," she calls.

I try to nod but can't even move my head. I hear the door shut. Allie's gone. She's left Eva and me alone together.

Eva still faces me, her chin lifted defiantly, yet as she stares at me, horrified tears fill her eyes.

"Eva," I finally whisper, unable to say anything else.

Her hair had been so long, reaching all the way down her back, thick, silky, onyx. Beautiful. And now what's left on her head is just a mess. Tufts and pieces, that's all there is, tufts and pieces, as if she were the dying Cosette in *Les Misérables*.

And next Monday is picture day.

As if she can read my mind, her lower lip suddenly quivers.

"Eva," I repeat, and it's the only word that comes to my lips. It's a plea, a protest, a refrain.

I think she's going to burst into tears, but instead she

forces a fierce smile, and the smile hurts her even more than tears. "I cut my hair."

I can see.

She turns on her heel and marches away, leading me to her bathroom, where she performed the act of butchery. The foot-long tresses are all over the bathroom floor, her hair nearly a yard long in places.

"I'm not like you," she says, chin jerking, eyes brilliant with unshed tears.

I see the scissors on the tiled bathroom counter. They're the kitchen shears, the ones I keep in my big wood knife block.

"I'm nothing like you," she adds, knuckles white, nearly as white as her face, and it crosses my mind that when people say childhood is the happiest time of your life, they've never met my Eva. And they never met me. My childhood wasn't much easier than Eva's.

I wanted so much then. I wanted so badly to be happy.

Yet happiness isn't something you chase, it's something you are. It's something you think, it's something you believe.

And I believe in Eva.

Just as I believe in me.

"I think it looks great," I say, because there's no way in hell I'm going to add insult to injury by crying about her beautiful hair now. Besides, she's more than the sum of the parts—hair, eyes, uncertain smile—she's also breath and heart, mind, spirit, and fire.

"You think so?" she whispers, some of the rigid tension in her shoulders going as she looks at me for hope.

Hope, I repeat silently. I can give it, I must give it, because this is what I do. This is why I'm her mom. "Yes."

She reaches up, touches her sheared head. "No one else has short hair at school."

"Your hair isn't that short."

She fingers the chopped ends again, one side far more dramatically mutilated than the other. "I don't look ugly?"

Even though my waiflike Eva looks like a poster child for famine relief, I can't tell her that.

I can't really tell her much of anything. I just have to be here for her.

"No," I say, wrapping her in my arms and hugging her until her arms reach for me and grip me just as hard. "You're beautiful. You're my beautiful girl, and you will always be."

It's easy to comfort her in the bathroom, but later that night I nearly cry in my pillow. I know it's just hair, but I'm upset, more upset than I'll ever let Eva know. I loved her hair. I loved how long and dark and thick it was. I loved how few children had hair as beautiful as hers. As mine.

And maybe that is what hurts, maybe that is what's rolling around inside me like a rubber ball on fire.

She changed us. She made it clear that she didn't want what we had. She wants something else.

She wants a mother that isn't me.

I'm not going to take this personally. That would be foolish. Eva's a little girl, a child, and children must try to separate themselves from their all-important parent figures. It's part of growing up. Part of becoming an individualized person.

But oh, it shakes me, making me feel vulnerable all over again, vulnerable in a way I hadn't ever imagined.

I knew in the teen years Eva would try some things, rebel as all teenagers do, but I didn't think it'd be like this, this personal, this painful, this soon.

Another half hour passes, and still tense, sleepless, I get out of bed and go to the great room where my easel's set up in the corner.

With a cup of tea at my elbow and the stereo on low, I squeeze great dollops of acrylic on the palette and I paint, losing myself in color and the picture in my head.

It's not until two hours have passed and my canvas has been set aside while I wash my hands to go back to bed that I realize what is eating me alive on the inside.

I'm afraid. I'm afraid that I'm going to ruin Eva.

Eva begs to stay home from school the next day, horrified all over again by her cropped head of hair. I tell her she can stay home, but only so we can go into a hair salon and get it styled a bit. She agrees.

While the stylist at Gene Juarez works on Eva's hair, I sit in the lounge, feeling as though a dark cloud has engulfed me. Yesterday started well—lunch with Luke was fabulous and fun—but then it all went downhill after that.

Thinking of Luke, I want to call him now. I want to hear his voice and have another of our semiridiculous conversations where I pretend I'm not interested when we both know I am.

I'd love to have him tease me now.

I'd love to have him give me one of those faint smiles I find so sexy, the one that just touches his mouth and makes his eyes warm.

But I can't use him for comfort. We're not in a relationship. I barely know him. I can't start depending on him or his smiles or sexy voice.

I call Shey instead. "Shey, help," I say the moment Shey answers.

"What's happened? Have you fallen in love?"

I nearly crack a smile. I love her twang and yet think I could hate her. "*No.* It's an Eva problem."

"What's she done now?"

"Cut her hair off, all off. The word *pixie* doesn't even cover it."

Shey whistles softly. "When did this happen?"

"Yesterday. We're at the salon now, trying to see if there's any way to make a style out of the mess, but it's pretty bad. She looks like a Romanian orphan."

"Why did she do it?"

I rub my forehead, feel my own heavy hair fall forward, against my hand. "She didn't want to be like me anymore."

I can hear Shey exhale. "I'm sorry," she says, and her voice is gentle. "You two are having a rough go of it. But it's a phase. You've got to know it's just a phase, Ta. It'll get better. I promise."

My eyes just keep burning. They feel like little onions popped into my head. "She's been trying so hard to make friends, she's even planned this big sleepover, but now she says no one will come. I don't know what to think anymore, but I do know this—if kids were making fun of her before she cut her hair off, it's going to be even worse now. And it's not just the kids who talk about her, it's the parents, too."

Shey's quiet a moment. "Let me think about this. There's got to be a way to turn it around, make it better. You're in advertising. What would you do if it weren't your daughter but one of the companies you represent?"

"I'm in advertising, not PR."

"But they're kind of the same."

"They're not at all the same. Advertising is about selling. Public relations is about building trust."

"Come on. PR is about putting a positive spin on things, including disasters. And that's what we need, a great reason Eva's cut her hair off, something honorable, like she's donating the hair to a good cause . . . donating the hair to make wigs for children undergoing chemotherapy—"

"A nice idea, Shey, but these kids are cruel. They'd never relate to that."

"Then let's give them something juicy. Something all the girls will be envious about. We make Eva a model."

"*What?*"

"We'll take some pictures, create a portfolio, find some print work for her—"

"Sure, and while we're at it, let's enter her in the Little Miss Beauty Pageants, too." I make a sound of disgust. "No, absolutely not. I won't have her modeling. I can't stand that world. It's even more fake than Bellevue."

"Ta, get over yourself. Think about it. Will the girls there be jealous if they hear Eva missed school because she had a modeling shoot?"

I close my eyes. Shey's such a pain. And she's always right. "Yes."

"And if she shows up without her hair, she can say it was for the shoot."

"The kids will still laugh."

"Not if they see her pictures. You know she's photogenic. She'd be stunning in black and white with her pale skin, strong cheekbones, and dark eyes."

Eva is beautiful in photographs. The camera sees something most people miss, and I cherish every photo of her. But to try to turn her into a model? To make her something she's not?

The receptionist at the front desk waves to me. "Henri says they're almost done. He'd like you to come see your daughter's hair."

"Shey, they're done with Eva. I'm to go see the finished product."

"Let me talk to Liza here at the agency. She's been in meetings all morning with the producers from the Discovery Channel, but if I can get a moment with her, I'll see who Liza recommends in Seattle. I know she's got a favorite kids photographer there, and I'll call you with the details."

"Fine," I answer grumpily.

"It's going to be okay," Shey repeats, Zenlike. "Just keep telling yourself these pictures and portfolio are for Eva's benefit, not yours." Shey pauses. "She's choosing her own path, Ta. Support it."

I stand behind Eva's chair and inspect Henri's handiwork. Eva's hair is so short that it's like a boy's, but at least Henri has created a style, and the wispy ends frame Eva's eyes, cheekbones, and mouth. Even if the hair is pixie short, there's no way to confuse Eva's face, with her big long-lashed eyes and full pink mouth, with a boy's.

Later that afternoon, I drive Eva to photographer Kira Stewart's studio in Seattle, a studio not far from the stadium where the Mariners play and the huge Starbucks corporate office.

ExpectingModels has used Kira for a number of her West Coast photo assignments as well as when they need to build a young model's portfolio. Kira's an expert with kids, and even I'm amazed at the shots Kira is getting of Eva, first in old-fashioned pinafores and then with Eva dressed in chunky turtlenecks and corduroy overalls with funky props like a wooden rake and an old red wagon.

While I don't want Eva to really model, I do think Shey's suggestion is brilliant. Instead of feeling hideous, Eva's beginning to smile and shine, and her confidence is growing.

By the time we're finished, it's nearly dinnertime. We stop at the Burgermaster drive-in for dinner, and as we eat in the car, Eva chatters away, thrilled with some of the digital prints that Kira sent home with her to keep as a souvenir until the real photos are ready.

"So Aunt Shey is really going to use me as a model?" Eva repeats for the fourth time between bites of hamburger and fries, her photos tucked beneath her leg.

"She says she wants to." I sip my Diet Coke, wishing it were spiked with rum. It's been one very long day.

"That's so cool." Eva slurps on her strawberry milk-shake, looks at me from the corner of her eye. "Modeling is cool."

I say nothing.

Eva says louder, "Jemma models, did you know that?"

"No," I answer wearily. "I didn't know."

"She does a lot for Nordstrom."

"Mmmmm."

"I just hope I get a real modeling job soon." Eva swirls her shake, her expression dreamy. "A good one. You know, maybe as a junior bridesmaid for a wedding ad."

*   *   *

Eva was right about the sleepover being ruined. The party cancellations start to pour in by voice mail and e-mail the next day, one right after the other. The excuses are lame, and some are barely excuses, just brief announcements that there's been a change of plans and Paige or Brooke (or whoever) can't come.

I don't announce each cancellation to Eva. It's not fair that she's been snubbed because of me. It's not fair that adults use children as pawns in their petty games.

By noon, I realize we don't have a party anymore. I haven't heard from two people, but if eight have canceled out, the other two can't be far behind.

Equally awful, the whole Walla Walla winery campaign is shot. We did the work, but we're not going to get paid.

I haven't had lunch yet and decide to use my lunch hour to escape. In the house I change into my boots, layer on an extra T-shirt, and grab my old leather bomber coat. I'm going for a ride.

Wheeling the motorcycle out of the garage, I see Chris standing in the studio office door. He doesn't wave or say anything, so I straddle my bike, stand it up, and kick up the kickstand.

I turn on the bike. Shift gears. One down, four up. The engine roars. I love that sound. I smile crookedly, and some of the tightness and hurt inside my chest eases.

I roar down the driveway, take a left onto 92nd Avenue NE, and head for the 520. I'm bummed we haven't heard from Freedom Bikes, but I won't panic, not yet. Everything's going to be okay. It always is.

After merging onto the 405, I head toward Snoqualmie,

where dairy farms fold into mountains and waterfalls tumble through a craggy gorge. I ride for over an hour, traveling past the town of North Bend, where *Twin Peaks* was once filmed, and on through the rugged Cascades until I reach the top of the pass. It's a beautiful fall day, the sky almost too sharply blue and the trees along the 90 every shade of red, copper, and gold.

The air's cold high up, and I wish I'd worn gloves. My fingers feel stiff on the handlebars, and everything in me rattles from the bone-jarring ride.

It's not a gentle bike, and it's not meant to be a soft ride.

On the way home, I stop in Issaquah at historic Gilman Village. Issaquah, once an old coal-mining town, has developed as the gateway to the "Plateau," which is a traffic nightmare unto itself. But it's early yet, not even two-fifteen, and traffic is light.

After parking my bike outside one of the village's restored farmhouses-turned-coffeehouses, I yank my helmet off my head and, carrying it loosely in the crook of my arm, enter the yellow-and-white-painted restored farmhouse.

As I wait for my order, I realize people are looking at me. It's been so long since I rode my bike, I'd forgotten how people stare when I'm in my biker gear. Men and women seem equally fascinated by the combination of long hair, scuffed lace-up boots, faded Levi's jeans, and black, macho helmet dangling from my hand.

Still waiting, I spot a young mom with her daughter, and I watch entranced as they sit at their tiny table for two and share a cookie.

The mother has a long dark ponytail, and the child—unlike Eva—is stunningly fair, Nordic instead of my coloring. The toddler dips her cookie crumble into her small paper cup of milk and nods seriously as if to say, *This is good*, and the mother smiles back and nods. Her nod doesn't say just that the cookie is good, but that the daughter has it right, that the daughter is good, that life—the two of them together—is good.

I feel a tug inside me, remembering how that used to be us, Eva and me, the two of us alone, against the world.

I remember how we were once our own little family, and it was wonderful and painful, hopeful and terrifying. It was just the two of us. In those early years in New York, I'd never been more courageous or more anxious.

I used to lie awake at night wondering what would happen to Eva if something happened to me. And then I'd wonder how I'd survive if something happened to her. I used to torture myself with thoughts like these until they made me ill, and then one day I decided I wouldn't play that game anymore. I refused to dwell on negative things, refused to give up one moment of life to sad, depressing thoughts. Nothing bad would happen. And if it did, I'd deal with it then and only then.

"Americano for Marta," the teenage boy announces.

My drink order is ready, and I step forward for my cup. "Thanks," I say.

"Is that your bike outside?" he asks, nodding to what would have once been a living room window with a view of the parking lot.

"Yeah." I lift the lid of the tall, steaming cup to help it cool. "Do you ride?"

"I have a Honda I bought secondhand. Kind of a girlie little bike. It's embarrassing. My dream bike's a Fat Boy."

"Good dream."

He blushes, nods, smiles shyly. "You have a good day."

I lift my coffee cup. "You too."

Outside, I blow on my coffee. It's hot. I won't have time to drink the whole cup before I have to go, but I'll get most of it down.

As I sip my coffee, crispy brown leaves play across my boots, tumbling into heaps with newly fallen ruby- and saffron-hued leaves. A nearby store has its front door open, and I catch a whiff of pumpkin and apple spice, and it's such a strong scent that I turn toward it, breathe in. It's fall. It's beautiful. Everything's going to be okay.

On my way home, I stop at the Chevron on Bellevue Way to put gas in the bike, and as I pull off my helmet, I spot a very familiar Land Rover already parked at the gas pump on the far side of the station.

Luke.

I just can't escape him.

He's got his back to me, and he's leaning against the side of his Land Rover, talking on his cell phone.

I keep an eye on him as I fill my tank with gas. Tall, tall, tall. So handsome. Look at that profile. Look at those legs. Oh, the things I could do—and would do—with him.

Finished, I turn off the pump, complete my transaction, and am just about to climb on my bike when he suddenly looks at me, making eye contact.

The corner of his mouth lifts, tilts. I smile back. He hangs up his phone. I walk his way.

"I should have known you'd have a bike," he drawls.

"I'm that bad?" I flash.

His smile grows. "You're that good."

His smile sends me over the edge. I hate him, I tell myself, I hate that I find him so unbelievably sexy and that for him I think I'd gladly break each and every vow I've ever made.

His smile makes me want to take a swing at him.

Makes me want to get his skin on mine.

Makes me want to fight, or make love, or both.

"But be careful," he adds. "Bikes are dangerous—"

"Thanks, Mom," I interrupt dryly.

"I'm serious."

"So am I." I give him a hard look so he knows I'm not messing around. I'm not a helpless woman, and I'm not a careless woman. "I've had a motorcycle since I was seventeen. I know the history of the American motorcycle, and I'm proud to be a bike owner."

"Knowledge won't keep you safe. I love bikes, too, but I don't have kids, and you do. You're a single mom."

"That's right, I am, and a good mom, too. And I could do without the guilt trip, thank you very much."

He shrugs. "There was no guilt trip."

"I love my daughter. I love her more than anything, and I'd never do anything that would hurt her."

"You're being defensive," he answers bluntly. "And you're taking my comment far too personally."

"It is personal. You implied—"

"I didn't imply anything," he cuts me off ruthlessly. "I care about you. I'm looking out for you. End of story."

Looking up at him, seeing the furious blue light in his

eyes, I don't think it's the end of the story at all. There's something else going on here, and it isn't comfortable. It's not platonic. And it scares the hell out of me.

I take a quick breath, struggle to calm myself. "I appreciate your concern, but you hardly know me—"

"Who broke your heart?" he demands. "Because someone did a number on you. You're a beautiful, intelligent woman, and yet you're as jumpy as an alley cat."

I don't care for his insight or his analogy. "I didn't have my heart broken."

"Then what are you afraid of?"

"I'm not sure what you mean—"

"You're a smart woman. Don't play stupid. It doesn't suit you." Then Luke does the unthinkable. He steps toward me, takes my face in his hands, and kisses me, really kisses me, holding my face between his hands and taking my mouth, tasting my mouth, tasting me.

It's all so hot, too hot, too much everything I don't know and can't hope to control.

Even when I wanted Scott most, it never felt like this. Electric and wild, a leaping, whipping sensation in my blood, in my veins. I shiver and crave. This is the kind of desire that isn't real, that doesn't exist. Lips—bodies—don't really feel like this.

Finally he lets me go, and I nearly sway on my feet.

"On second thought," Luke says, a flare of fire in his eyes, "maybe you should be scared."

His gas pump clicks off, and I climb back on my bike.

After tugging on my helmet, I start my bike up and pull out of the station, knowing Luke, Man as Big as a Mountain, is looking at me, and I feel even more wound up than I did before.

I'm starting to feel undone, and the kiss didn't help. The kiss was good. The kiss was great. The kiss just makes me think more of the thoughts I don't want to think.

It's been so long since I felt like a woman, and there's something about Luke that makes me feel very warm, and very soft, and very real. And the softer I feel, the more I want Luke's strong arms around me.

It's probably just a mile from the Chevron station to my home, but it feels like forever because the entire ride home I'm battling with myself. I hate him. I want him. I hate him. I crave him. I hate him. I need him.

I *don't* need him.

At my house, I park the bike in the garage and sit there for several minutes without moving. I don't need him, I repeat silently. But I do want him. Badly.

Chapter Seventeen

Back at home, I see I have just minutes before Eva returns from school. I quickly hang up my jacket, straighten one of Eva's jackets in the closet, and find a rolled-up book in her coat pocket.

I pull out the book, and it's what I expected: her beloved copy of *How to Be the Most Popular Girl in Your School.* And she's got little sticky notes from my studio desk marking pages.

Leaning on the kitchen counter, I leaf through the book to read her latest sticky notes.

1. Be smart and funny.
   Just because you will become popular doesn't mean you have to be nasty to the not-so-popular girls.
2. Eat lunch with your friends.
   Talk, don't stay quiet. Make sure you get the conversation going.
3. Be pleasant when you meet new friends.
   Ask questions about what they like, and just smile and listen to what they say to show you're interested in them.

4. Never be a snob.

   If you can afford to buy more expensive things than
   others can, don't brag about what you have.

I stop reading as the back door opens and Eva walks
into the kitchen, shrugging off her backpack and dropping it on the floor.

"Hi, Mom."

I shut the book but can't exactly hide it. "Hi, honey."

"What are you doing?"

"Uh, reading."

She comes to the counter, lifts the book, and then looks
at me, puzzled. "You're reading this?"

"I found it in your coat in the closet."

She glances down at the book and then back at me.
"How much did you read?"

"I was just, um, skimming."

"What do you think of it?"

What do I think of it? Half a dozen thoughts come to
mind, but none of them are nice. "It's, um, interesting."

She leans on the counter, looks up at me worriedly.
"Does it make sense?"

"Uh, some of it."

"Would you want to read more? We could read
it together. You and me. Talk about this stuff if you
want."

I feel a weight lift off my chest, and I find myself smiling. Reaching out, I ruffle what's left of her hair. "Sure.
It'd be . . . fun . . . to read it together and then talk about
it. Let's do that."

Hope shines in Eva's eyes. "When? Tonight?"

I don't see why not. There's nothing else we'll be doing later. "Okay."

"Great." Eva presses the book to her chest. Her smile grows bigger. "I'm going to go get my notebook, write down some more things so I can be ready. Okay?"

"But what about your homework?"

She waves me off. "I already did it on the bus. It was easy." She blows me a kiss. "Talk later."

In the studio, Chris asks if I've heard from Freedom Bikes yet. I say no and, sitting at my desk, check for voice messages.

There have been a number of calls on my private line, including several from Tiana, who is arriving tomorrow in Seattle but won't be free until Saturday, and one from Taylor, who has two things to say: First, it's my turn to photocopy the class bulletin in the school office tomorrow noon and then assemble it with another mom; and two, Jemma will not be able to attend Eva's party next weekend because Jemma is having a big party herself.

As I discard her message, I can't help muttering, "Bitch."

That evening, Eva doesn't forget that I've promised to read her popularity book with her. As soon as dinner's over, she whisks out the book along with her notebook and sits on the couch and calls me over.

"Ready?" she asks cheerfully.

Why do I feel as if I'm being dragged to a wedding gown fitting? Eva's too happy, too excited about this book. I try to look enthusiastic as we start on page one.

" 'Popular girls aren't born, they're made,' " Eva reads aloud. " 'They've learned the secret to being popular, and now you will, too.'" She pauses, glances up at me. "Sounds good?"

"Oh. Very good."

She taps the page. "Popularity isn't something everyone just knows. It's something we have to learn, it's something we have to do."

I smile, but I'm not so sure I like her plural pronoun "we." We learn. We do. Shouldn't she be saying I learn? I do?

"'Remember,'" she continues, reading again, "'becoming popular will take some work. But the payoff is huge. If you follow these steps, soon you'll be the most popular girl in your school!'"

Eva quickly flips open her notebook, clicks her pen, and looks up at me. I make sure my smile is frozen in place.

"I've already done some work and made a list of the things we'll—"

"We'll?" I interrupt, hearing the plural pronoun that made me nervous.

"I'll," she corrects graciously, "I'll need. Makeup—lip gloss, blush, eye shadow. Good looks. Good grades. Social skills. Manners. Cool clothes. And lastly, AOL Instant Messenger, MSN, MySpace, or whatever."

I fold my arms across my chest. "Are you sure this book is for fourth graders?"

She shrugs. "It's for whoever needs it. Just listen to this: 'Remember that first impressions are important, and you've got to always present yourself with complete confidence. Don't ever put yourself down, and don't let anyone know you're less than perfect.'"

"Wow."

Eva ignores me and keeps reading. "'Gain the trust of

your new friends by being nice to them, and once you're a better friend, you can show a tiny bit of your bitch. Not for long. Just a second. Because you never, ever, show anyone how bitchy you can be. All you want to do is hint at it.' "

I shift on the couch. "Why? Why be a bitch? Why play these games?"

She sighs and looks at me over the top of her book. "Are you being negative?"

"I just don't agree with being bitchy. I don't think people have to be mean to get ahead."

"But you do, Mom. Look at us. We're nice, and we're nobodies."

"I'm not a nobody!"

Eva sighs again, a long, drawn-out sigh. "I thought we were going to go through this together."

I glance down at the page and see what's coming: more ridiculous stuff about bitch power. But what do I do? Tell Eva I don't care, I'm not interested? And if I shut her out, who will listen to her then? "Okay, let's keep reading."

Eva sits taller. "Your turn to read."

I want to roll my eyes, but I don't. Instead I start to read:

1. Be a bitch.
2. Don't be above sabotage.
3. Have a backup plan.
4. Sneaky is good.
5. Consolidate your power.
6. Execute revenge in secret.
7. Be clever.
8. Keep others off balance.
9. Stay sexy.

10. And most important, remember that being the girl that rules the school is the best. It's fun!

I stop reading and look at Eva, who has been listening closely. "Eva, you can't really like this, can you?"

She shrugs. "It sounds a lot like *Mean Girls*."

"And the mean girls in the movie *Mean Girls* were really horrible." I close the book and hand it back to her. "Why would you want to be horrible?"

"I don't want to be horrible."

"So why this book? Why all the notes? It's not teaching you anything you can use."

She's already shaking her head. "But it is. It's teaching me things I have to know."

"Like what? Black is slimming? Wear brooches and scarves to accessorize? Carry a designer purse and get a MySpace account?"

"But that's important," she answers. "I need to know everything. I need to know how women think."

"*Why?*"

"Well, how am I going to help you if I don't know how women think?"

"Help *me?*"

"Yes. Help *you*. Why else do you think I'm doing all this?"

"Wait. Wait, wait, wait." I scramble off the couch and pace up and down the floor before turning to face her. "All this stuff, all those notes in your notebook—"

"I knew you'd looked," she says under her breath.

I shake my head. "It's for *me?*"

"Why are you so surprised?"

"I thought you were the one who wanted to be popular, Eva. I thought this was for you. The slumber party. The cool purse. The lip gloss."

"If I have to be popular to make you friends, then I will."

"*What?*"

"Mom, face it. You're in trouble. You need help."

"I'm not in trouble."

Eva rolls her eyes and begins ticking off each finger. "You don't have any friends. You don't go on dates. You don't go to dinner. You never dress up. You don't even drive a nice car."

"My truck is beautiful!"

"It's not what popular moms drive."

"But popularity is for little girls, not mothers."

Eva's shaking her head hard. "I've read this book, Mom. Everything I thought, everything I suspected, is true. Being popular makes your life easier. When you're popular, you get invited places. When you're popular, people ask you out. When you're popular, you're never lonely."

"Well, that's a bunch of baloney! Popularity might mean you're invited to lots of parties and have boys who want to date you, but what if these so-called popular people aren't people you enjoy? What if their interests aren't your interests? What if being around people like that makes you feel lonelier?"

"That wouldn't happen."

I collapse into a chair facing the couch and lean forward, feeling utterly useless. "What makes you such an authority on everything, Eva? What makes you so sure you know everything—and don't mention the book. Don't use this book as a resource because it's wrong. It's hurtful. And it's unkind."

"Mom, you're taking this the wrong way. You have to be positive. You have to *think* positive. These tips might sound dumb to you, but they're to help you take charge—"

"I have taken charge."

"So why don't you ever go anywhere? Why don't you date? Why don't you have a boyfriend?"

"Because I don't want one!"

"Why? That's not normal. You're not being normal."

I'd pull my hair out, but then I'd look like Eva and we'd both hate that. "Eva, being single is a choice I made years ago. No one forced me to be single. No one is making me not date."

"But you don't even know any men. You couldn't even go out if you wanted to."

"That's so not true. I have had a date. I went out last month, the night you stayed at Grandma and Grandpa's." I see her jaw drop, and I take advantage of her stunned silence to plunge on. "He called me earlier this week. We even had lunch. We might go out this weekend."

"I don't believe you."

"It's true."

"What's his name?"

"Luke."

She wrinkles her nose. "You're making that up."

Does my daughter think I'm that weird? That I'd actually make a man up just to humor her? "His name is Luke Flynn, he's a Big Brother to a boy at your school, his parents are farmers, and he went to Harvard."

She folds her arms across her bony chest. "So call him."

"What?"

"Call him. Right now. I want to hear this for myself."

"Why is this so important to you? Why do I have to have a man?"

She looks at me perplexed. "Grandma has Grandpa. Shey has John. But you're not married. You don't have anyone."

Our conversation ends there.

Later that night, I think of all the things I should have said earlier. I should have told Eva that marriage isn't a tonic or panacea. I should have said getting married isn't like waving a magic wand. Problems don't go away. Sometimes problems are just beginning. But I'm not married, so why would she listen to me?

And then there's the fact that she's still just a child, as well as a devotee of *Modern Bride* and *Southern Living*, and in her mind, marriage resembles Cinderella's Castle at Disneyland. You go there and it's beautiful. Romantic. With fireworks exploding above the castle towers and spires every night.

What good would it do to burst her girlish bubbles and dreams? Just because I've chosen to go the single life doesn't mean I'd want her to.

In fact, I'm not even sure *I* want the single life anymore, but I'm not yet ready to really put my heart out there, either.

In the meantime, I tuck Eva in, kiss her good night, and head to my room. As I climb into bed, my thoughts turn from Eva to Luke, to my parents, and back to Eva again.

It makes sense that Eva worries about the future, especially with Mom sick and Dad caring for her. But I don't think this is just about me. It's about Eva, too. She's trying to see what would happen to her.

If I got sick, who would take care of her? If I died, where would she go? Questions she's smart enough, perceptive enough, to ask. Questions that must worry her when she lies in her bed in the dark.

But I don't want Eva worrying, as I know what it's like to lie sleepless in the dark, the mind racing, thinking, imagining.

I worry that if something happens to me or my company, we could lose our house.

I worry that maybe I am too different from other moms and that my way of thinking, doing things, will harm rather than help Eva.

I worry that if I couldn't care for Eva because of illness or death, she'd be completely uprooted—and yes, she could have a good life with Shey (her backup guardian), but Shey isn't me.

Maybe everyone worries about these things—death, illness, disaster—but when you're single, you can't complain that all the pressure and responsibilities fall on you. Of course they fall on you. That's what I wanted. To be in charge. To have control.

The funny thing is, I don't have that much control. I never did. I just didn't know it back then.

It's nearly eleven and I'm just about to fall asleep when the phone rings. My first thought is, Luke.

My second thought is, Don't let it be about Mom.

It's Tiana, actually, and she's just returned home from an industry awards dinner and she's in a chatty mood.

·"Have you read Nora Ephron's latest, *I Feel Bad About My Neck*?" she asks, not even bothering to check and see if maybe she woke me up.

"No," I mumble, flopping back into bed.

"It's brilliant," she continues blithely, "and you've got to read it today."

"Tits, it's after eleven," I answer grumpily, thinking that it's fine for Tiana to suggest I go buy something I have to read today when I'm forced to read Eva's *How to Be Popular* in secret every afternoon just so I can stay a chapter or two ahead of her. "Even Barnes and Noble is closed now. And my neck is fine. My neck looks great."

"That's because we're still in our mid-thirties. The turkey neck comes in the mid-forties." She pauses, takes a thoughtful breath. "Apparently forty-three is the magic age."

"Thanks."

Tits pauses again. "You okay?"

"I'm good. Just sleepy." It's eleven, Tiana. E-l-e-v-e-n.

"So what have you been reading lately?"

Tiana is the bookworm. All she ever wants for her birthday or Christmas is a gift card for more books. Rubbing my eyes, I try to clear my head. What is the last book I've read? "I've been reading about how to get popular."

Tiana snickers. "You want to be popular?"

"Shut up."

"You, the one voted most likely to burn down the school?" She laughs harder, before stifling her fit of giggles. "Okay, seriously, the point of me mentioning Nora's book is the chapter on parenting. Even though I don't have kids, I thought it really nailed the whole parenting craziness going on in the world, because even here in

La-La Land, parents have gone crazy. Parenting here is a profession. A calling. You wouldn't believe the articles in newspapers and magazines this year looking at this whole phenomenon of alpha moms and helicopter parents."

"What's an alpha mom?"

"An overachiever mom, a mom who takes charge of everything, including the kids' world, school, teachers, everything."

I think of Taylor Young. Alpha mom. "Ephron's book sounds good. I'll look for it." I yawn again. "So are you still coming this weekend?"

"You better believe it."

The next morning, Robert chuckles when I tell him I've got to spend my lunch hour at Points Elementary photocopying the school newsletter. "Now that's a wise use of your time and talent," he taunts me as I head out the door.

"It's not my choice. It's part of my volunteer job," I answer, grabbing my keys and wallet.

Chris glances up from his computer screen. "You know a man would never do that."

"I know." I flash a smile and wave good-bye.

Mrs. Dunlop, the school secretary, greets me as I walk into the school office. "Let me show you the way," she says, rising from behind her desk. As she leads me to the copy room, she whispers, "We saw Eva's hair. I know it was for a modeling shoot, but it's short, isn't it?"

I plaster a smile. "It was a surprise."

"You didn't know ahead of time?"

"No."

"It's just that she had such beautiful hair."

I just nod. What else can I say?

Another mom is already in the copy room, pushing buttons, keeping the massive copier running. When she looks up, I'm delighted that it's Kathleen, the woman from the cotton candy booth.

"You," Kathleen says with a smile of welcome.

"Yep. You're stuck with me again."

Mrs. Dunlop leaves us, and Kathleen explains the system. "We're copying four hundred and eighty of everything. I've already done the green cover sheets and the orange Halloween letter. All that's left is the lavender page, which is the library, chess club, and soup can info, and the cherry-colored page, which has the play info. Then we start laying it out all, stapling it together, and start counting them out for each class."

I survey the enormous stacks of paper towering everywhere. "We're to do that all in an hour?"

"Whatever we don't finish gets passed on to the next set of mothers."

It's tedious but easy work, and Kathleen and I talk as we finish copying and then start collating and stapling.

Kathleen lines up the next stack of handouts. "Thank you for coming in. This is a horrible job to do on your own."

"You volunteer a lot, then?" I ask.

"As much as I can. It helps pass the time."

"You have a son, right?"

She nods. "Our only one. It took us four years to make Michael, so when I discovered I was finally pregnant, I really wanted to stay home with him. And I have."

"What did you do?"

"Hard to believe now, but I was actually a vice president with a big accounting firm."

I pause and flex my fingers, which are getting numb from stapling so much. "Why is that so hard to believe?"

Kathleen shrugs tiredly and laughs. "Now the only thing I count is Scholastic book orders."

We start in on the next pile of copies. "Do you ever regret staying home?"

She shrugs. "I think there are always regrets, no matter what we do. But after seven and a half years of being home, I'm comfortable with being a full-time mom. Not that I don't sometimes envy the moms that have managed to keep their career. Working moms have it better."

"You think?"

"Working moms get recognition and perks that stay-at-home moms don't. Paychecks. Promotions. Expense accounts. Travel opportunities. Job reviews. All of those things validate the professional in the workforce. But for a mom who stays at home with her kids, who recognizes her? What are the rewards?"

"But your husband appreciates you, right?"

Kathleen's expression turns wry. "He's a man. You know what I mean?"

I like Kathleen. She, like many of the moms at Points Elementary, has the obligatory rock on her ring finger and shimmery foiled hair. I don't know what she drives, but I imagine it's a spotless luxury model, and these are the perks the stay-at-home mom gets: shiny hair, white teeth, big house, nice clothes, great skin, good body, new car.

It's a trade-off, of course. Working moms are harried, their cars frequently dirty, their voices a tad shrill, their skin a little more lined, but they do get paychecks and bonuses and travel perks. They get to escape the domestic mundane for goal-setting meetings and sales calls and consultations, whatever they might be.

One life isn't better than the other. They're just different. Each woman must decide what's right for her in life.

I couldn't not work. I had a taste of being trapped at home when I was on maternity leave after having Eva. After just two weeks, I started to go crazy. I had too much time on my hands. Too many hours in the day to fill. I hate watching TV. I didn't want to look at another magazine. And I missed thinking about something other than my baby, my leaking breasts, and my wild mood swings.

At work I suit up, pull back my hair, and I'm a brain, not just a body.

At work I have ideas that are good, valuable, influential.

At work you have to respect me.

For the stay-at-home moms, where is the respect? How many men really respect their wives? How many men understand the sacrifices their wives are making to keep the house clean, and raise the kids well, and make sure dinner's always on the table, warm and waiting?

A half hour later, we've finished stapling and counting the copies for each class, and Kathleen and I grab our coats and keys and head out.

"You do this every week?" I ask as I button my coat. Clouds have gathered overhead, and the sky is dark, threatening rain.

"I'm here almost every day." She grimaces. "Gives me something to do."

"You'd never consider working part-time?" I ask, bundling my arms across my chest. "It sounds like it could be good for you."

"It would"—she sighs—"but Michael needs me."

We part just as it begins to rain. It's a cold rain, too. Winter is on the way.

Reaching the house, I spot a huge, exotic floral arrangement at the door. After parking, I head to the front step and pick up the enormous glass vase teeming with flowers—it's heavy—and smell the opulent perfume of plumeria and tuberose.

I carry the deep purple vase into the house to open the card tied to the front of it.

After flicking on the kitchen lights, I open the envelope. The card looks like Albrecht Dürer's work, and it's a woodblock print of a huge brown chicken

I open the card and read, "Marta, scared yet? Luke Flynn."

My lips twitch. Extravagant flowers. An artsy linen card featuring a big brown chicken. And a taunting one-liner.

Interesting. Luke must like playing with fire.

Chapter Eighteen

I return to the studio without the card or flowers. Since it's Friday and the team works only a half day on Fridays, Allie and Chris have already left, and Robert is just shutting off his computer and cleaning off his desk.

"It's going to be a wet weekend," he says as I enter the studio, fat raindrops pinging against the studio's glass door.

I drop into my chair at my desk, still thinking about Luke and his card. "It's cold, too," I answer, thinking that I very much like the sexy tension that sizzles and crackles between Luke and me.

I like that Luke's bigger than me.

I like that he's not scared of me.

I like that my motorcycle doesn't have him running in the opposite direction.

I think I like him very much.

Robert grabs his leather satchel, shoves his laptop and paperwork into it, and, after throwing me a kiss, exits.

As leaves blow into the studio, I reach for the phone and the scrap of paper with Luke's number and give him a call.

He answers on the third ring. "Luke Flynn."

His voice sounds distant, and he seems distracted. "Luke, it's Marta."

"Marta, how are you?" The distance and detachment are gone. He sounds amused now.

The fact that I amuse him just makes me want him more. "Thank you for the flowers. Very thoughtful of you."

I can feel his smile across the line. "That's what I am. A very thoughtful man."

That fizzy rush returns, and I find it hard to breathe. "You like chicken, then," I say, my heart hammering so hard that I'm grateful my voice doesn't come out a squeak.

"Are you inviting me to dinner?"

The husky sexiness in his voice has me running mental circles. Go-go-go, and I don't even know where I'm going. The headless chicken racing around the poultry yard.

"I'm sure you already have plans for a Friday night," I answer, and this time there is a faint catch in my voice, my crazy rush of adrenaline more than I can handle.

"I don't. What time should I be there?"

I laugh and nervously tuck hair behind my ear. "You're not serious."

"I like chicken, Marta." His voice has dropped, and it practically caresses me, flooding me with yet another rush of desire. Hope.

Luke Flynn is making it very difficult for me to remember why I chose a life of celibacy.

"But I'm serving pizza or pasta, something easy like takeout."

"Even better. I'll bring a bottle of red."

"Luke."

"Yes, my chicken?"

I'm blushing furiously even as I cough. "That's horrible. Don't say that again."

"Would it sound better in French?"

"No. But if you want to come for dinner, be prepared for a boring girls night. Tonight it's just Eva and me hanging out, probably watching one of her teen angst movies."

"Can't wait."

"Sevenish?"

"Sevenish it is."

Hanging up, I go weak all over, flabbergasted at my ballsy move. Not only do I call Luke, but now he's coming for dinner.

To say Eva is excited about us having a male guest for dinner is like saying someone's anxious to get off the sinking *Titanic*. Once I told her the news, she hopped around the house, asking questions and then making rapid-fire decisions on her own.

What are we going to eat? What will you make? How about your lasagna? That's always good. Okay, lasagna.

If we're going to make lasagna, we have to go to the store right now. Need to buy cheese and all the other stuff. What stuff do we need? I'll start a list. Mom, tell me what we need.

And what will we have for dessert? What about that chocolate Kahlúa cake? Or the rum cake? Men like cake. And pie, too. I could make a cake or pie if you just show me how.

So what will you wear? I think it should be something pretty. Let's go look at your closet now. Maybe the red dress? Yes, the red dress with high heels.

That's when I put a stop to her plans. Lasagna will be fine. Cake is good. But no high heels and no red dresses. Yes, it's Friday night, but this is my house, not a brothel.

We leave for the store. Eva wants to go to Whole Foods, but I don't have time for such a megastore right now, so we hit the QFC close to our house, the one near the Chevron from the other fateful day.

I pick up the ingredients for lasagna and salad and garlic bread while Eva studies all the boxes of cake mix.

On our way home, she keeps tapping her foot. "How are we doing on time?" she demands, shifting restlessly on the bench seat.

"It's not even four yet," I tell her.

"Good." She nods firmly. "We've got a lot to do. *A lot.*"

I glance at my daughter with her dark pixie cut and her gamine features, which will one day become more mature, and reach over to pat her knee. "I love you, Eva. Even if you make me crazy."

She smiles back at me. "I love you, too, Mom. Even if you don't know what you're doing."

At home, I get to work making my famous homemade meat sauce (okay, famous in my own home, but that still counts for something), and Eva runs around straightening up the house. She vacuums while I put the noodles on to boil, and then while I start assembling the layers she pulls out the cake box, the mixer, eggs, and oil.

Eva and I have fun making the cake together. She loves baking and is the most serious measurer I've encountered yet, bending low to gaze eye level at the water and oil, scraping the bowl diligently, timing the beating to the exact second since it's science.

As I watch her divide the cake batter between the two pans, I smile, amazed, awed, proud. This is my little girl. This is my Eva, who gave me such a scare and put me on bed rest. My Eva, who insisted on walking early, talking early, who was so determined to grow up fast.

"Stop looking at me," she says gruffly, her cheeks darkening to a gorgeous red.

"I can't help it. I love looking at you. You're my girl." And I mean it in that deep, bone-aching way where I can't imagine myself without her, can't imagine how I'd get through a day if anything ever happened to her.

Do other mothers ever torture themselves this way? Do all mothers love their children so much that the love brings you to your knees?

She shakes her head, but she's smiling. "Do you still hate my hair?"

"I don't hate your hair. I think it's cute. It suits you. But do *you* hate your hair?"

She sets down the bowl, her fingers covered with chocolate cake mix, and licks one sticky finger. "No. I actually kind of like it. It's different." Her shoulders rise and fall. "I kind of like being different."

My heart catches, a funny little trip, and even though I never cry, my eyes burn and sting. "You do?"

"Yeah. Like you always say, why be like everybody else?"

With the lasagna and cake baking, I go to my room to shower and change into something a little fresher, and there on my bed Eva's laid out her favorite dress, the cherry red linen sheath with the halter neckline.

It's a dress I've worn just once in New York for a summer party at Shey's place, and Eva loved it so much that she talked about it for months after. She said I looked so beautiful, more beautiful than even Aunt Shey, and I looked not like a mom, but like a model from a magazine, and now it's the dress she wants me to wear.

I touch the linen fabric, see how it curves at the waist and shapes the breasts, and I feel such a pang for my daughter who craves a glamorous mother. But I never wanted to be that Betty Crocker–Martha Stewart perfect woman, never wanted to be whipping up recipes in the kitchen in my 1940s frock and pearls and heels.

Eva has what she has—a mom who truly loves her—and I won't feel guilty, I refuse to feel guilty, for being who I am.

Out of the shower, I blow my hair dry, smoothing it with a laminate-style polish, and go to my closet to find something else that might work for tonight, something not so cocktailish but still pretty, something that would please my fashion-conscious Eva, and I settle on a long dark brown suede skirt and a chocolate silk-and-cashmere-blend turtleneck. With my hair loose and brown boots, I think I look okay.

Eva knocks on my door before sticking her head inside my room. "You're not wearing my dress!" she protests.

"It's too summery," I answer, even as I gesture to the skirt and sweater. "But what do you think of this as a backup? It's a skirt, and it's dressy."

She studies me for a long moment before nodding and breaking into a smile. "No. It's good. Actually it's better than the red dress. You're right. You don't want to seem like you're trying too hard." With a blown kiss, she dances out again.

I turn to the mirror just in time to catch sight of my expression, and I look so startled, so confused, I burst out laughing.

Sometimes I don't know who is in charge here. Don't know who is raising whom.

The doorbell rings at seven-fifteen, and Eva rushes to the door before I can get there. "Hello," I hear her say in her most grown-up voice, "I am Eva Zinsser, please come in."

"Luke Flynn," I hear him answer. "Pleasure to meet you."

I come around the corner in time to watch Luke shake hands with Eva. Luke is so comfortable chatting with Eva that neither sees me there watching them.

Eva's cheeks glow dusky pink as she looks up at Luke. He's been here maybe two minutes and she's already smitten. I'm smitten, too. I knew I liked him, but it wasn't until I saw him making my daughter smile that I realized how much I like him.

How much I want him to fit in.

How much I want this to work.

My throat squeezes closed, and an intense pressure fills my chest. It all aches so much that I inadvertently make a sound. Luke hears, lifts his head, and looks at me.

The fire's still there in his blue eyes, but it's a fire I crave. "Hi," I say shyly, my voice strangely faint.

"Hi," he answers with a smile.

"He brought flowers and wine," Eva says, "and sparkling apple cider for me!"

My gaze still holds his. "That's very nice of you."

His grin deepens, fine lines etching at the corners of his eyes. My belly flips over. My knees knock. When am I going to sleep with this man?

Eva leads us into the kitchen, and while he opens the sparkling cider I rummage in a drawer for the corkscrew.

"Do you play any sports?" Luke asks Eva, filling a wineglass with sparkling cider for her.

"I did last year, and I might play basketball again," she answers. "But I decided against soccer this year."

"Why?"

"It wasn't my thing."

I take a vase from her and fill it with water, and as I do, Luke's eyes meet mine above Eva's head, and the look is so warm, so intimate, I nearly drop the vase with the flowers.

Wow, I think, walking on shaky legs into the living room to place the flowers on the coffee table. Wow.

Luke opens the wine, and I pull the lasagna from the oven and pop in the bread. The cake's already cooling, and the salad has been made but not dressed. Things, I think, are going a little too well.

But what's funny is that it continues like this all night. Eva and Luke act like old friends, and I'm comfortable, and laughing, and cracking up at Luke's jokes, even his very bad jokes.

And while I'd never admit this to anyone, it's really nice to see a gorgeous man in my house, sitting at my dining table. It makes the fizzy good feeling in me feel even more legit. I'm happy hanging out with my close friends, but I'd forgotten what the company of the right man can do. Forgotten that intensely female sensation, of being smooth and soft and real.

After dinner, I clear dishes and Eva runs to grab the game of Scrabble. She loves Scrabble, and maybe it's because she's scarily good. In the last year, Eva's begun giving me a run for my money, and I'm a savvy Scrabble player.

"What do you think?" I ask, turning around in the kitchen to find Luke there with the place mats and napkins from the table. "Scrabble okay or do you want to duck out now?"

"Why would I want to duck out now?" he asks.

"You might find us a tad overwhelming."

"You're not reading my mind very well."

"No?"

"Look at me and try again."

I have to force myself to look at him, to meet his fierce light blue eyes, and when I do, I flush but don't look away.

I can't.

There's so much life in his eyes, so much fire and intelligence and emotion. It's almost too much. He's strong and intense.

I take a short, quick breath, knowing I've sworn off men, sworn off all involvement, all hoping, wishing, dreaming, and yet with one look Luke's made me rethink my decision. With one look he's broken my heart wide open.

I'd vowed I would never do that romantic fall-in-love-and-be-disappointed thing again, yet as I stand, the kitchen counter against my back and a dish towel in my hand, I'm falling.

"Do I look bored?" he asks quietly.

I look into his eyes, and no, there is nothing bored there. Hungry, yes. Curious, yes. Bored, not at all. "No."

"So why would you want to send me away?"

I don't answer, as I feel as though I'm running, running from something so fierce, so frightening, and yet beautiful at the same time.

"Unless we're back to the whole chicken thing," he answers.

The corners of my mouth curl up. He smiles, too, creases fanning from his eyes.

I drop the dish towel on the counter. "All right, you want the truth? I am chicken. I should be chicken. You're everything I've avoided for the past ten years, and yet after two dates here you are, in my house, having dinner with Eva and me. She obviously already adores you . . . not that she'd be a hard sell at this point, while I'm—" I swallow, break off, try to find the right words, and I can't. I don't know how to make him understand how momentous this is for me, and how frightening. I'm so protective of Eva, so protective of our little world, and I'd rather be alone forever than have anything hurt her.

"You're what?" he prompts.

"I guess I'm still trying to understand just what is happening here."

He leans against the counter. "What do you think is happening?"

"Girl stuff. Boy stuff. The usual."

Luke laughs that husky laugh of his and leans back, triceps hardening beneath his shirt. "I'm thirty-eight. You're thirty-six. I'd hardly call this boy and girl stuff."

He's not being as reassuring as he could be.

Eva, in the meantime, has finished setting up the Scrabble game, and she shouts to us in the kitchen, "Are we playing or not?"

"I am," Luke calls back, giving me a rather pointed look.

Isn't he the confident one? I respond in an equally mature fashion. I stick out my tongue. "I'm playing, too," I answer, grabbing my wineglass and heading back to the table. "And watch out. Tonight I'm going to show you how the game is played."

I'm in for a surprise. Luke's a master of the game, jumping out far in front of us by his fourth turn. "You're cheating," I mutter when Eva disappears to use the bathroom.

"I'm not cheating." His eyes spark. "I'm just better than you are."

I lean on the table. "How's that for modesty?"

"It's not, and that's because false modesty is the worst sin of all."

"Says who?"

"I don't know." He shrugs. "I just made that up."

I laugh and I feel warm, and as we sit there smiling at each other, my heart does yet another sharp, painful free fall.

Eva returns, and we resume playing. We're still engrossed in the game an hour later when the doorbell rings. I get up to answer it, and it's not until I've opened the door that I remember Tiana was supposed to be up here this weekend but she's arrived early. I hadn't expected to see her until Saturday.

"Tits!" I cry, flinging my arms around her. "You're really here."

"I told you I was coming." She hugs me back before drawing away to peel off her coat and drop it on the antique painted chest in the hall. "I got lost—"

"You drove here?"

"No, I had a driver, but he was lost. Saw a lot of your neighborhood. Very nice. Very New England–ish. I can't believe all the big homes."

"Aunt T?" Eva says, coming around the corner and leaping into Tiana's arms. She hugs Tiana hard, grinning up at her delightedly. "You're here!"

Tiana kisses Eva's forehead. "That's exactly what your mom said. You're two of a kind." She pauses, touches Eva's shorn head. "Except for your hair. What did you do? Where did it go?"

"Oh. I cut it off." Eva makes a face, shrugs philosophically. "I was mad at Mom."

Tiana looks at me, and I make a face. What can I say? I have a drama queen for a daughter, and that's just the way it is around here right now.

Luke appears in the entry, and Tiana looks at him and then at me, and her dark arched eyebrows rise even higher.

I vow to kill her later. "Tiana," I say as nicely as I can, "this is my friend Luke Flynn. Luke, meet one of my best friends from high school, Tiana Tomlinson."

Tiana is barely five three, and Luke looks humongous next to her as he extends a hand. "Tiana Tomlinson the journalist?" he asks.

Tiana smiles broader, dimples deepening on either side of her mouth. "It's a pleasure," she says, shaking his hand, and she's just become Luke's fan. Few people call her a journalist, even though she's one of the brightest minds out there. Years ago, she covered the war in Afghanistan and was shot at, threatened, and even held hostage for a mind-numbing seventy-two hours before being released.

Now Tiana is the anchor for an evening newsmagazine that competes with Deborah Norville and *Inside Edition*, but she bristles when her program is dismissed as fluff. She's smart, she works hard, and she knows how to nail, and deliver, a story.

"Luke Flynn," she repeats, head tipped as she studies him, and I can tell she's intrigued by Luke. But why wouldn't she be? He's six feet seven, beautiful, built, and brilliant.

"I should go," Luke says. "You all seem to have some catching up to do."

"Pah," Tiana answers breezily. "Don't let me chase you out yet. We'll be up all night gossiping anyway."

"And we haven't had my cake," Eva chimes in. "And last time Grandma came, she didn't eat my cake, either."

I guess Luke's not going home anytime soon. "Let's have that cake, then," I say, and lead everyone back into the living room.

While Tiana and Eva sit on the couch, Luke takes one of the chairs opposite, and I go to the kitchen to make a pot of coffee and cut the cake.

I'm slicing the cake when I feel eyes on me. Looking up, I see Luke watching me, his expression so steady, so serious, that my hand grips the knife tighter, harder, as I try to keep my emotions in check.

I like him here. He looks good here. Even better, he feels right here, and I'm ready for this, ready for a man to be in our lives.

But what if I get attached and he doesn't?

What if my heart gets clobbered again?

Chapter Nineteen

Luke leaves after ten so I can attempt to put a rather hyper Eva to bed. While Tiana corrals Eva in Eva's room, I walk Luke to the door.

"Thank you for having me over," he says, reaching into his jeans pocket for keys. "I'm just sorry I had to embarrass you at Scrabble, what with it being your best game and all."

"And I was just about to tell you I'm glad you came."

"You're still glad."

"Not *as* glad."

"I'd call you a liar, but I want to be invited back." His eyes meet mine and hold.

I note the rather sly curve of his lips. "Oh, don't worry," I answer sweetly. "You're not coming back."

"Now I know you're a liar." Luke closes the distance between us and dips his head, briefly covering my mouth with his. Even though it's a fleeting kiss, it still sends sharp, needlelike tingles up and down my spine.

For the past ten years, I haven't missed this crazy adrenaline rush of desire. I haven't missed breathless, erotic sex. Haven't thought twice about passion. But that's changing with every Luke Flynn kiss.

By the time he lifts his head, I'm a quivery, sex-starved mess and he's got a mocking glint in his eye. "Good night, my chicken."

My heart's pounding. "Get lost, Luke."

Laughing softly, he leaves, and I close the door behind him, my knees knocking. For a minute I just stand there, trying to catch my breath. He makes me feel like the oil painting I bought in a SoHo gallery ten years ago, a big red-and-brick canvas with an even bigger pumping heart.

With Eva in bed and Luke gone, Tiana and I sprawl on the couch in our PJs, open another bottle of wine, and talk, talk, talk. I built a fire earlier, and it's crackling happily away now. As we sit and talk and laugh, I know there's nothing better than being with your very best friends, especially those friends who go way back to childhood, back before you even knew who you were.

"So Marta has a boyfriend," Tiana teases, elbow propped on a big smushy pillow.

I shove another pillow behind my back. "He's not my boyfriend."

"He likes you."

"I barely know him."

Tiana giggles, and her gold brown eyes twinkle at me over the rim of her wineglass. "So what's it like dating after a hundred years of solitude?"

"It was ten years, thank you very much, Gabriel García Márquez, and we've had maybe two dates."

"Two dates or two hundred, he's quite a catch."

"Because he's tall? And built?"

"And handsome as sin?" she adds, sipping her wine.

"That's all good, but I'm more impressed by his brain. The man's brilliant."

"How do you know?"

She rolls her eyes. "Oh, come on, Marta."

"Because he went to Harvard?"

"Because he's only one of the most successful, gorgeous, and eligible bachelors in the country."

"A gross exaggeration."

"You don't know who he is, do you?" Tiana grins at me and leans forward to say in a stage whisper, "I profiled him last February in our 'Hot Hunks and Dreamy Bachelors' show. Women are nuts about your Luke Flynn. They're always throwing themselves at him. Drives your honey crazy—"

"He's not my Luke Flynn, and he's not my honey."

"Because he's p-i-c-k-y. He doesn't want just anybody, he's waiting for the right body, and sweet pea, I think you're that body."

"Tiana, I swear to God, I will smother you with this pillow if you keep talking."

"Don't believe me? Google him."

"I'm not going to Google him." I take a huffy breath, not telling her I'd meant to but life got in the way.

She snorts with laughter. "You look so mad."

Every word she says just makes my skin go cold, and for some reason my heart starts to hurt, my chest growing tight and heavy. I press the pillow closer to my heart. "Why are you doing this?"

"Doing what? Telling you the truth? Telling you that you just spent two and a half hours playing Scrabble with one of America's most successful and gorgeous men?" She leans forward, smacks a kiss on my forehead. "My poor, dear darling. Your Luke Flynn is the founder, president, and CEO of BioMed, a company he started in his twenties and has taken international. He's . . . huge. Rich. Millions. Billions—"

"No." I jump up, get to my feet. I don't want to hear this. I don't want Luke to be this. "No."

"Why not?"

Tiana doesn't understand. She works with celebs and the rich and famous every day. She's used to the spotlight, has grown comfortable in the limelight. I just want a regular guy, as in a regular medieval warrior guy. Like Luke in his battered truck and with his long, steady gaze, the man in the school gym who stands too big and tall at the back.

That's the Luke I want. That's the Luke I need.

Not some rich guy. Not some Bellevue man.

"What?" Tiana asks, her laughter fading. Her glossy brown hair swings across her cheek. "What's wrong? Don't tell me you're really upset."

But I am. It was scary enough falling in lust with Luke, and that was when I thought he was just some ordinary Viking Highland warrior guy. But now that I know he's founder, president, and CEO of a billion-dollar international company and one of America's heartthrobs? Can't do that. Don't want any part of that.

I want low-key.

I want simple.

I want no boxes, no traps, no games, no pretense. The moment you're in a position of power, the moment you make serious money, you're surrounded by people who want something from you, who see your stuff and your bank account and what you represent rather than who and what you are.

People with serious money have a different playbook and rule book.

People with money think they can buy anyone and anything, and maybe they can't actually own you, but they try.

I know. Just look at my dad.

"Marta, he's nice." Tiana's voice is low and urgent. "He's a good person, and he clearly adores you. What is there to be afraid of?"

Everything.

Absolutely everything.

Exhaling, I sit back down on the couch and squeeze the pillow again. "Can we now talk about something else?" I gulp some wine and smile at her. "Like your interview with the First Lady?"

I drag myself out of bed, wrap myself in my white fleecy cotton robe, and head to the kitchen. It's a gloomy morning with a thick layer of fog concealing the red and yellow leaves of the Japanese maples outside the window.

Eva's up, tucked beneath a blanket on the couch. Tiana must be still sleeping in.

"Morning, baby," I greet Eva, bending over to kiss her on the lips.

"Uck, morning breath," she complains, making a face.

"Thanks, doll, love you, too," I answer, covering a yawn, and that morning breath she hates, before heading to the kitchen to start the coffee.

In the kitchen, I clean out the filter and grind fresh coffee. Dumping the ground beans into the clean coffee-maker, I spot the vase of flowers Luke sent me yesterday afternoon, and then I think of last night and dinner and then that kiss. My stomach does an immediate flip.

That kiss . . .

That kiss was so good.

Determinedly, I push the flowers back on the counter so the vase and fragrant scent are no longer directly in front of me.

"So how long is Aunt T going to sleep?" Eva asks, glancing up from her movie, which from this angle looks like *The Princess Diaries*, the one where she's got to get married or something bad happens to the kingdom.

"I don't know. As long as she wants. We have nowhere to go."

"How long is she staying?"

"I didn't ask. I was afraid she'd say she'd have to go."

Eva suddenly mutes the TV. "Mom, I have an idea, and don't say no until you hear me out. This is serious. I want to take Aunt T to school with me."

The coffee machine makes a snort behind me so I don't have to. "You're not going to take Tiana for show and tell," I say.

"Show and share," Eva corrects, rising to her bony knees. "And why not? Other kids do it. They take baseball players and ballerinas and stuff like that."

"I think that's called Career Day."

"They don't just do it for Career Day, they do it when they want to, and Mom, Aunt Tiana's famous. Even more famous than Aunt Shey. T's on the news every night. Everyone knows her."

"And this will help you how?"

"Help *us*," she corrects. "People will want to meet her and get her autograph, and to get her autograph, they'll have to talk to me."

I just look at Eva. She can't possibly be my daughter. She's either ridiculously smart or absolutely pathetic. I haven't figured out which. "You're going to use Tiana to make people like you."

"*Us.*"

"No."

"Mom, in the book—"

"*How to Be the Most Popular Girl in Your School?*"

She inclines her head, smiles. "You do what you have to do. It's a fact."

My Eva, the social climber.

"No," I repeat, and I grab my coffee and head through the back door for the studio, where I sit answering e-mail until Tiana walks in an hour later, still wearing her pajamas and carrying a cup of coffee.

"Eva said you live out here," she says with a smothered yawn.

I grab a chair for her and roll it toward my desk. "It's my office."

"How's business going?"

"Good." I roll back from my desk, face her. "By the way, congratulations again on your Emmy last year. I did send you flowers, didn't I?"

"And champagne. And Cheryl's Cookies. Balloons, too."

"I was happy for you."

"I could tell." Tiana blows on her coffee. Without makeup Tiana's freckles show and she looks like a little kid curled up in the office chair.

She looks up at me, dark bangs falling in her eyes. "Heard you walking around last night. Figured you needed some time to yourself, so I didn't come out."

"I would have loved your company," I answer, reaching behind me to click off the Internet and close up the screen. "I was making myself crazy. Thinking too much."

"About Luke?"

I make a face. "I Googled him."

"Didn't like what you saw, huh?"

"No." I rub my face, see his Web site in my mind's eye, the page with his bio and photo, the mission statement written and signed by Luke. "It was impressive. He's impressive. He's really into philanthropy. One of the biggest donors to disadvantaged youth programs in the Pacific Northwest."

"That's good."

Too good, I silently flash. He's too smart, too successful, too everything for me. I'm a rabble-rouser. I have a tiny tattoo on the back of my shoulder. I once had a pierced tongue (it grew in years ago).

I smile crookedly. That life in New York was so long ago. Before Eva. Before Mom's illness. Before anything big and significant.

"Eva asked me about visiting her class," Tiana says. "But I've got to fly out late tonight. We're shooting new segments first thing Monday morning, and I have a lot of reading to do, but I did tell her I'd send a stack of signed photos to her and she could pass them out. And the next time I have a break, I'll fly back up and we can do a party or school visit or whatever she wants then."

"That's very nice of you."

"Hey, anything to help the cause."

"Eva's popularity quest."

"Well, that and getting you married."

I choke on my coffee. "Who said anything about marriage?"

"Eva's pretty determined." Tiana glances at me from beneath her lashes. "She really likes Luke, too."

"I'm not getting married, and she definitely shouldn't be getting too attached to Luke."

"Why not?"

"Not interested in marriage, and definitely not interested in becoming one of these rich Bellevue wives. Now that I know Luke isn't just handsome Luke, but one of Bellevue's wealthiest executives . . ." My voice fades away.

Tiana leans forward. "You honestly feel different about him now?"

I nod. "I don't like all the money around here, don't like how people worship money—"

"And how do you know Luke does? He drives an old car. He wears Gap clothes. There's nothing flashy about him."

"I know, but still."

Tiana gives me a look of disgust. "You're so damn judgmental. You always have been."

"I'm no more judgmental than other women here. Everyone here is so perfect. So competitive. They talk about you if you wear different shoes."

"Ridiculous. This isn't junior high."

I shrug and mutter, "They don't like me, Tits. They don't want me involved or near their precious A team."

"Marta darling, has it ever crossed your mind that they're *afraid* of you? That you scare the shit out of them?"

"That's not why they don't like me—"

"No? You dress the way you want. You don't mince words. You've the longest legs, incredible hair, a great figure. You own your own company. And you ride a motorcycle. You scare women to death."

"This is how I've always been."

"But you're not just living in the 'burbs, babe, you've bought a home in Eastside's crown jewel. If you want Eva to have more friends, if *you* want to have more friends, you've got to be less rabble-rouser and more PTA."

"Become like them," I grouse.

Tiana doesn't answer, just sits.

Her smile makes me want to punch her. Lovingly. "*Tiana.*"

She just smiles wider, her grin illuminating her face and revealing the deep dimples on either side of her mouth.

I shake my head. "We shouldn't have to change to make other people feel more comfortable." And I mean this with all my heart. I've felt this way since I was just a kid, a little girl who couldn't sleep at night because I hated the system, a system that gave more freedom to boys, a system that taught boys to fight, to struggle, to succeed, and taught girls to make peace, compromise, and not make a scene.

"I shouldn't have to change me," I add insistently, "so others will like themselves better. That's wrong, not right." Because isn't this the very lesson I'm trying to teach Eva?

Don't change to please others. Don't become less you so others won't feel threatened.

"I'm not saying I like the system, Marta, I'm just reminding you that there *is* a system. And to make the system work, we've got to find ways to get along with other women so you—and Eva—don't get hurt."

"Because if I don't play the game, my daughter gets hurt." The bitterness in my voice is almost as sour as the taste in my mouth. This makes me furious. Absolutely furious. I grip my mug tighter to hide that my hands are trembling.

"Ta, you can't change the bitch factor."

"The bitch factor" was a phrase coined by Tiana and Shey years ago when we were in our early twenties, just starting our careers, and encountering firsthand how catty even "professional" women could be. Even though none of us were sheltered, we were all surprised by the aggression—both direct and indirect—we experienced in the workplace. Women weren't half as supportive of other women as we expected. There weren't the mentors we'd hoped to find. There wasn't a support system. I honestly think Shey, Tiana, and I have succeeded because we have one another. We're one another's biggest fans.

Tiana shrugs. "The bitch factor might not be PC, but it's real. The brighter you are, the harder you've got to work to make others comfortable. The prettier you are, the more you have to put others at ease. The more successful you are, the less attention you can afford to draw to yourself."

"And this is what I'm to teach Eva?"

"That's your call, but what you can do is help her

navigate the system. Make it easier for her. And you can, because you understand what's going on. You get the game, even if she doesn't."

God, I'm pissed off. Pissed off that men don't have to play these damn games, that it's perfectly okay for them to be assertive, that they're expected to succeed, and fight hard, and reach for that top, brass ring.

Men can and do scramble up the totem pole of success faster—and it's not because they have more upper-body strength. It's because they don't have to expend this ridiculous mental and emotional energy trying to make sure all the other men are okay with their agenda.

A man doesn't have to comfort the other guys who haven't climbed as high or as fast.

He doesn't have to pretend that he got to where he wanted to go by luck or accident.

He doesn't have to push the attention away from himself, insisting his good fortune is really everyone else's.

"You're getting all worked up." Tiana smiles at me.

I smile weakly because she's right. But I can't help it. One hundred years ago, Virginia Woolf wrote that women need a room of their own. But Virginia's wrong. Women don't need a room of their own. What they need to do is get out of the goddamn building.

Tiana leaves later that night, and after Eva and I drop her at the airport, I know we working women have paid a price for our success.

Shey's and Tiana's work might appear glamorous to the outside world, but they both work long, long hours, and they're constantly giving up sleep, passing on evenings out, pushing back vacations. Lots of women could be as successful as Shey and Tiana, but I don't think most would be willing to make the sacrifices they've made.

On the way home from the airport, I stop at the grocery store, and while Eva pushes the cart, I grab the groceries—milk, eggs, bread, yogurt, Fuji apples, bananas, grapes, chicken breasts, broccoli. You'd think at nine o'clock on a Saturday night we'd be the only ones shopping, but there are at least a few dozen people pushing carts up and down the aisles.

Thank God I'm not the only one without a torrid social life.

We're just heading to the checkout stand when I spot Taylor pushing her cart in the opposite direction. She doesn't see us, and her head is bent as she studies her list. Her hair's swept back in a teased ponytail, and she's wearing a black Juicy Couture sweat ensemble and black slip-on Pumas with white topstitching.

She's frowning at her list, her perfectly plucked eyebrows pulled in concentration, and for the first time I notice how really tired she looks. But not just tired, she looks emaciated, even old.

I know she's not old—in fact, Eva told me she's several years younger than me—but between the fluorescent lighting and the black tracksuit, she looks sallow, leathery, and worn.

Maybe she's had a bad day.

Or maybe she and her lovely husband (I hear way too much about him for my taste) had a fight.

Maybe she just got sad news from a friend.

Whatever it is, I feel almost sorry for her. She's too thin and tries too hard, and I wonder if all that trying really makes a difference.

We get our groceries checked out and bagged and out to the truck without Eva spotting Taylor. But on the way home, I keep thinking about her and how much work it is to be Taylor Young.

Taylor, like other Bellevue moms, is busy all week and then absolutely frantic on weekends with sports, games, and endless activities. I know during school holidays they all travel to magazine-perfect destinations, but their vacations are expensive and time-consuming, and they usually come home more exhausted than when they left.

Nothing in me wants that life or the pressure these women must feel.

Must be thin.

Must be tan.

Must have smooth forehead and unlined skin.

Must have great house.

Must have great kids.

Must have successful husband.

Must, must, must.

Oh yes, and must take that daily antidepressant pill.

Sunday morning, we go to the Points Country Club to meet my parents for brunch, something we've been trying to do once a month while we can.

I'm not a country club kind of girl, but along with the usual golf club offerings, the country club itself has festive brunches during the holidays, twice-a-year bingo nights for families, and the swimming pool in the summer.

Eva and I get to the country club early. The dining room is practically deserted, and we're seated at one of the prime tables in the bay window alcoves that overlook the golf course. The hostess gives Eva a cup of crayons and pages from a coloring book to keep her busy until my parents arrive.

After the waitress takes our drinks order, I glance around the dining room and realize with a little jolt that the family seated just two tables away is Bill and Melinda Gates and their three children. Bill's reading at the table and Melinda's chatting with the kids.

One table to the right of the Gateses is the Young family, another family of five. Last night at the grocery store Taylor looked tired and too thin but this morning her makeup is flawless, her hair is glossy and straight, the honey highlights catching the light, and she's smiling at something Nathan has said to one of the girls. Nathan's wearing a salmon-colored Polo that would be wimpy on someone else, but his bronze tan, sun-streaked hair, muscular frame, and square jaw somehow make it okay.

I covertly study the family, both intrigued and repelled. Taylor and Nathan together are striking, and their three little girls are all quite pretty. Almost too pretty. And I think they know it. The whole family has the glossy polish of a *Town & Country* magazine ad, something that only happens with a lot of hard work.

"There's Jemma," Eva whispers, darting a nervous glance at the Youngs.

"I know, but just keep coloring," I tell her. "Pretend you don't see them."

My parents arrive just then, and it takes me all of five

seconds to realize I've forgotten something very important. I failed to warn Mom and Dad about Eva's hair.

"What in God's name has happened?" my father booms. His voice has such an impressive range, perfect for getting the attention of young grunts and humiliating sensitive granddaughters.

Eva stops coloring, startled.

"Dad," I say.

He doesn't hear. "You look like a refugee," he barks.

My mom is peering at Eva with some bewilderment. "Who is this?"

If we were taping a TV sitcom, this is when they'd play the laugh track. "Mom, it's Eva."

"But this is a boy."

Mom is beginning to remind me of Edith from *All in the Family*, my father's favorite show when I was growing up.

"Eva, your granddaughter," I repeat.

"*Who?*"

I feel Eva stiffen next to me, as it sinks in that my parents are going to make a scene. Of course they're going to make a scene. Isn't this how they raised me? "Mom, Eva, my daughter, your granddaughter."

"But Eva has long hair, and this boy doesn't."

And that's about all Eva can take. Letting out a devastated huff, she whirls around and runs off, out of the dining room and probably toward the country club's front doors.

My mother makes a peculiar little sound and lifts her hand to her throat (very Edith-like, if I do say so myself). "What's wrong? Why did he run away?"

"It's not a he, Mom. That was Eva."

"Eva's a boy?"

"No, Mom, but you said Eva looked like a boy."

"Eva doesn't look like a boy. That boy looks like a boy."

"That boy and Eva are one and the same."

My mother lets out a horrified cry. "So Eva is a boy!"

It just keeps getting better.

I'm of two minds right now. I could just go outside, get Eva, and go home. It'd be easy and fast, and we'd be free of any more unfortunate scenes and uncomfortable conversations, especially with Taylor and family sitting only a couple tables away.

But Mom's not going to get better. Mom's only going to get worse. And that's why we're here, having family time. Eva and I moved to Seattle so we could be part of this journey, or whatever you want to call what's happening to Mom.

I try again. "Eva was upset this week, and she cut her hair off," I say, hoping a simple explanation will eliminate any more confusion. "I took her to a hairdresser to get it shaped up, but it's going to take some time to grow. Eva's sorry she cut it, but there's nothing we can do now but be supportive and patient and let it grow."

Sadly, my dad isn't strong in the empathy suit and isn't making this process any easier. "But why would she cut her hair off? What's the matter with her?"

"Nothing's the *matter* with her. She just wanted a change."

"Well, it's not flattering at all. She looks like a mouse."

"Not like a mouse," my mother corrects. "More like an orphan."

"Yes," my dad agrees. "A refugee."

"Or like Little Orphan Annie," Mom adds, now smiling tenderly at me. "Remember when we saw *Little Orphan Annie* at the Fifth Avenue theater, Marta? It was one of the first musicals I took you to."

"I do remember." I hated it. All those little orphans singing, and Annie with her disgustingly red, curly hair. It gave me the creeps.

My dad suddenly takes my arm. "Is that Bill Gates and Melinda?" he asks in a whisper.

"Yes."

Dad's shoulders straighten, and he looks like a retired officer. "Why didn't you tell me they were here? We should be sitting, enjoying our meal, allowing them to finish their breakfast in peace.

"Sit, Marilyn," he says to my mother, pulling out a chair for her and holding it while she sits down. "Now go get Eva," he tells me, "and let's act like a family that has some manners."

I go outside to cajole Eva into returning. It's a chilly morning, the air damp and cold, and even though Eva's shivering, she doesn't want to come back in.

"I knew I looked ugly," she says glumly, seated on the cement planter by the front door, picking at the purple and green cabbage foliage around tiny purple pansies.

"You don't look ugly. You look different."

"Huh. Same thing."

I smile down at her and riffle her hair, the dark ends wispy. My little gamine. Like a young Audrey Hepburn before Audrey Hepburn was pretty. I smile a bit more. "Come inside and eat. I need you there. Your grandma is going to drive me crazy."

The mention of her grandmother reminds her of her humiliation. "Grandma thought I was a boy," she says bleakly.

"Grandma's losing her marbles."

"What does that mean?"

"It means Grandma has dementia, and little by little she's losing her mind."

Now Eva glares at me reproachfully. "That's not nice. Grandma can't help it. It's the disease."

"I know. But losing your mind isn't nice, so we're just going to love her anyway."

We return to the dining room, and Mom and Dad are suddenly absolutely delightful company, and I know—because my dad keeps sneaking glances Bill's way—it's because we're trying to impress the Gateses. Not that the Gateses even know we're there.

Chapter Twenty

Monday morning, it's back to work in the studio. Robert's taken the week off. It's his anniversary, and he and his partner have gone to Costa Rica.

I wish I were going to Costa Rica. What I actually wish is that I'd hear from Freedom Bikes. It's been a couple of weeks, and we should hear something soon, even if it's just a request to schedule another meeting, give me a budget, and ask for a more detailed proposal.

Tuesday, I present a proposal to Trident Conglomerate. I'm not really thrilled about the proposal because I don't want to get their account. Trident's a huge company undergoing tremendous change, which also means tremendous stress. Executives are being laid off quarterly, which is why we've been approached about handling their advertising. The last director of sales and marketing was just given the boot, along with the ad agency, and now they've got a new (panicked) director who is good at sales but doesn't have a clue about advertising.

Tuesday evening, I get a call from Luke but don't have time to call him back, as Mom's disappeared. I hear the panic in Dad's voice, and Eva and I throw on coats and rush to Laurelhurst to help look for her.

By the time we get to Laurelhurst, Mom's home. A neighbor three blocks over found her in his driveway and thanks to Mom's MedicAlert bracelet was able to escort Mom back to her house.

Eva takes Grandma upstairs while Dad and I confer in his study. Dad is absolutely sick. He sits ashen in a leather chair in his study, his head in his hands.

"I only went out to get the newspaper," he keeps repeating. "I was gone just a minute. How did she slip out? Why didn't I see her?"

"It was dark, Dad—"

"But she didn't say a word. She just left."

"That's part of the disease."

"I've already put locks on all the doors. I already watch her like a hawk. What else can I do?"

"I don't know."

He lifts his head and looks at me, eyes hollow. "It scares me, Marta, scares me half to death. It's dark out, she's not wearing a coat. She could have been hit by a car, attacked, raped—"

"But she wasn't, Dad. She's here now. She's safe."

"If something happened to her, I couldn't live with myself. I couldn't. She's a fine woman, your mother. A fine woman." His voice deepens, breaks. "You don't get much better."

I've always known my dad loved my mom in his way, but until now I had no idea how attached he was. When I was growing up, my parents weren't particularly lovey-dovey, but I always had the sense that they liked each other, enjoyed each other, even if they didn't make a lot of jokes or even laugh all that much. Maybe it was the way my dad's mouth turned up or the way my mom's eyebrows lifted, but when one talked, the other listened.

"Dad, everything's going to be fine."

"But it's not. I'm losing her, every day, bit by bit. And I have to watch."

A cold knot settles in my stomach. "Maybe it's time you got more help. You can't do this on your own anymore."

"I have help."

"The housekeeper is here to clean the house, not take care of Mom, and Mom's going to need more and more care soon. She can't be left alone."

"But what I want to know is where is she going? What is she doing? The specialists say she's looking for someone, but what . . . where?"

I clasp my hands together, feeling terribly useless. "I don't know, Dad. I don't know if we'll ever know."

I eventually leave and get Eva to bed, and I know I should go to the studio and work—I have dozens of e-mails to be returned—but I can't make myself do it. I'm tired, and like Dad, I'm scared. I don't want to see Mom in a hospital. I know they eventually have to "lock up" their Alzheimer's patients, but Dad's right. Mom could have been badly hurt tonight.

Thinking about Mom's future, thinking about what's happening to her—to all of us—I put my head down on my arms and cry.

I don't cry. But I can't seem to help it tonight.

I miss my mom, and the mom I knew isn't coming back.

* * *

The next day is Wednesday, a day I haven't been looking forward to, as it's the first auction class project meeting. As first assistant head room mom, I'm apparently the fourth-grade co-chair for the class project. Not quite sure how that distinction was made, but here I am at Tully's on Points Drive at ten-thirty in the morning, waiting for the rest of the moms to arrive.

I hate all these meetings. There are way too many meetings. Haven't these women heard of e-mail or voice mail?

While I wait, I can't help studying a cluster of women at another table.

They're all very well groomed and certainly polished, but they don't look quite normal. No one in the group looks quite like what a woman in her late fifties, sixties, or seventies should look like.

I'm reminded of those funny picture books made for kids, the ones where you can flip different heads and torsos with different feet and legs. These lovely, sophisticated women seem to have stepped from that book. Faces don't match bodies, and bodies don't match wardrobe. Skin is too taut in some places and droops too much in others. Some women with softening jaws and softening eyes are toned and taut. Other women with small shoulders and widening waists have the smooth, shiny complexion of a twenty-year-old. How is this possible?

It's plastic surgery, and I know it's plastic surgery, but something in me rebels. My stomach knots.

There's nothing wrong with plastic surgery, yet when I look at these women, all "seniors," it's obvious that they work very hard at taking care of themselves. It almost seems indecent the amount of work involved. Such devotion, such dedication, such personal sacrifice.

Aging gracefully—surely an oxymoron if ever there was one—is wonderful, but this is beyond graceful. It's *Star Wars* meets *The Swan*. Weird. Sad. Unnerving.

Finally, the other moms start to arrive, and our one table becomes two tables and then finally three as more tables are dragged over to accommodate all the binders and planners and calendars.

I don't want to say it was a waste of time being there, but I've nothing to contribute. I'm not even sure I understand the point of yet another school fund-raiser. How much money does the school really need? And how much time is this auction going to take?

But this time, wisely, I voice no opposition and sit there instead, taking notes and nodding my head, trying desperately to fit in and be a good Bellevue mom.

It's not until a half hour later when my phone vibrates in my purse that I actually come to life. Checking the phone, I recognize Frank Deavers's number and my insides jump.

I've been waiting for this call.

Motioning to the others that I've got to take the call, I start walking toward Tully's glass doors even as I answer. "Frank," I say. "How are you?"

"Good. And you?"

"Great."

"Is this a good time to talk?"

I push open the doors and step outside. It's a gray day, overcast, with the big trees lining Points Drive pale and nearly leafless. "Yes. I'm glad you called."

I wait for him to make the standard preliminary

chitchat we always have before we launch into business, but this afternoon Frank's abrupt and right to the point.

"We didn't go with you." His rough voice sounds almost like a bark on the phone line.

For a moment, I think I'm going to drop the phone. I go cold and numb. My heart plummets. "No?"

"No. And I called as soon as I found out. I didn't want to leave you hanging, and I didn't want you to hear it through a third party."

I'm quiet and shaking inwardly. I should have expected this—who doesn't prepare for failure?—but I didn't. I hadn't. I never attempt anything that doesn't have a chance of succeeding. I never doubt my ability to succeed. It doesn't make sense to think anything but positively.

"You had some good ideas, great ideas, but the general consensus was that Z Design doesn't have the resources to get Freedom Bikes where we need to go."

I'm still silent. I'm holding my breath, trying to take it all in. I've thought of nothing but Freedom for weeks. I've worked, eaten, slept, dreamed this deal. I wanted this deal.

"It wasn't personal," Frank adds even more gruffly.

I suppose I'm silent because I'm afraid I'll blurt out something stupid, somehow make things worse. I'm silent because a little part of me hopes that this isn't happening, that it can't be true.

"If anything, Marta, we respect you tremendously and admire the passion and vision you brought to the meeting."

"I'm sensing a strong 'but' here," I finally say, finding my voice and gratified it sounds almost normal.

"As I said, you have some fantastic ideas, and obvious

energy, but the overall feeling was that you're pulled pretty thin and we need someone who can give Freedom their all."

"I can. We can."

"Marta . . ." Frank's deep sigh is audible, and I can almost picture him rubbing his salt-and-pepper-speckled beard. "You're a single mom."

"I am."

"Most of us are married. Most of us have kids."

"Uh-huh."

"We know what it's like to juggle work and home." He pauses, and the silence lengthens. "Marta, I don't know how to put this."

"Frank, just say it. Get to the point."

"Leaving the meeting early hurt you. I know it had to be important for you to walk out in the middle of the presentation, but for the management members riding the fence, it cast the deciding vote."

This is not what I want to hear. I want to have a family and a career. I don't want to have to make a choice between them. Men aren't forced to make these choices. "I didn't leave in the middle. I left near the end."

"Regardless—"

"You said, and Chris said, that the rest of the presentation went well," I protest, clamping my elbow to my side. I'm trying to keep my teeth from chattering, as I'm shivering from cold and shock. Glancing into Tully's, I can see my coat hanging on the back of my chair.

"It did. But Chris isn't Z Design. Chris isn't a bike enthusiast. Chris isn't *you*."

"And you have me."

"Then you should have stayed till the end."

"Despite Eva throwing up like Linda Blair?"

"Kids throw up. It's what they do."

And he doesn't say this next part, but I sense it, hearing the unspoken: *Daddies don't race home from the office just because Timmy has the stomach flu.*

I shake my head, my teeth gritted. My throat feels raw from swallowing so hard.

This is ridiculous. This is so unfair.

"Marta."

I can only shake my head silently. I don't trust myself to speak. I'm too hurt, too disappointed.

Frank sighs tiredly. He doesn't like playing the bad guy. It doesn't help that we've known each other for years. "It would have been better if you'd had someone else pick her up from school," he says flatly. "It would have looked better, Marta. Would have solved a lot of problems."

I don't think he's reprimanding me, but I do know he's disappointed, maybe even feeling let down.

"I had high hopes," he adds. "I'm just sorry it didn't work out."

"It's fine, Frank," I say, eager to just get off the line.

But after I hang up, I know it's not fine.

It's not fine because men aren't penalized for working and being a father.

It's not fine to have a man criticize me for going to pick up my child when she's ill.

It's not fine to assume that just because one day I drop a ball, I can't juggle my commitments.

It's time corporate America realized that working moms offer our companies the same thing we offer our families:

ethics, integrity, and loyalty. Just because we love our children doesn't mean we don't love our jobs.

Still shivering, I go back to the class auction project meeting, sink into my chair, and wrap my coat around me, but I sit catatonic for the rest of the meeting.

I wouldn't say I'm shattered. But I'm certainly not all here.

The next day is hard. I'm working the same long hours, but now the time seems to crawl by, and before it's even lunch I'm aching to cut loose, leave the office, and do something else.

I think about calling Luke back. It's been two days since he left me a voice message, and while I want to call him, I'm not sure what I'd say now. He's not who or what I thought he was. He's far wealthier, far more powerful, and I don't know that he'd even understand just how bad I'm feeling right now about losing the Freedom Bikes account. With his company and success, could he relate to my disappointment?

I don't call him. And I finish the week at work knowing that everyone's walking on tippy-toes.

By the time Friday afternoon rolls around, I'm just glad it's Friday, although everyone's staying late today to cope with four deadlines that have all hit at once.

Eva, not knowing that my bad mood has infected the rest of the team, trips happily through the studio door. "Hey, Mom," she sings as the door bangs open. "Look what I have!"

Chris, who's on the phone, looks up irritably and hushes her even more irritably. Allie sighs, rubs her temple. Even Susan frowns at yet another interruption.

Poor Eva, I think, shutting the door quietly and drawing her toward my desk. It's got to be tough enough having a mom who works from home without being made to feel as if you're a nuisance in your own home. "What do you have?" I whisper.

"What's wrong with everybody?" she whispers back, rummaging through her backpack. "It's like somebody died or something."

"It's just work." I smooth the wispy brown black hair from her pale oval forehead. "Everyone's really stressed."

"Why?"

"It's the end of the month, and it means everything's got to wrap up or roll over."

"Crunch time," she says wisely.

"Exactly." A better answer, I think, than explaining to her that I laid out a fortune to land Freedom Bikes and we still didn't get it, which means we're in the hole, and people will be mad if there aren't holiday bonuses.

Eva finds what she is looking for, retrieving a small square orange envelope from the front pocket of her backpack.

"An invitation," she says triumphantly, opening the envelope and pulling out the card, which is black and white with dancing skeletons on the border. "Phoebe's having a Halloween party on Halloween before everyone goes trick-or-treating!"

The invite's cute. I admire the font and print style. It's been professionally done, and I like the card stock. "See, you have friends."

"Well, she invited the whole class, but still." She flops into Robert's chair and sits Indian style. "She lives in Clyde Hill on this big acre and a half, and kids were saying there are ponies and a tractor pull and lots of games. Phoebe's family has a Halloween party every year, and everyone dresses up."

"Sounds fun."

"Can we go buy my costume tonight? Halloween is just five days away."

The phone on my desk rings. I glance at the number. Jet City Coffee. I don't pick up. I need to finish running some numbers before I can call them back. And before I can run their numbers, I've got to upload the winery's holiday calendar to the printer and double-check the PowerPoint presentation for Ewes and Lambs Maternity Clothing Store. They're a regional upscale clothing chain about to take their stores, and brand, national. It'd be a great account, and I could use Shey and her models, which would be fun for me.

"So can we get my costume tonight?" Eva repeats.

Frowning, I look at her and run my hand over her head. "Baby, I'm so behind. I'm going to have to work tonight."

"Again?"

"Unfortunately."

"But why? Why are you working so much at night?"

I think back on the week, on the parent meeting at school and the case of the blues with not getting the Freedom Bike Group. "I'm working as hard as I can."

"But all you do is work."

"That's not true."

She clamps her jaw. She's furious with me. "Fine," she says smartly. "Whatever." And she marches into the house.

The next morning, I'm back at my desk the moment I wake. It's Saturday, and hopefully Eva will sleep in so I can get a jump on the work still piled high on my desk. But Eva doesn't sleep in. She's at my desk in less than a half hour, a gloom-and-doom expression on her face.

"There's no milk," she says tersely. "And no bread. No frozen waffles, French toast, or microwave bacon left. There's nothing to eat, Mom."

"How about eggs?"

"They're old."

I lean away from my computer, sigh, rub at my neck and then my nape. "Can you eat cereal dry?"

"No!" she explodes. "No, I can't. And I'd go to the store myself if I could drive, but I can't. I'm nine. I'm your kid. I'm a child."

Oh. Right. Right. I know that.

I push hair behind my ears, struggle to smile. "You want me to go to the store?"

"Yes. Please."

"Now?"

"Right now."

I nod. I expected that. I knew it was coming. "Do you want to come? Keep me company?"

She's still angry with me, angry that I'm working too much and not spending enough time with her. Angry that she's an only child living with a single mother. "No," she answers bluntly.

I should have expected that, too. I reach for my sweater, tug it on. "I'll be back soon."

I race around the aisles of QFC, trying not to feel guilty that we have no groceries and that I've left Eva home. Eva, being nine, has already taken a junior baby-sitting class at

Overlake, where they taught her basic CPR and infant and child care tips, but I'm never quite comfortable with her home alone, even if she is.

I shop quickly, grabbing bagels and bread, frozen waffles and French toast, fruit, milk, yogurt, eggs, butter, cereal, coffee, and just for good measure, I go back for a box of doughnuts.

It's while I'm deliberating on the kind of doughnut— miniature chocolate-covered or miniature powdered sugar—that I sense someone behind me. Turning, I see Luke examining loaves of bread.

He sees me about the same time I see him, and he straightens, broad shoulders just getting wider, bigger.

His head's taller than the top shelf, and he dwarfs the bakery section, making the aisle even narrower.

He's wearing a navy cotton shirt, long sleeved and clean, and faded jeans that just barely outline the hard quads and hamstrings beneath.

How can this man be a CEO with millions (billions?) in the bank? It's impossible.

"Hi," I say, my voice less than steady.

His expression is somewhat quizzical, definitely reserved. "You're bad at returning phone calls."

"I'm sorry," I apologize. "I, uh, wanted to call. I meant to call—" I break off, shake my head. "It's been a bad week."

"You could have called and talked to me about it."

There's a definite rebuke in his voice, and I flush. I really, really like him, yet I'm also mad at him.

I'm mad that I didn't know he was Luke Flynn of BioMed.

I'm mad that he's not just a medieval foot soldier, but the powerful lord.

I'm mad because I don't want him to be more successful, more wealthy, more anything than me. It makes things harder, more complicated. I liked it when I thought the power was equal, that we were equals. Now I'm scared again. Scared and vulnerable, the two emotions I never want to feel.

"I didn't know you were the founder of BioMed," I blurt out, my face still blazing hot.

"Tiana told you," he guessed, his expression even more shuttered than before.

I nod.

"She interviewed me for a piece last February," he adds.

I nod again, emotion running hot and cold inside me. I'm scared. Scared to care so much, scared to want so much, scared to think he's got it all together while I'm still just trying to figure life out.

"And that's why you didn't call," he continues.

I manage the briefest of nods.

For a moment, we stand utterly silent in the middle of the bakery section, in front of the freshly baked breads and glass case of doughnuts, Danishes, and breakfast rolls, and I'm sad, really sad, because I know I've hurt Luke, and I didn't mean to hurt him. It's just that I'm so confused.

I need to say something, apologize. My hands flex around the cart's handle as I struggle to find the right words. But Luke doesn't seem to have the time or patience.

"I've got to get going," he says with a cordial nod. "You have a good weekend."

My tentative smile freezes. I feel that terrifying cold *swoosh* of disappointment. I don't want him to just leave, not like this, not without him understanding.

"Luke," I say, and he stops, turns to look at me.

"Do you ever have one of those weeks where everything goes wrong?" I say to him. "Where you lose a huge account and your daughter's furious with you and your mom gets lost because she keeps forgetting who she is and where she lives?"

Luke just keeps looking at me.

I'm feeling so scared and nervous, but I hate being afraid, so I take a deep breath and press on. "I really did want to call you. I thought every day about calling you, but my life is so messy, and I'm still trying to carve out a niche for myself in business, and you're . . . you're . . . you."

"Me," he repeats, stepping back toward me.

"Yes."

His forehead furrows, and he looks at me long and hard, the blue gaze narrowed. "You know what I liked about you, Marta? You were sexy and smart and funny, and you didn't care about who I was or what I had. You liked me for me."

"And I still do," I whisper.

"No, you don't. Not if you can't call me when you're having a bad week because you're afraid I won't care because I'm Luke Flynn, founder of BioMed."

My face burns. My insides feel icy. A huge lump is filling my throat, pressing down into my chest. He's mad at me. He doesn't understand. This whole dating thing is so new and it's scary, but I'm trying, I'm really trying. Six months ago, I wouldn't have even considered a date, much less opening my life for a relationship, but I want to change my life, I want to change me, though it doesn't happen instantly. I don't change that fast.

"It was a really bad week," I repeat, mortified that my eyes are burning and tears aren't far off. I haven't cried in front of a man since I was a teenager. Please, God, don't let me cry now. "My mom has Alzheimer's, which is why we moved back here, and Eva hates me right now because we don't have milk and she doesn't have a Halloween costume yet. My staff wants to mutiny over this lost account, and they blame me because I did leave a presentation early, but Eva was sick and I'm a mom first and will always be a mom first now—"

I break off as Luke closes the distance and wraps his arms around me.

My chest heaves, and I squeeze my eyes shut as the tears are so close.

I feel lost.

Really lost.

Luke's hand rubs my back. "Everyone has bad weeks."

I'm ashamed I'm near tears, yet his arms feel so good and he feels so warm and so strong, and for the first time in days I don't feel as if I'm going to snap in two.

"I'm sorry," I say against his chest. "I'm sorry for not calling. I really did want to call you. I wanted to hear your voice. It would have been so nice."

"Okay," he says.

"It's not okay. Forgive me."

"I have." And he releases me.

I step back and look up into his face. "Really?"

He smiles, and he has such a gorgeous smile. His teeth are straight and white, and they make his blue green eyes deeper. "Really."

I smile back, and as I smile I feel a burst of fizz inside

me, as though I were a can of carbonated soda, and my sadness lifts and dissipates like our morning coastal fog.

"So you'd go out with me again?" I venture.

"Any time, any place."

Hard to believe a moment ago I was near tears, as suddenly I'm happy, that giddy, light, dizzy kind of happy where everything feels good and looks good. I don't even know why except that I'm standing here with Luke and he's said he'd go out with me and he's not mad at me anymore.

"Do you have plans for tonight?" I ask.

"No."

"Would you like to do something tonight?"

"Yes."

"Okay." I'm blushing, and my cheeks burn hot. "I'll call you about where and when." I catch sight of his expression. "I *will*. I *promise*."

His eyes crease. "I believe you."

"I just need to find a sitter," I say. His eyes meet mine and hold. "But I will call you, and we will go out, and I won't forget."

"I said I believe you."

"Then why are you looking at me like that?"

His smile grows. "Because I'm glad to see you, and glad I'll see you later tonight."

Chapter Twenty-One

I arrive home with groceries to find Eva waiting at the door, holding the school's parent directory. "Guess what?" she says, twirling around me as I head to the kitchen with the first of the grocery bags. "Guess who called and invited me to a sleepover?"

"Jemma?"

"*No.* Jemma hates me. Jill. Jill Hunter. She said you met her parents in my class at Back-to-School Night."

I think back, trying to recall the meeting, and then realize the Hunters must have been the parents who told me who Steve Ballmer was. If I remember, I found Lori Hunter's honesty refreshing. "That sounds great. What do we have to do?" I ask, putting the bags on the counter before heading back to the car for the rest of the groceries.

"Just call Mrs. Hunter back and confirm that it's okay for me to go."

I grab the last bags from the floorboard of the truck. "You dial the number," I tell her, "and I'll talk."

Eva closes the truck door behind me and runs ahead to open the door to the house. "Ready?"

"Yep." I get the rest of the groceries to the kitchen just before I've got to take the phone from Eva.

Lori Hunter is as friendly on the phone as she was at Back-to-School Night. "We'd love to have Eva stay the night. Jill's been wanting to have Eva over for the longest time, but we've been short-handed at the restaurant and it's been hard to get a free weekend night before now."

"You have a restaurant?"

"Three." She laughs. "But let's not talk about that. I've made my escape for the weekend, and I don't want to think about work until Monday."

I understand completely. "So what's the plan for tonight?"

"I was thinking we could come pick Eva up on our way to a matinee movie and then dinner, if that's okay with you."

Eva's jumping from foot to foot, and I smile. "That sounds great."

"Is four too early?"

Eva's hands are folded in a prayer pose, and I have to fight to keep from laughing. "No. Not at all. Eva's very excited. Thank you for including her."

"We'll see you at four, then."

"Great."

As I hang up, thinking that the Hunters just solved my child care issue for tonight's date with Luke, Eva throws her arms around me. "I'm going to a sleepover!" she cries.

"And a movie and dinner."

"I'm so happy. Jill's really nice, and her mom is great. Mrs. Hunter coaches Jill's soccer team and makes up the recipes and everything for the restaurant. You'll like her."

"As much as Taylor Young?"

Eva hugs me tighter. "Better."

I call Luke an hour later. "Eva's been invited to a sleepover, so I'm free tonight. Are you still up for going out?"

His laugh is husky. "Yeah, I'm still up."

I flush all over again. "So should I pick you up since I'm in charge of this date?"

"I'll pick you up, and actually, I'm in charge of this date. You were in charge last Friday. Tonight's my turn."

"But—"

"Four-thirty. See you then." And just like that, he hangs up.

Luke arrives at four twenty-five on a gorgeous, classic 1960s chopper. I practically run out of the house to get a proper look at it. "You have a bike," I say accusingly, "and it's a Freedom." I crouch next to the engine to take a look.

He's smiling as he tugs off his helmet. "You're a Harley girl, though."

I shake my head. If only he knew the real story. Standing up, I circle his bike again. The chrome gleams, and there's miles of it. The spokes shine. The gas tank is burnt orange surrounded by a diffused yellow line that goes black. The handlebars, ape hangers, are huge, spread so far out that it's definitely a bike only a big man could ride.

"Wow," I keep repeating. "I think I'm in love with your bike."

He grins at me and drags a hand through his hair, riffling it on end. "So a ride sounds good?"

I glance from him back to the bike. It's a two-seater,

unlike my bike, which has one of those small solo seats. "We'll go to dinner on your bike?"

"If you're not scared."

I stand tall and whip my hair back over my shoulder. "Those are fighting words, baby."

His smile flashes, and he doesn't look the least bit remorseful. "Damn if I don't say all the wrong things."

"That's to be expected. You're a man."

"Ouch."

"It's called tough love."

"Is that what it is?"

"Yeah." Impulsively, I lean forward and stroke the bike's leather seat and then kiss him. "But maybe I'll be nice tonight. Seeing as you brought my favorite bike."

He catches me in his arms for another kiss, and this one is longer, slower, and it makes my insides melt.

"You really like Freedom Bikes?" he asks a long time later.

My lower lips quivers. "Love Freedom Bikes," I breathe, very aware of his big—hard—body against mine. Tonight, I think, let's take this all the way tonight.

Luke pushes hair back from my eyes, and I see something in his eyes that nearly undoes me. It's not exactly sympathy, but it's definitely a strong emotion. "So why the Harley?"

The lump in my throat is back, the one that makes it hard to talk or swallow. I really wanted the Freedom account, wanted it more than I've wanted anything in a long, long time. But I can't tell him, can't talk about it. "It's cheaper—" I try to laugh it off, sliding from his arms. "I'll go get my helmet."

"And your coat."

* * *

Seated on the bike, we take the 520 bridge to Seattle and then exit on Mercer and travel past the Space Needle, down toward the water. The sun is beginning to set, and the sky turns red behind the ragged line of the Olympic range beyond Puget Sound.

We travel along the waterfront, passing the Edgewater Hotel, the trolley line, the fishing and cruise ship piers, and then the aquarium.

Luke takes a right, turning into Pier 52/Coleman Dock, which is the entrance for the ferry to Bainbridge Island. Motorcycles board before cars, and we're allowed to bypass the long line of cars to go to the front to join the other bikes.

After parking the bike, Luke takes my hand and we walk into the ferry terminal to buy a pass for the five-thirty ferry to Bainbridge.

"You've got this all planned out," I say as we buy cups of coffee to sip while we wait for the half hour to pass.

"I know what I'm doing, if that's what you mean."

The way he smiles down into my eyes, I think he does know what he's doing, and that's both exciting and nerve-racking.

On the half-hour ride across to Bainbridge, the sky turns shades of red and orange and purple, and we stand at the front of the ferry, the wind buffeting us, and laugh with the cold.

"Everybody else is inside," I cry out, trying to hold my wild hair in one hand while wiping my cold, stinging nose with the other.

"They're bigger chickens than you are."

Luke stands behind me, his body not quite touching mine, but I feel his warmth and it is wonderfully distracting.

Being with Luke like this feels right. We just click, and I can't even explain how or why, but it seems as if I've known him forever. I feel free, young, happy, and while I hadn't thought I was unhappy before, I can see now I've been lonely.

"This is fun," I say, the wind catching my words and spiraling them away.

"It is," he agrees. "Bainbridge is one of my favorite places."

"You do this often?"

"It's easy to get to, especially when you walk on, or take your bike on, the ferry."

Despite growing up in Seattle, I've been to Bainbridge only one other time, and that was so long ago that I'd forgotten the shape of the island and the way the shingle and clapboard houses cling to the inlets and coves. It's very New England, very New Hampshire, and I lean on the rail to get a better look.

The ferry warning sounds. We're less than ten minutes from disembarking. Luke and I head back downstairs to his bike, pull on our helmets, and prepare to unload.

Once on Bainbridge, we travel up Winslow Way, past a beach and fishing pier to the quaint downtown once known as Winslow but that now is just Bainbridge.

Luke parks the bike and we walk the length of town, which I'm surprised to see is already closed. The only places still open are restaurants, a coffeehouse, and a lone drugstore.

I peek into the window of the dark bookstore. "I wish something was open. It's so pretty here!"

"We do have dinner reservations," Luke says, glancing at his watch. "In fact, we should probably head to the restaurant now."

"Is it far?"

"Nope. Just a couple blocks from here. We could take the bike, but it's such a pretty night I'd like to walk."

I shoot him a swift side glance. Luke Flynn, Man as Big as a Mountain, rides a Freedom bike, drives an old Land Rover, heads a multibillion-dollar company, and also happens to be a romantic. "Good." I smile at him, a giddy sensation in my heart again. "Let's do it."

Dinner's at the Four Swallows, an amazing restaurant tucked inside a historic little house. Each room of the house has tables and booths, and each room has a different ambiance, too.

The menu's spectacular, everything sounding so mouthwatering, ranging from an appetizer of kiwi, pears, and feta cheese dipped in toasted pine nuts and served with crackers and roasted garlic, to succulent lamb and freshly prepared northwest seafood.

We eat by candlelight, squeezed into an antique booth that looks as if it came from an island church. We talk and laugh over dinner and dessert.

"Tell me about your mom," he says, sitting with a black coffee in front of him. "How long has she been diagnosed?"

I think of my mom, picture her slim elegance, her once impeccable manners, and my smile falters. "Five years, I think." My shoulders lift and fall. "My dad ignored the symptoms as long as he could. He didn't want to believe it, especially as my mom was definitely young to be diagnosed."

"I take it you and your mom were close?"

Another stab in my heart. It takes me a long moment to answer. "Not as close as we could have been." I'm silent again, and I think about all the could-have-beens and should-have-beens. "I was a rebellious teenager."

"What teenager isn't?"

He has a point, but I know how I behaved, and I know it's because I thought we had so much time. I took my mom for granted. I guess I thought we'd all live forever. "Dad doesn't want to put Mom in a home, but even with help, he's having trouble managing her. Mom wanders a lot right now. Some specialists say Alzheimer's patients wander because as they regress, they go back to another point in their life, to an earlier point, and they're looking for someone or something."

Luke's expression is concerned. "What would your mom be looking for?"

And I suddenly know. "Eva," I murmur.

"Your daughter?"

"My sister." I look up at him, candlelight flickering, throwing shadows off and on his face. "I had a sister named Eva. She died just before her second birthday. I was four."

"Do you remember your sister?"

I feel hollow inside. "I remember her being gone." Which is true. No one talked about "Sissie" after she died. She was never mentioned again, and all her baby things were quickly removed from the house. I don't think I really even remembered I had a sister until my daughter was born and the only name I could think of in the hospital was Eva. I held my six-pound-five-ounce baby girl against my chest, and as I held her, I kept hearing over and over, Eva Rose.

Mom was livid that I gave my daughter my sister's name. For weeks after Eva's birth, she wouldn't speak to me, and when she finally sent something for the baby, she didn't include a card.

I thought Mom was such a bitch for doing that. I don't think I forgave her for a long, long time.

We're still sitting deep in conversation when the waitress brings us the bill. "Just a reminder that the last ferry to Seattle tonight leaves in a half hour."

It's a scramble now to pay and hustle back down the hill to Winslow to get the bike.

By the time we reach the ferry, they're already boarding and we're waved on and parked in record time.

We're laughing as we pull off our helmets. I'm laughing so hard that Luke's arm goes round to steady me, and then we're kissing.

As he kisses me, my legs give way, my mouth trembling beneath his. I slide my arms around his waist, beneath his leather jacket, and as the kiss deepens, I hold him close and closer still. It's been so long since I was kissed like this. So long since I felt what I feel.

Later, we climb the stairs, heading for the top deck to watch as we sail toward the spectacular Seattle skyline, the lights of the city glittering beneath a sky full of stars.

Everything tonight is perfect. The wind's crisp and cold, yet the moon overhead shines fat and full, and our ferry pushes through the water, humming and creating a white foamy wake that looks iridescent in the moonlight.

Luke stands behind me, his arms around me, and I hold his arms against me, hold him tight, hoping I know what I'm doing, hoping no one will get hurt, hoping this amazing, happy feeling will last at least till morning. That Luke will maybe stay till morning.

On the doorstep of my house, I invite Luke in.

"I'm not sure this is a good idea," he says, cupping my face. "It might be too soon."

"I think you're chicken," I taunt softly.

His body hardens almost instantly against me. I hide a smile. I always did like playing with fire.

We end up inside, kissing against the front door. Then, still kissing, Luke walks me backward, step by step, through my living room and down the hall. "Which is your room?" he mutters, tugging my black cashmere V-neck sweater over my head.

I shiver in my black lace bra. "That way—" I indicate toward my room, and after sweeping me into his arms, he pushes open the door and carries me in, dumping me unceremoniously on the bed.

He strips off his shirt and then stretches out over me on the bed. Our chests are bare, yet we both still have jeans and boots on, and the feel of his chest with its warm skin over taut thick muscle makes me want all of him just as bare.

Luke kisses me more deeply, his tongue teasing mine, and I arch against him. Reaching up, I clasp his face and then slide my hands down to his shoulders, amazed at the feel of him. He feels amazing. Unreal. Perfect.

I caress down until my hands reach his belt. "Can we dispose of these?" I whisper against his mouth, tugging on the belt and jeans.

"You're so impatient," he answers, kissing the hollow beneath one ear and then lower, on the side of my neck, making me shudder beneath his delicious weight.

"I've only waited ten years, baby."

He pushes up to prop himself with his elbows. "How long has it really been?"

"Ten years."

"Ten years without sex?"

I cringe at his incredulous tone. "I do have toys, some very nice toys—"

"Pocket Rocket?" he guesses.

I grin and nod. "Among others."

He drops his head to kiss the swell of one breast and then the other. "Are you nervous about making love?"

"No," I answer without hesitating, and then I wait until he looks me in the eye. "I just want it to be good."

Luke laughs that deep, sexy laugh of his and runs his hand through my hair. "No pressure there."

"None at all," I agree solemnly. "Oh, and Luke?"

"What, my darling chicken?" he asks, now unzipping the zipper of my jeans and leaning lower to kiss my abdomen just above the lace of my very low-cut black thong. I shiver as his tongue snakes across the lace, going low, lower, until the tip of his tongue hits right where I'm most sensitive.

"I want to come, too," I pant, the air now strangled in my throat.

He slides off my jeans and parts my knees. "You'll come, baby. You just leave it to me."

I do come. Not just once, but twice, and I think I could even have another orgasm, but Luke teases me that I don't want to be sore, and he's right. He doesn't have a problem staying very big and very hard, and it has been a long, long time.

Luke stays the night, sleeping next to me, his right arm wrapped securely around me.

I don't sleep, though. Instead I lie there, strangely at peace.

I've missed this so. I've missed being someone's woman.

I've missed belonging somewhere, to someone.

Luke leaves early in the morning before I can even make him coffee. Turns out he has a flight to the East Coast in just three hours, and he's got to get home, pack, and grab his computer.

I wander around the house until Eva returns at ten.

"What did you do last night?" she asks me.

I feel myself redden. "Had dinner with Luke."

She turns on me eagerly. "Was he here, or did you go out?"

Oh, he was here all right, I think, biting my lip and hiding my smile. "We went out. He took me to a restaurant on Bainbridge."

"Was it fun?"

I picture his bike, the dinner at Four Swallows, the ride home on the ferry, and then I remember the feel of his mouth on me. I go hot, and the breathless feeling is back, the one that makes me want to find Luke and strip off my clothes and beg for a repeat of last night's performance. He was good. And he was right: He knew exactly what to do with my body. "Very," I croak.

She looks at me from the corner of her eye but says nothing more.

But she knows something's up. How can she not? I can't stop smiling.

We spend the rest of the day at Mom and Dad's house, making roll-out sugar cookies that Mom helps us frost and decorate for Halloween. Dad's housekeeper has put a roast in the oven for us, and I whip up mashed potatoes and green beans and salad.

Mom goes to bed early, though, almost as soon as we eat, and Eva and I go home to watch *Desperate Housewives*. It's not a show for kids, but Eva loves it. She thinks she's Eva Longoria.

Monday morning I get another big call at work. Trident wants to go with us.

How's that for getting exactly what I don't want?

We don't get Freedom Bikes, but we do get Trident.

I should be thrilled that we've got new business, but my gut has told me from the beginning that Trident's going to be a mistake. They're based in New York, and they'll require some serious travel. Fortunately, Chris likes to travel, and since he once lived in Manhattan, he's looking forward to getting home more.

But as the team pow-wows after the phone call, I don't feel better about the deal. I feel worse. I mention my concerns to the group, and Chris shoots me down with a dismissive, "Without Freedom we need them. We don't have a choice."

I shuffle papers, change subjects, but my gut says we're in trouble. My gut says we've just boarded a sinking ship, which is always a bad, bad, bad decision.

Monday evening, I get a text message from Luke. *When can I see you again?*

I text back, *When do you get back?*

He texts right away, *Tonight. But I leave in the morning again for 10 days.*

I stare at the screen on my BlackBerry for a long time before texting my reply: *Then stop by tonight on your way home.*

Luke arrives late enough that Eva's already in bed sound asleep. I quietly close the door to Eva's room before leading Luke to the kitchen. "Hungry?" I ask.

"Yes," he answers, backing me up against the refrigerator. The kiss is explosive. Hot, so hot that I grab on to his shirt and hang tight.

"Let's go to my room," I whisper.

"Eva's here."

"We'll be quiet."

"You're not that quiet."

My eyes flash. "You shouldn't be so good."

We head to my room, and Luke barely gives me time to lock the door before he's sliding his hands from my waist down my hips and over my butt.

I gasp a little at his touch and grab the ends of his hair, tug on them, before covering his mouth with mine.

I feel like a savage, but as he strips the clothes from me, he seems just as fierce and hungry.

Making love is wild. When he enters me, I'm not even properly on the bed, but somehow it's right. Everything about being together is right, as long as we are together.

It's the being apart that's getting hard.

Luke leaves at midnight, and I stand beneath the hot, steamy spray of the shower.

I won't see him again for at least ten days. He's heading in the morning for Europe, and this is what he does. He's on the road more than he's home.

I touch my breast, still feeling the imprint of his hand on my skin. Ten days until he touches me again. Ten days until I see his blue eyes again.

After turning off the shower, I grab my towel and press the terry cloth to my face. Even if I wanted to see Luke more, I couldn't.

And that thought somehow fills me with despair.

Luke calls me Tuesday noon from Hamburg. It's evening there, and he's just wrapped up a day of meetings. "How are you?" he asks.

"Good," I answer, taking the phone and heading from the studio outside so I can have some privacy. "How about you?"

"Long day, but productive."

"Good."

His voice drops. "I can't stop thinking about you."

I wrap one arm across my chest. "I feel the same way."

"Ten days is too long."

"I agree."

"Come see me."

I laugh. "Can't. I have a business to run. Come home."

"Can't. Have a business to run."

I laugh again. So does he. "I'll call you tomorrow," he says.

"You don't have to."

Luke makes an exasperated sound. "I know I don't have to. I *want* to."

"Okay. Be careful."

"You too."

The rest of the afternoon passes, and before long it's six o'clock Tuesday night and we're all still buried in the studio, even Susan, and she's got three kids at home waiting for her.

"Susan, get out of here," I tell her, rubbing a knot at the base of my neck. I'm currently on hold with Gord from Jet City—he's going to round up his partner to continue our unhappy conference call.

Jet City Coffee feels as if we're dropping the ball. We're not as creative or responsive as we used to be. They're not getting phone calls returned. They don't like the numbers on their last ad campaign. And frankly, they're beginning to think it's time they moved to another agency, one with fresh ideas and new blood.

Susan does eventually leave, but Allie, Chris, Robert, and I remain to finish the conference call.

By the time the call ends, it's seven and Eva's curled up in a bean bag chair that she's brought from the house, reading a book.

"That was a long call," she says.

"Tell me about it." I look over her head at my exhausted team. They all are grim and gray. There's no way anyone's in the right mind frame to discuss the call tonight. "We'll talk about it in the morning," I tell them.

Nodding and muttering good-byes, they grab their coats and go.

Eva watches everyone leave and then looks at me. I smile tiredly down at her and then stoop to give her a kiss. "You must be starving," I say.

She shrugs. "I made myself a peanut-butter sandwich."

"Good for you."

She reaches up, touches my hair and then my face. Her dark hair curls in little wisps around her face. "Mom, I know you're tired and you've just had a really bad conference call, and I don't want to bother you . . ."

Eva reminds me of Natalie Portman right now with her big dark eyes and pixie cut. "What, baby?"

"Tomorrow's Halloween, and Phoebe's party," she blurts out. "And we never got me a costume."

Oh, *shit*.

We head out immediately to Redmond to look at mermaid costumes, princess costumes, cowgirl and Native American costumes. We look at scary, gory, bloody, pretty, charming, classic, silly.

As we shop at the cavernous Halloween Outlet, I catch a glimpse of my image in one of the tall, skinny mirrors and hardly recognize myself. I still feel so young, yet right now I look disturbingly middle age, with shadows under my eyes and creases at the corners and pinched lips that look as if they could use some collagen.

Suddenly, I remember the older ladies I saw at Tully's and how each looked so stretched and pulled and tucked. I remember how I vowed I'd never do that, never chop me up and pull me back together again, but I don't want to look old, either. Don't want to look . . . beaten.

And maybe that's how those older ladies ended up getting all that work done. Maybe one day they looked into the mirror and they didn't recognize the face they saw anymore. Maybe one day the face in the mirror wasn't familiar.

Last year, Shey told me a story about aging and our faces. She said she and her mom were talking, and Shey said on the inside she still felt thirty, and her mom laughed and said that was good, because she only felt like forty.

Perhaps that's the difficulty with aging gracefully. Our hearts don't age, yet the rest of us does.

Which sends us to the doctors in search of miracles, drugs, and cures. Nips and tucks and little fixes. A bit of Botox here, a touch of filler there. Yet no matter how little or much we do, we can't ever stop time, so in the end we must make peace with the little girl inside us, the one that doesn't want to grow up, or age, or ever die.

"There," Eva says, plopping a witch's hat on my head. "Now you look like that lady. Morticia. The mom from *The Addams Family.*"

If I recall, Morticia didn't exactly look young. In fact, I thought she was downright old. But I don't say any of that to Eva. I just pat her head and murmur, "Isn't that fantastic?" even as I wonder what time Luke will call tomorrow from Hamburg. Will it be day or night?

The next day, I'm so buried with work that I totally forget I'm supposed to be helping with Eva's class Halloween party until she calls me at one-forty.

"Where are you?" she whispers tearfully into the phone. "Everyone's here but you, and you're in charge of the drinks."

"What?"

"The *drinks.* Mrs. Young said you volunteered to bring the drinks today, and we have our cupcakes and popcorn and treats, but there's nothing to drink and everyone's sitting around with an empty cup and Mrs. Young is mad."

Frankly, I'm more worried about Eva's feelings than Taylor Young's, and right now, I can't believe I've let her down. Again. Things are just so stressful right now. It's like I can't get a break and can't catch my breath.

"Give me two minutes," I say. "I'll be right there. Okay? Two minutes. I promise, baby."

As I hang up, everyone looks at me. "You going somewhere again?" Chris asks flatly.

"Eva's class party. I'm in charge of the drinks."

"What about the Ewes and Lambs call?" he asks pointedly, placing his hands on top of his head. "What do I tell them now?"

"That I'll be back in an hour."

"Marta. This is a business."

"Yeah, Chris, I know it's a business because this is how I pay for my house and my car and my groceries." I yank on my coat, nod at the others, my jaw flexed. "I'll be back soon."

I grab whatever sodas we have in the refrigerator in the garage—a case of 7Up, a case of Coke, a case of A&W root beer—load them in the truck, and head up to school in a pouring rain.

I stack the sodas and carry them, three cases high, through the school to Eva's classroom in the fourth-grade wing.

Eva's delighted to see me, but Taylor Young pulls me aside and tightly asks me what I plan on doing with the "soda pop."

I rip open one of the cartons and look at her. "The soda

pop is for the kids' party." I smile with lots of teeth to show I'm not in the mood for her fun and games right now.

"Do you really think the kids need more sugar now?"

I turn and face her, one hand still resting on the soda boxes. "Do you think they needed all the cupcakes and treats, Taylor?"

She folds her arms, her chin lifting righteously. "They always have treats for Halloween."

"Fabulous! And now they're having another." I turn my back on her and see a boy getting a drink from the water faucet near me. "Would you mind helping me pass these out?" I ask him, dropping the case of root beer into his arms.

As he heads off, Eva comes running, and I give her the 7Up cans. Another girl shyly asks if she can help, and I hand over the Cokes.

There. Mission completed. I find Eva, tell her I've got to get home, to have fun and I'll see her later. Grabbing my keys, I'm out of there.

Who said working moms can't do it all?

I'm away from the studio for the Halloween class party for maybe twenty, thirty minutes total, but when I get back to the studio, Chris is gone, and Allie, Susan, and Robert look at me gray faced.

"What's wrong?" I ask, dropping my coat on my chair and turning to face the others.

Allie shakes her head. Robert shuffles the papers around on his desk before clearing his throat. "Chris quit," he says quietly. "I'm sorry."

It's that gob-smacked feeling again. Crazy, disorient-
ing, off-kilter. I sit down heavily, my hands falling to my
knees. "Quit?"

"He said he couldn't work here like this." Allie's voice is
small.

"Is it that bad?" I ask, leaning back in my chair, my gaze
moving from one face to the other.

"No," Susan says loudly, briskly, from her desk across
the room. She lives surrounded by copiers, faxes, printers,
and filing cabinets. "It's not bad at all. This is just life, and
Chris isn't living in reality."

I'd smile if I weren't so stunned, and sad. Chris is a huge
part of this company. A big part of what I do.

Sitting at my desk, I pick up the phone. I hear the beep
that says I have a voice mail on my personal line and check
messages. Luke called. He said it's late there in Germany
and he's going to bed, but he wishes me a Happy Halloween and will try again tomorrow.

Chapter Twenty-Two

With Chris gone, I start having to travel to New York for the Trident meetings. They'd said travel would be minimal, maybe a few days every month, but it's not even December yet and I've already been to New York twice, for a total of a week.

The first trip to New York, Susan had Eva stay with her for the Friday and Saturday I was gone. The second time, November 12 through 14, my dad and Allie juggled Eva between them. Eva wasn't thrilled with living out of her backpack, but I promised her that I was trying to hire someone new to fill Chris's position, and as soon as I had someone new, I wouldn't have to travel anymore.

But filling Chris's shoes is harder than I anticipated. One, he was really good. Two, apparently my team is working as slave labor. No one with a good résumé is interested in what I'd pay.

The third weekend in November is dark and gray and rainy. I'm home this weekend but working, and when Eva asks if Jill can come to our house for a sleepover, I readily agree. I've got so much to do that if Eva's occupied, I can work without feeling as guilty.

Now Jill stands on our doorstep with her sleeping bag clutched beneath one arm and her pillow under the other. "Am I too early?" she chirps. Jill's a small, round-faced girl with apple cheeks, dense dark eyelashes, and light brown eyebrows that arch delicately over startling blue eyes.

"Nope," I answer with a smile.

Jill smiles back before bounding into the house.

The rain is pelting down as I walk outside to the car, where Lori's trying to calm her youngest so she can make it to the door to greet me.

"Hi," I say, leaning down to wave at the preschooler in the backseat. The boy stares at me and then bursts into tears all over again.

"He wants to join the sleepover," Lori says apologetically.

I bend down again and look at three-and-a-half-year-old Mike. He's cute. He looks just like his big sister. "Mike, it's just girls. It's not going to be that much fun."

But Mike only cries harder.

"You're getting wet," Lori says, sliding regretfully behind the wheel. "And I better go. I've got to be at the restaurant by five. We don't have a cashier tonight, so I'm working."

"What about Mikey?"

"He's going to his aunt's house."

"Do you want me to watch him?"

Lori looks over her shoulder, monitors the ear-splitting tantrum for a moment, then turns back to me. "No. And you don't want to watch him, either." With a cheerful wave, she's off.

Luke comes over later after he arrives back in Seattle following a week-long trip to Dallas, Raleigh-Durham, and

Boston, that trip coming only three days after the ten-day trip to Germany. We've been apart far more than we've been together, but every time Luke walks through the door I'm absolutely thrilled to see him.

The girls and I went out earlier for Chinese, and Luke now stands in my kitchen eating the leftovers straight from the white cartons.

"I wish I had more," I say as he finishes off the chow mein and spicy beef. "I should have realized you'd be hungry."

"It's okay." He leans over and kisses me, tasting like Mongolian beef. "I'm just glad to see you."

Looking into his face and those light blue eyes that I always find so reassuring, I reach up to touch his cheek, and a little spark goes through me. "I could make you something. I've got pork chops and ground beef—"

"I'm not that hungry. I'd rather just be with you."

We sit on the couch and find a cable movie to watch, but halfway through the movie I notice Luke's fallen asleep. I go to cover him with a fleecy blanket I took from the linen closet, but Luke catches my hand and tugs me back onto the sofa again. "Come here," he growls, pulling me closer.

I settle in his arms. He's warm. Hard. Muscles everywhere. I sigh appreciatively. "I've missed you."

"I've missed you, too," he answers, moving my hair off to the side to kiss my neck.

Shivery sensations race up and down my spine. "And I've missed that, too," I breathe unsteadily.

"So I'm not just a one-night stand?" he asks, his voice humming against my skin.

I turn around on the couch to face him and place one

hand on his chest. I can feel his heart. His heart beats steady and strong. "You're *not* a one-night stand."

His hands slide from my hair to my face. He pushes one long strand back behind my right ear and then another strand behind my left, and all the while he's studying my face. Then his lashes lower, and I can tell he's interested only in my mouth now.

Luke pulls me forward onto his lap, so that I feel the heat in his jeans, the rigid length of him, and the sinewy strength of his thighs. He's aroused, but then so am I.

I take his face in my hands and kiss him, my thumbs stroking across his amazing cheekbones and then down the hollows between cheekbone and jaw. He feels so good. He feels so right.

I love kissing him. I love being this close with him. "You're not," I repeat, sitting up to look down at him, "a one-night stand."

A lazy heat burns in his blue eyes, and color darkens his skin. "Then what am I?" he asks, touching my mouth with his finger.

My lips part, and I touch the tip of my tongue to his finger. The blue light in his eyes burns hotter, brighter.

"Mine," I whisper wickedly, flicking my tongue across his finger again. "You're mine."

Suddenly the door to Eva's room opens and the girls' voices sound in the hall. Luke immediately lifts me off his lap and back onto the couch. He picks up a magazine, and I reach for my computer. The girls run toward us with their pillows and sleeping bags.

"Can we watch a movie in here with you?" Eva asks.

I look at Luke. His eyes flash at me.

"Of course," I answer.

Luke leaves partway through the movie. I walk him out onto the front porch. The rain is still coming down, and it's cold. I shiver in just my T-shirt. After shutting the door, Luke turns me so that my back is against the house, and as he kisses me, he leans against me, one of his knees between mine.

I can feel his thighs, his hips, his chest, and I hold on to him, my hands clasping the thick cut of his bicep.

"We need more time together," he says, his voice hoarse.

"I know."

"How?" he demands.

"I don't know."

"Not good enough."

I reach up, touch his cheekbone. "We'll find a way."

But we don't find a way, at least not anytime soon. The grueling pace continues, but at last it's now late November and we're facing Thanksgiving weekend.

After too many hours on airplanes and in hotels, in taxis and in conference rooms, I've promised Eva it'll be a traditional Thanksgiving Day with Grandma and Grandpa and then a girls-only weekend.

"Well, you can invite Luke over," Eva says. "He's okay. I just don't want you to do e-mail and work on your computer."

"I promise."

"And no conference calls."

"Scout's honor," I vow again.

Eva looks at me suspiciously. "You were never a Girl Scout."

"No, I was. For one week. And then they kicked me out."

"Mom!" She shrieks with laughter, and I just smile with her.

I fully intend to keep my promise to Eva, too. There will be no business phone calls. No e-mail. No faxing. No photocopying. It's just going to be mother-daughter stuff, girl stuff. Bake cookies and paint our toenails and shop and go see the newest Amanda Bynes movie.

But then Thanksgiving Day arrives and my cell phone and house phone won't stop ringing.

I'm in the middle of making gravy and trying to mash potatoes, and all I can hear is the telephone ringing, ringing, ringing.

"Eva," I finally shout, "can you please answer that for me?"

"But what if it's work?" she answers, emerging from the pantry, where she's been looking for the perfect set of candle holders for the table.

"It's Thanksgiving. Can't be work."

I'm wrong. It is work. I turn down the heat beneath the gravy, turn off the mixer, pray the potatoes won't get cold, and go outside to take this call. "What do you mean they're calling everyone into the office? It's Thanksgiving weekend."

"The meeting's not until Saturday." It's Eric, the VP of sales with Trident. "You'll still have tomorrow off."

"I'd have to fly out first thing tomorrow to make the meeting."

"That's okay."

I close my eyes and hold my breath, feeling nothing, nothing, because if I stay very calm, this will be a nonissue. "No, it's not okay. It's Thanksgiving weekend."

"It'll just be a quick turnaround. Out, meeting, home again. No one will notice."

Not notice? Who is he kidding? "Eric. There's no way."

He pauses, and then when he speaks his voice is flinty. "Your attendance is required. Everyone on the team must be there."

"On a *Saturday*." My voice drips venom. "Thanksgiving weekend."

"Sucks, I know."

"Eric, I have a daughter—"

"We all do."

You all have another parent at home, too. You all have someone else to be there to comfort your son or daughter. I totally get the whole stay-at-home mother or father thing. One person works, the other stays home so kids aren't alone. Got it.

But that's not what I get.

It's not the path I took, and right now I don't know how to swallow that when I'm asked to make sacrifices, especially when it's Eva being sacrificed.

I go back inside. Turn the heat up under the gravy. Finish the potatoes, even though they're lumpy. It's okay, Marta, everything's going to be fine.

But as I dish up the stuffing and sweet potatoes, I glance at Eva, who is putting the finishing touches on our Thanksgiving table, and my heart just falls. I'm letting Eva down again.

The turbulence during the flight from Seattle to New York has us buckled into our seats for three of the four and a half hours.

The cab ride from the airport to the hotel isn't much better.

The taxi driver has adjusted his rearview mirror so he can look at me while he drives, and he spends more time staring at me than out the window at the road.

I just want to get to my hotel. Alive.

The Saturday meeting goes well enough. Although I still don't know why I had to be there, as it had very little to do with anything I'm doing for them.

After the meeting I hop on a late night flight back and get home that night, pay the sitter, someone Lori Hunter recommended, and then fall exhausted into bed.

The morning after I've returned from New York, Eva and I meet my parents at the club for Sunday brunch, and she watches the families around us with more wistfulness than usual.

On the way home from the club, she turns to me. "Mom, do you ever think I'll have a brother or sister?"

I tighten my grip on the steering wheel. "I don't know, Eva. I really don't know."

"But if you marry Luke, you and Luke will want a baby, right?"

Oh God. What a question. If I married Luke. If Luke married me. If we even see each other enough to get that far. . . .

"I don't know if Luke and I will ever be that serious," I finally answer.

"But you like him. You've kissed him."

"Eva!"

She gives me a long-suffering look. "Relax, Mom. It's okay to like a man. Especially since you aren't a lesbian."

That night after Eva's gone to bed, I work for a few hours in the studio before turning in. On the way to my room I stop at her door, open it, and peek in.

She's curled up in a little ball, her baby blanket nestled in her hand.

She's had that blanket since she was born. It used to be pink. It's somewhere between gray and grungy now.

I go to her bed and adjust the comforter to make sure she's covered. Just looking at her makes my heart hurt. I used to think I could never love anyone as much as I love her, but what I'm finding is that what I feel for Eva is so different from what I feel for Luke.

Eva's my baby. Luke's . . . my man.

And yet my baby won't be my baby forever.

One day, this gorgeous, divine human being will leave me.

Sometimes it blows my mind. Imagine falling in love with a man, an amazing handsome loving man who makes you feel like the best thing in the world, who gives your day purpose, *hope,* and yet you know from day one of meeting him that you'll have only eighteen years with him.

One day, about eighteen years after meeting him, falling in love with him, he'll go. Move on. Do whatever it is he was meant to do.

And this is my job as a woman, as a mom, to love her, prepare her, and then, once she's ready, push her out of the nest and make her fly.

Heart in my throat, I lean over and kiss her cheek. She's so warm, her skin's soft, and in sleep she's my baby again.

I watch her for another moment and then go to my room, the master bedroom, the place that says I'm the adult here. I'm a woman. And this woman very much wishes a certain man were here to spend the night with her.

December arrives and I'm scheduled to head back to New York. This time Jill's mom, Lori, invites Eva to stay with them the four days I'm to be gone. "Are you sure?" I ask Lori. "That's a long time to have to watch her."

"When you have three kids, what's one more?" she answers with a laugh.

Eva isn't as sad about me leaving now that she'll be staying at the Hunters'. I, on the other hand, take the separation much harder.

In my hotel room, I sit with my laptop and work on my notes for the Trident meeting in the morning. It's nearly two New York time, but that's only eleven West Coast time, so I force myself on.

Yet as I type, inputting changes into the graphs and spreadsheets, I can barely concentrate.

I don't want to be here.

I want to be home.

I want to be with my daughter.

It's reached the point that it's too much. I'm so tired of saying good-bye to her. So tired of not having enough time with her. The experts are wrong when they say it's not about quantity time, it's about quality, because I need the quantity, too. I need to be with her more. I literally, physically, miss her.

My body, arms, heart—all of me misses her.

Soon, I tell myself. As soon as we hire another ad guy. As soon as the business is back in a solid position. As soon as I can get rid of this nightmare Trident account. . . .

My second night in New York is worse than the first. I call Shey, thinking we can get together, but she's taken her brood to France for an impromptu ski trip. I think about all the other friends I used to have here, but frankly, I'm not feeling that sociable.

The problem is, I'm not merely lonely, I'm homesick for Bellevue. I'm homesick for my daughter and my home and my life there.

I don't want to be in a hotel. I want to be in my own house, tucking Eva in at night and making her lunch in the morning. I want her to bound into my office at the end of her day. I want to see her face and her eyes and her smile.

I want to be a mother again.

To distract myself, I open up my laptop, pull up the Google toolbar, and type in "Luke Flynn, BioMed, Bellevue," and wait.

It takes less than a second to deliver me not just to the BioMed Web site, but to Luke Flynn's biography. And there he is. Luke Flynn, co-founder and CEO, Harvard grad, sponsor and organizer of the huge annual bike rally Bikes-to-Tikes.

I exhale and sit back, every nervous, anxious emotion alive and well inside of me.

I'm still staring at his photo when my phone rings.

"Bad time?" Luke asks when I answer.

I'm so glad to hear his voice, I could hug myself. "Not at all. I was just thinking of you."

"Good things?"

"Very good."

"So what are you doing?"

"Working on my computer," I answer, guiltily clicking off his company Web site. Not that he knows I've been staring at his photo, but still. "What about you?"

"Just trying to figure out my evening plans."

"Do you have a business meeting?"

"No, I just got out of one." He pauses. "Feel like dinner?"

If only. "Sure," I flash back. "Where should I meet you?"

"How about downstairs in the lobby in twenty minutes."

"Dude, I'm in New York."

"Dudette, I am, too. I'm overnighting in New York before I head to Dublin tomorrow morning."

"*You're* in New York."

"I'm just a ten-minute cab ride away."

"Then get over here!"

He laughs again, that great, sexy rumble of his. "Baby, I'm on my way."

When Luke steps into the hotel lobby, New York suddenly feels like home all over again. He's bundled up, a heavy coat, a scarf, gloves, with a dusting of snowflakes on his shoulders and head.

"Hi, stranger," I say, hugging him and smiling up into his face.

"You're the stranger," he grouses. "Every time I come home you're jumping on a plane."

"I'd rather not be traveling. I'd rather be home."

"Then let's do something about this Trident account of yours."

Laughing, I just hug him again. It's so wonderful to see him.

"Will you be warm enough?" Luke asks, indicating my leather coat.

I nod. "I used to live here, baby doll."

"So you like to remind me."

With Luke's arm wrapped around me, we head to a Greek restaurant around the corner from my hotel. Luke and I both love Greek food, and we order an appetizer sampler, just so we can enjoy a taste of everything.

Over the flaming saganaki, Luke says bluntly, "I think we need to coordinate our business trips. This going two weeks at a time without seeing each other is for the birds."

I nod. I couldn't agree more.

"How much longer will Trident need you here in New York?" he asks.

I shake my head. "I don't know. Frankly, I don't think they need me here at all. Their VP of sales doesn't know what he's doing and keeps calling these all-hands-on-deck meetings. It's a huge waste of time, never mind their money."

"Is there a way to get out of it?"

"Not for a year."

"Can you hand it over to someone?"

"I'm trying."

He raises his beer glass. "To finding a replacement," he says.

I clink my glass with his. "I'll drink to that."

After dinner we walk back to my hotel, the snow still falling, the streets quieter than usual, the street noise muffled by the snow. We're so far from home, Bellevue a whole world away, but it's right being here like this together.

"Come to my room," I say as we reach my hotel lobby. "Come to my room and stay the night with me."

"My flight—"

"Push it back." We stop by the elevator, and I wrap my arms around him, tilt my head back to look up into his face. "I want you, need you, to stay."

He kisses me. "Done."

I laugh as the elevator doors open. "I closed the deal?"

"Closed it?" he mocks, stepping into the elevator with me. "Hardly. We've only just sat down for negotiations."

Chapter Twenty-Three

The happiness doesn't end the next day. Luke announces that he's pushed his flight to Dublin back a day, and I call in sick to work. We start the day with a huge breakfast at a great deli, and then Luke accompanies me while I do some Christmas shopping for Eva and my parents. Laden with bags and packages, we take a carriage ride through Central Park, and then after an afternoon nap and a long, lazy bath together, we have a romantic dinner at Tao and then later drinks in the dark, intimate lounge at the Mark Hotel.

We sleep together again, Luke sharing my hotel room and bed for the second night, and it's the first time we've ever been together for twenty-four hours straight, and it feels so natural. It feels the way it should.

"You're not sleeping," Luke's voice sounds in the dark. He rolls onto his back and brings me on top of him. "Work worrying you?"

It's dark, but I know his face well enough now to know it in the dark. "I hate that you're leaving tomorrow."

I feel his hand in my hair. He loves my hair. "I'll be back in Seattle in less than a week."

"I just would love a week where we could see each other every day. I know it sounds greedy, but I feel greedy right now. I feel like time is always so short and we're both always so busy."

"We both have careers," he says.

Is that why we don't see more of each other? Because we both work? I'm not so sure, but I don't want to argue.

The next morning, Luke leaves for Dublin, and after a day spent at the Trident office I catch the six p.m. flight back to Seattle.

I'm upgraded to first class thanks to all my recent miles, but even the relative comfort of first class doesn't ease my mind.

I don't want to be single anymore. I don't want to have to do it all. I want a real relationship with Luke, one of those that look so achingly traditional: man, woman, and child all living in the same house.

Please God, let Luke feel the same way.

Back in Bellevue, I work even more hours than I did in November and early December. I also catch cold after cold. Thank God Luke's traveling or I would have gotten him sick, too. Eva catches a cold once, but she's better in days, whereas I drag myself through the weeks feeling dead on my feet.

Dad talks to me about taking a sabbatical from work. I can't do it—it'd kill us financially—but I wish there were another way. I wish I weren't spread so thin. I wish I could just enjoy Eva more.

Luke calls me from all over the world. He's in Beijing one day, Tokyo the next. Then it's Perth, Sydney, Auckland. He offers to fly me out to see him in New Zealand.

"It's gorgeous here, Marta. It's summer, and absolutely beautiful."

I'm tempted, but I've passed my cold on to Allie, and Robert is stressed out of his mind.

"It'd be good for you, too," he adds. "You could use warm weather, and a break."

He's right. I could. But I can't. "Next time," I tell him, praying there will be a next time.

Luke is finally heading home, but I fly out the same day he's supposed to fly in. I nearly cry with frustration as my airplane takes off. It's only a day-and-a-half trip to Los Angeles, but it feels long enough.

I'm home again, just a day and a half later, and I try to call Luke, but he's wrapped up in meetings. I take the evening off, but Eva's out, she had plans.

I wander around my house feeling ridiculously lonely. I miss everyone It's the holidays, and instead of feeling happy or grateful, I feel stressed out of my mind.

But in just five days you'll be in Whistler, I remind myself. In five days you'll have a full week off, a week to do nothing but relax with Eva.

I'm taking Eva to Whistler for skiing the week between Christmas and New Year's. We've already got reservations at the Fairmont Hotel, and it'll be fantastic to get away for a whole week. Seven days no work. Seven days no desk, no computer, no cell phone. I swear.

Thinking of no cell phone reminds me of Luke, though, and while I don't want to work for a week, I do want to see him. I even casually mentioned Whistler to him during one of our last phone calls, suggesting that he join us for a few days, possibly hook up with us New Year's Eve.

Restlessly, I turn on the Christmas tree lights. Dad and Mom came over a few weeks ago to help put the tree up. Dad and Mom don't do a tree anymore, but Mom still enjoys the festive lights.

I touch one of the red Christmas bulbs and then a gold one.

Christmas is almost here, and although I did some shopping in New York, there's still more to do. I haven't bought Eva anything for her stocking, and I still need to go through our winter ski stuff to see what works and what Eva's outgrown.

It's too much, I think, staring at the tree. Everything is just too much.

I'm still staring blankly at the tree when my cell phone rings. I pick up the phone, hoping it'll be Luke. Instead it's Frank Deavers.

I haven't talked to Frank since he told me in October that Freedom wouldn't be going with Z Design. I've never been nervous taking Frank's calls, but my stomach's full of icy butterflies now.

"Hey, Frank," I say, answering his call and trying to sound casual.

"Have I caught you at a bad time?"

"I'm just thinking about hitting the mall. I still have more shopping to do."

"Is Eva there?"

"No, she's at the ballet. Friends took her to *The Nutcracker.*"

"That's nice."

It is, but I would have rather taken her to *The Nutcracker.* I would have rather taken her to holiday tea. I would rather be the fun mom than the mom who works too much and doesn't smile enough and never has any energy.

"What's up?" I say, forcing myself to speak.

"We've pulled the Super Bowl spot."

I close my eyes, not wanting to hear details about an ad campaign that isn't mine, so I keep silent, not sure what Frank wants me to say.

"There's been some delays, and we're not ready to start taking orders. It seemed premature to start an advertising blitz."

And still I say nothing. I gave them a great ad campaign and they passed on it, so I don't really understand why Frank is calling me now. He's not saying that they've changed their mind about ad agencies. He's not saying they want our ideas. He's actually not saying much of anything.

"Why this friendly Freedom Bikes update?" I ask, barely able to mask my bitterness.

"I don't know how you're going to feel about this, so I'll just throw it out there. You might even want some time to think about it. But we've come up against some problems, and it's been decided by the exec committee that we made a mistake. We want you, need you, involved."

"But you already signed a contract with Lowell Bryant."

"We did. But we're willing to break it."

"That'll cost you six figures."

"Or more."

The icy butterflies are warming, heating up, but I'm nervous, very, very nervous. Because I can't handle another account, not now, not when we're all stretched too thin.

"I don't know," I tell him, because I don't know. I need to figure out how we could take on one more thing when it's just Robert, Allie, and me handling some serious accounts.

"Would you take the Christmas holidays and at least think about it? We don't need an answer till January third. That will give you two weeks," he persists.

I've known Frank too long to play games, so I take a breath and consider how I want to answer. "I took it pretty hard, Frank."

"It was business."

"And this is business still." After hanging up, I hide the packages in my closet before dialing Luke's number. I want to know what he thinks. I want to know what he'd do.

I reach Luke, he's just on his way to the gym, but he sits in his car and talks to me for a few minutes about the offer I've just received.

"So what do you want?" he asks when I finally stop talking.

I shake my head. I wanted the Freedom Bikes account, badly, but they burned me, and we signed Trident and lost Chris, and it's been hell ever since. "I'd love to work with Freedom," I answer cautiously. "They're here in Seattle. They wouldn't require travel."

"But . . . ?"

"I can't add another client, not without replacing Chris, and I've spent six weeks interviewing people without much luck."

"But you said you found a couple of people, only that they were out of your salary range."

"That's true. By nearly ten to twenty thousand dollars."

"So up your salary range. Pay and hire great people."

"What about Robert and Allie?"

"Are they traveling? Are they doing the presentations? Are they going to be the one on the road, or will they be at your office here?" He knows the answer. He knows how we work.

Luke pauses, adds, "If it makes you feel better, give everyone raises, but remember, a salary should be commensurate with the job demands."

Hanging up, I know he's right. I could afford to pay more for a senior partner, someone to take over the Trident account, which would leave me here at home with Eva.

Christmas Day is spent quietly at our house. Mom and Dad spend most of the day with us, although Mom naps in the afternoon for several hours.

Dad and I have another slice of my homemade carrot cake while Mom sleeps.

"I'm glad you came over, Dad. It was really nice having you here with us."

"It's different not celebrating Christmas at our house, but it doesn't make sense anymore."

"No, I know. When I first moved to New York, Christmas felt strange there, and now that we're back here, it's strange again. All these changes." I twirl my fork on my plate, collecting crumbs and cream cheese frosting.

"You look tired," Dad says gruffly. "Sound tired, too. I hope you're not going to be on the road as much as you've been these past couple months."

I glance toward the living room where Eva is stretched out on the couch, reading a new book that Luke gave her for Christmas. "It's been hard," I admit.

"Have you hired someone new? I know you've been interviewing to replace that loser who quit on you on Halloween."

Trust my dad to call it as he sees it. "There are actually two people I like. A man and a woman."

"But the job has lots of traveling—"

"A woman can travel, Dad." Sometimes I think he's just one generation away from our ape ancestors. "Women can do whatever men do. We're smart enough, strong enough, and we communicate a hell of a lot better."

"She's not a mom, is she?"

"No. She's not married."

He makes a rough sound. "She will be."

"Someday. Maybe. But maybe not. Look at me."

He makes an even more scornful sound and leans forward, one arm resting on the dining room table. "You like to think you're so independent, but you're not that much different from anyone else."

I lick the cream cheese icing from the prongs of the fork before pushing the plate away from me. "Meaning?"

"You need people. Even if it'd kill you to admit it."

It would kill me to admit it, but he's right. I do need people. I need more time with people I love and less time on the road. I need to be with family, friends, those who let me know I'm good and cherished. Loved.

Dad's absolutely right. I do need people. I just don't know how to let others know it. Something else I'd never admit, but I'm tired of raising Eva on my own. More and more, I think she'd benefit from a two-parent household. *I'd* benefit from a two-parent household.

I look up into my father's weathered face. The face of a man who has lived much of his life outside, on ski slopes and boat decks and golf courses. "You know, Dad, if something happened to me—"

"Nothing's going to happen."

My mouth curves. I don't believe that horseshit anymore, and neither does he. "Eva would go to Shey," I continue, "but I'd want you to spend as much time with her as you could. Weekends. Holidays. Whatever you could. Whatever worked."

"Marta . . ."

"I travel all the time. There could be an accident. Plane, car—"

"Of course I'd take her," he interrupts gruffly. "But I wouldn't just want weekends and holidays. She's my granddaughter. She's *you*. She's your mother." And then his face tightens, lines deepening everywhere. "She's all that I love best."

I bite down hard. My dad isn't a complicated man, and he's not a particularly deep man, but he has spent most of the last fifteen years taking care of his women. "I've met someone, Dad."

"Mister Tall, Dark, and Handsome with a Harley?"

I crack a smile. "It's a Freedom bike. And how did you know?"

"Your daughter tells me everything."

"Does she?"

He nods, but there's a soberness in his eyes that tells me he's worried, he's worried about all of us. Here he is at sixty-eight, and nothing in his world seems as secure as it once did, not with Mom slowly disappearing, not with his only child single and raising a child of her own.

"Why aren't you spending Christmas with him?" he asks bluntly.

"He's coming over later tonight."

"After your mom and I leave?" Dad guesses.

I smile wryly. "He's a good person." And just thinking of Luke, I get that blasted lump again, the one that fills my throat and makes my chest hurt. My feelings for him have gotten so strong and there are times, like now, where I don't want to feel this much.

"Why don't you invite him over sometime when we are here?" Dad's trying to sound blasé. He's not succeeding. I know he's interested. He told me once he wouldn't sleep properly until he had me settled.

Settled.

The expression used to annoy me, but it's actually beginning to sound better and better, because settled no longer means settling, but comfortable. Safe. Secure.

Maybe at thirty-six going on thirty-seven, I'm ready to settle down. "Maybe I will."

"How about dinner the Sunday after you get back from Whistler?"

"*Dad.*"

"I'll throw some steaks on the grill. We'll keep it casual and friendly."

"Dad."

"Afraid we'll embarrass you?"

I think of Luke, and my heart turns over. "*No.*"

He waits, silent. And knowing him, I know he'll just continue to wait. He'll wait forever. I sigh, push the hair back from my face. "If I do invite him for dinner at your house, it'll just make everything more serious. You know, take it to the next level."

Dad collects the dessert plates and stands up. "'Bout time."

The week we spend in Whistler, British Columbia, between Christmas and New Year's is better than the best medicine in the world. Eva and I have a great time. We ski and ice-skate and sit in the hot tub outside the hotel and laugh as the snow falls on us.

One night we indulge in fondue at a little Swiss style restaurant. Another night we eat steaks and ribs and huge potatoes. The next night we stay in our room and watch a movie and get room service.

Then Luke arrives, the day before New Year's Eve, and he has his own hotel across town, so we shuttle back and forth, comparing his accommodations with ours. We, Eva concludes gleefully, have the better hotel.

New Year's Eve, the three of us attend a party hosted by someone none of us know, but Luke being Luke Flynn gets invitations to all sorts of things, and Luke thought Eva might enjoy a proper New Year's Eve gala, one of those parties where everyone dresses black tie and dances in an ornate ballroom and drinks expensive champagne.

I hadn't brought anything so fancy with us, so Eva and I go shopping in downtown Whistler and hit every boutique we can, searching for a proper party dress.

I find a simple black gown that's cut on the bias and hugs the figure, and Eva falls in love with a midnight blue velvet dress with a lace collar. With dresses and new shoes, stockings and coats and purses, we head to the hotel to dress.

The New Year's Eve party is crowded and very posh, but Luke's wonderful sense of humor keeps Eva and me in stitches.

With the clock and crowd counting down the time, I stand with Luke and Eva with our party hats and noise-makers and wait for the New Year.

The hour strikes, brilliant bits of confetti fall, and Luke lets me kiss Eva, and then he kisses me, and as we stand there, the three of us, I think, This is what I've been waiting for all my life.

My man. My child. My family.

By the time we drive home on New Year's Day, I've made up my mind. I'll hire that young ad executive I liked so much, the woman who wants to relocate from San Francisco to be closer to her boyfriend in Seattle. I'm going to give her the Trident account, and I'm going to take Freedom Bikes. And the New Year will be prosperous, less stressful, and happy.

Especially happy.

I do exactly what I resolved to do.

I hire Beth on Tuesday, put her on a plane to New York Thursday, and Friday afternoon I jump in my truck and head to Seattle to attend my first meeting with the Freedom Bike Group's executive board.

I'm definitely nervous, though. Frank had sent me bios on everybody, and I'm the only female in the bunch. But I wouldn't be here, I remind myself as I park and take the elevator up, if I didn't have something to contribute.

The meeting is held in Freedom's new office space, and everyone's already in the conference room, mingling.

I recognize a few faces from the last time I was here, but I don't see Frank, and I'm disappointed because he's at least one person I know.

Then I freeze, and my smile falters. I do a double take. Luke. *Luke?*

What the hell?

My pulse quickens as everyone begins to take a seat. I wait for Luke to look at me, make eye contact, but he doesn't. It's not until everyone's seated and I'm the only one left standing that I force myself to move. Into the last open seat, the seat at his left.

Hell. Hell, hell, hell.

My legs feel like fire pokers as I make my way to the table. I'm so upset that I can hardly see straight. What is Luke doing here?

How is he connected with the Freedom Bike Group?

"Join us, Marta," a voice booms from the far end of the table, and it's the man I recognize from the first dinner I had with the group, the one with thick gray hair and an equally thick gray handlebar mustache.

I shift my briefcase to the other hand and slide uncomfortably into the seat next to Luke.

His half-smiling eyes meet mine as I sit down.

I'm not smiling. I'm livid. Beyond livid. What the hell is going on?

Little spots dance before my eyes. My head swims.

"Breathe," Luke mutters. "You're about to turn blue."

I'd object, but I can't. He's right. I am holding my breath, and I force myself to exhale and then inhale, and exhale.

But the breathing isn't helping. I'm just getting more and more upset.

I know he's looking at me, but I refuse to glance his way again. I'm shaking in my seat. My arms, legs, and hands tremble with shock and fury. I don't want to be sitting here feeling this, either. Freedom is business. I'm here for business. I'm here to work.

Which leads me back to Luke. Why is he here? And what is his part with Freedom?

The man with the mustache, R.J., calls the meeting to order, and we're to go around and introduce ourselves, giving our name, our title, and anything else we feel is pertinent. R.J. starts, and the introductions go to his right. I'm listening to the introductions but taking in only about half of what everyone is saying, as I'm too aware of Luke to my left.

When it comes to Luke, he says the least of anyone so far. "Luke Flynn." And that's it. That's all he says.

R.J. laughs. "Our Luke is a closemouthed guy."

Our Luke. So R.J. knows him well, quite well, if he refers to Luke Flynn that way.

Luke meets my gaze and arches an eyebrow.

Deliberately I turn away, my gaze sweeping the table. "I'm Marta Zinsser, president of Z Design, a Seattle-based advertising agency. I met many of you in October, and as you know, I'm a big fan of Freedom Bikes."

From the corner of my eye, I see Luke shift abruptly. He's scribbling something on the pad of paper in front of him and slides it toward me.

I look at the paper and what he's written: *"Even though you ride a Harley?"*

Looking up, I meet his eyes, but I can't smile. I feel sick. Dead. This is a trick, I think, but I don't know what the trick is yet to understand it.

"*What are you doing here?*" I write on the pad of paper.

He scribbles back, "*I'll tell you after.*"

I don't think I can wait until after. Thank God we have a break at the one-hour point, and before Luke can get caught in conversation, I tell him we have to talk now.

"After the meeting," he answers, waving to R.J. and another heavyset fellow.

"No." I smile at R.J., nod at the heavyset fellow. "Now."

We step out of the conference room together and walk down the semidark hallway. Luke attempts to put his arm around me, and I pull away sharply. "What have you done?" I choke, grateful the light's dim or he'd see the pain in my face. "What have you done?" I repeat, unable to think of anything else to say.

"Nothing," he says, stopping me at the end of the hall.

One of the gentlemen is heading our way to get water from the cooler. "That's not true," I whisper. "You're part of this somehow, you're here at this meeting, which means you're part of Freedom—"

"I'm the owner."

My God. My legs wobble, and I fall back a step, even more unsteady. Luke puts a hand out to my elbow, but I won't let him touch me.

"So you did all this." I can't speak above a whisper even if I wanted to. "You were behind Frank's call and the money and terminating the other agency's contract, weren't you?"

"No."

"Luke, don't lie to me. Not to me, of all people. I'm not stupid—"

"I never said you were."

"Then tell me the truth. Did you talk to Frank?"

"Yes, and no."

That's all I need to hear. I lift my hands. I surrender. "Then I'm done. I quit. I'm out of here."

I start walking for the elevators as fast as I can. I'm shaking so badly, I'm afraid I'll fall out of my high heels, but I don't stop out of fear that I'll fall apart. But I can't fall apart here, not in front of men who build motorcycles.

Luke's walked with me to the elevators. As the doors open, he tries to grab my elbow for a third time. I raise my hand warningly. "Don't."

My Mountain of a Man puts his hands on his hips, his red gold hair flaming. "So what do I tell everyone?"

My eyes burn and my throat burns, and I swallow hard. Luke has disappointed me more than anyone has in years. "You tell everyone you made a mistake, and you're going to do everything in your power to get Lowell Bryant Agency back."

Chapter Twenty-Four

I'm shaking as I drive home, both furious and heartbroken. How could Luke do that to me? How could he pull a power play like that?

Fine, he can be founder of BioMed. He can be a billionaire. But don't be God and manipulate my jobs and whip up magical contracts to "make things better" for me.

I don't want a fairy godmother for a boyfriend.

Arriving home, I'm just glad Eva's in bed. I couldn't handle trying to act normal in front of her right now.

I spend the next two weeks avoiding all contact with Luke. I don't return his calls or answer his e-mails or his text messages.

I'm done with him, so done that I delete him from my BlackBerry and go through everything I have and toss anything he might have given to me, anything that might remind me of him, even putting my bike up for sale on Craigslist. It's not a Freedom bike, it's a Harley, but I never want to ride a motorcycle again.

Eva knows I'm upset, and she knows it's about Luke,

especially as she doesn't see him anymore or hear me speak to him on the phone.

It's not easy, though, for me to erase him that fast. I might have blanked him out of my BlackBerry, but I can't get him out of my system that fast. I do miss him, far more than I anticipated, far more than I can handle.

But getting rid of the bike will be the first step to really moving on.

The bike has found a buyer. I read the e-mail from an Al Pancetti of Lakewood, Washington. He'll pay asking price with a cashier's check, and he'll be here the day after tomorrow in the afternoon to pick it up.

Wow. That was fast. So that's it. Bike is gone. Well, almost gone.

I leave my desk and head to the garage, pull back the dropcloth, and, crouching next to my bike, run my hand over the chassis. I feel a twinge of pain as my fingers glide over the chrome and glossy paint.

I need to go for one last ride. Sticking my head in the studio, I shout that I'm taking an early lunch and will be back before one.

I'm already wearing jeans and a sweater, so I layer on a black leather coat and my black combat boots and set off. I head north on 405, passing Bothell and Mill Creek, continuing on to where 405 and 5 merge, up to Mount Vernon, before turning around and heading home again.

I'm on 5 South, passing the University District and getting ready to take the 520 on ramp, when my bike begins to sputter. It's making a coughing, skipping sound, and from the way the engine starts racing, something's loose.

Glancing down, I look for the screw in the carburetor, and once I find it, I run my fingers across it. It feels tight. I'm going to need to back it off, but I can't do it driving.

I pull over to the side of the freeway, hoping I can make the adjustment now without having to go to a gas station. It's dangerous here on the side of the road, but I work quickly, first tugging off my helmet and then kneeling next to the bike.

I use my fingernail to try to turn the little screw. It doesn't need a lot, just a small adjustment would work, but the screw doesn't budge. I try again without success. I'm still kneeling next to the bike when I hear a truck pull up behind me.

"Everything okay?"

I know that voice. Very well. Karma, I think, pushing hair off my face to look up at an unsmiling Luke.

I wipe my cold, stiff hands on my knees and sit back on my haunches. "Hey."

Luke towers above me. "Break down?"

"The carburetor needs adjusting."

"Need a hand?"

"I've got it. Thanks."

His scrutiny deepens. "Where are your tools?"

My skin grows hot, and I hate this feeling, so anxious, so nervous, so not in control. "I don't have any." The beat of silence is hugely uncomfortable, so I add flatly, "I'm using my fingernail."

"Your fingernail," he repeats.

I know it sounds funny, but it's what I've done before and it was fine. "Yes, my fingernail."

His expression doesn't change, but I can tell he's laughing on the inside. "Is it working?"

"It will," I answer, surprised by the crazy weakness in my knees and thighs as I stand. I'm shocked by the sight of him and hope that my brisk tone communicates that I'm a professional and completely in control.

He doesn't buy it. "What if it doesn't? What will you do then?"

It must be a rhetorical question, because he doesn't even wait for an answer. Instead he heads to his Land Rover, retrieves a toolbox, and returns with a screwdriver.

He steps around me and crouches next to my bike. With a quick twist, he adjusts the screw on the fuel filter, shakes it once to make sure it's on tight, and then stands up.

"All done," he says, looking down at me, his expression as cool as the frost on my lawn this morning.

"Thank you," I answer stiffly.

"You should carry tools," he adds. "If you're going to ride—"

"I know," I cut him off. "I should. But I wasn't going far, and I didn't expect any problems."

He stares down at me, and I can tell he's just as angry as I am. He's quiet so long, I don't think he's going to answer, and then he gives his head a single shake. "You make so many assumptions, and most of them are so wrong, so wildly off base, that I sometimes wonder what we were doing seeing each other."

Luke's words hit hard, each of them a slap, the consonants and vowels like stinging hail. "I wonder who it is you think I am," he continues, "and why you always think the worst of me."

I open my mouth to protest, but there's enough truth in what he says that I can't defend myself. Instead I stand there, chin lifted, even as my insides fall, icy cold.

"I have ethics, Marta, and I wouldn't sell out, not even for you. I'm proud of the way I do business. I'm proud of how I conduct myself. Maybe it's time you looked at the way you conduct yourself." Finished, he turns and heads back to his truck.

Shaking, I watch him put away his tools and then open his door. "So what did happen with Freedom Bikes?" I call to him. "If you didn't go in and wave your magic wand, who did?"

The traffic is thick and loud and zooms past, and for a split second I think Luke hasn't heard me, but then he pivots away from his truck and faces me.

"Frank," he answers.

I'm not sure I heard him right over the roar of traffic, so I walk toward him. "Frank?" I repeat.

Luke glances at a huge semi truck that has just sounded its horn. "It was Frank's idea to toss out the other agency and bring you back in."

"So you didn't ride roughshod over the executive committee?"

He makes a sound of disgust. "God, no. I wouldn't be in business today if that's how I operated. First, I delegate decision making, and second, Frank came to me, telling me he'd made a mistake. He wanted you back. I told him there was nothing I could do, that it was his and the board's decision."

Shivering, shaking, I cross my arms over my chest. "But the timing was just too good."

Luke's expression hardens all over again. "Sometimes life is good, Marta. Sometimes life is freaking fabulous. Don't you know that? Life isn't just bad things. Life can also be wonderful."

I feel my throat and nose burn. "I'm sorry."

Luke just shakes his head. "Yeah. Me too." He takes a breath. "If your bike doesn't start, call me. Otherwise . . ." He doesn't finish the thought. He climbs behind the steering wheel and drives off.

Al Pancetti arrives Thursday afternoon at two o'clock with a black truck and trailer to pick up my bike. I stand off to the side and watch him load it into a trailer. My chest feels so hot and tight, I can barely breathe. I cross my arms, squeeze, try to stay calm. This is right, I tell myself, this is smart. I'm being a better mom this way. Becoming more like everybody else.

Yet as Al slams the back of the trailer closed and slides the lock across the back, I nearly cry out, *Don't take my bike, don't take it.*

I don't cry out. I just stand there, still, cool, controlled. My dad would be so proud of me.

"I guess that's it," Al says, wiping his hands on the back of his jeans before extending one hand to shake mine good-bye.

I shake his hand, nod. "It's a good bike."

His warm brown eyes meet mine. "I know it is. You take care now."

"You too."

I go inside before he drives away. I have to. Otherwise I'd be bawling like a baby.

The loss of the bike is the final straw. I'm shattered and angry, mostly angry at myself because I didn't have to sell the bike. I didn't have to walk out of the meeting. I didn't have to cut Luke out of my life, either.

Why, oh, why do I do these hard-core, knee-jerk masochistic things? Why do I respond to life this way? All or nothing? Throw the dice, baby, all or nothing . . .

But I don't want all or nothing.

All or nothing has just about broken me.

I finally call Tiana because she's single and I hope, pray, she'll understand what I'm talking about and hope, pray, she can tell me how to get through this.

"I've goofed," I tell her. "I've goofed so bad." My voice is shaking and I'm shaking, and for the first time in a long time, I think I'm really going to crack. "What I did . . . what I said . . . Oh, Tiana, what have I done?"

"What did you do?"

"I walked out of a huge meeting, walked out on a job I wanted more than anything, walked out on Luke. You name it. I did it."

"Why?"

"I was upset. Confused. And now I find out I had it all wrong. I didn't understand it, and I thought the worst, and oh, Tiana, I hate myself right now. I feel so bad. I'm so crazy about Luke, and I've screwed everything up."

"I'm coming," Tiana says crisply. "I have the weekend off and no plans. I'll be there first thing in the morning."

*   *   *

Tiana is as good as her word. Eva and I pick her up, and as soon as we get home, Eva has Jill over so Jill can meet her famous "aunt." Once Jill is done gawking, Eva and Jill disappear into Eva's room to play.

Tiana drags me into my room to talk. "So what exactly happened," she demands.

I tell her all, as briefly and concisely as possible. Tiana listens to the whole story and then asks, "So what's the bottom line, Marta? What do you want right now?"

"Luke." There's no hesitation on my part. "I want the bike account. It was my dream job. But it's just a job. Luke's . . . Luke's . . ." I try to smile, yet even trying to smile makes me nearly cry. "Luke's wonderful, and I don't know why I did what I did. I don't know why I didn't trust him."

"Oh, Marta, you've always had a huge issue with trust, especially after Scott duped you."

"But this isn't about Scott, it's about me."

"It's *all* about Scott. He was a bad apple. He started seeing you before he was even divorced—"

"I don't want to talk about Scott."

Tiana slams her hand on my dresser. "But we're going to talk about Scott whether you like it or not. We need to talk about him because he's messed up your life long enough. You loved him. You wanted to marry him. You wanted to have kids with him, but the bastard already had a wife, a wife he didn't tell you about—"

"They'd been separated for over a year."

"But he was still seeing her, wasn't he? Still going 'home' on weekends and just possibly, still sleeping with her."

I feel as if I can't breathe, and it's not the sexy, excited

I-can't-breathe, but the elephant-is-standing-on-my-chest-and-crushing-me kind of feeling. "Tiana."

She shakes her head. "He was the worst kind of man, Marta, the kind of man that needs so much that he'll string women along, have girlfriends, mistresses, wives, women who all think they're the only one when in reality they're just one of a half dozen he woos and wins, women he needs to support his fragile ego and self-esteem.

"He hurt you," she continues furiously. "He lied to you. He cheated. He was an ass. A pig. A prick. A jerk. But he's not all men. And you can't let one rotten prick haunt you forever. You can't let that rotten prick keep you from being loved."

Tiana takes my hands in hers, squeezes them. "For ten years you've been afraid of men, afraid of being hurt, afraid of being rejected because of one lousy man. Okay, you thought Luke let you down and you behaved childishly, but have you tried to apologize? Have you really tried to fix things? Or have you just crawled into a hole and played dead?"

It'd be so easy to hate Tiana when she's in her righteous mode, but Tiana has been through hell and back and she's a survivor. She knows what it is to love and lose and try again. Shey might be the sister I never had, but Tiana's the guardian angel. I couldn't go through what she's gone through, and I know she's suffered.

"But I don't know how to fix this," I confess. "I think it's gotten out of hand."

"Maybe in your mind." Her eyes search my face. "And maybe it's uncomfortable, and maybe it'll hurt your pride, but don't give up. Don't throw in the towel. What kind of attitude is that?"

"It's my inner chicken talking."

"You're not a coward at work, why be a coward with men?"

She has a good point there. "I don't know."

"I don't know, either, and maybe it's time you had some balls when it comes to relationships. Maybe it's time you take what you learned about the world and apply it to love."

"You make it sound easy."

"It ain't easy." She smiles wryly, her deep dimples appearing and disappearing. "Being married wasn't perfect, but I loved being married, and I loved my husband, and I want to have that again. Not because I'm weak. Not because I can't make it on my own, but because love feels good. Love makes me a better, and happier, person."

I picture Luke, picture us together and how I feel when we're apart, and I finally get it. It's not that two halves make a whole, but that two wholes can definitely increase happiness.

And happiness is worth fighting for, just as Luke is worth fighting for. Now I've got to put my biker girl attitude back on and make this work.

Tiana promises to take Eva and Jill shopping while I try to call Luke and have a real conversation with him.

Of course, I remember his number, despite erasing it "forever" from my home phone and BlackBerry.

I dial his number, and he answers. "Marta," he says.

"Hi, Luke."

"What can I do for you?" His voice is pretty dang hard.

I take a quick breath for courage. "Could you meet me for coffee?" He doesn't say anything, so I add, "So we could talk?"

"What are we going to talk about?"

My mouth's so dry. I'm so nervous. "Us. What happened. With Freedom Bikes and all."

"You know, Marta, we should talk sometime, but I don't know that this is a good time. I'm packing, and I've an early flight to catch."

"Where are you going this time?"

"China and Australia."

My heart tumbles and falls. "For how long?"

"Probably a couple weeks."

"That's so long."

He doesn't say anything, and it hurts. I can't bear to think he's angry with me. "Please meet me for coffee," I say. "Fifteen, twenty minutes is all I'm asking for. The Starbucks near the mall, the one next to See's Candy?"

"All right. I'll be there in half an hour."

The Starbucks across from Nordstrom's is always packed, partly because you can park out front and partly because it's big and has a fire and is famous for its hookups.

Once I arrive at the Starbucks, I don't even know why I chose this location. There are half a dozen other Starbucks within a mile radius. I should have picked something smaller, quieter, darker.

It's blustery outside, with steely skies and a whistling wind that becomes a howl every time the glass door opens.

Before I can even find a table, Luke arrives. It's like seeing him again for the first time. He's so big, so rugged, he takes my breath away.

"What would you like?" Luke asks, taking a place in line.

"Green tea. Hot, please." I keep darting glances at him as we wait for our order. He barely looks at me.

When our drinks are ready, Luke finds a tiny table for us near the fireplace. "Your teeth are chattering," he says.

He's right. They are. I'm that nervous. "I'll be better now that I have the tea."

But Luke still shrugs out of his big leather jacket and drops it around my shoulders. I nod appreciatively. "Thank you."

He sits across from me, and he's so big, and his legs are so long, that he looks like a giant at a children's table. "You walked out on a business meeting and then go weeks without a call," he says bluntly. "That's pretty rough."

I look at him, see the fierce glint in his eyes, and realize the glint's there because I hurt him. He's angry because I hurt him. And I hurt him because he hurt me.

My teeth still chatter, and I circle my paper cup to warm my hands. "Why didn't you tell me you owned Freedom Bikes?"

He focuses that flinty blue green gaze on me. "For the same reason I didn't tell you I'm a majority shareholder in Trident."

Luke's just knocked me sideways all over again. *What?*

"Marta, whatever contracts you get, whatever clients you acquire, whatever accounts you lose, that's business, your business, and it doesn't involve me. But when you walk out on me, won't talk to me, won't return my calls—that's personal. And that didn't just hurt us, it pretty much killed us."

The doors open, and a group of teenagers race in to escape the cold wind outside. Their voices are loud as they push one another and laugh at something that happened outside. Several of the older patrons frown at the kids, but I welcome the interruption, as it gives me a chance to gather my composure.

"So there's no us anymore?" I ask, trying to be brave but feeling rather faint.

Luke shakes his head and takes so long to answer that I'm afraid to hear what he's going to say. "I don't believe in games, and I don't give people the silent treatment. I believe in respect and honesty, integrity and loyalty—"

"I thought you'd lied to me," I blurt out, my hands twisting. "I thought you'd been dishonest, and I handled it all wrong. I should have asked you before I judged you—"

"Yes. Yes, you should have."

This just keeps getting worse. I feel like hell, I really do, and I don't want us to travel down this path, going to an awful place of no return.

"I'm not good with trust," I say, feeling as though I'm stumbling around in the dark. "It's my weak link, and I could blame it on someone from my past, someone who did hurt me, but I don't want to make excuses. I realize I'm wrong, and I'm sorry for not giving you a chance, and I'm asking you now, please, Luke, to give me a chance. Don't give up on me. Don't view me as a lost cause. I'm trying to learn. I really am."

He looks at me a long silent moment and sighs. "Marta, I don't know. I really don't know. Just like you, I have a lot of responsibilities. I have pressure. Problems. This whole thing has been really hard. It's been distracting."

I suddenly lean across the table and kiss him. His lips are so warm and firm, and it's Luke, the Luke I fell in love with, the Luke who isn't sure he wants me anymore. "I goofed," I whisper, my eyes filling with tears. "I goofed bad. Please understand that I'm sorry, deeply, truly sorry." My eyes search his face for any sign of emotion or tenderness. "I want to make this right. Just give me a chance to make this right."

He shifts uncomfortably, and I slowly sit back, my hands balled in my lap.

"I can try to talk to Frank." He speaks flatly. "Maybe he can get you on board with the Freedom team again."

"This isn't about Freedom. I don't want Freedom Bikes. I want you." My chest hurts so much that I can hardly get air in or out. "I love you."

His head turns. He looks at me, and finally, a flicker of expression in his eyes. "I don't play games."

"Neither do I. I'm miserable—*sick*—because I screwed up. And you don't have to love me back. You don't have to forgive me immediately, but you do need to know that I'm sorry that I hurt you, and sorry that I humiliated you, and promise you that I will never run away from a problem or conflict again. I'm going to have balls from now on. I'm going to stop being a chicken, and I'm going to suck it up."

The corner of his mouth very nearly lifts. "You're too pretty to have balls."

I nearly burst into tears. "Luke, please don't give up on me. I need you. I do—"

He cuts me off with a kiss, thank God. For moments it's just his mouth on mine, and warmth, and relief.

When he eventually lifts his head, his eyes are the most brilliant blue. "I haven't given up on you," he says gruffly. "Not by a long shot."

My hand slides into his, and when he holds my hand tight in his, I finally feel as though I can breathe for the first time in weeks.

"You want to know how you got the Freedom Bikes account?" Luke asks, still holding my hand.

I nod.

"I was in a meeting with Frank a while back, and I happened to mention that I had dinner with you in New York. Frank wanted to know what you were doing in the city, and I filled him in. But instead of being pleased that you had a big new account on the East Coast, he was upset."

Luke's eyebrows lift to emphasize the point he's making. "*Frank* said you were a single mom, and it was wrong for you to be on the road that much, especially when he knew you loved your little girl as much as you did. Frank was the one who put the wheels in motion to bring you back. I just supported him."

I look up at him, and Luke's expression is still somber but a little less hard. "And this is the truth?"

"I'd never lie to you, Marta, never, not even to protect your feelings. And something else you should know is that Frank was bitter about the executive committee's decision from the start. He said the ad agency they'd hired was second rate compared to Z Design and he'd regretted not fighting harder for you when some of the good old boys complained about putting a woman in charge of a motorcycle ad campaign."

I sit up taller. "They didn't want to work with me because I was a woman?"

"Some men can be sexist pigs. And some men can be your greatest champion. Frank is one of your champions."

"And you?" I whisper. "Are you one of my champions?"

"Your biggest."

He's just about to kiss my hand when the doors open again, and suddenly it's Tiana and Jill and Eva walking in loaded down with shopping bags from Nordstrom's and Gap Kids and Limited Too.

Eva's wearing a new purchase, a faux spotted Dalmatian coat, no doubt a present from Tiana, and her cheeks are ruddy from the cold, and her hair is a shaggy pageboy around her face, and I don't think I've ever seen her so alive or so happy or so original. Eva's going to be okay.

Eva now spots me, and she cries my name. "Mom!"

She's running over to give me a hug, and she's just about to fling herself at me when she spots Luke.

Eva freezes and stares at Luke so long and hard, I'm afraid she'll burst into tears. But then she throws herself into his arms and hugs him harder than she's ever hugged anyone.

"Where have you been?" she cries, her skinny arms wrapping around his neck. "We've been missing you!"

"Maybe China can wait," he says, looking at me over the top of Eva's head. His gaze holds mine. "Maybe I need to stay home and spend some time with my girls."

His girls.

His girls.

I smile back at him, and as I smile I realize, I belong somewhere, I belong with someone. I'm not the odd mom out anymore.

Five Months Later

"I have a birthday present for you, too," Luke says as I finish opening my last birthday gift, a gift for a Mother-Daughter Spa Day courtesy of Eva, who is still trying to turn me into a proper mom—her lifelong quest, I fear.

"What?" I ask, smiling indulgently.

"Come see." He stands, extends his hand to lead me to the garage. Eva jumps up, giggling. She knows something, and she's excited.

"You're a big girl now," Luke says, turning on the garage light. "You might as well have a big-girl bike."

I freeze. My breath catches. It's my bike, but . . . *better*. The Harley engine is gone, replaced with a Freedom engine, and the handlebars are larger, higher, cooler. The body is shinier. The paint sparkles.

Crouching next to the bike, I touch the chrome finish on the new engine, and I can't quite catch my breath.

My bike. My bike is a Freedom bike.

I look up at Luke, absolutely stunned. "How did you find my bike?"

He shrugs, smiles that faint, sexy smile. "I have my ways."

"But it's been . . . months."

"Yeah. And you've been working on the Freedom account for months now." His gaze holds mine, and he's never looked more heroic. "I've gotten to know your team at Z Design really well. They coughed up all your secrets. Including Craigslist and Al."

I nod, completely overwhelmed, because he doesn't just get it, he gets *me*. He gets that I'm proud, fierce, loyal. A *fighter*. But he also understands that I have a tender side and a strong need to be wanted. "Thank you." My voice cracks. "I love it."

Luke extends a hand to me, tugs me to my feet. "Happy birthday, baby." He drops a warm kiss on my lips. "You deserve it."

Eva bursts into a cheer, and I laugh. Luke's right.

I do deserve it.

But don't we all?

About the Author

I never planned on being a single mom, and I'm one hundred percent certain my boys would *not* want me to be known as an odd mom, but even they will tell you I'm a bit different.

Personally, I like being different. *Different* and *eccentric* are compliments in my book. Which is probably how I ended up a novelist. Ever since I was little, I've made up stories and walked around with plots and characters running around my head. I do hear voices, and yet the fact that I get paid to write these voices down convinces me I'm not crazy, I'm just . . . special.

The writing life suits me. Some of the most obvious advantages to the writer's life include: not getting dressed if I don't want to; not leaving my house if I don't feel like it; and being able to drink gallons of coffee and tea, since the bathroom is conveniently close.

But before you think I'm the luckiest woman alive, let me be honest: My kids don't let me stay in my pajamas all day because they say it's annoying to look at me dressed that way at four in the afternoon; I sometimes forget I haven't left the house in days and that's why I'm talking to myself (again); and lastly, I can't color my hair properly or grow my own fruit and vegetables at home, so I do eventually leave the house to run errands and pretend I'm a normal mom.

Normal, though, is a state of mind and I encourage all women to embrace their quirks, enjoy their uniqueness, and be proud of any eccentricities. I firmly believe the more you are yourself, the less you have to worry about what other people think.

For more from this odd mom and *Odd Mom Out* come visit me at my Web site, www.janeporter.com.

Jane

5 WAYS YOU KNOW YOU'RE THE ODD MOM OUT

 1 Every year the principal asks if you're new to the school.

 2 Your kids know the inside scoop weeks before you do.

 3 You've never shopped nor even known when Nordstrom's big semi-annual sale is (it is twice a year though, right?).

 4 You don't own a pair of designer jeans and couldn't tell Prada from Gucci if you tried.

5 You make up your own rules as you go . . . and ignore real lists (like this one!).

If you liked
ODD MOM OUT,
here are 2 more books that will hit the SPOT

5 SPOT ● ● ● ●

"Brilliant...hugely enjoyable. It's romantic, funny, intelligent, believable, and gripping"
—MARIAN KEYES, bestselling author of *Angels*

frenemies

a novel

MEGAN CRANE

On the cusp of 30, Gus has it all, until her boyfriend dumps her and her friends become enemies overnight—is her grown-up world entering a quarter-life crisis?
"Brilliant . . . hugely enjoyable . . . It's romantic, funny, intelligent, believable, and gripping."
—Marian Keyes, bestselling author of *Angels*

Cassie has good reason to believe in The Plan: perfect job, man, and engagement. But what's a girl to do when The Plan fails her? Go to Buenos Aires, of course!
"Funny, fresh, enchanting, and real, this is one fabulous debut."
— Lani Diane Rich, award-winning author of *Time Off for Good Behavior*

JESSICA MORRISON

A Novel

The Buenos Aires Broken Hearts Club